Helping the community, one book at a time

# THE ~~Billionaire~~ BOSS NEXT DOOR

### max monroe

*The Billionaire Boss Next Door*
A Romantic Comedy

Published by Max Monroe LLC © 2019, Max Monroe
All rights reserved.

Without limiting the rights under copyright reserved above, no part of this publication may be reproduced, stored in or introduced into a retrieval system, or transmitted, in any form, or by any means (electronic, mechanical, photocopying, recording, or otherwise) without the prior written permission of both the copyright owner and the above publisher of this book.

This is a work of fiction. Names, characters, places, brands, media, and incidents are either the product of the author's imagination or are used fictitiously. The author acknowledges the trademarked status and trademark owners of various products referenced in this work of fiction, which have been used without permission. The publication/use of these trademarks is not authorized, associated with, or sponsored by the trademark owners.

Editing by Silently Correcting Your Grammar
Formatting by Champagne Book Design
Cover Design by Kris Hack with Temys Designs

Author's Note:

***The Billionaire Boss Next Door*** is a full-length romantic comedy standalone novel.
Due to the humorous nature of this book's content, eating and/or drinking and/or operating heavy machinery while reading is not recommended.

Happy Reading!
All our love,
Max & Monroe

# Dedication

To The Bookworm Box and The Bookworm Box Subscribers: Thank you for being so amazing. We're so excited about putting our *goodies in your *box.
*These are in no way related to songs from Justin Timberlake or Ciara. They are books. And the box is cardboard. Gah, this is awkward.

To intimidating women: May you find your superfish and harpoon that fucker right in the heart. Also, we know this doesn't make the most sense to you right now, but it will when you're done reading.

To billionaires: Thank you for being so fun to write.
*P.S. Hi. *winks* We have husbands, but they won't mind if you pay us to come spend time on your yacht and eat fancy cheese.
*We're not hookers, even though this makes us sound like it. We swear. We're just writers who like yachts and cheese.

To Colleen Hoover: Thanks for doing such a good job being us. Or maybe we do a good job of being you?
We're confused.

# Intro

My name is Thatcher Kelly, but my friends call me Thatch. You might know me, or, if you're new here, you might not. So, I'll just take this time to tell you about myself.

I—*and pretty much everyone else*—would describe myself as an insanely handsome, crazy successful, addictively charming, and irresistible man of many talents.

I'm confident, maybe to the point of cocky, but I'm not the kind of guy who gets lost in the logistics of people's opinions.

I take life by the balls. I live without regrets or hesitancy. I do what I want, whenever I want, without fear of judgment or societal constraints.

Basically, if Lenny Kravitz were an insanely successful billionaire banker and had an extra two inches of length behind his zipper, he'd be me. Now, I'm no bullshitter—*or* rock god, for that matter—but what I lack in musical expertise, I more than make up for in all aspects of *giving pleasure*.

I'm aces at fucking. Amazing with my tongue.

And so damn generous with gifting orgasms, you might as well call me Santa Thatch.

Simply put, I'm all the good and delicious things.

But before you start licking your lips and getting amped up to know me, I need to tell you one very important thing: this story isn't mine to tell. It's not even about me, really.

I know. I know. What a fucking disappointment, right?

But I've had my time, and now, I'm told, it's best if I pass the torch.

And I guess, if I have to give up the limelight, there's no better person than the guy in this story to turn it over to.

See, while I'm not the main player in *this* game, one of the best guys I know *is*.

And, while I know it would be considered "mannerly" to tell you his name, I've never really been one to play by the rules. Plus, I'm a big fan of surprises *and* teasing, if I'm being honest.

But don't worry, I *never* tease without the certainty of satisfaction and pleasure in the end. With me, a little teasing goes a long, long, *big huge climax* way.

So, what can I tell you about the leading fella of this little tale?

With a chiseled jaw, svelte physique, and striking green eyes, he's almost as attractive as me. He's got a great sense of humor and impeccable taste—he knows me, after all—and a heart of fucking gold.

He's a bit of a workaholic, but he's smart as a fucking whip.

**This mystery man is the kind of eligible bachelor that would've made Prince Harry look like a British schmuck before he committed himself to one beautiful American for the rest of his life.**

No offense to the royal ginger, but he ain't got nothing on my homeboy.

And if the world's hospitality industry were stationed in Buckingham Palace, this guy wouldn't even be Harry. No way. He's a William all the fucking way.

**His last name stands for a billion-dollar empire, and my buddy will one day take the throne and be in control of *all* of it. We're talking the kind of success and appeal that would give that dude who hosts *The Bachelor* a boner.**

Yeah, Chris Hansen would definitely tent his pants over this guy.

*Wait.* Is Chris Hansen the host for *The Bachelor,* or is he the one who catches sex predators in a staged kitchen with cookies and Kool-Aid?

Meh. It doesn't really matter.

**What matters is Mr. Mystery.**

All he needs is a woman who can show him there's life outside of the office.

To help him let loose. To challenge him.

To bust his balls and call him on his bullshit.

A sexy, curvaceous woman to blow his fucking mind.

And you know what? I have a feeling, a gut instinct so to speak, that just might be what he gets…

This might be my perfect, addictive, literary greatness of an introduction, but **this is one hundred percent *his* story. And *hers* too.**

Fluffing hell, guys. You're in for one hell of a ride.

## Chapter ONE

## Greer

It's the end of December—otherwise known as the Bermuda Triangle of the calendar—and still, I find myself outside of my bed, wearing business attire rather than pajamas, and acting as a functioning member of society.

*Insanity, I tell you.*

A notification pings on my phone, and I snag it from my kitchen counter to glance at the screen. After spending the entire night in my office—with the door locked because, you know, weirdos—and then rushing home with exactly one hour to pack a suitcase, I'm praying the news from Uber isn't grim.

"Don't say *known for great conversation*, don't say *known for great conversation*, don't say *known for great conversation*," I chant to myself.

After a night of going over my company's books, there's nothing I want to do less than make up stories to entertain some stranger with a lot of questions this early in the morning.

**Nelly in a silver Chevrolet Equinox is here.**

The Uber notification thankfully says nothing about Nelly's conversational skills, but I have no idea what an Equinox is. The last time I had a car was never, and the last time I was interested in them was sometime before that.

I've lived in New Orleans all my life, and most everything I've done has been possible on foot, on public transportation, or via taxi.

And now that ride services are a thing, I just pretend I'm rich enough to have personalized chauffeurs all the time.

Which, after what Hudson Designs' accounting records had to say last night, I am *not*. If those fuckers get any redder, the New Orleans homicide division will be confiscating them as evidence.

Thankfully, though, when I open my front door and drag my suitcase over the threshold, my driver is out of her vehicle and introducing herself.

"Gree Hudson, right? I'm Nelly." She flashes a toothy grin my way and crosses her arms below her chest, revealing a giant, sparkly-silver horse head on her white t-shirt.

"Nice to meet you, Nelly," I say and pull the cheap suitcase I bought off Groupon for fifty bucks toward the sidewalk. "But it's actually Greer."

"What is?" She raises one of her bushy gray eyebrows.

"My name," I explain in the friendliest voice I can manage. "It's pronounced *Greer*."

At a whopping five letters, it's one of the simplest names in the greater New Orleans area. Thanks to a heavy Creole influence, I went to school with a Fabienne and an Adelaida and a Eulalie, and Nelly's having trouble with Greer.

She must be new to the area.

"Oh, sorry about that," she responds, and her smile turns apologetic. "Greer-er."

"*Greer*."

"Gree-ware," she tries again.

*Screw it. As long as she gets me to the airport in time for my flight, Nelly can call me whatever she can get past her tongue.*

"You got it." I force a smile and stop beside the hatch to the cargo area, but she gestures me toward the back-passenger door.

"Sorry, but the back is filled with stuff for my horses."

I blink three times as if that simple movement might help me hear better.

# THE *Billionaire* BOSS NEXT DOOR

*Did she just say stuff for horses?*

Living inside the city that hosts Mardi Gras, it's safe to say I've experienced some pretty insane Uber rides, but I can't deny this is the first time horses *and* stuff for horses have ever been an obstacle.

"So, if you don't mind," Nelly continues. "You can put your suitcase in the back seat and sit in the front." She takes my bag from my hands. "I mean, you're a petite little thing and could probably fit in the back *with* your luggage, but I figure you'll be more comfortable up front."

To be honest, I might be *most* comfortable if I called a new Uber, but I'm already running significantly behind schedule and have zero time to question the contents of her trunk.

Anyway, as long as it's not an actual horse or a dead body or a dead horse body, we're all set.

Once my suitcase is securely in her back seat and we're both seatbelted into the front, Nelly pulls away from my place and out onto the main road.

Instantly, our drive has a soundtrack that includes the sounds of swishing and swashing coming from the cargo area. It's like a sound machine, only it's not raindrops or the ocean but some mysterious fluid.

And whatever it is, there's *a lot* of it.

*There're not, like, jugs of gasoline back there, are there?*

No way. That'd be ridiculous. She said it was for her horses. I'm no veterinarian, but I'm pretty certain they're powered by hoofs and hearts. Not fossil fuels.

"Beautiful day, right?" Nelly asks, her eyes not on the road and staring directly at me.

I mutter a simple *uh-huh* and bury my face in my phone, hopeful that'll encourage her to keep her eyes focused on driving and possibly save me from hearing about the history of the hoof or something similar.

But it's hard to scroll through Amy Schumer's Instagram page when my driver is speed-racing through yellow lights and fucking up the flow of traffic.

I look up to find my driver glancing around at the scenery like it's a fucking Sunday morning walk.

"Oh! Look! It's the new Target!" she exclaims and takes one hand off the wheel to point toward the right side of the road. "If you haven't had a chance to check it out, you definitely should, Greer-ware! They even have a Starbucks inside."

It's not so much that my Uber driver is distracted but more I don't think she is aware that she's actually driving.

"Oh, uh, *watch out!*" The words tumble out of my mouth on instinct, and I point toward the vehicle right beside us. The one she's mere inches away from side-swiping because, *apparently*, Nelly is an "I'm going to use all the fucking lanes" kind of broad.

"Hey there, buddy!" She honks her horn and jerks her wheel to the right. "Bastards don't know how to drive!"

Simply put, her driving isn't exactly aces, and I'm gripping the edge of my seat before we even reach the highway.

And, sadly for me, the ride doesn't get any smoother.

The road is apparently a deterrent for Nelly's eyes. Her foot consists of lead. Her turns are rough at best, and she sticks with the mindset that everyone on the road *but* her is a terrible driver.

"What the hell!" she shouts toward the car in front of us. The car that she cut off no less than two minutes prior, mind you. "For goodness' sake, no one can drive today!"

I grip the edge of my seat tighter and close my eyes and start chanting *namaste* in my head.

But my attempt at finding solace and calm is brief at best. I pop my eyes wide open when my body is catapulted toward the passenger door as Nelly takes a sharp left turn and accelerates onto the highway.

*Whoa, Nelly.*

All the while, the swooshing from the back turns into the equivalent of Niagara Falls, and I white-knuckle the handle above the passenger door and glance toward my driver. "What did you say you have in the back again?"

*Please don't say gasoline. Please don't say gasoline.*

"Two big tanks of water for my horses," she answers like it's the most normal thing in the world and switches lanes without the use of her blinker. A horn honks behind us, but Nelly gives zero fucks about other drivers' horns. "I was at my mom's place this morning, and I always get my water from there because it's cheaper. She has a well." She grins over at me. "And since I'm planning on seeing my horses after my morning Uber shift, I figured what the hell. Might as well kill two birds with one stone today."

*Metaphorical birds might not be the only thing she kills today.*

On the bright side, I suppose, if I never make it to the airport, I won't have to worry about my interview with Turner Properties.

*Hah. My anxiety must be at a new, all-time high if I'm considering the possibility of death as an upside.*

Yeah. But that's because things are looking pretty damn grim from where I sit.

Even though I have plenty of happy return clients and referrals for small bathroom renovations or sunroom decoration available for work, the profit margin on those kinds of jobs is barely enough to keep my doors open for a month or two.

I need a large-scale job with notoriety and name recognition, and the new Vanderturn New Orleans hotel is it. The outcome of this interview is the difference between struggling to stay open for another thirty days without bankrupting myself and setting up my firm to thrive.

My stomach spasms.

*Yeah, no pressure or anything.*

Instantly, my stress level skyrockets, and Nelly's driving only gets worse.

Not to mention, she keeps talking to me.

It's the longest twenty minutes anyone has ever experienced, and all I can do is hold on for dear life and answer her questions. The last thing I want to do is upset her and cause some sort of accident.

Honestly, I never would've thought drowning was an actual possibility in a motor vehicle collision, but here I am, inside Nelly's water bed on wheels.

By the time she pulls the Equinox into the airport entrance, I've seen my life flash before my eyes a good seven times, and I've run the conversational equivalent of a marathon.

I know the names of all five of her horses, her retired parents' favorite vacation spots, and that her sister Marion makes her money by selling homemade scarves on Etsy.

Once she pulls the SUV to a stop at the departure curb, I hop out with about six times as much energy as the carcass formerly known as my body feels, but also, I *hop the hell out.*

*Five stars.* That's what you do with Uber, right? Just be thankful you arrived at your intended destination alive? What the fuck do I know.

I'm tempted to get on my knees and kiss the concrete, but my body isn't up for that kind of physical challenge. My legs and lower back ache as I yank my suitcase out of the back seat, and a sigh escapes my lungs of its own accord.

I feel like I've been ridden hard and put away in one of Nelly's water tanks.

Simply put, my mood is shit.

My business is failing. I've had zero sleep. And I'm headed to New York for the biggest interview of my life.

But I put on a smile for Nelly's sake. It's not one hundred percent her fault I'm such a bitch today. I mean, she could've not been such a shitty driver or asked me so many questions or told me her whole life story, but still, she is just a woman trying to earn a living and keep her horses hydrated.

"Thank you for the ride," I say and grip the handle to my luggage with my right hand. *Thank you for not killing me.*

"Have fun in New York, Gree-ware! And good luck with Hudson

## THE *Billionaire* BOSS NEXT DOOR

Designs!" She offers a little wave and a big ole grin before hopping back into her SUV.

And not even a minute later, she sloshes her way back toward the highway.

*Good luck with Hudson Designs,* her words repeat in my mind.

*Yeah. Pretty sure I need a hell of a lot more than luck, Nelly.*

Hudson Designs is my baby. The company I birthed from my proverbial womb. It is my pride. My passion. And the biggest reason my shoulders feel like I'm walking around with Dwayne "The Rock" Johnson hanging on, piggyback-style.

Normally, I have nothing against The Rock.

He's big. He's handsome. And if I had to smell what he was cooking, I'd venture to guess it would have an aroma of success and a multimillion-dollar bank account.

But his weight perched on my shoulders is no fucking joke, and everything I've ever worked for is at risk of crashing into the fiery pits of hell if I crumble under it.

It's almost hard to believe it all went so wrong.

When I graduated college, I was practically high off excitement over the possibility of future success. I mean, I had landed a huge internship turned full-time employment with Clarise Beaumont, one of the foremost interior designers on the Gulf Coast.

It was a big fucking deal, and in my naïve eyes, success skyrockets were already in flight.

After a few years working under her, I realized how impressive her work ethic and accomplishments were—and how much better they could be if I'd done them my way.

Eventually, I opened my own firm, motivated and hopeful about what opportunities being in business for myself could bring. And for the first couple of years, I chalked any and all hard times up to getting started. I had a client base to build, infrastructure to get in place. A few bumps in the road were more than understandable—they were expected.

Unfortunately, the next few years didn't improve.

The design business isn't the same as it was ten years ago, and everyone in the industry has taken a hit.

But when you're a one-woman show like me, there's a lot more overhead involved in making suppliers happy by taking sample stock at wholesale cost and keeping the daily operations of the office running.

Other than my assistant, Rosaline—who I had to let go three months ago—I couldn't afford to keep a staff for the work I couldn't spend my time doing personally. As a result, I had to outsource most of it, and the markup on the cost doubled.

And the bottom line of my books this morning confirms what I already knew—without a miracle, the last five years of my life might as well have been for nothing.

I haven't dated, I haven't traveled. I haven't even been to the Cheesecake Factory they built at the mall. All I've done is work, desperate to build something I'm proud of, and now it could be over.

My lip quivers unexpectedly, and I grind the gears in my mind straight into reverse.

*Do* not *cry, Greer. Breaking down on the sidewalk of the New Orleans airport is* not *acceptable.*

Besides, other than the whole *my business is failing* thing, today isn't *all* bad.

For one, I didn't die in Nelly's Equinox, and secondly, New Orleans is playing its most impressive hand of cards on what should be a cold winter day. The sun is surprisingly strong, and it makes my skin feel crisp, like I could crease it down the middle to match my slacks.

It feels good. Warm. *Cozy.*

This is my favorite city. The place I grew up. The place I started my business. My *home*.

And today, I'm minutes away from seeing my best friend Emory and flying first class to New York with her, courtesy of her family's

## THE *Billionaire* BOSS NEXT DOOR

money. They have old money, new money—all the fucking money—and Emory never flies anywhere in the back of the plane.

Luckily for me, she also doesn't like to fly alone, and her boyfriend is already there.

The loose wheel on my bargain luggage clatters behind me as I drag it up the ramp to the automatic door and inside the bright lights of the ticket area of Louis Armstrong International Airport.

People scurry back and forth around me in varying states of distress, but it's there, in the center of the chaos, that I find Emory, waving wildly from her spot in front of a pile of Louis Vuitton luggage.

Her red hair is so big, it's got to be full of something—I'm guessing money—and her signature blood-red lips pop against her ivory skin. She's got a look all her own, and each detail is centered around making her light blue eyes look misty gray.

I know this ridiculous information because she told me one night when we were a bottle deep in wine.

"Greeeeer!" she yells, obnoxiously enough that everyone in the vicinity turns to look.

My cheeks burn and sting as I make my way toward her reluctantly, avoiding any and all eye contact from the curious gazes she's garnered due to her big fat mouth.

I am a people person who kind of hates people. A conundrum in any country, on any day, in any language, but all the more complicated when you do what I do for a living.

But the work is what I love. The art, the creativity—the chance to do something different with each and every design.

It's what gives me life.

"Hello, hello," I greet as I pull my bag to a stop next to her five, and I smooth a hand down my wrinkled blouse and slacks. "Have you been here long?"

Automatically, her eyes engage, sliding into their default setting whenever I am around—an intensely obvious roll. And I can't even really blame her.

Her palate is refined, her heart is endlessly open, her workweek consists of *occasionally* going into the office to do god only knows what at one of her family's successful marketing firms, and her idea of discount shopping is a sale at Bergdorf's. I eat ramen at least two times a week, avoid men at nearly all costs, spend eighty hours a week in my office, and splurge at Target. But when it comes to personality, I am, without a doubt, the high-maintenance one of the two of us.

"You know I have. You're twenty minutes late."

"Well," I respond. "I think we should both just be happy I didn't drown."

She scrunches up her nose. "What?"

"It's a long story," I say. "And I'm twenty minutes late from the time you told me. Which is exactly what I always am. You know this, you've known this for years, and you should totally be able to factor that into your arrival time. So, really, it's like you're early."

She guffaws, and I transition my smirk into a smile. "You only have yourself to blame."

"Sometimes I really hate you."

I wave off the comment as if it is no more than a buzzing fly. "Yes, but that's nothing new either. And yet, you keep coming back for more."

Emory and I have been friends for what seems like forever—we're talking since tutus and closet costumes and an innocence the world had yet to crush. With only the all-male influence of my grandfather and my brother to guide me after my parents died, I clung to Emory like a female beacon of hope.

"Must be brainwashed."

"Hmm..." I pause for a moment and grin at her. "Pretty sure if I were going to brainwash you, I'd definitely use it for something other than this. Like convincing you to give me all of your money."

She rolls her "misty gray" eyes. "Why is it I wanted you to fly with me again?"

"My wit and charm, mostly."

# THE *Billionaire* BOSS NEXT DOOR

"No. It's definitely not that."

I pretend to purse my lips thoughtfully. "My delicately angelic good looks?"

"No."

"My—"

"Oh, right. I have no other friends. That's why."

"I wonder why that is. Maybe you need to reevaluate how demanding you are," I say sarcastically. Sarcastic or not, Emory's glare is hotter than a thousand suns. "I'm joking, E. Geez. You're a gem. The purest form of—"

"Shut up, Greer."

"Fine," I say with a laugh. "Go on, lecture me. I know that's what you've been waiting on."

"I'm not going to lecture you."

I scoff. "Sure, you're not."

"Well, if you don't want me to lecture you, you could at least show up in clothes that don't look like you slept in them. Did you even shower this morning?"

In an effort to avoid getting sucked into a steaming crater of pity and despair, I decide it's best not to tell her just how accurate she is and focus on complaining instead.

"Why do I have to go to New York for an interview for a job in New Orleans anyway?"

"Because your potential boss is a busy guy, and that's where he's going to be. I used my connections to get you this thing for a reason. Turner Properties is the real deal. A Vanderturn hotel in New Orleans is a *big* deal, especially if *you* get to design it," she says with a little smile, but that quickly vanishes when she continues her train of thought. "And *have to*? You act like you're going to war. It's New Year's Eve in New York, for shit's sake. You should be excited!"

"You're right. New York does sound amazing."

"*Thank you.*"

"I'm just—"

"I know." Her eyes turn soft and understanding. "I know what's riding on this, and I know it's weighing you down a bit."

*Weighing me down a bit?* If the stress of my financial situation gets any heavier, I might actually become my own gravitational force.

"If this doesn't go well," I say on a near whisper, "I'm not really sure what I'm going to do."

Because I don't. If this job interview isn't a success, I honestly have no idea what my next move will be. And that is *terrifying*.

"It's going to go well! You're the right person for the job. There's no way he won't see that."

I chew my lip.

"As long as you bring sweet Greer and leave the bitch at home..."

I feign a gasp.

Emory's lips crest up into a smile. "Oh, come on, put a smile on that pretty face. This is going to be the best trip of your life! Everything is about to come up roses! I can feel it!"

I just stare at her.

"Smile, Greer."

I half-ass an attempt at a smile, but it's brittle and forced and probably looks like Chandler Bing's engagement photos.

"Repeat after me," she says. "I am a brilliant designer."

I furrow my brow, and Emory nudges my arm with one of her pointy fucking elbows.

"Ow." I rub at my arm, but she ignores her assault completely.

"Say it, Greer. Say, *I am a brilliant designer*."

"I am a brilliant designer." The words come out monotone and unconvinced, but my newfound motivational speaker isn't deterred.

"Say, *I am going to nail this interview*."

"I am going to nail this interview."

"But before I go to said interview, I'm going to remove this resting bitch face and put on my strong, confident woman face."

I can't not smirk at that. "That is incredibly specific."

"Just say it."

## THE *Billionaire* BOSS NEXT DOOR

I oblige *and* silently pray that Tony Robbins will leave my best friend's body so I can attempt to enjoy this first-class trip to New York.

"Who's the best interior designer in New Orleans?"

I stare at her, but she threatens to dig one of her pointy elbows into my skin again.

My eyes roll heavenward. "Me."

"Who's the best woman for this job?"

"Me."

"Who is going to flaunt her perfect tits around New York and land herself a kick-ass job and nail a hot guy all in one weekend?"

"Me…wait…*what?*"

"Don't you worry, sweet cheeks, no one at Turner Properties will be able to resist you." Emory winks. "Now, let's go catch our flight to your future success!"

*Minus the nailing a hot guy part, I hope she's right.*

Because, fuck, I *need* this job.

# Chapter TWO

## Greer

After two-and-a-half hours on a plane, an hour-long slog in a death taxi—*without mention of horses, mind you*—a long line to check in at the Vanderturn Manhattan hotel, and eleventy-billion interview pep talks from Emory, I'm on the very brink of insanity.

My skin feels tight, my hair hurts, and my eyeballs seem to be operating independently from each other.

Apparently, I'm not the only one to notice.

When the bellman leaves to head up to our rooms with our luggage, Emory gets bossy and points in my face.

"Go work out. You need some Elle Woods thinking in your life. Exercise gives you endorphins. Endorphins make you happy. Happy people don't murder their husbands."

I scoff and tilt my head to escape the virtual laser beam shooting out of her finger. "Grumpy people without husbands don't murder their husbands either."

"You're going to have one someday, I'm telling you. So, you should start training now."

"Training? To be happy?" I frown. "Isn't that the sort of thing that should come naturally?"

"For you?" She snorts. "Probably not. You have a nasty habit of being a miserable shrew, and habits are hard to break."

My sigh is heavy as I grab the tops of her slender arms and squeeze *affectionately*. "You really say the nicest things."

# THE *Billionaire* BOSS NEXT DOOR

She ignores me and shoves me in the shoulder.

"Go. Change out of last night's clothes—"

I grin contemptuously.

"And sweat out all of that toxic energy you're carrying around. I'm going to need you to be in a better mood when I introduce you to Quincy."

"Ah, the boyfriend," I hum. "You're finally done hiding him?"

My best friend has been dating the illustrious Quincy for a few months, and this is the first time she's even *mentioned* introducing us. The guy also lives in New Orleans, yet she's waited until we're in New York for the big meet-and-greet. It's like she's afraid I'm going to do something crazy and doesn't want me on my home turf or something.

"I haven't been *hiding* him," she corrects. "Just making sure he's good and hooked before you scare him off."

I plaster a sugary-sweet smile onto my lips. "I resent your insinuation that I'm anything but pleasant and easy to get along with."

"If by *resent* you mean accept and acknowledge its validity, okay."

"Hmm…" I pause and tap my chin pointedly. "Webster's must have come out with a new version I'm unaware of, but I'll go with it for your sake."

She subtly applies a sheer shade of imaginary lipstick with her middle finger.

"Quince and I will meet you at the party at nine."

*Son of a bitch.* The New Year's Eve *"Mask-erade."* Obviously, I'd blocked out the fact that this trip includes a social engagement where an actual grown-ass human decided it would be a good time to take a traditional masquerade-themed party and sleaze it up by making the masks be made out of rubber and celebrity likenesses instead of exquisite lace and beading. But Emory's reminder ensures I can't ignore it now.

It takes every ounce of willpower not to dive into a long-winded, snarky rant about it.

But I suck it up and remind myself of the silver lining.

*A New Year's Eve party equals alcohol, Greer.*

"Be on time, please," Emory adds, but the *please* completely contradicts the stern, motherlike tone in which she delivers it.

"As if I'm ever anything else."

Her responding scoff echoes around us.

"Just enjoy yourself," she says. "Have a positive attitude for once. If you do, I guarantee it'll be great."

"You got it, Mom."

"Hey," she says, and her eyes turn soft as she steps forward to wrap me up in a hug. "You're my best friend, and all I want is for you to be happy. I know I'm pushy, but it's only because I love you."

I hug her back. "Love you too, E. Even when you sound like you're gearing up for a career in direct sales."

She snorts and lets me go with amusement shining in her eyes.

"Working out before a party gets results, people! Four out of five farm animals can't be wrong!" I use a far too high-pitched voice to mimic hers. "Happy people make happy choices, and this tea is the answer to happiness at least once a day! Your tits will be perky and your energy rejuvenated! Try the gel pads under your eyes for a fresh day feel!" I finish off my little act with a set of a jazz hands and a cheeky grin.

"I feel like you might have exaggerated a bit there…"

"Nah." I grin and shake my head. "I'm pretty sure that's what you said."

Emory rolls her eyes and laughs at the same time. "I'll see you tonight at the party."

She departs without another word—probably in an effort to avoid another smartass comeback or impromptu jazz hands—and leaves me to my own devices.

Once she's gone, the interior designer in me kicks in, and my surroundings become my companion.

And let me tell you, she's a real bitch.

The lobby is ostentatious in its design, and I'm practically offended by the maroon and green color scheme. Honestly, even Santa Claus would be offended, and that jolly mothershucker is all about the green and red.

The décor is more pretentious confusion than anything else. And if I have to come face-to-face with one more gilded sailboat painting or ornate statue, I swear on everything, I might puke.

*Jesus.* These people are never going to want me to do the design work for their New Orleans hotel. We have completely different tastes.

My style is what the design world would call *comfortable minimalism.* Not minimalism like Kim and Kanye's morgue-like mansion, but warm light, rich textures, and clean lines. My designs revolve around making a space feel light and airy yet so warm and cozy you feel like you're cocooned inside of a womb.

A space you not only want to look at, but you want to live in, be in, *thrive* in, too.

But this? This flashy and ostentatious gilded-clutter of a design scheme is giving me a headache.

If this space is a womb, I'm smack-dab in the center of Satan's uterus.

Discouraged again, I head for the elevator, intent on ordering a hamburger the size of my face and devouring it like the classy lady I am—wearing nothing but a bathrobe while lounging in bed, mind you—when I get to my room.

When the elevator door opens, I step inside and turn around, only to realize I've been followed in by what must be a supermodel convention.

The five women are tall, slender, and artfully put together. Sexy heels. Sexy dresses. Perfect hair. Perfect nails. Perfect lashes and lips. They are ready to do it up New Year's Eve-style in New York City.

And standing beside them is *me*—a woman wearing wrinkled clothes, who stinks of airplanes and bad news.

*I'm basically the cover model for pathetic right now.*

And it's that bleak thought that sparks something inside of me.

Emory's right.

If I have any chance of going into that interview in two days with an attitude even slightly better than the Grim Reaper, I need to shake it up.

Make different choices. Get some endorphins or whatever shit Elle Woods has, and give myself a chance to turn it around.

I have tonight and all day tomorrow to get myself in order. Get my mind right. Get my confidence up.

In terms of time, it's not a lot.

*You better get your ass in gear, girlfriend.*

The elevator slows to a stop and announces its arrival at the twentieth floor, and I move past the flawless women, out of the cart, and toward my hotel room without looking back.

This isn't a time to dwell; it's a time to take action.

And my first New York action? Throw on some workout gear, figure out where in the hell the hotel gym is located, and get some damn endorphins all up in my bloodstream.

*You got this, Greer.*

It only takes five minutes inside the hotel gym to realize why my original plan was to eat a hamburger in bed.

I do *not* got this.

I'm not good at working out, I've never been good at working out, and I'll never *be* good at working out.

I don't know what to do with the equipment, and it doesn't know what to do with me.

Clearly, it's been designed for people with half a foot more height and fifty percent more muscle, and even on the lowest of settings, I fumble my way through biceps curls like an uncoordinated inchworm.

I can barely reach the handles, so I have to kind of stoop to get

# THE *Billionaire* BOSS NEXT DOOR

in position, but the newly formed curve of my spine makes me have to arch and wiggle to complete the curl. If it weren't for my kick-ass Metallica T-shirt, I might start to worry that I look foolish.

The ten-pound weight clanks as I drop it the inch and a half I managed to lift it in the first place, and I stand up to find a different machine. Surely there's something in here I can operate without having a special license.

I find some kind of seated thing with weights on one end and a padded face rest on the other. I sit, lay my face down, and attempt to slide my legs underneath the weighted bar. But it's completely awkward and uncomfortable, and I start questioning what in the fuck this thing is even supposed to do.

Just before I give up completely, a throat clears deeply beside me, and I look up to see a far too muscular man staring down at me in confusion. "Uh…wow…I didn't realize you could use it that way…"

*Huh?*

I nearly ask him what he's talking about, but his actions answer any and all questions I might have.

He sits down on the machine beside mine—*an identical machine to mine*—and it's then I realize the face rest is *not* a face rest.

It's a seat. For *asses*.

A seat for sweaty, workout asses.

*Jesus Christ.* I shudder and disentangle myself from the machine.

"You okay?" Arnold Schwarzenegger's long-lost brother asks, but I just nod off his question and put some much-needed distance between us.

Also, I scrub my face with the hand towel I brought down from my room like it's a fucking Brillo pad capable of removing the ball sweat that's probably found itself a home in my pores.

*Note to self: take one thousand scalding-hot showers tonight.*

With a deep inhale, I try to regain some of the pride I lost back there to Mr. Muscles and peruse the room until I find a machine that's labeled with instructional pictures to boot.

Hip. *Abduction.*

*Do I need aliens to use this thing?*

Against my better judgment, I study the pictures and peptalk myself into sitting down on the seat and swing my legs over to the inside of the knee pads.

*No face-to-butt-sweat mistakes happening here, folks!*

The weight is set on one hundred and fifty pounds from the person before me, and it makes me wonder if Thor is staying at this hideous hotel too.

I pull out the pin and put it on forty instead.

After a quick test push with my legs, the setting seems doable, so I take out my phone and start scrolling through it to set up some music to accompany me.

*Yes. Yes. That's exactly what I need. Some workout jams.*

Of course, once I'm on it, I get distracted by Instagram, and five minutes go by before I realize I'm sitting on a machine, not a couch, and the purpose here is to do something other than lounge.

I glance up from my phone and scan the room, wondering slightly if anyone knows how long I've been sitting here. Mr. Muscles has moved on to a new machine, but a different guy across the room makes eye contact and smirks.

*Busted.*

Normal human decency dictates he should let me off the hook and go about his day, but this fit, Adonis-looking, sweat-covered, brown-haired, green-eyed—*good God, he's attractive*—man apparently has no manners.

*Shit.*

His sleeveless white T-shirt clings to his tanned body as he strides my way, and his athletic shorts conform to a muscular set of thighs and ass.

I look everywhere but at him, fiddling with the machine as though I'm doing something productive, but he still doesn't get the hint.

# THE *Billionaire* BOSS NEXT DOOR

Raspy and firm, the clearing of his throat sounds right next to me.

I look up as innocently as I can manage and pull out my earbuds as though I had music playing.

"Um, hi," I say with a cute little manufactured laugh. "I'll be done in just a second."

He laughs too, but his seems genuine and undeniably directed at me. "If you keep up your current pace, I think it's going to be a little longer."

"Excuse me?"

"Come on," he says good-naturedly—*the prick.* "You're just pretending to work out."

*Oh no, he did* not *just say that....*

"I'm not *pretending* to work out," I deny. "I'm just getting warmed up."

He nods knowingly.

"And setting up my music," I continue.

He hums.

"I'm just about to catch my stride."

"Sure you are." He calls bullshit with his smug, green-as-fuck eyes, and for the briefest of moments, they glance down at my chest and my legs before meeting my gaze again. "But there are people who would like to *really* use it, so if you're done…"

What. The. Fuck.

Who does this guy think he is?

"Are you always this rude?" I question, and his green eyes lighten a bit.

"All right, you're right. I'm really not trying to be a dick," he says and runs a hand through his hair.

*Should it really take that much effort* not *to be a dick?*

"Let's start over…" He pauses and pushes a small smile to his full, kissable lips. "How are you enjoying the hotel?"

*Start over? How about let's never have started at all?*

Still annoyed, I don't censor my answer. "It's…*swell.*"

21

He laughs at first, but when I raise an eyebrow in contention, he frowns. "You don't like it?"

"Maybe ugly décor and a whole buttload of pretention are good for some people, but not for me."

"Ugly décor? Really?"

*How can he be shocked by this? Anyone with eyes could see the design flaws here.*

"Are you kidding? I feel like I'm in my ninety-year-old grandmother's living room, except it's a waking nightmare and I'm about to be eaten alive by the curtains."

"I don't think it's that bad. It's timeless."

Normally, I'm not such a snob about design, nor do I make a point to make other people feel bad for their likes and dislikes, but for some reason, this handsome prick and his dickish attitude just bring it out in me.

Before I know it, I'm channeling Regina George.

"Well…" I pause and scrunch up my nose dramatically. "I'm sorry to break the news to you, but the design of this place looks like it was done by a blind rat. Gilded sailboat pictures and tapestries with oxen on them aren't timeless. They're old."

His eyebrows pinch together, highlighting the otherwise perfect features of his face. *Goddamn this ugly hotel for housing such perfect-looking humans.*

"What did you say your name was again?"

*Shit.* Emory will absolutely murder me if she finds out I got into some kind of confrontational tête-à-tête with a random Romeo in the hotel gym.

*Let's also not forget this hotel gym is located inside a hotel that is owned by the company you're about to interview with…*

Shit. Yeah. I'd better cut and run while I can.

"I didn't." I jump up from the machine with the exact agility I've lacked during the rest of my workout and offer a saccharine smile. "But, hey, good news. Machine's all yours."

"Aren't you going to wipe it down?" he asks as I walk toward the door, and I can't help but turn around for my parting shot.

"Why?" I smirk at the pouty-lipped asshole. "After all, I was just *pretending* to work out."

Because you know what dicks can do?

They can go fuck themselves *and* wipe down their own workout equipment, tight asses and chiseled jaws be damned.

*Suck on that, workout Romeo.*

# Chapter THREE

## Greer

At ten thirty on the dot, I glance at the clock and tell myself it's time to get a move on. Even though Emory might strangle me for being so damn late, I focus on the fact that I'm starting to feel kind of good.

It's quite possible Lady Luck has decided to grace me with her presence.

*Maybe, just maybe, things are starting to look up.*

I've only been in New York for half a day, and I'm starting to feel like the Greer I used to know way back when. The Greer who had vigor and a lust for life. The Greer who felt like she could conquer anything.

I've showered. Well, showered *and* most likely scrubbed off a layer or two of skin from my face.

And I've made myself look presentable, pretty even. My long brown locks are fixed into gorgeous waves, and the long, snazzy gown I'm wearing is hugging my curves in just the right way.

Simply put, I'm Beyoncé.

Okay, fine, I'm *Greer* in a rubber Beyoncé mask.

But that's not the point.

The point is that inside the city that never sleeps, I'm starting to feel like me.

Maybe *this* is what Billy Joel would call a "New York State of Mind"?

## THE *Billionaire* BOSS NEXT DOOR

*Or was that Sinatra?*

Eh, screw it. No matter who said it, I'm feeling it.

*Start spreading the news, bitches! Greer is feeling herself!*

*Figuratively* feeling myself, that is. My hands are nowhere near my tits.

With my head held higher than it's been in months and a hitch in my hard-to-wear-stilettos-clad step, I hurry out of my room and head for the elevators.

From the hallway, I hear the arrival bell ding, and my red satin dress drags on the carpet behind me as I run for the available cart and slide in just before the doors close.

Several partygoers fill the cramped space with an overpowering mix of perfumes and cologne and pompous attitude. It's obnoxious, but maybe if I'm lucky, the particles will cover my tardiness like a cloak.

I wish I knew what I was getting myself into by attending this insane New Year's Eve Mask-erade party at the Vanderturn Manhattan hotel, but Emory lives for the element of surprise.

*Meet me up there*, she said.

*It'll be great*, she said.

*This party is hosted by the people you're interviewing for, and I'll kill you if you mess this up*, she said.

Nerves flutter in my stomach as laughter and chatter carry on around me. The people filling the tight space around me are in Emory's circle. They're rich and happy, and I can guarantee none of them are faced with looking for a new place to live because their house is being foreclosed on.

*Fuck.* Instantly, my thoughts send my upbeat mood into a nose dive.

*Hold the presses, bitches. It appears there is no news to spread.*

Not to mention, Emory has a new boyfriend to take her arm, a man to take her back—a shield to deflect some of the attention.

I am a one-woman Beyoncé show. In a fabulous dress, mind you, but still a lonesome party of one all the same.

The elevator dings its arrival on the top floor, and the people behind me push out with the consideration of a herd of buffalo.

I bob and weave, trying to find my footing in these stupid fucking heels I decided to wear, and I finally make a dash out the doors just as they're closing.

One deep breath is followed by a second as I take in the room and engage a commanding step forward.

At least, I *try*.

The train of my red satin dress tugs back violently, and I stumble like a newborn colt.

Sweat breaks out in beads on my brow as I scan the room to see if anyone noticed. All eyes safely averted, I try again, jerking on the material with a demanding hand, only to be denied once more.

*What the ever-loving hell?*

Now manic and desperate, I follow the satin like a dive line until I reach the end—clamped by the fucking vise of the outer doors of the elevator shaft.

*Oh my God. Why is this happening?*

I tug and tug with my back to the doors in an attempt to be discreet, but people are starting to look, I can feel it.

The anxiety is intense, pricking at my skin and clamming up my hands and making my throat close in around itself.

*Oh my God. I'm going to die, right here, dressed like Beyoncé!*

I look to my right and find a rubber-masked Batman, but all hope of the Caped Crusader offering a superhero hand goes out the damn window when I notice he's tongue-kissing a guy dressed like Robin. My heart drops to my fucking feet.

Since when is making out more important than saving a damsel in distress? Gotham City would be ashamed.

I'm just about to knock myself out by slamming my body into the doors in a feat of sheer self-preservation when a Kanye-masked mountain of a man appears and pushes the button to call the cart.

Within seconds, the ding of arrival sings, and the doors pop open to free me.

*Why didn't I think of that?*

"Jesus," I mutter more to myself than anyone else and put a hand to my chest to calm my racing heart. "Thank you, Kanye. I'm certain Beyoncé wouldn't have wanted to go out that way."

"No worries." The man's responding chuckles fill my ears. "Beyoncé had one of the best videos of all time!"

I smile at his use of Kanye's exact words to Taylor Swift, when the blond-headed singer herself steps forward and takes his arm in hers.

"I guess it's a good thing we were standing near the elevator, waiting on your notoriously late arrival," the girl on Kanye's arm says, and instantly, I know it's Emory, dressed like Taylor Swift. "You okay, friend?" she asks, and I nod.

"Quince, this is Greer," she says, and I smile, but it's useless behind the rubber Beyoncé mask covering my face.

Seriously. Whoever thought wearing rubber celebrity masks to a fucking party like this would make it a good time is a total moron.

"I like your mask, Greer," Quincy says behind his Kanye mask. "Isn't it fun?"

"The masks were Quince's idea," Emory moons, and the ironic timing of my thinking almost makes me choke.

"Wait...are you Greer Hudson?" Quince asks suddenly, turning to look at Emory and then me, like somehow staring into the eyes of my Beyoncé mask is going to uncover the truth.

"Uh, yes. Should I already know you?"

"No, no, I'm just a fan of your work."

"Seriously?"

"Definitely," he says, and his voice vibrates with honesty. It warms my cold heart, but unfortunately for him, it also leaves me one hell of an opening.

"Well, this is embarrassing," I respond with feigned nervous giggles. "I honestly thought none of those tapes were circulating anymore…"

"What?" he questions.

"I swear, I only did it briefly," I add. "After college. To pay rent."

"Oh God." Panicked, his eyes dart between Emory and me like a ping-pong ball. "No, I… I don't… I—" He clears his throat. "I haven't seen any *tapes* of you. I don't watch *tapes*. Well, I mean, not since high school anyway. I—"

Emory spears me with a glare and takes her flustered boyfriend's bicep in hand.

"Relax, Quince. She's kidding. Greer never had a porn career. Only a sick sense of humor."

I smile and stick out a conciliatory hand. "Nice to meet you, Quince. And now I'm one-hundred-percent interested to know which *tapes* you watched in high school. *Hefty Jugs? Tight Taints? Bangin' Blondes,* perhaps?"

"I'm sorry," Quince mumbles. "I think I just swallowed my tongue."

"Jesus Christ, Greer," Emory grumbles. "Can I not take you anywhere?"

"What?" I shrug. "I'm just making friendly conversation."

"It's fine, Em," Quince says. "I'm kind of in love with her now."

I can't exactly see Emory's face clearly under her Taylor Swift mask, but I don't have to. She is undoubtedly ordering a voodoo doll of me from an Etsy shop tonight and stabbing it right in the vagina.

"No, no, she's right, Quince. You guys are adorable together, and it really is nice to meet you. I'm surprised but honored that you've heard of Hudson Designs, and I appreciate the excitement about my work. I'm also digging the Kanye, Taylor Swift couple irony you have going on here."

"That was Em's idea," he says admiringly and tucks her closer to his side. The two of them lock gazes and sway toward each other with fairy-tale precision.

# THE *Billionaire* BOSS NEXT DOOR

And I officially need a drink.

I excuse myself pretty easily since they're ensconced in their canoodling and slink toward the long marble bar along the windows on the far side of the ballroom. Free drinks are one of the bright spots of attending this party, and I fully intend to enjoy the opportunity to consume them.

The line is long and the people are chatty, so I take the time to retreat deeper into myself. The bartender works the crowd and smiles readily with everyone, and he seems like the kind of easygoing guy I could get along with.

His name tag glints in the light, and I ready myself to regale him with charm by studying his name.

When I finally belly up to the cold gray stone, I lean my elbows into the counter and announce cheekily, "Chardonnay me, Kevin."

Kevin's eyebrows pinch together, and his fun-loving demeanor suddenly seems a lot less fun. "My name's not Kevin."

*What?*

I glance back to the name tag I was so sure had set me up for success and read it again.

*Karen.* Her name is Karen, and Karen is a girl.

*Dear God, I need to get my eyes checked.*

"Heh. Whoops." I laugh nervously. "I have…uh…cataracts. And you look lovely tonight, Karen."

Her scowl is scary, but I'm not leaving without my Chardonnay. I tap my fingernails on the counter as she prepares it, and I watch with an eagle eye for spit or poison.

Thankfully, the open setup of her workspace makes it hard to achieve either form of sabotage, and she slides the half-full glass toward me.

Her intense loathing of me won't make getting another drink easy, but maybe I can sweet-talk Emory into switching masks with me in the bathroom before I need more.

I turn to leave the bar and smack right into a hard wall.

"Excuse me," a tuxedo-wearing Albert Einstein says. I can't see his face, obviously, but the fit of his formal wear is superb. I can feel the hot muscle of his chest through the expensive fabric as I force myself to step away.

I smile flirtatiously on instinct, but it's not until he speaks again that I realize he can't see a goddamn thing thanks to Beyoncé.

"Are you okay?" The mask does a good job of muffling his words, but it does nothing to disguise the deep, rich, masculine edge of his timbre.

"Oh, sure, sure. Just a little elementary particle interaction," I tease flirtatiously. "Nothing I can't handle."

"What?"

Jesus. Don't tell me my eyes have failed me again.

I squint through the tiny holes in Beyoncé's rubber skin. "Aren't you supposed to be Albert Einstein?"

"Yeah."

I frown under my mask. "I was referencing the theory of relativity. Albert's kind of famous for it…"

"Oh. Yeah, I just went with the first mask I found."

*Wow.* Note to self: don't be lured into the trap of svelte physique, Greer. He may be pretty, but some people really are all looks and no brains.

Not even bothering to formally excuse myself, I turn and head for the darkest corner I can find. Luckily, it also happens to be right outside of the kitchen—perfect for getting first selection of hors d'oeuvres as the servers bring them out on shiny silver trays.

When I've had almost more than my dress was built to accommodate and the waiters start to subtly shield the trays with their arms upon exit, I mosey back toward the dance floor and try to find Emory and Quince.

I'm due for a new drink anyway.

Thanks to Quincy's size and Emory's blue tulle gown, I locate them effortlessly. They're swaying in the center of the room with champagne glasses tucked close to each other's backs, and interrupting them in the name of alcohol suddenly doesn't seem like such a good idea.

Emory's been searching for a man of worth for nearly as long as I have, and in the process, she's dated some real dogs.

With a parade of cheaters, gamblers, drinkers, and a few money-hungry clingers, she's sampled from quite the mixed bag. She even married one in Vegas for, like, fifty-five hours just like good ole Britney Spears, but her parents' lawyers got it annulled before he could ruin her life.

From what I can tell, Quincy seems different. A little goofy, sure, but altogether a really good guy.

She deserves to have a romantic New Year's Eve with her long-awaited Prince Charming.

Even if it means I have to suffer through the rest of this party sober…fucking hell.

"Excuse me," a man says as he runs into my back thanks to my decision to reroute midstride. Flashbacks of Ignorant Einstein turn the corners of my mouth down into a grimace as I turn to face him, but upon inspection, I'm thankful to find a different scientist entirely—Walter White of *Breaking Bad*.

He's tall. Fit. His shoulders are the perfect kind of broad beneath his well-fitted and dapper tuxedo. Even though I have no idea what his face looks like beneath the mask, the rest is a welcome sight for my eyes.

"My *bad*, Walt," I apologize. "I'm the one who switched directions."

He laughs and rubs a tanned, long-fingered hand across the black-and-white material at his chest. "Well, in that case, I *Better Call Saul*."

I smile at that, Beyoncé and her rubber-masked cockblocking be damned, and look to the ground self-consciously.

My feet feel like they're bleeding, my dress might as well be painted on, and I'm starting to sweat under this stupid mask, but finally, the evening seems to be looking up.

"Would you like to get a drink?" Walt asks, and I can't contain the fervor in my nod.

"God, yes."

He holds out a hand to indicate I should lead the way when I remember my little mishap with the bartender and the possibility of, you know, poison.

"Ah, hell."

"What's wrong?"

"Oh. Well, see, I didn't make the best impression on Karen earlier, and I don't really think she's going to do cartwheels at the idea of serving me again."

"She's an employee of the hotel. It's her job."

"Yeah." I laugh. "I guess you haven't seen the movie *Waiting*."

He's silent for a moment, perhaps considering the absolutely disgusting subject matter of that movie, before changing his tune. "Okay. You wait here. I'll get the drinks. What do you like?"

"Tropical vacations. Reruns of *The Office*. New Kids on the Block. Kittens—"

"*To drink*." I swear I can hear a soft chuckle escape his lips, but I can't be sure over the music pounding from the speakers. "What do you like to *drink*?"

"Ohh, *that*," I say with a knowing laugh. "Chardonnay."

Not being able to take advantage of facial cues when bantering with a new partner is disconcerting to say the least, but Walter seems to be up to the challenge and properly versed in humor. I decide to trust that he'll understand mine.

"Great. Be right back."

I weave among the dancing couples as he makes his way to the bar and hover creepily behind Ed Sheeran and Miley Cyrus while Walt orders from Karen.

I can almost sense the moment he says the word Chardonnay—because her eyes surreptitiously scan the room. I slouch farther behind Miley and peek again.

# THE *Billionaire* BOSS NEXT DOOR

Reluctantly, Karen smiles and grabs a bottle from the shelf behind her to pour my glass of wine and then gets to work making a complicated concoction for Walt.

My back aches from hunching, and Miley might have to consider adopting me by the time he finally turns around to make his way to me again.

I kind of want to tease him about it, but the desperate little bird on my shoulder reminds me what that will do to my prospects for having someone to kiss at midnight, and I seal my sarcastic mouth tight.

There's not much worse than standing around watching everyone else in a room toast to the future with someone they love while you whither in your lonely destitution.

A little dramatic? Probably. But my dismal business situation has me riding quite the emotional wave. *Cowabunga, dude* and all that.

Walt hands me my glass, and I take it gratefully. "Thank you."

"You're welcome."

I lift the bottom edge of my mask and slip the glass underneath to take a hearty gulp, and he does the same.

Lost for words now that I've forbidden myself from saying anything too sarcastic, I flounder in my awkwardness and fidget obsessively. A tug at the fabric on one strap of my dress, a smoothing hand across my stomach, and a tap of my toe on the marble floor later, the lights of the room finally flicker their absolution.

"Ladies and gentlemen," a disembodied voice says over the speakers of the room. "Make your way to the windows and find your companions. The ball will be dropping in one minute."

I'm half expecting Walt to excuse himself to find his wife or girlfriend or someone else, but he doesn't. Instead, he holds out a gallant arm. "Shall we, Beyoncé?"

*Oh, Walt. We definitely shall.*

With my hand tucked into the crook of his elbow, he guides me across the room and to the windows, even managing a spot for us right up front with an unobstructed view.

We face forward silently as a countdown begins from thirty.

Lights flash in Times Square below, and the crowd in the room gets restless. They chant the numbers exuberantly, but with each progressive number of their countdown, I retreat deeper into uncertainty.

Disquiet about why I'm here and what I'm doing with a guy I only know as Walt and insecurity about the big interview with Turner Properties.

*What if I fail?*

*What if I put everything I have into this business of mine, and I walk away with nothing but years of stress and aging?*

I'm so lost in my thoughts, I almost don't notice when the crowd turns bloodthirsty for satisfaction and winds their way down from ten.

A roar of noise penetrates the windows from below, and still, I don't flinch.

It isn't until the touch of a warm, gentle hand slides across my back and puts pressure on me to turn that I realize Walt has rolled up the very bottom of his mask and is reaching for mine with the hand not at my back.

Seconds masquerade as millennia, and cheers take over the room. The transition of one year to the next is official, and Walt's lips are on mine.

Slow and exploratory, he teases and tastes and builds energy in the bundle of butterflies at home in my stomach.

The kiss is…exquisite.

It's new and unfamiliar, but satisfyingly *right*.

It's everything I'd want out of a midnight kiss with a stranger and more.

There's a buzz between us—a hum of electricity or energy or some other new age shit—and my body sways toward his naturally. His big hands move down my sides and over my hips until they're gripping the silk material covering my ass, and a soft moan escapes my throat.

He feels so good. Tastes so good. Like mystery and excitement and promises of sex and sin.

# THE *Billionaire* BOSS NEXT DOOR

I slide my hands to his broad shoulders, letting my fingers explore the firm and taut muscles of his upper body.

Time is nonexistent. The partygoers around us go poof. And the music coming from the speakers of the dance floor disappears entirely. This mind-blowing, deepening kiss commandeers all of my senses until the only thing I can hear is the excited rhythm of my heartbeat pounding inside my ears.

Our lips tease and explore and take all of my breath, so that when he finally pulls away, when the moment finally ends, when we finally come back down to earth, I don't even have the air left to sigh.

All sorts of reckless possibilities run through my mind and pulse in my vagina as I work up the nerve to ask Walt back to my room. It'd be a night of wild chemistry if nothing else, and a good cleaning for these dusty pipes.

With his hands gently gripping my fingers, he leans back and looks down at me, and I can't stop my gaze from fixating on his now visible mouth.

*God, no wonder he's such a fan-fucking-tastic kisser.*

His lips are full and round and just...*perfect*.

Damn near entranced, my eyes follow the path of his tongue as it sneaks out and runs across his bottom lip, almost like he's savoring the taste of our kiss.

It's incredibly arousing. Even my vagina agrees. The horny little bitch is already throbbing and aching over the mere idea of spending the night with him.

"Hmmm...interesting..." he says on a near whisper, and I honestly get the vibe that it's more for himself than for me.

But I can't be sure.

And *interesting*? What does that mean?

Good interesting? Bad interesting? "You are an incredibly weird person, and I never want to kiss you again" interesting?

I have no idea, but I can't stop myself from trying to find out. "What's interesting?"

He doesn't answer. Instead, his eyes search mine for a good ten seconds.

And he squeezes my fingers with his hand as his attention snags for the briefest of moments over my shoulder. But he quickly recovers and brings his gaze back to mine.

Before I can urge him for an explanation or for his name or for him to let me see the face behind the mask, he leans in closer to my body, and his warm breath brushes across the skin of my cheek. "If we were anywhere else," he whispers, and his soft lips just barely tease against my ear. "If we were anywhere else in the fucking world but here, my next kiss would be between your legs."

*Holy fuck.*

Instantly, a shiver rolls down my spine, and every damn cell in my body is shouting for him to make an exception.

*We can go anywhere but here!* my vagina basically shouts from beneath my dress. *Just let her get her purse, and we'll be on our way!*

"Happy New Year, Beyoncé." His tone sounds so final. Too final.

Instantly, my stomach takes a nose dive into disappointment.

A part of me wants to urge him to reconsider. But another part of me, the larger part of me, is all about keeping my pride intact.

So, I do the only thing I'm capable of. I swallow down my discomfort and keep it locked beneath the rubber of my mask.

"Same to you, Walt," I whisper back.

After one last look into my eyes, he lets go of my fingers and walks away, disappearing into the crowd of happy people and leaving me to wonder all alone.

*Is it better to have been kissed and left or to have never been kissed at all?*

## Chapter FOUR

### Trent

It's the second official day of the New Year, and I've already hit the ground running.

There's no rest for the wicked and the work-driven, and I have an entire hotel to get off the ground in New Orleans and a short-as-fuck timeline in which to do it.

And, apparently, this morning, I also have an impromptu meeting with my father.

As I walk down the marble hallway of the sixteenth floor of Turner Properties' New York headquarters and toward my father's office, my phone buzzes in my jacket pocket, and I pull it out to check my messages.

*Cap: Do you know the name Sophia Moran?*

I smirk and shake my head at the same time. Caplin Hawkins is one of my best and most ridiculous friends. With my fingers to the screen, I type out a quick response.

*Me: That's Quince's college girlfriend.*

*Cap: Quince had a girlfriend in college?*

*Me: Uh…yeah. They dated for two years.*

**Cap:** *Ah, fuck. I knew that name sounded familiar. How firm do you think Quince is on Bro Code?*

I can see the text bubbles in the chat box move up and down, and I hurriedly type out a response before he can say anything else.

**Me:** *Keep whatever details you're about to tell me to yourself. I do not want to become an accessory to your crime.*

**Cap:** *Who says I did anything wrong?*

I laugh to myself. And as I step into the reception area of my father's office, I type out one final text and slip my phone back into my pocket.

**Me:** *Everything you've ever done in your entire life.*

Helen, my father's assistant, is busy typing something out on her computer, but the instant she looks up from her screen, a genuine smile consumes her face.

"I'll let him know you're here."

"Thanks." I nod and move toward the large floor-to-ceiling windows overlooking the massive city.

With leftover snow from last week's storm dusting the rooftops and buildings and streets, New York oozes winter. But the cold weather doesn't stop her liveliness. The sidewalks are littered with people, and the streets are filled with yellow taxi cabs and delivery trucks navigating the early morning rush.

Eventually, I move away from the windows and make myself comfortable in one of the chairs positioned across from Helen's desk.

In a weird way, waiting outside of my father's office is almost like sitting in my own living room. The taupe-gray walls house pictures of familiar faces from all over the world—a sort of shrine to all of the connections my dad's made over the years—and the feel of the cushion of the leather chairs reminds me of all the years I've spent sitting in them.

I've spent more hours in this building than I have in houses in my lifetime, and I have my dad's ambition and drive to thank for that.

Trent Turner Senior is a man who could be the poster child for the American Dream. His family wasn't poor, but they weren't well-off either, so it was only the power of his determination and perseverance and drive for success that allowed him to create the multibillion-dollar empire that is Turner Properties.

The company was established back in the late seventies when my father opened his first hotel in New York. A boutique hotel, at that. It began with a two-hundred-thousand-dollar debt, a second mortgage on his and my mom's house, and an insane amount of stress and failures from what I've been told. But within ten years, he'd turned that debt into a million-dollar profit and ten more hotels across the country.

And with Turner Properties' last evaluation as a solid twenty-billion-dollar company, it's safe to say the momentum hasn't stopped since.

No matter how big his company got, no matter how many employees he acquired, he's always kept an ear to the ground and a hand to the work. As a kid, I went with him everywhere he would let me, and I have to admit, that meant I went a lot of places.

He flourished under my attention, and I worshiped the ground he walked on.

All in all, that foundation for our relationship is probably the reason why I am the way I am. He is a self-made man—something, as his son and employee, I'll never be able to say I am—but he's the man who made me.

I work long hours, and the ones I don't spend at the office, I usually spend plotting and dreaming about new ideas to implement when I'm there.

But all of the hard work isn't for naught.

One day soon, I want my father to be able to retire. He's reached the age where he shouldn't be spending the majority of his days and nights in the goddamn office. He should be at home with my mom. Spending time with her. Taking care of her. Enjoying the time he has left with her.

But getting to the point where he trusts me enough to take over Turner Properties currently feels like a nearly impossible feat. One I've been trying to overcome for the past decade.

I'd never personally label myself a workaholic, but it's a term I've heard thrown around more than once or twice among my friends.

I don't have to wonder where I got it.

In addition to hardworking and dedicated, my father is also incredibly loyal. When he finds an employee he loves, he makes sure they never have a reason to leave.

Which probably explains why I've known my dad's assistant, Helen, since I was a baby.

The shine of her hair glints in the bright recessed lighting as she completes numerous tasks behind the shield of her white-marble-topped and gold-legged desk.

She's a hard worker and even thicker-skinned, and she runs such a tight ship, sometimes I wonder who's really running the company—her or my dad.

"He's ready for you," she says, touching her ear with a nod, but I hesitate.

Is she talking to me?

Someone else?

God, Bluetooth technology is fucking unnerving. I never know if people are talking to me or the person in their ear.

"Trent," she says, and still, it doesn't really clear anything up.

My dad and I share the same name, and ever since we started working together, it's been a point of confusion on many occasions.

## THE *Billionaire* BOSS NEXT DOOR

She snaps her fingers and points at me, clear as fucking crystal, and I feel like a fool for not responding earlier. "Get in there, kid."

Only Helen and my mom can get away with calling me "kid" without it boiling under my skin. At thirty-three years old, I'm not exactly old and gray, but after a decade in the business, I feel like I've earned my stripes. Anytime anyone says anything to suggest I haven't, it grates.

Confident and quick, I stride into the office and shut the door behind me with a click.

My dad is going over a report and retucking his shirt into the waistband of his pants. He's always worked sloppy, but he'd never let that show to anyone else. Not even me.

*Look put together, feel put together*, he always used to say. I apparently took the words to heart because my black suit is one of twenty just like it hanging in the master closet of my loft in lower Manhattan, and I've never worn flip-flops in my life.

"Have a seat," my father orders, and I do. I'd rather stand, since I don't know the nature of this meeting and being on my feet makes me feel quicker on them, but I'm not in control here.

My dad's obsessive need to control everything is the ultimate trump card in every conversation or meeting I have with him.

And that's exactly what he's trying to tell me as he rounds the desk and leans into the heavy wood so I have to look up at him. His stormy gray-blue eyes sparkle behind his glasses, highlighting the silver flecks in his black hair. We don't look particularly alike other than our bodies—slender hips and broad shoulders—because as far as my features are concerned, I heavily favor my mother.

"How's construction going?" he asks without preamble, and for once, I appreciate the omission of bullshit.

"Fine. George gets lazy if you don't push him, but we're on schedule so far."

"You need to be in New Orleans," he huffs. The fact that I'm still living in New York, working remotely and only traveling to New

Orleans when absolutely necessary, is a huge point of contention between us. He knows damn well why I've stayed, but it doesn't matter. If the time you're living on isn't *his* time, it's wrong.

"I know. I'll be there by the end of the week."

"You should have gone two months ago."

I grind my jaw against his insensitivity. Every time he pushes me on this, I get a little bit closer to feeling like we're not even related at all. I cannot comprehend why can't he understand why I've stayed. She may be his wife, but she's my mom, and she's sick.

"Mom—"

"Would have understood. She's been with me long enough to get it when work comes first."

And this is a perfect example of where his bullheadedness and indelible work ethic go too far.

It takes everything inside me not to offer up a rebuttal to his fucked-up mind-set, but I take a deep breath and stand up from my chair. I move behind it and lean into the leather back pointedly.

I'm done lying on the ground and taking my licks. If he wants to continue this meeting, we're at least going to do it on the same level.

"What do you need?" I ask, hoping to speed up this painful process.

"I just wanted to let you know I'll be finishing up staffing for the New Orleans team today."

*He* is going to finish up staffing for the hotel *I'm* in charge of.

*Fucking hell.*

My eyebrows draw together, and tension pulls my spine straighter. This is the first time I'm hearing anything about his involvement in the staffing for *my* hotel, and apparently, he's already almost *done.*

"I thought I was doing the interviews."

My dad shakes his head, but he doesn't make any excuses. It doesn't matter what the plan was, this is the way it is now. Period. "You thought wrong."

"Dad—"

# THE *Billionaire* BOSS NEXT DOOR

"Staff is important, Trent. You should know that by now."

My jaw aches as I clench my teeth together in an effort not to say something I'll regret. "I do."

"Your track record says otherwise."

The urge to toss poison and bullshit right back at him is so fucking strong, I can taste it. I'm tempted to tell him about the woman from the gym the other day. The one who said his pride and joy was ugly.

She was attractive, even beneath that baggy Metallica T-shirt of hers, but rude as fuck. And her opinions of the Vanderturn Manhattan were obnoxiously bad.

But the mere idea of her pisses me off too much and repeating what she'd said to my father would result in the opposite of satisfaction. The criticism that came out of her pretty but vile mouth was a fucking slap in my face too.

And *my track record? Really?* The only track record I've established is a strong work ethic and a willingness never to rest until the job is done.

"I think you might be forgetting about what I did in Tokyo. Or Paris."

"Those were small projects, Trent," he retorts, like all of the time and effort I put into those was bullshit.

"They're five-star, highly successful restaurants."

"Yeah, but they were restaurants *inside* the hotels, not the entire hotel," he retorts with a smugness highlighting his jaw. "Not to mention, they have nothing to do with the actual hotel you're working on. The one you've already delayed development on by sixty days."

Nothing is ever fucking good enough for him.

After thirty-three years, I thought I'd be used to my dad's thinly veiled insults, but it never gets easier.

Trent Turner Senior is one of the most liked men in the hotel business. His smiles come easy, his employees are valued, and he's smart enough to stay down-to-earth despite growth and wealth.

He's "the best"—as long as you're not his son.

I've been trying to crawl out of the shade of his shadow for the better part of the last five years, but every time I think I'm getting close, he gets up and moves.

I'm dying to tell him what I think of his domineering bullshit, but if there's one thing he really hates, it's back talk. So instead, I stand tall against the onslaught and bear it. It won't do me any good to get into it with him now. I'm on the cusp of finally being far enough away to do something without him, to make a name for *myself*, and I don't need my impatience to derail it. "So, you're finishing the interviews today."

"Yep," he responds. "We'll have a meeting when all the staffing is finalized, and then it will be your project."

My project with a staff full of people *he* chose.

"Great."

He purses his lips and shakes his head before rubbing at the tense skin between his eyebrows and taking a seat in his chair. In my effort to keep things civil, I've taken my concise responses too far.

"You don't have any idea, Trent," he chastises, "what it takes to run a multibillion-dollar company like this."

I clench my fists in my pockets and prepare for the speech he can't stop himself from giving me. If I've heard it once, I've heard it a million times, and I don't know that there will ever come a time when he thinks he can stop.

"It's more than strong-arming and thinking you know what's best. It's collaboration and humility. Listening and learning instead of ordering people around. Sometimes you're *not* the expert, and you have to be okay with that."

I laugh inside. Is he even listening to himself? He should try following his own fucking advice sometime.

"I'm making sure you've got the best group of people around you. Experts in their field."

The pointed statement rubs against my skin like sandpaper, and

# THE *Billionaire* BOSS NEXT DOOR

I can't help but throw out a sardonic question. "Who do you think I was planning on hiring?"

He rolls his eyes. "I'm sure you would have hired people who *seemed* like experts. But it's not always as simple as a fancy resume and smooth-talking, Trent. I've had years and years to get an eye."

"Through *experience*," I stress. "If you don't ever let me fully take the reins, how do you plan on having me learn it?"

He smirks then. "Through observation. If you want to learn through trial and error, you'll have to do it with your own money."

And that's the real crux of our issues. Trent Turner Senior doesn't think it's possible for anyone else to invest as much interest and care into the business he built. He thinks I'll take what he's made and run it into the ground with carelessness and laziness and entitlement.

But none of those things are true of me.

There's nothing that means more to me than the business he built on his back, and there's no one, despite our disagreements, who respects him as much as me.

That's why I put every ounce of blood, sweat, and time I have into it.

That said, all I have to give him is a tight nod. I don't trust myself to respond any other way.

"I'll let you know when you can meet them."

*Fan-fucking-tastic.*

"You have nine months, Trent," he says in closing. "*Nine*. Don't fuck this up."

## Chapter FIVE

### Greer

Vomit pools in my throat as I move my purse from one side to the other and back again in the bulky leather office chairs in the waiting room outside of Mr. Turner's office.

Helen, his bob-sporting assistant, smiles at me awkwardly, and I know she's noticed my fidgeting.

*Great.*

I sit up straighter and smooth my smart pencil skirt down over my knees. Helen pushes a crinkly plastic-covered candy toward the edge of her desk and then turns back to her computer.

Helen, it's now obvious, is someone's mom. That kind of care and compassion is nothing short of maternal, and it's the sort of thing I missed out on as a kid.

My brother and my grandfather did their best, don't get me wrong, but there's only so much motherly instinct inside a body with a penis.

Grateful, I get up to take the candy, regardless of whether I want it or not. My stomach hasn't decided, but accepting the gesture seems like the right thing to do either way.

When I get back to my seat and look at its contents, red and white pinwheeled together, I realize Helen really has thought of everything.

Peppermint soothes nausea.

I pop it into my mouth and suck until it disappears, and by the time I finish, I'm feeling a little better.

# THE *Billionaire* BOSS NEXT DOOR

Helen types furiously on her computer without looking at the screen, clearly transcribing something for Mr. Turner, and then stops immediately.

She touches the Bluetooth piece in her ear. "Yes, Mr. Turner?"

A brief pause.

"Of course. I'll send her in."

I gather my purse and portfolio and stand as Helen gestures me forward with the curl of two fingers, saves the document on her computer, and rounds her desk to hold open Mr. Turner's office door for me.

She is efficient to the point of madness. I hope I can live up to the employee standard she's set.

Trent Turner is an attractive older man who's started to gray around the edges. His temples and hairline are more salt than pepper, and a wire-framed pair of glasses sit perched at the end of his nose.

Helen knocks on the frosted-glass pane of the door to announce my entrance, and he looks up and tosses his glasses to the surface of his massive desk before rounding it to greet me.

"It's nice to meet you, Mr. Turner," I say as I shake his hand.

His grip is firm, a quality I appreciate, and he indicates I should take a seat with the other hand. "You too, Greer. And please, call me Trent."

I smile nervously and settle into the soft leather chair in front of his desk before tucking a curled lock of hair behind my ear. My knee bounces—thankfully out of his sight—and I put a weighty hand on top of it to slow it down.

"Okay. Trent." I test out his name to make sure I can say it without dropping to my knees and begging for the job. It's close, but somehow, I manage. "I really appreciate you taking the time out of your busy schedule to meet with me."

He waves me off and sits in the large desk chair on the other side of the mahogany island between us. His desk is so massive, I wouldn't be surprised if he had hermits camped in the middle of it that he doesn't even know about. "Please. I need a designer, and you come highly recommended."

*Really? By whom?* Clarise Beaumont doesn't hate me or anything, but she's not the kind of person to speak *highly* of anyone. Other than her, the only person I've ever worked for is my grandfather, and if he's giving me references from the grave, I'm officially freaked out.

I'm careful to cover the shock in my heart with a smile on my face, but he's too keen and too experienced to miss the subtle clues.

"I've spoken with several of your clients."

"My…" I swallow a sudden flood of saliva. "You've spoken to my clients."

He grins, comfortable in a position of power. Clearly, he didn't get to the place he is in the hotel business by playing by the rules, and I didn't get into the trouble I am by expecting the unexpected. We're a match made in hell, and he's the devil who plays all the chords.

Each and every one of my client relationships is important to me. I've been a part of creating the perfect home for a new couple just starting to build a life together, making a space for a new life to live out its days and nights in several nurseries, and restoring a foundering home left ravaged by Katrina to its former glory. My design expertise even turned a barely surviving gallery in NOLA's Arts District into a thriving, successful business that now attracts some of the most popular artists in the country. But I've never done anything with the magnitude of a hotel, and I'm afraid the limitations of my past experience will work against me.

What does Trent Turner, one of the richest men in the country, care about Genevieve and Ford Amant's nursery? Or Lisette Ellois's kitchen remodel?

"I've always hated references from employers and coworkers and industry professionals because they're good at feeding bullshit in whatever direction benefits them. You were good, you weren't, whatever. Their opinions are based on *their* needs and wants. Not the needs and wants of your clients. And I'm in the market to be a client, not an employer."

# THE *Billionaire* BOSS NEXT DOOR

"I…" I frown and put a hand to his desk, swirling a smudge onto the wood with a fingertip before coming to a conclusion. He's not holding anything back, and neither should I. I'm either going to save everything I've been working toward or go down in a blaze of glory.

Go big, or go home.

"Would you mind explaining to me how you see those as different? To me, my clients *are* my employers. I work for you and your goals. I'm only meant to be an expert in all the areas you're too busy to get lost in."

He smiles, and for the first time since I landed this fucking interview, hope actually sprouts in my chest.

"I knew I liked you."

"You did?" I'm dumbfounded. Hardly anyone ever likes me based on my first impression. I'm crass and inappropriate, and I don't do the best job of following normal social cues.

"I've seen your exemplary work, and your clients spoke highly of your work ethic and designs," he responds. "You see the world the way few people do, I can tell, and that means you've got a good head on your shoulders. My son is heading up the New Orleans project, and he really needs someone like you on his team."

"I'm hired?" Shock laces my words, and I'm powerless to stop it. As much as I've been counting on this job—*dreaming of it*—I never really thought I'd land it.

Designing the Vanderturn New Orleans is a *big* deal. Way bigger than Greer Hudson and a totally new endeavor for Hudson Designs.

"Indeed. It won't be easy. We're on a tight timeline, but I'm excited to see what you can do for us down there."

I jump up from my seat and shove out a hand again. I'm too excited not to. This is *it*. The kind of moment I'll never get to experience twice, no matter what I do with my career from now on.

This is the kind of turning point I'll *never* forget.

Thankfully, he takes my overzealous hand with a smile.

"You won't regret this," I say as I shake.

He laughs. "I hope not, dear. Why don't you head out and see my assistant again? She'll get you a cup of hot tea while I gather the rest of the New Orleans team to introduce you."

I absolutely despise hot tea, but I nod anyway. I'd drink a cup of toilet water at this point if Trent Turner wanted me to.

He's just given me a shot. A second chance at making my dream a reality, and really, a chance to make it better than I've ever imagined.

This isn't the kind of thing most designers have on their resumes—and certainly not something they add to them at thirty-three.

But for as sarcastic and cynical as I am about everything else, I'm three times as grandiose with my expectations for my work.

I'm going to put everything I have into this and then some, and when I'm done, people will know my name all over the Gulf Coast.

Now, I just have to win over the rest of the team.

# Chapter Six

### Trent

Quincy Black and Caplin Hawkins split the space on my enormous twenty-seven-inch computer screen, and thanks to the breadth of the display, they're about the size they are in real life. Except in real life, we never sit this close to one another.

"Emory has a friend. I know you're not into being set up, but I haven't technically met her, so really, this isn't a setup," Quincy, my longtime friend and hotel supplier, says. Just like always, a huge smile is permanently tattooed on his face.

Not, like, literally. But Quince is the kind of guy who never lets the world get him down, even in the worst of situations. He's a positive force and a positive source for someone like me, one who definitely forgets to look on the bright side sometimes. Some days, it seems like I've known him forever.

"How can you *technically* not have met her? Isn't it a you have or you haven't type of thing?"

"I met her at the Mask-erade. She was dressed like—"

"No, no, Quince," Caplin Hawkins interjects, paying attention for maybe the first time throughout this whole call. "Turn only dates women with the personality of a turnip. Remember?" He smirks at me patronizingly. "And I know a lot of instances of *technically*. My first high school girlfriend was *technically* a virgin, but it was like she wasn't, you know?"

It's official. What was once a business video conference call with my supplier and my lawyer about merchandise liability for the bath products we plan to carry in all of our hotels has become an episode of *Singled Out* from the 1990s. Which is appropriate, I guess. That's around the time we all became friends, and around the time they decided I needed a name different from my father. I blame the nickname Turn on junior-high-level creativity. We may have gone to a private school on the Upper East Side, but we were just as maturity-stunted as the rest of the kids our age.

Truthfully, we may not be all that much more mature now. Outside of our careers, we're all still basically a bunch of big kids.

"What personality does a turnip have, exactly?" I ask, rubbing my chin with the tip of my middle finger meaningfully.

"Bitter, mostly. A hint of spiteful. Fairly good-looking, but about as interesting as a fucking *turnip*."

"They're not all that bad," Quincy, the goofball with the good soul, defends.

Cap scoffs. "None of them are good."

I'd be tempted to take Cap's words personally if they weren't so true. I've dated a fair number of women, but the depth of those relationships was practically nonexistent.

Cathy Hounds was after my family's money, Tina Gabriel was after my dick and then my family's money, and Sadie Billings was after an appearance on Page Six. I was a means to an end to them, and I guess, if I'm honest, they were the same for me. I can hardly distinguish one's bland personality and plastic parts from another's, and looking back, I don't want to.

They weren't worth more than a mediocre fuck, and these days, I'm too busy to even go looking for that.

*What about the enticing woman at the party the other night?* my mind taunts, but I slam the brakes on that thought just as quickly as it appears.

"What do you care? It's not like you're searching extensively to find your soul mate," I challenge Cap. "You sleep with any woman who purrs in your direction."

If Caplin had a vagina, it'd be the size of the Holland Tunnel. He's looser with his physical affection than most hookers, and he doesn't even get paid.

Though, I'm half convinced he would if it wouldn't get him disbarred.

But just like with Quince, our friendship goes back a long way. The three of us spent the majority of our formative years together, horsing around and giving each other shit about everything.

As an only child, they are the brothers I never had, and I wouldn't recognize my life without them.

"Yes, but that works for me. Really well."

"And it doesn't for me?"

Cap laughs right in my face, the bastard. "You're painfully monogamous, Turn. And if you're going to insist on fucking one woman, I'm going to do my part to make sure it's a good one. Flexible. Acrobatic. *A true joy to be around.*"

"So, according to your description, I'm supposed to date a gymnast or a bendy straw," I retort with a smirk, and Quince laughs.

But Cap, well, he keeps rolling with his outrageous *and* nonexistent point. "Both sound like better options than your usual."

"Just so I'm clear on your suggestions…" I pause and lift up a paper clip from my desk. "It bends. Hell, it's even shiny. Should I fuck this, too?"

Cap grins. "Some action is better than no action, Turn."

"You're off your fucking rocker, you know that?"

"That might be true, but…" His grin only gets wider. "My dick is a happy and entertained lad every-fucking-day of the week."

"Your dick is one bad hookup away from shriveling up and falling off."

"Meh." He shrugs. "At least he'd go down with a smile."

Quince sighs. "It'd be great if we could have one conversation where your dick isn't discussed like it's an actual person."

"Aw, don't worry, Quince," Cap retorts. "I'm sure your dick is a real nice guy. A little boring, far too predictable, but there's a real sweetheart inside that barely average-sized core of his."

"Barely average-sized?" Quince scoffs. "You—"

"Hey, I've got an idea," I chime in before they start getting out rulers and measuring shafts. "How about someone lets me know if we should sign the contract with Essence Skin Care? Hell, if Cap's dick is well-versed in legalese, that'll work at this point."

"It's all good in the hood, baby." Cap winks. "I have a few recommendations for the contracts that I'll send your way, but it's all pretty minor shit."

I look toward Quince, who is now smiling.

"The report from product research came back with no areas of concern related to liability."

"Great." The line goes silent for the briefest of moments, and I can't stop myself from veering the conversation back to the ridiculous. "Oh, hey, Quince. Guess who Cap saw the other day?"

*Goddamn, I'm just as bad as they are.*

The instant the question leaves my lips, Cap glares and Quince tilts his head to the side.

"Who did you see, Cap?"

"He saw Sophia Moran." I kindly offer up the information on a silver platter.

"No shit?" Quince responds. "How is she doing?"

"Uh...good." Cap clears his throat. "She's doing real good."

*Doing real good? Yeah. Nice one, Cap.*

I have to bite my lip to hold back my laughter. And, fuck, this is too entertaining not to continue. So, I do. "What did you guys talk about?"

"Well..." Cap pauses and flashes me another glare before moving his eyes across the screen to Quince. "We didn't get a lot of talking in..."

*Realization in...*

5
4
3
2
1

"Are you kidding me?" Quince snaps when he connects the dots of Cap's passive innuendos. "You slept with my ex-girlfriend?"

"Dude." The big bastard raises both hands in the air. "I promise you we didn't sleep at all."

Quince looks at me and then back at Cap before an annoyed laugh escapes his throat. "You're a real asshole, you know that?"

"I do, actually." Cap nods, and his eyes turn apologetic. "Honestly, Quince, I didn't know. I mean, she looked kind of familiar. Her name sounded familiar, but I had no idea she was your ex."

"I think your dick is stealing your brain cells," Quince retorts, and I laugh.

"Yeah. That, right there, is a likely scenario."

Cap just shrugs. "He does have a mind of his own."

"Trent," my dad says after peeking his head in my office without knocking. "I've got someone for you to meet."

"Gotta go," I say and hit end on the conference call without giving Quince or Cap time to interject.

But they've been around long enough to know about the tense, tumultuous relationship between my father and me. They know he can be a demanding, controlling bastard and that I spend most of my time trying to keep the fucking peace between us. They also know I'm not completely above hiding one of their bodies if they ever decide to ride my ass about it.

Without another word, my father steps back out of my office with the expectation that I'll follow.

And, of course, I do.

*Always the fucking peace-keeper.*

I shove back in my chair, grab my suit jacket from the rack I keep behind my desk, and head out the door.

I would have loved to have a minute to prepare to meet the group of people I'm going to be spending all of my days and many a long night with over the next nine months, but Trent Turner Senior waits for no one, least of all his son.

Tight-jawed and tense, I make my way down the hall toward the conference room as quickly as possible, bumping carelessly into a woman as she's stepping out of the break room.

"Ow," she umphs, groaning as I step on her toes.

*Shit.*

Instantly, I grab her by the waist to keep her from falling. "I'm sorry. Are you okay?"

She flips her hair up and out of her face, a smile prepped and ready to forgive me, when our eyes meet.

"*You,*" she growls.

And at the exact same time, I spit *"You"* through a clenched jaw.

It's *her*. The woman from the gym. The smartass in the Metallica T-shirt with the all-consuming hate for my father's prize hotel. I've been thinking about the flippant way she talked about everything my family's business is built on ever since she sauntered out of the fitness center, and seemingly, it hasn't done anything to diminish how annoyed she makes me.

Not to mention, she didn't even wipe down the equipment she was *pretending* to use, and I had to spend the last twenty minutes of my workout inhaling her sweet fucking perfume.

I mean, it was a good sweet. A soft and seductive kind of sweet.

But fuck, she should've stuck to gym etiquette.

"What the hell are you doing here?" Once again, our timing and our words are completely in sync.

"I asked you first," she argues snottily and settles her red-painted fingers into the perfect crook of her skirt-covered hip.

I snort. "I think not."

Her impressive blue eyes turn cold, and my blood pressure

## THE *Billionaire* BOSS NEXT DOOR

skyrockets. Today of all days—the beginning of the next phase of my career—I have to run into her again. Talk about the last thing I fucking need.

"What are you doing here?" I demand. "At my company."

"Your company?" she shrieks, her wavy brown locks swaying with the agitated forward motion of her upper body. "I work here."

My heart pumps twice instead of once, and my vision tunnels around her words. Her awful fucking words. "You…you work here?"

"Oh good," my father says, appearing out of nowhere. Apparently, the strength of my surprise and disdain at the sight of the rude woman from the gym was enough to completely block out the action of him walking down the hall toward us. "I was hoping I'd get a chance to introduce you two before you meet the rest of the team."

His smile is as radiant as the sun, and sweat drips appropriately down my back.

"Greer, this is my son, Trent. And, Trent, this is Greer Hudson. She is going to be heading up the design in New Orleans."

Heading up the design in New Orleans? At *my* hotel?

*You have got to be kidding me.*

"Trent," she sneers.

"Greer," I snarl, memorizing the name that goes with my enemy's face.

It's a showdown worthy of any old Western, and I can practically hear the clank of our spurs as we take our positions opposite each other.

High noon and the fastest draw, winner take all.

Oh man, if only office politics were that simple.

Reluctantly, knowing my dad is watching, I stick out a hand for her to shake. She takes it roughly, digging a fingernail into the back of it. I'm almost certain her attempt at skin mutilation is on purpose.

My father is oblivious to our silent showdown. "It's safe to say the two of you are going to be working very closely together over the next year, so the sooner you can get to know each other, the better."

Greer's face is a mirror of what I imagine my own looks like—sheer horror.

When it comes to a hotel, there's no more important relationship than the one between the project head and the designer. Together, those two roles on the team are building an experience that is supposed to translate to everyone who steps inside. Most of all, they need to be able to work together.

Instantly, the logistics of my new reality become crystal clear.

Me and this woman. Working *together*. Side by side. For nearly a year.

This is so fucked.

"Come on," my dad says, somehow unscathed by the singe of our eye lasers. "Let's meet the rest of the team."

Greer nods and smiles, which is more than I can say for myself. I'm still locked in a nightmare and struggling to wake up, and my body acts accordingly.

Either that, or I'm having a small stroke.

My dad, of course, notes the lag and files it away as yet another mark against me.

"Jesus, Trent. Did you not sleep last night or something? Look alive."

I jolt into action, but not before I notice Greer's smirk. My dad's castigation of me amuses her.

Something inside me ignites and starts running at high idle.

She might think she's ready, but she has no idea what she's getting into with me—how much animosity I'm built to withstand when it comes to working at Turner Properties.

For the first time ever, my father's criticism of me may serve a greater purpose.

I stay put, giving her and my father a minute to make their way down the hall without me, adjust my tie, and take a deep breath.

*Greer*, my mind rumbles.

If she wants a battle, I'll give her a damn war.

# Chapter SEVEN

## Greer

Nerves jump up and down in my stomach like a million chaotic bouncy balls set to work by a bunch of manic kids. I am freaking *the fuck* out.

The green-eyed, good-bodied, trash-talker from the gym is my boss.

As in, in charge of me at work.

As in, signs my paychecks.

*As in*, he is the *only* thing standing between me and a new job at the Stop and Pop gas station where I will have to drown my life's failures in cheap beer, cigarettes, and cheesy curls.

I don't even smoke, never even let a cigarette touch my lips, but from where I stand, a life filled with dirty ashtrays and cheese-stained fingertips is a strong contender for my future.

Holy bitchtits. This is bad.

And like a spoiled high schooler who actually has parents who pay for all of their stuff—*like a woman who doesn't have everything on the line*—I gave him attitude. I talked back. I dug my fingernails into his hand when he shook it.

*What the hell is wrong with me?*

My breathing kicks up a notch, and I glance around the conference room to see if anyone has noticed how close I am to hyperventilating. After my altercation with his son and with my heart beating a million miles a minute, Trent Senior led the way down the hall and into this room. I'm sure employees made eye contact with me, but the only thing I could see was my career going up in flames.

Five people other than me circle the large marble table in the center of the room, not a single one of them a woman.

I'm the only hen at this cock party, and that spurs my anxiety further.

The reality of what I'm up against crashes down on me all over again, and my breathing breaks down into uncoordinated gulps.

I study the faces around me, but they're all ensconced in their own conversations and unconcerned with me.

Desperate for a lifeline, I scour the refreshment cart in the corner, but there's not one paper bag for hyperventilation purposes in sight. I can only hope I weather this storm on my own.

Breathing may sound instinctive, but I wouldn't put it past myself to forget to do it. And I do *not* want to be known as the woman who passed out on her first day for the rest of my employment with Turner Properties.

In a room full of men, I refuse to be the fainting to the floor, fucking damsel in distress.

Especially not when one of those men is that rude, bastard prick from the gym.

Trent Turner. Well, Trent Turner *Junior*, I guess is his full name.

If I weren't so amped up on anxiety and dread, I might take the time to laugh silently at the fact that his full name includes Junior. Like he's a little boy. A fucking kid.

Unfortunately for me, his tight muscles and sexy jawline and piercing green eyes are the exact opposite of what a boy should look like.

*No sirree Bob, he is all man, Greer. All-fucking-man.*

Pfft. Whatever. The fact remains that he's a Grade A asshole.

The titter of conversation dims as the green-eyed devil himself steps inside the glass-walled conference room and shuts the door. I didn't get the chance to really take him in when he bumped into me

## THE *Billionaire* BOSS NEXT DOOR

before, but as a mere member of the crowd, I more than have the chance now.

His suit is pressed and a crisp black in a way that isn't maintainable without a hefty dry-cleaning bill. Below the edge of his jacket sleeves, the white of his shirt cuffs sticks out ever so slightly, and a shiny silver clip holds the emerald green of his tie in place.

It matches his eyes almost perfectly, and my knees feel weak. I'm almost certain the two are completely unrelated.

"Hello, everyone," he greets simply, and we all respond with nods and hellos of our own. At least, everyone else does.

For some reason, I'm having a hard time forcing the civil exchange past my lips, and my hello comes out more like a stuttered *"e-low."*

What is it about him that rubs me so wrong? I mean, I barely met the guy the other day. It's not like we've got some long-standing rivalry that dates back to pigtail-pulling and shoves on the playground.

He poked fun at me. *Big deal.*

It *shouldn't* be a big deal.

It is, though. I feel the weight of my agitation toward him deep in my gut, right next to the two mini donuts I shouldn't have shoved down my throat in the employee break room.

It's burning and achy, and I don't recognize it at all. For the greater part of the last five years, my emotions have avoided the extremes. If I were to make a line graph to represent myself, Greer's numbness would be a great big tick mark right across the middle.

Suddenly, now I can't seem to stop bouncing off the sides of the scale.

"I'm looking forward to working with you for the next several months to make Vanderturn NOLA our most enjoyable and profitable property yet. The work may get grueling, thanks to the timeline that we're working with, but I know you're all up to the challenge."

He's barely even begun his speech, and already, I'm rolling my eyes at his management spiel.

*He knows I'm up for the challenge?*

Besides our altercation in the fitness room, he doesn't know anything about me. I mean, unless he's a fucking fortune-teller, he can't possibly know that I'm up for the challenge.

Hell, *I* don't even know if I am.

I've never taken on a workload like this, and my previous assistant Rosaline already moved on to another job. If I'm going to find a staff to help me manage it, I'll have to start from scratch.

But with the schedule we're on, I might have to go it alone.

"Five days from today, we'll convene in New Orleans at the property site to get started. I'd like it if we could all go into that day with at least one thing we can contribute to making this the best property in the country. One specific, plan-oriented thing. Take the next few days to consider it, to strategize, and Wednesday, we'll start implementing."

His smile is big but completely devoid of warmth as his father steps in front of him in a gesture of dismissal. "Thanks, Trent."

*Junior* only hesitates for a second, his features strangely confrontational as he focuses on the back of his dad's head, before turning to the glass door, heaving it open, and retreating down the hall.

*That's weird.*

Fortunately, I don't have the time to focus on their freaky exchange or my panic attack as chatter fires up once again.

The rest of us stand up from our seats and start to mingle as Senior makes a point to talk to each of us individually.

It's clear he's known Marcus and Harold for years, but Brad, Frederick, and Isaac all seem to be new like me.

Still, he treats us all the same, inquiring about our personal backgrounds with a thorough warmth.

Marcus is the only one who'll actually be on site with us, everyone else's role centered in the financial and business aspects of the build, but by the time Senior's done making the rounds, I feel like I know little pieces of everyone's lives. Their families. Their work experiences. Their personalities.

# THE *Billionaire* BOSS NEXT DOOR

Everyone but his son *and* the actual boss of the New Orleans project.

No, other than the bothersome way he makes me feel, that asshole is still a complete mystery to me.

---

Mr. Turner finishes getting to know everyone just before lunch and dismisses us for the day.

After a quick call to Emory, who's been shopping all day on Fifth Avenue—the lucky bitch—we decide to meet for lunch at the 51st Street Deli.

It's no surprise that Emory is waiting for me in a booth at the back of the restaurant—built soundly for a party of eight—when I walk in. Most of the seats are filled with bags from designer brands and boutique shops I could never afford, but she manages to leave just enough space for her ass and mine.

"You're late," she accuses as I sit down to a hot pastrami sandwich and a half a dozen pickles—a personal weakness—already waiting for me. I roll my eyes in a secret gesture of appreciation.

I'm the only one who knows the secret, but I'm thankful in my heart, and that's what really matters, *right?*

Right.

"And?" I laugh caustically. At some point, she's got to realize this is never going to change. "If you're surprised, you should be really disappointed in yourself."

She huffs, banging her hands on the table and innocuously rearranging her silverware. I smile, amused by my friend's closet OCD.

"I just don't understand. You were done when you called me. You were closer. We agreed to meet here as soon as we could. How on earth do you end up taking double the time?"

I shrug. I really don't know. "I guess I just come by my tardiness naturally."

I've always had a gift for shitting away time. Two hours in front of the TV, an hour and a half in the shower, forty-five minutes on my bed in the middle of the day for no reason—I'm an Olympic-level athlete at all of it.

It's no wonder I haven't a clue what I did between the time Emory called me and the time I got here to delay myself.

Seriously. Time just disappears.

"Whatever," she finally sighs, delicately spooning a mouthful of her side of chicken noodle soup into her mouth and swallowing. "Let's talk about the job."

"What about it?" I furrow my brow, and she rolls her eyes like my question is the dumbest question that's ever existed.

"Aren't you excited?" she asks, and her voice rises three octaves. "Relieved? Anything? I mean, I feel like there should be some kind of emotional evidence of your success."

I shrug. In a way, I am relieved. But in another, much bigger way, this is just the beginning. And the rest of the story includes finding some way to lose the animosity I feel toward my new boss. *Trent fucking Turner.* He may be a stuck-up prick, but I doubt his opinion of me is much better. "I didn't make a great first impression with my boss."

"What do you mean? You got the job, didn't you?"

I choke down an overly large bite of pastrami in my haste to answer and have to grab my throat as it burns.

"You're not a snake, you know," Emory teases. "You don't have to swallow your food whole."

I scrunch my face into a fake hysterical laugh and sneer. "I've hardly eaten anything all day," I retort. "And if you keep up that kind of bitchy food judgment, I'll assume you want me to start eating your food too."

"Greer." Emory just stares. I swear, if her eyes get any bigger, they'll pop straight out of the sockets and literally push me for the answer to her initial question.

I waver between ending or prolonging her misery, but it doesn't

## THE *Billionaire* BOSS NEXT DOOR

take long for me to decide that it's best if her eyeballs stay secured inside her head.

"Yes, I got the job," I finally answer. "Mr. Turner loved me. But it's his son who's running the New Orleans hotel and, well, it's *that* Trent Turner I fucked up with."

"How?" She scrunches up her nose. "How have you already fucked up *so* badly in a day?"

"Because I sort of met him the other day at the hotel, when *you* sent me to the gym…" My voice is needlessly accusatory. "And I *might* have said a thing or two I shouldn't have."

She pulls her sandwich away from her mouth and glares. Sometimes she really knows me too well. "What did you say?"

I shrug in an effort to play it off and pick at the seeds in my rye bread. "Just…you know…that the décor in their hotel was so hideous, I felt as though I might actually die from it." My laugh is scary. "No big deal, right?"

Emory drops her head into her hands. "Jesus Christ, Greer."

"I know! Gah!" I wail. "But I didn't know it was him! He never introduced himself, and he was really fucking rude to me about my fitness. It just came spewing out like lava. You can't blame me, really. It was a volcano!"

She's skeptical, and it shows. I can't blame her, really, but I'm actually telling the truth this time. Green-eyed, good-bodied Trent is a Grade A prick. "Rude to you how?"

"He said I was pretending to work out!"

Her raised eyebrow is nothing but accusatory and calling me on my bullshit. "And were you?"

"What does that matter?" I screech.

Her sandwich hits the plate so hard, it falls apart and rains corned beef on the table. I reach out to pick it up—no meat left behind and all that—and she smacks my hand.

"Here's what you're going to do. First day on the job in New Orleans, you're going to march right up to him and apologize."

"What? No! I'm not apologizing to that asshole. If you hadn't been so busy primping, we would have been able to fly up here earlier with Quincy. I would have had more time to stabilize the bitchiness."

"Don't you dare blame this on me and my spa day!" she snaps. "This is on you, and you only have one option."

I raise a skeptical brow and grimace. She doesn't even bother to soften the blow.

"Take your pride and shame and stubbornness and eat it, Greer," she instructs. "Pretend they're all fried and pickled if you have to. For God's sake, don't you remember what you have riding on this?"

*Everything*, my mind remarks. *Literally everything.*

"Fine," I huff, shoving her hand out of the way and grabbing her meat defiantly. "When we get to New Orleans, I'll apologize. And then I'll be on my best behavior. But I'm not going to like him. No buddy-buddy exchanges and shit. This is business. Period."

Emory nods.

"And for the love of God, he better be open to suggestions. I refuse to stamp my name on the puke-worthy design they have going on in the Vanderturn Manhattan. I'd rather starve to death in my newly renovated cardboard home on the streets than do that."

"Of course," she says with a hum, and I decide to ignore the fact that she's humoring me.

"I *would*," I retort. "If I'm going to do a good job, he's going to have to trust me to make decisions. I can't work creatively when everything I come up with is being turned down."

She rolls her eyes. "You're assuming a lot here. You haven't worked with him. He might be a great team player. Just because the two of you bumped heads in the hotel fucking gym, doesn't mean he's not open to suggestions."

"It might. Trust me. You didn't see him when his father introduced him to the rest of the team today. He was so cocky. So removed. So…managerial. Plus, no one should be that obsessed with the cleanliness of workout equipment."

# THE *Billionaire* BOSS NEXT DOOR

"Workout equipment?" she questions. "What in the hell are you talking about?"

"At the gym," I respond.

"For the love of God, Greer, forget about the encounter at the gym." She shakes her head as if she's literally shaking away my words. "And I'll bet during the meeting, he was confident *not* managerial. Your first encounter is probably coloring your opinion of him."

"I guess." I frown and breathe a deep, heavy sigh. "I just need this to go smoothly, and a better start would have really helped things along."

"You're used to rough starts," Emory reasons kindly. "Look at the way your life started, Greer. Most people would have let it sour them. Not you. You fight harder than anyone I've ever met," she says with a little, knowing smirk. "*Sometimes* when you don't need to."

I roll my eyes.

"Just try to put away the boxing gloves," she pleads. "Only for a little while. You might be surprised what it gets you."

"But I'm pretty good at boxing…"

Emory snorts. "Greer, just try to approach this with a less cynical mind-set. And definitely leave the sass and sarcasm at the door."

"All right," I agree. "I'll try." Skepticism and sarcasm come naturally; niceties and kind exchanges do not. The effort to change will likely be Herculean, but for Emory's sake—and mine—I've got to try.

"Good." She takes a sip of her water and switches conversational gears. "Now, tell me something good. I barely saw you at the party the other night and since you *refused* to come to Marquee with me yesterday, I haven't heard anything about how your New Year's Eve actually went. Please tell me you didn't bail and go to bed early."

I roll my eyes at her insinuation that I was *actually* invited to Marquee with her and Quince—as in, in some other way than *I'm just being polite, but if you come, there's a chance you'll see us tongue-fucking each other*—and think about the New Year's Eve party instead.

I think about Walt. I think about that incredible kiss.

Hell, I can still practically feel his lips on mine.

And those delicious, teasing words of his have been popping into my brain for the past thirty-six hours.

*If we were anywhere else in the fucking world but here, my next kiss would be between your legs.*

I blush unexpectedly as the delicious memory wakes up my underused loins, and she notices. "Oh my God. What happened?"

I shake my head. My vagina wants to sing about unexpected "feelings" and "a new lease on life," but winter in New York means I've covered her big fat mouth in several layers of clothing.

The rest of me is far less chatty.

Emory slams her hands down on the table and leans toward me. "Greer Hudson, you tell me right now!"

Avoidance is usually the easiest way out of things I don't want to be a part of, but with Emory, I have to sink to new levels of low. Specifically, a transfer of blame. It's an old trick I've used one too many times, but she's left me with no other options. "If you weren't so drunk on Quince, you might already know."

She smacks me. "Stop trying to make this about me."

*Goddammit, she knows me too well.*

"Well…"

She smiles and leans forward in her seat, perched on the edge almost comically. When it takes me more than a beat and a half to answer, she yells. "Well, what?"

A few patrons in the diner look in our direction, and I sigh.

"Fine."

I guess the most concise, base-level details won't hurt.

"I kissed someone," I say, my voice a whisper compared to hers. "At midnight. It was good."

"*Oh my God!* And you're just now telling me this? What the hell!"

If I'm being honest, it was more than good. It was, like, masturbation-worthy good.

But no way does Emory need to know those dirty details. Her

# THE *Billionaire* BOSS NEXT DOOR

overzealous reaction makes it obvious she wouldn't shut up about it if she did, and I don't have time to put out some kind of New York search party for a guy I kissed...*once.*

A guy whose face was hidden behind a rubber Walt mask.

A guy whose name I don't even know.

"It was nothing," I say, my voice easy breezy. "I mean, we only interacted for about ten minutes beforehand and none after. It was... weird. He said 'Happy New Year,' and then he left." I shrug. "I don't know."

He also insinuated he wanted to eat my pussy, but that's a minor detail, *right?*

"What don't you know? I mean, come on, Greer. You're not exactly prospecting to be on *The Bachelorette*. You haven't even thought about a man in the last five years that I know of. Now, you're kissing strangers at midnight, and it's just *no big deal?* I'm sure he had a reason for walking away."

I shrug again, and it only amps her up more.

"Greer!" she shouts, and when I don't respond right away, she reaches across the table and smacks my arm.

"What?" I ask with annoyance in my voice. "It's not like it's going anywhere, you possessed nutcase. I don't live in New York. I don't know who he was. I don't even know his fucking name! All I know of him is his knowledge of Walter White and *Breaking Bad* and that he's not a complete moron like Albert Einstein. For all I know, he hated every moment of our interaction," I huff out, but my brain reminds me of his sexy words and even sexier mouth in a rebuttal.

*Stupid brain.* I shake off those pointless thoughts. It doesn't matter what he said or how good the kiss was. *Or that he talked about putting his face between my legs.* It was a one-time thing.

Plus, he was the one who walked away, not me.

Emory scrunches up her nose. "Okay, half of what you just said doesn't even make sense, but you're forgetting something else you know."

"What?"

"That he's a good kisser."

I groan and drop my face into my hands. I don't want to be discussing this at all. In fact, I'd rather be harpooning myself with one of those guns they use to tag sharks and shit.

She smacks my arm to get my attention. "That's a pretty important detail, friend."

"Sure. Whatever you say," I agree just to make her happy and lift my eyes to hers. "But you really need to wrap your mind around the fact that there's nothing else there, E, no matter how much your romantic heart wants there to be."

Her only answer is a frown heard 'round the world.

And if I'm honest, I'm kind of sad too.

But I don't have time for a man, and I don't have the investigative skills to find one I don't actually know. This is a job for a Sherlock, and I'm really more of a Shirley.

Fuck, that's not even true. I'm a Laverne.

Regardless, I need to focus on my firm, the hotel, and turning things around with my new boss.

It's going to require long hours and personality adjustments and a lot of hard work.

I don't have time to stop and smell the roses, and I don't have time to fall for someone random, good kisser or not. Especially not someone who walks away before I can invite them to sleep with me.

Love, it seems, will just have to come later.

## Chapter EIGHT

### Trent

Greer Hudson.

The new designer for the hotel in New Orleans, the snarky—*albeit gorgeous*—woman from the gym, and my waking nightmare.

She made pouty, disapproving lips at me for the entirety of the meeting with the new team, and the weight of her stare makes me want to shove it off and slam it to the ground like body builders do after snatching.

Well, probably something less violent, but just as visually significant.

The more she stared at me with those big, blue, judgmental eyes of hers, the more annoyed I became and the heavier my chest felt. My mind might as well have been a hoarder's house for all the clutter and garbage filling every thought.

Perhaps the worst part? This is just the beginning.

In less than a week, we will be spending all of our days, week after week, month after month, working as closely as two people can work.

It's intimate and inescapable, and the whole idea of being crushed by inexplicable ire and manic, annoyed thoughts for the next nine months is nearly unthinkable.

I retreated to the familiar feel of my office to contemplate my options, but the gray walls and clean lines of my desk haven't had anything to say.

Paper clips litter the reclaimed wood surface in a trail generated by my anxiety, and three empty coffee cups sit mockingly in the corner. Busying my hands and readying my mind felt like the only options since the moment that meeting ended and my new staff left for the day, but all I'm left with now is an overexaggerated coffee buzz and no idea what to do about Greer.

It's only taken two interactions for me to know she's outspoken and obstinate and her every opinion appears to be the opposite of my own. She hates the design of the Vanderturn Manhattan, one of our most successful hotels and the crown jewel in my father's empire. She's beautiful, sure, but trusting her taste for every single element in this hotel feels like a career death sentence.

*What am I going to do? Can I really do my best work like this?*

Everything is on the fucking line—*my career, my relationship with my father, the success of Turner Properties, my mother's happiness*—and making sure this hotel is everything it should be and more is the most important thing I will ever do.

*And I'm supposed to just, what, rely on this infuriating woman to design it?*

My phone pings from in the middle of my desk calendar, and I pick it up to check the message.

The name **Caplin Hawkins** fills the tiny bubble, beckoning me to open it, but the action it sparks is different altogether.

*Fuck the message. I need to see him in person.*

I shove back in my desk chair and rise, turning in one fluid motion to grab my suit jacket off the coat rack behind me, dropping the phone into my pocket, scooping my keys out of the top left-hand drawer of my desk, and striding out of my office with a new sense of purpose.

Caplin may have texted me as a friend, but he's about to get a visit as my lawyer.

# THE *Billionaire* BOSS NEXT DOOR

"There's got to be a way!" I shout, pacing the herringbone tile floor so furiously, Caplin might have to regrout his office.

Fifteen minutes ago, I forced my way past his assistant when I arrived and barged in during the middle of what was apparently an "important" call.

I explained quickly that this was an emergency, a four-alarm fire, and he reacted accordingly by asking the president of ABC to reschedule.

The problem came when I explained that the fire was more like a *firing*—of an employee.

A new employee.

A very annoying employee with a menacing influence on the retention of my sanity.

Greer Hudson, I explained to him, is the devil in angelic clothing.

With her cerulean blue eyes, tanned skin, and dark brown hair, she's everything a man should be fighting to keep.

Except that she's quite possibly the most maddening, rudely forthright, boldly sarcastic person I've ever met. And I *cannot* spend nine months fighting with her while I'm trying to complete the New Orleans project.

Since my arrival, I've suggested every reason for firing an employee I've ever heard of. My supposed friend and hotshot lawyer has turned down every one of them, the bastard. It's like he *wants* me to punch him right in the center of his proportionally featured face.

Undisclosed pregnancy?

*She's not pregnant,* he says. *Plus, if she were, that's about as low as you can fucking get, Turn. And you might be a dick sometimes, but we both know you're not an insensitive tool.*

What about damaging company property?

*What property? Your fucking pride?*

Theft?

*Stealing your sanity doesn't count.*

He tries telling me to give her a chance, but I'm still on a roll.

I know it's insane. I know I've quite possibly lost my fucking mind, but goddamn, I don't see Greer Hudson and me working side by side for nearly a year and it ending in anything but absolute disaster.

The Vanderturn New Orleans hotel needs to be a success.

*But how can the designer of said hotel be someone who called the appearance of our most popular hotel ugly?*

If only my father weren't such a controlling, prideful son of a bitch when it comes to his business decisions. This would be a much easier scenario if I could just *tell* him that his choice in designer isn't going to cut it.

But me taking a bullet to the heart would end better than giving him that kind of constructive criticism.

*Fuck, I have to figure out something here.*

If there are a billion, trillion stars in the sky, there have to be at least a million and one legal loopholes for every situation. I round the proverbial third base and head for home, trying my last few reasons with an even deeper sense of desperation.

"A slander clause," I suggest.

He frowns and tosses the tiny basketball he keeps in the bottom drawer of his desk up like he's shooting. When he doesn't give me anything else, I move on to the next.

"Or…misappropriation of taste!"

He quirks a brow. "And that's what, exactly?"

"There's no way my father knows how she feels about the Vanderturn Manhattan. Isn't that something she'd have to disclose?"

"When did Turner Properties start using protocols from fucking *Gossip Girl?*" he tosses back with a far too knowing smirk. "You and I both know her not liking the design of a hotel she had no part in designing is utter bullshit."

God, he's right, *and* I'm seriously losing it.

*But fucking hell. I need an out.*

"Goddammit, Cap! Work with me here. There's got to be something."

# THE *Billionaire* BOSS NEXT DOOR

He shakes his head. "I don't—"

"No, no." I point an accusatory index finger toward him. "Don't you say it."

"Look, Turn—"

"No!"

"You already know this, but since you're obviously having some kind of psychotic break that I'm praying is temporary, I'm going to say it. You can't fire her without opening a whole shitcan of shitworms. She hasn't done anything wrong." He says what, deep down, I already know. "You're just going to have to ride it out. I'd suggest literally if you weren't such a prude."

"A prude?" My face contorts into confusion and annoyance. "Can a man even be a prude?"

"You're what I like to call evidentiary support."

"Fuck off."

"Dude, you're in *my* office. If you want me to fuck off, you'll have to do the fucking. Oh, whoops. Forgot. You're a prude." He laughs like a hyena, and I decide immediately to cut him from my life with a savagery and ruthlessness that rivals the most oppressive tyrant.

"What I *can* do for you," he continues, "if you insist on carrying on with this whole insane charade rather than fucking the insanity out of your system, is a background check. I've got a PI I've worked with on occasion, and he's licensed in forty-nine states."

Hmm. Maybe his offer holds merit, even if I'm supremely curious as to why one state has refused this guy credentials.

"Is the state he's not licensed in this one?"

"Would I be involved with someone like that?" Caplin asks, and I nearly snort.

"Yes. Yes, you would."

He smiles, secure in the questionable parts of his morals. Hell, that's probably why he's the main counsel for pretty much every fucking billionaire and millionaire around. Not to mention, a successful lawyer who turned a million-dollar idea of creating an app to assist people with cheap *and* quick legal counsel into a thriving company he sold off for a measly 2.2 billion dollars.

"And what about Louisiana?" I ask and he chuckles.

"He's licensed in the states you need him to be. Trust me."

I don't trust him one bit, but I have only two options at this point—use the resources he's suggesting to dig up dirt on Greer Hudson, or turn tyrannical against him while also losing my sanity.

*Bloody torture will have to wait for another day.*

"Fine. Do it."

"Please? Thank you?" he prods.

"You're welcome," I goad back.

His brown eyes deepen with sin and enjoyment, and his voice is eerily calm. "I know people, Turn."

I roll my eyes, and he smirks.

"Just don't act shocked if you wake up behind bars one day."

"I'll prepare nightly."

"By sticking things in your ass? Because that's what will happen to you. You're a real pretty boy, and they love those in there."

"Fuck you, dude."

"Yes, that *is* what they'll call the game they play with you. Because you'll be the prettiest boy there."

"I know it's hard for you to admit that I'm better-looking," I say with a sly smirk. "But don't worry, over the years, I've learned to understand your backhanded compliments. And thank you."

Cap laughs, and just as he opens his mouth, I quickly cut him off.

"Anyway, don't you have better things to do today than to compare our good looks?" I ask, knowing we'll be stuck in this vortex of nonsense and insults all day if I don't.

"Yes, in fact, I do. I was in the middle of an important call when you barged in here with a hard-on for termination, remember? Stroke that thing a little tonight, and it might just go away."

"Prick."

"Prude."

"I'm not a prude, fuck you very much." I roll my eyes, and he challenges me with a smirk.

"Prove it."

"How?" I raise an amused brow. "You want me to pull out my dick or something?"

"We both know that's the kind of thing I would do, not you."

I nod. "Because you have zero fucking shame."

"You got that right, Turn." He smirks. "There ain't no shame in my big-dick game."

"Jesus," I mutter, and Cap just laughs, his entire fucking body vibrating with humor.

"Anyway, it's been what? Five? Six? Twenty months since you've even touched a woman?"

"It's been exactly one day."

He furrows his brow.

"I kissed someone at the New Year's Eve party the other night."

"Ooh, kissing," Cap croons in an annoyingly fake voice. "Did it happen under the bleachers or in the back seat of your car?"

"I had just met her, dude. We kissed at midnight, and she was wearing a Beyoncé mask because of Quince's terrible fucking idea. What was I supposed to do, fuck her in the bathroom?"

He laughs. "That's what I did."

"You're ridiculous," I say, but it's mostly in an effort to hide my jealousy. The truth is, Caplin's not that off base. I was so into the woman at the party, so into the kiss we had at midnight, I was considering all the ways we could spend the rest of the night. Visions of her in my bed played vividly in my mind, and if I'm honest, still do.

I wanted to take her up to one of the penthouse suites and spread her legs.

I wanted to touch her. Taste her. Slide my cock inside of her.

I wanted to do a lot of fucking things, but my father's stare was weighty, even from across the room, and despite the protection of my mask, it felt like he could see right through me.

His judgment about my behavior at a work function—a party we as a company were responsible for putting on—was more than I was willing to risk.

I know I shouldn't give him that much control over my personal life, but the fact remains, he's finally giving up enough control to let me run the show on something big. And right now, the New Orleans project is my main priority. My entire focus. And, quite possibly, a huge turning point in my career that will result in my dad *finally* trusting me and realizing I am more than capable of running Turner Properties.

Random sex with a random woman, no matter how irresistible she was, was not a good enough reason to put that kind of future on the line. No matter how fucking worth it her perfect, satin-covered body and plush, warm mouth made it seem at the time.

"You know what?" Cap asks, but apparently, the question is for himself. "I *am* ridiculous. Because you can't say ridiculous without saying dick, and you can't come without getting your dick wet."

I laugh. "You can't get genital herpes without sticking your dick in random pussies either."

"Geez, Timmy. Back away from the well. That's what condoms are for."

"For fucking random strangers without contracting diseases? I'll suggest that to Trojan for their new campaign," I say with a little smirk. "I'm sure their marketing department is just waiting for that kind of million-dollar idea."

"I'd buy forty cases," Cap retorts, and another laugh escapes my lungs.

"And go through them in a week."

"Glad to see you're starting to understand just how virile my big cock and I really are, Turn."

"I swear to God," I say through a laugh. "One day, I will get a wedding invitation for the impending nuptials of you and your dick."

"And I will look fucking gorgeous in a wedding dress. Satin and silk, though. No fucking sequins and tulle."

# THE *Billionaire* BOSS NEXT DOOR

"So that's how it would work." I grin. "You would be the bride?"

"Of course." He snorts. "My cock is far more of a man than I am."

"Touché, Cap. Tou-fucking-ché."

He smirks like he's the smartest man in the room, and I shake my head when I realize just how far off track he's managed to take us.

"God, sometimes I really do kind of hate you."

"I love you too. Now get the hell out of my office, and don't come back until you've fucked the new chick."

I laugh. "I know your general inclination is toward absolute insanity, but I'm not going to have sex with her."

"Why the fuck not?"

"For about a million different reasons…not only are intraoffice relationships a hell no, but she's literally the last person I would consider having sex with."

"Is she ugly?"

"No," I admit. "She's beautiful."

"Does her pussy have actual fire ants living inside?"

"Not that I'm aware of."

"Then why in the hell would she be the last person on earth you'd have sex with? Because I personally never say never until I see a vagina with fangs and venom. Even then, I'd consider it. Sometimes freaky, kinky shit is just what the good doctor ordered."

"She's an employee, Cap," I repeat. "*And* she's obstinate. Stubborn. Fucking *infuriating*."

"Mm-hmm. And you, what? Have the employee handbook memorized and say your prayers over it nightly?"

I shake my head. "You don't get it."

"Oh no. I get it perfectly."

"No, you don't."

"Oh, trust me, I do." He smirks like the devil. "I'm even going to start a countdown on my desktop."

"To what?"

"The fucking," he says with the biggest grin that could fit on his giant head. "Because that's exactly where you're headed, Turn."

Pfft. That's not happening. *Ever.* I'll be rolling around in my grave before I have sex with Greer Hudson.

But this is a useless conversation where Cap is concerned. He's convinced something nefarious is going to happen, but he's a moron when it comes to shit like this. The bastard thinks every life scenario ends with sex. Funerals, business meetings, trips to the fucking grocery store, sex is always a possible outcome for ole Cap.

"You're getting the PI, right?" I ask, and he tilts his head to the side and smirks like a bastard.

The instant the question leaves my lips, the inklings of regret start to roll around in my stomach. *A PI? Really, Trent? She might be a big fucking problem, but isn't a PI a little over-the-top?*

It might be. Okay, it probably is.

But what could it hurt, really? Just because I'll get the information doesn't mean I'll actually do anything with it.

"Is this your way of telling me you're done here, sweetheart?" Cap asks, and I nod.

"Yep."

"Consider your dirty work done." His grin grows wider. "And consider yourself mere weeks away from knowing what pretty little Greer feels like—"

Instantly, I cut him off before he can say any more obnoxious shit. "Goodbye, Cap."

Without another word, I head for the door, but not without lifting my middle finger over my shoulder.

Cap, however, has one final comment before the door closes behind me.

He's laughing as he says it, and his voice carries all the way to the other side of the building.

"Sexual destruction in five, four, three, two, one…KABOOM!"

# Chapter NINE

## Cap

The instant Turn leaves my office, I lean back in my chair and have a good laugh at his expense. I don't make a point to laugh at my friends behind their backs, but fuck, he came in here with guns blazing and insanity predicting his every word.

Greer Hudson. A woman who, apparently, holds the power to turn an otherwise intelligent man crazy.

I like her already.

I might've told Turn a little white lie about hiring a private investigator to hunt down some dirty secrets on his sexy archnemesis, but that doesn't mean I actually planned to follow through.

Sure, I know people, all kinds of fucking people, but my good buddy doesn't need a PI.

He needs to get laid.

Eventually, though, curiosity gets the best of me, and I snag my phone off my desk and type the name *Greer Hudson* into the search bar on Facebook.

Instantly, thirty Greer Hudsons fill the results, and I start the process of elimination.

**Hometown: Portland, Oregon.** Nope. Next.

**Age: Sixteen years old.** Not her. Although, that would really make this interesting.

**Occupation: Kindergarten teacher.** Unless she's schooling Turn on humbleness, this forty-year-old Greer Hudson isn't her.

By the time I reach the fifteenth Greer Hudson, I'm certain I've found my match.

**New Orleans, Louisiana.**
**Thirty-three years old.**
**Owner of Hudson Designs.**

*Bingo.*

Without any preamble, I click on her profile and scroll through the pictures I can see without being Facebook friends. And it doesn't take long for me to understand Turn's momentary insanity.

While she may be a real stubborn pain in his ass, she is, without a doubt, a fucking beauty.

Long brown hair. Crystal-clear blue eyes. Greer Hudson is what most would call *stunning*.

Perfectly proportioned and curves in the most delicious of places, this fury-inducing designer is sex on a pair of mile-long legs, topped off with a great set of perky tits.

I laugh hard. I can't help it.

*Trent is so fucked.*

Hell, it's no wonder he came in here shouting about firing her for shit like property damage and undisclosed pregnancies.

*Goddamn.* I probably shouldn't be so amused, but I am.

And I'm more certain than ever.

These two enemies are in for the fucking of their lives. Hell, I'm almost jealous of their future orgasms.

When my assistant buzzes my intercom to let me know my next conference call has been rescheduled by thirty minutes, I click out of Facebook and type out a text to the one and only person who needs to be pulled into Turn's wild web.

# THE *Billionaire* BOSS NEXT DOOR

*Me: You still pissed about Sophia?*

His response is instant. And far more forgiving than I deserve.
But that's Quince for you. Always kind. Always calm. Always positive.

*Quince: Nah. I know things like thinking get hard when your dick is involved. Consider yourself forgiven, you bastard.*

"Get hard when your dick is involved." Fucking hell. It takes everything inside me to hold my sarcastic, witty tongue and stay serious.

*Me: Thanks, Q. You're a real class act.*

*Quince: I know.*

I grin and type another message.

*Me: Now that we've kissed and made up, I have some news. Meet me after work at Murray's Pub.*

*Quince: Your news is going to have to wait. I have dinner plans with Emory. I'm taking her to her favorite New York restaurant before we have to head back to New Orleans tomorrow.*

*Me: Aw, look at you all romantic and shit.*

That's cute and all, Q being a good little boyfriend and taking his gal for a night on the town, but it's not helping me. Though, with me being the brilliant bastard that I am, it doesn't take long before I get an idea and send the bait.

*Me: What's her favorite New York eatery?*

And, as expected, he bites like a fucking fish.

**Quince:** *Le Bernardin.*

"Hey, Liz," I call out to my assistant through my intercom system. "Call Le Bernardin, act like you're Quincy Black's assistant, and find out what time his dinner reservations are tonight."

Her response is quick and to the point. "On it."

"Oh, and get them to change the reservation from two to three."

"Only if this doesn't lead to me being an accessory to a murder."

I grin and hit the intercom to answer. "Would I ever put you in that kind of situation?"

The only response I get is silence. Fucking *crickets*.

"Fine, Liz," I chuckle into the intercom. "No murders. Promise."

She sighs, literally sighs, into the receiver. "I'll call Le Bernardin now."

I smirk at her lackluster response, and before I get lost in the rest of my work day, I grab my phone and begin one last but very important text conversation.

**Me:** *Full check complete.*

Lucky for me, he responds right away.

**Turn:** *Huh?*

**Me:** *The PI. He completed his check. Very thorough. FBI, CIA, FB, IG, 23andMe. You name it, and he did it.*

**Turn:** *I just left your office, like, an hour ago...*

**Me:** *My guy is good.*

My guy is me. And I am good. So, yeah, technically, I'm not lying.

# THE *Billionaire* BOSS NEXT DOOR

*Turn: Did he find anything?*

*Me: Well…I'm not sure how to break this to you…*

*Turn: Break what to me?*

*Me: She's wanted.*

*Turn: WHAT?*

I grin like the devil as I type out another cryptic message.

*Me: In all fifty states.*

*Turn: WANTED FOR WHAT?*

Fuck, I wish I could keep this going for just a teensy bit longer, but I have too much work to catch up on. So, I throw in the towel and give him what I know.

*Me: Just kidding. She's clean as a fucking whistle.*

Greer Hudson isn't anything but a thorn in his side.
Not a criminal. Or a drug addict. Or some freaky dominatrix who ties people up and whips them. She's simply a beautiful woman who makes Trent Turner crazy.

*Turn: You didn't hire a PI, did you?*

Obviously, I didn't, but that doesn't mean I shouldn't be allowed the opportunity to slow roll him a bit.

*Me: Are you calling me a liar?*

Not even twenty seconds later, my phone vibrates in my hand.

*Turn: Yes, you lying motherfucker, I am. No PI completes a "thorough" check in one fucking hour.*

I can see the text bubbles moving up and down on the screen, indicating he's primed and ready, and I send another quick response before he can shoot me a ramble full of *fuck yous*.

*Me: You're welcome for saving your ass and preventing you from doing something stupid.*

Instantly, the text bubbles stop and never return.
Obviously, I *do* know people. But I'm not hiring a PI because Trent has a hate-boner for his new employee.
*And everyone thinks Quince is the most reliable friend.*
Pfft.

## Chapter TEN

## Emory

I look at the time on my phone and see it's quarter after seven. Instantly, my eyes move toward the entrance of the restaurant and then take a quick detour heavenward when my boyfriend is nowhere in sight.

And here I sit, inside Le Bernardin, one of my favorite New York restaurants, all by myself.

A sigh escapes my lungs as I pick at the white napkin wrapped around my cutlery.

For some reason, I spend the majority of my life waiting on people.

My best friend Greer can't be on time to save her life, and it seems, now that they've met, her tardiness has spread to my boyfriend like a parasite.

I look at my phone to see if Quince has texted or called to let me know how long he'll be, but I'm redirected when my sassy sister from another mister slides a text into my inbox.

**Greer:** *I can't believe you're ditching me to have dinner with your boyfriend.*

**Greer:** *In New York, of all places, btw. It's like you're just asking me to get mugged or kidnapped or something.*

This snarky bitch grew up in New Orleans. She spent her weekends working at her grandfather's restaurant, which means she also spent her weekends strong-arming drunk Mardi Gras tourists.

I've literally seen her punch a guy three times her size in the balls.

A punch to the face you'd expect.

Even a kick to the family jewels is understandable.

But a fist to some drunken asshole's balls? That's the kind of crazy shit I've learned to expect from Greer.

Needless to say, this isn't the kind of chick who would get kidnapped. If anything, the kidnapper wouldn't last two minutes before returning her.

I scoff to myself and type out a quick response. Giving attitude is, without a doubt, her most readily available skill.

She serves it as both a means of self-preservation and amusement, and she's been that way for as long as I can remember.

And that's a long time.

**Me: Why is that something you can't believe? Quince is actually nice to me.**

Greer and I first met at St. Augustine School in the first grade. She was toothy and full of piss and vinegar back then. She cursed and spat and did everything my mother had told me a lady never did. At the time, I didn't understand it was because she was being raised by a man and a boy in the absence of her parents, but I didn't need to.

As a first-grader born into privilege and swanky parties, I thought Greer's aggressive take on life seemed almost otherworldly cool.

She was outspoken and didn't take shit off anyone.

She was the six-year-old who stood up for me with a mouthful of sass and curse words a child her age never should've said when Sara Ruey told me I had ugly hair.

She was a shit-talking, outrageous enigma, and I wanted to be her with a desperation I didn't understand.

Ironically, she would have given anything to be me.

# THE *Billionaire* BOSS NEXT DOOR

I had two parents who loved me and everything material the world had to offer at my fingertips. She had pictures of the parents she'd never met, a uniform that was a size too small, and a pair of gym shoes her grandfather snagged from the Goodwill. Scuffed-up, beaten-down Nikes that she snazzed up with black-inked doodles of hearts and skulls and her name.

But for as much as we wished for the traits of each other when we were kids, our dynamic still hasn't changed today.

Greer is still the same cursing girl with a secret heart of gold, and I'm the friend who loves her for it.

*Greer: I'm nice to you! The amount is just expertly tailored to make sure you don't get spoiled by it.*

I roll my eyes. She may not think so, but she's so fucking predictable, it's ridiculous.

*Me: Sure, that's it. Just like I'm sure you're not already in your pajamas, eating room service, and giving me shit just for the hell of it.*

*Greer: What kind of person would do that?*

I smirk and tap one manicured finger on the table while I use my free hand to type out a three-letter text.

*Me: You.*

*Greer: Fine. I'm halfway through a cheese quesadilla and a brownie the size of my head. This hotel may have shitty taste in decor, but they've got good food. I'll give them that.*

*Greer: Seriously. You can't deny this hotel's style is like Exorcist-level scary.*

I shake my head at her inability to get out of her own way and glance to the door again for Quincy. Still nothing.

I sigh and type out more advice she probably won't heed.

**Me: Maybe you should practice not calling it shitty now.**

**Greer: That's no fun. I like my way.**

**Me: Whatever.**

**Greer: Is this you being done with our conversation?**

**Me: Yep.**

**Greer: P.S. Enjoy your date with my superfan.**

I'm typing out a response when a feel a gentle hand on my shoulder. I drop my phone into my purse and look up instead.

"Hey, baby," Quince greets, pushing his lips to mine for a quick kiss that makes me shiver. Even after three months together, I *still* get goose bumps when he simply says hello.

The mere realization of that urges a smile to kiss my lips.

Unfortunately, the sweet little swoony pebbles on my skin turn into the R.L. Stine version as he steps to the side to reveal his friend Caplin. Dressed down in jeans and wearing an actual flannel shirt, he looks more like a farmer than the top corporate lawyer and billion-dollar entrepreneur Quince has painted him to be.

I force a phony laugh and look to Quince imploringly. I was expecting this to be a date, not boys' hour at the tractor pull. "I know we're still kind of new, honey, but I should tell you now—one man is absolutely all I can handle."

Quincy's smile grows, and he's really fucking lucky I like the way it looks on him so much. "That's fine. Because I can't handle any."

# THE *Billionaire* BOSS NEXT DOOR

I grin—I can't help it when he looks at me like that—and he mouths the word *sorry*.

The chair scrapes across the carpeted floor as he takes his seat. Caplin has already made himself at home, not letting the exchange between Quincy and me deter him at all. His brown hair is messy, and a five-o'clock shadow is in full effect on his chin, but I suppose it rounds out his impression of Farmer John quite well.

A handsome-as-hell Farmer John who, from what I hear, way too many women drop their panties for, but still, he looks ridiculous.

And fucking oblivious that he's the third wheel.

I watch as he snags one of the two menus sitting on the table and just starts scrolling through his food options.

"Cap wants to have a quick chat with me after dinner, and since he managed to find his way to the restaurant, he decided he might as well use this opportunity to make a really great impression on you before we head back to New Orleans," Quincy offers in an attempt to give me an explanation. It's not the real explanation, I'm almost certain of that, but it's an explanation all the same. "Isn't that right, Cap?"

Caplin jerks his head up. "What?" he says, complimentary bread from the table hanging haphazardly from his lips. He pulls the excess away, sets it on his plate, and chews quickly. "Oh. Yes. Best of impressions. That's really important to me."

Dear *God*.

"Did you have some kind of laundry mishap?" I ask. "An explosion at your dry cleaner's, perhaps?"

"Nope." If he has any shame, it's somewhere else—across the globe. The corners of his lips curl up as he holds eye contact until I look away.

"Just another person who wouldn't know fashion if it smacked them in the face, then?"

"You look at it how you want, honey. I like the way I dress just fine." He smiles around another bite of bread, completely unaffected by my words or the fact that he is ruining my dinner date with my boyfriend.

My eyes widen as I implore Quincy to do something. He just grins like his gal and his pal are getting along better than he ever could have imagined.

"Maybe you should introduce me to one of your female friends who hasn't managed to meet your standards," he suggests with an ease that makes my blood boil a bit. "Although, that might be a big ask, huh? I mean, you probably don't allow those kinds of people in your inner circle. Gotta keep up the right appearances and shit like that."

"Don't be an ass." I roll my eyes. "Anyway, the only friend of mine who might possibly understand your current attire isn't looking for love. Especially with a New Yorker. Greer made that clear at lunch today."

"I'm not looking for love either—wait. Did you say Greer? Her last name wouldn't happen to be Hudson, would it?"

How the fuck does he know her *full* name?

Immediately, I stiffen my defenses. "Yes. Why?"

His chuckle is big enough that he actually has to stop inhaling the free bread basket for a second and a half. "Oh, nothing." He smirks.

"You have no idea, dude. No idea," he says to Quince with a bro-curated expression of *I'll tell you later.*

"Tell me," I say and lock eyes with him from across the table.

His obstinance appears in the form of a raised eyebrow. "No."

"Tell me right now."

He looks to Quince again, but this time, the line of his jaw is all *control your woman.*

This is a nice restaurant and I'm wearing a five-thousand-dollar dress, but desperate times call for desperate measures.

Quick as a flash, I stand and lean, over the bread carcass and carafe of wine and all manner of stain possibilities, and clasp my fingers onto the peak of his nipple.

He jumps and howls, and Quincy rears back in his chair, apparently shocked by this new side of me.

"You tell me what you know about Greer Hudson, and you do it now."

His smile is overwhelming. It beams. And, if I'm not mistaken, it's even a little bit salacious.

An image of Quince's friend engaging in rough sex appears uninvited in my mind, and my hand jerks back as though his nipple burns. I sit back in my seat again.

"Fine. Whatever. What's the point of attorney/client privilege, anyway?"

I scowl and tap my toe on the floor.

"Turn came in today to talk about her around lunchtime. That's all."

"Turn?" I ask.

"Trent Turner," Quincy explains and reaches out to rest his arm affectionately around my shoulders. "It's the nickname we gave him when we were kids."

Jesus. While Greer was dining on pastrami with me, Trent Turner, Greer's new boss, was seeing his lawyer about her. Mere hours after she was hired for the job.

*What the hell did she do to this guy?*

"And?" I prompt. "What happened?"

Caplin rolls his eyes and takes another piece of bread from the bread basket. I have to wait an entire thirty seconds as he slathers the thing with an ungodly amount of butter before he answers. "Well, he wanted to fire her—"

"What?" I nearly shout. Several patrons turn to look at us, and I feel the subtle heat of embarrassment as it pools in my cheeks. Quincy and Caplin don't even notice. Evidently, they're completely unfazed by uninvited attention.

"Relax," he says through a chuckle. "He can't. He knows he can't. Hell, he knew it wasn't possible before he even stepped foot in my office this afternoon. Still didn't stop him from unloading his baggage full o'crazy on me, though."

A relieved breath leaves my lungs. "Okay, well, that's good."

"Although," Cap continues. "I did tell him I could hire a PI to find out more about her."

*What the fuck.*

A private investigator? Jesus. Greer is the last person who needs some snoop digging around in the bowels of her life. They are shit-filled and clogged.

My only option is to protect her.

"Do that, and I will personally see to relieving you of a testicle."

Cap smiles. "Like, in a kinky way?"

"*No*," I say just as Quince jumps in with a *"Hey!"* of his own.

"All right, all right, all right," Caplin agrees, a regular Matthew McConaughey. "Let's all just calm down because I was never going to hire a PI. I only offered it to appease his temporary insanity."

"So, no PI?"

Cap shakes his head.

"Well, what else did he say, then?" I continue my interrogation, because son of bitch, I'm mentally freaking out for my best friend. "Is he planning on making her life there miserable?"

"Couldn't tell you." He shrugs off my questions. "After I destroyed his irrational dreams of wrongful termination, he started talking about some chick he kissed at the party the other night."

"He kissed someone?" Quince chimes in with a question of his own. "At a work function?"

"You know, I'm going to tell him you said that, Quince." Cap winks. "More evidentiary support that he is the epitome of a man prude."

"Who did he kiss?" I ask.

"I don't know. Some fuck decided masks were a good idea," Cap says, flashing a mocking wink at Quince, who gives him the finger back. "All he said was that she came as Beyoncé."

# THE *Billionaire* BOSS NEXT DOOR

Quince and I both freeze, statues in human form. "Beyoncé?" I ask to confirm.

"Yep."

"As in Beyoncé *Beyoncé*? The singer?"

Cap smirks. "Is there more than one Beyoncé?"

"Wait…" I pause and blink through the utter shock of it all. "Are you sure it was Beyoncé?"

"How many times do I need to say Beyoncé before you stop saying Beyoncé?" he tosses back. "And what's the deal? You got a thing against Bey or something? You really don't want to mess with the Beyhive. They can stir up some shit."

I ignore Cap completely and look at Quince. "What was Trent wearing at the party?"

I mean, I'm pretty sure I already know the answer to that question, but I have to make certain. This realization is too crazy not to double-check the facts.

"Walter White. From *Breaking Bad*."

Good God, this is bananas.

"Nothing beat my Thor costume," Cap chimes in with absolutely no valuable information for this conversation. "I was the tits."

*God, why is he here again?*

Because, apparently, he does occasionally provide valuable information.

I'd bet on the fact that it's rare, but I can't deny it just happened.

"Holy shit." I look at Quince. "I definitely didn't see that coming."

"Well, I'll be damned," Quince says, a rolling laugh vibrating his stomach a bit. "You're a dick *and* a shitty lawyer for offering up that info, but I can't deny I'm glad you did."

"What?" Caplin asks. "What in the fuck are you talking about right now?"

Quince grins. "It seems our friend might not dislike Greer Hudson quite as much as he thought."

"What does that mean?" Caplin asks again, slightly agitated that he's out of the loop.

I resist the urge to laugh in his face now that he's the one on the outside of the know.

Quincy, however, is too good of a guy to let him suffer. "We know who came to the party as Beyoncé."

"Who?" Cap furrows his brow, and I chime in with the answer.

"My best friend. *Greer Hudson.*"

"Are you serious?" The words fly out of his mouth. "The chick Turn kissed at the party is the same one he went on and on about finding a way to fire?"

Quincy laughs. "Sure sounds that way."

"Well, fuck me sideways and call me Sally, it looks like I was right." Caplin reaches for his phone, shaking his head in actual glee. "Oh, man, I can't wait to tell him about this shit."

And suddenly, it hits me like a flipping lightning bolt.

I reach out quickly, smacking Cap's phone out of his hands, and he scowls. I don't bother apologizing.

"Don't tell him."

"What?" Quince asks.

Instead of answering, I ask a question back. "Didn't you say Trent is renting one of the apartments in my parents' building while he's working on the Vanderturn New Orleans hotel?"

His brows pull together as he answers. "Yeah."

"Well, boys," I say, rubbing my hands together. "I've got a plan."

It's a bit evil.

And I'm going to have to keep one hell of a secret from my best friend.

But something just feels *so* right about this.

What Greer doesn't know won't kill her.

*Yeah, but she might kill you…*

Meh. She'll have to catch me first.

# Chapter ELEVEN

## Greer

Thirty-three years and it's come to this.

Moving in to an apartment a friend's family owns, rent-free, while I try to sell the house I've put all of my time and effort into.

The letter from the bank I found in my mail upon my return from New York four days ago made it pretty clear, though. Sell soon, or lose the house to foreclosure and send your credit to the depths of hell forever.

In fact, I'm pretty sure there was a doodle of the devil standing beside a car with a "Credit" decal holding a pair of hedge clippers and everything.

So, I did the only thing I could do—contacted a Realtor friend and started moving out my shit so I can make my house, my pride and joy, market-ready.

*Fuck my life.*

A lot of people toss around those three words in moments of menial crisis. When they're having a bad start to their week or dealing with a summer cold or when freaking gas prices go up by ten cents. Over things that are annoying, maybe even a little bad, but not end-of-the-world scenarios.

But my current depressing situation is truly worthy of *fuck my life*.

When Hudson Designs really started to struggle a couple of years ago, I took out a loan against the equity in my house to cover expenses in the interim. I figured it was a short dry spell, and if I could bridge the gap, I'd come out on the other side okay.

When that didn't work, I took out another, and before I knew it, I was drowning in personal debt, in addition to the loans for the business.

When it came down to eating or paying the mortgage, I chose the one that would keep me functioning, keep me scrapping to save what I'd built.

Unfortunately, when things didn't turn around like I'd hoped, all of those short-term-focused decisions eventually caught up with me.

I look around the insanely big apartment, my new apartment, and my stomach rolls with discomfort.

The floors are original but beautifully restored wood, and the trim woodwork throughout the vast living space is original but impeccable. The cabinets in the kitchen are custom-made, the counters expensive marble, and the bathroom is roughly the size of a streetcar.

Emory's parents could be pulling in a hefty amount of rent each month for this place, and instead, they're letting me stay in it for free.

*Good God, this feels like more than I deserve...*

"Are you sure it's okay I stay here?" I ask Emory uncomfortably. I appreciate her generosity, but that doesn't mean I feel good about it. I've worked hard for everything I've ever had in life, and somehow, taking her offer in this time of need seems like a concession of morals.

"Of course. There hasn't been a tenant in a couple of months, and my parents love you."

"They do?"

She laughs. "God knows why."

"Very funny."

Emory grabs my arm and shoves. "Well, when you ask a dumb question, you get a dumb answer. My parents have known you almost as long as they've known me, Greer. You're like a second daughter. I'm not sure why you're surprised by that. Especially after I already told you before we left for New York that they were more than willing to help you out."

God, the Collinses are fucking generous. Too generous. And there was no way in hell I could take them up on their offer to help me climb out of my garbage financial situation. It was way too much, and I didn't feel worthy of that kind of charity.

Also, I didn't want to feel like a charity case either.

My pride is far too thick and strong to allow that.

Insecurity of my vulnerabilities makes me play off her words. "You're right. I mean, I'm entirely lovable. I'm probably even their *favorite* daughter."

She squawks and drops one of my boxes unceremoniously. I set mine down gently and jump forward to put my finger in her face.

"That thing better have pillows in it, Emory Marie!"

Arms flailing, she comes at me like a wrecking ball, and I leap over boxes like an Olympic hurdler to get away.

"Favorite daughter, my ass!" she yells, chasing after me on a hyena-like laugh.

"All right," I yell, dodging her fist with a bob and a weave. "All right, you lunatic! You're the favorite daughter, obviously! I'd definitely respect someone who came out of my vagina more than someone who didn't!"

"Oh my God!" she exclaims on a cackle. "Why are you so gross?"

"Because I was raised by wolves, Emory."

"You were raised by men." She wrinkles her nose, and I grin.

"I'm pretty sure we're saying the same thing here."

Emory's eyes roll toward the ceiling. "We both know that's not it. Your brother has way more manners than you do."

I shrug it off. "I guess I just don't conform to the societal ideal of a lady, then."

"No kidding." She snorts. "Quince and Trent's friend Cap is right. You probably would get along great with him."

"What?" I ask, stopping short as suspect rosiness colors her cheeks and her mouth closes. "Did you just say Trent? As in Trent Turner?"

"You know he's friends with Quincy. And I'm dating Quincy. I can't help it if my boyfriend is good buddies with your new boss."

I glare. "So, you've been talking about me with my boss's friends?"

"No, of course not," she says. Too bad, her face says another thing.

"You have! Why were you talking about me?"

"We weren't," she refutes.

"*Emory Marie!*" I shout, arms raised like a lunatic. "What did you say about me?"

"It was just casual conversation—small talk—not the combination to your safety deposit box. *Jesus.*"

"My safety deposit box has nothing but lint and an old Altoid in it. I'd honestly rather you'd given them the combination," I retort. "And when did all this happen?"

"That night I had to suffer through dinner with my lovely boyfriend and his, obnoxious, third-wheeling, caveman buddy, Caplin Hawkins. I already told you all of this." She puts a defiant hand to her hip. "And you act like the details of our friendship are a state secret. Are you a Russian spy? Do I need to ask the FBI to conduct an investigation?"

"I just…" I pause and look down at my Converse sneakers as I try to formulate what in the hell I even want to say. "I just don't like wondering what other people know about me," I say seriously, and the tone of my voice sobers Emory up quickly.

"I wouldn't say anything bad about you. I'm your best friend, and I'm always looking out for your best interests."

"Talking about me with my boss's best friends doesn't feel like my best interests."

"I swear I didn't say anything bad."

I mull over her words for a long moment. "So…Quincy is good friends with Trent?"

She nods. "Friends since they were kids."

"So…he talks to him a lot?"

"I guess, yeah…" She pauses and searches my eyes. "What are you getting at here?"

"I don't know." I shrug one nonchalant shoulder. "Maybe Quince could, like, you know, talk me up to his asshole friend. Put in a good word."

She quirks a brow. "You want Quince to talk you up to Trent?"

"It couldn't hurt," I respond with another shrug. "He could tell him I'm wonderful and a brilliant designer and have impeccable taste and shit like that. Basically, just the facts, you know?"

"Just the facts, huh?"

"Yes. Just the facts," I repeat. "Then, maybe, my bastard boss will pull that giant stick out of his tight, firm ass and stop throwing shade my way."

She smirks. "His tight, firm ass?"

"Shut up."

"Okay…" She pauses for a moment, and before she can continue, a soft, amused laugh escapes her pretty red lips.

"Stop laughing, you biotch." I glare, and she raises both hands in the air.

"I swear, I'm not laughing at you, just at the situation," she explains through another fucking laugh. "And I am truly hearing what you're throwing down here, but there's a pretty big hole in your plan…"

"And what's that?"

"Trent Turner can't be the only one to stop throwing shade."

I scoff. "I don't throw shade."

She eyes me for a long moment, and I sigh.

"Ugh. Never mind. Forget it."

Emory grins and wraps me up in a tight hug. "I promise, it's all going to be okay. I've got your back, friend. Hell, I'll always have your back, even in the moments you might not realize."

My eyes narrow at the careful construction of her wording, but I decide to let it go and focus on the important shit.

Tomorrow is a fresh beginning—the first official day of my new job and a chance to open up new doors.

I'll own a house again one day. I'll be on my feet soon.

And life as I know it is going to be bigger and better than ever.

# Chapter TWELVE

## Greer

The very first day of my new job has arrived, and the sun is shining, the birds are chirping, and some other shit that happy people notice is definitely going on just outside of my new apartment.

Normally, I would focus on the drunk guy puking against the building across the street, but not today. Today, I am a shimmering beacon of positivity.

My new apartment is still a bit of a mess with boxes and stuff scattered around, and I've had exactly zero opportunity to put my own little design touches throughout the massive space, but last night, I managed to sleep a solid six hours.

Sure, it's two hours short of the recommended amount, but a miracle considering the circumstances.

This is a big day. A monumental day, in fact.

I have everything to prove.

*Yeah, you also have everything to lose.*

I shake off my inner-bitchy-subconscious and revert my focus back to positivity.

*Today, you are a positive ray of sunshine, Greer.*

*A real beacon of light. So bright and shiny that if you lifted your skirt, your crotch could be used as a flipping flashlight.*

I ignore the tightness in my chest and give myself one last final pep talk.

*Today, you will be light and airy. Focused but breezy. Serious but ecstatic.*

*You are going to nail this first day so hard, it'll be screaming your name by the time you get home tonight.*

Quickly, I nab my keys from the counter, sling my blazer on over my blouse, and drop my cell phone into the outside pocket of my purse.

I heft it off the counter and nearly crumple under the weight of everything I've got inside, but you never know what you're going to need on the first day of work for a new company.

I have my sketch pad, pencils, fabric samples, previous blueprints, furniture catalogs for my favorite designers, lighting brochures, and one tiny bag of cashews—just to give me something to chew on if the nerves turn my stomach.

I considered packing a change of clothes, a drink, lunch, and maybe a Toyota Supra, but the limits of my shoulder strength are finite, even if the bounds of what my anxiety about the first day has pushed me to are not.

I take one last peek in the mirror to assess my appearance.

Sharp black skirt, smart white blouse—that I actually ironed—panty hose, and a black blazer with gold buttons make up my ensemble, and my eye makeup is light but striking.

It's exactly what I wrote down when I woke up at two a.m., dreaming about my outfit, and even if I hate it, it's all I have time for.

I take a deep breath, grip the knob of my front door, and prepare myself to face the music.

"Here goes nothing."

My door squeaks a little as I open it to step outside, and I make a mental note to apply some WD-40 to the hinges when I get home.

The manic part of me wants to do it now, but the realistic part of me knows I don't have time.

That's the kind of shit that's always making me late, and there is absolutely no room to be tardy today.

# THE *Billionaire* BOSS NEXT DOOR

*No*, I think with a sardonic shake of my head. *Your new boss already dislikes you enough.*

I'm putting my key into the lock and turning it into place when the door to the apartment next door opens with the same squeak as mine.

Instinctually, I lift my gaze and turn to get a quick look at my new neighbor.

Time stops. Just up and fucking stops.

My breath freezes in my lungs, and I have to blink several times to understand that what I'm seeing is real.

*That can't be real. He* can't *be real.*

Surely, the pressure of this day is making me hallucinate or something…*right?*

Wrong.

I know that ass, those thighs, that brown hair, and sharp jaw. I know the expensive fabric of his suit, and I *know* when he turns around, those emerald-green eyes will be all too familiar.

It's Trent Turner. My new boss.

The asshole. The prick. *Here.* In the flesh.

*What in the actual hell?*

Did I conjure him with some kind of witchcraft?

I can't stop the little bark of discomfort as it bubbles up my throat and spills from my mouth, and nothing, it seems, can stop him from noticing it.

Poised with a smile for his new neighbor as well, he halts in the middle of his turn like he's been shot.

Once again, our timing is in sync as we engage in some kind of shocked stare-off.

"*You*," we both say and not the least bit kindly.

I look around the hall, but my mind can't slow down enough to stop on any one object.

It's like I no longer know where I am or what's happening or what planet we're on.

My mind takes off at a gallop, and my mouth follows close behind.

"What the... Did I somehow teleport to the hotel?"

Trent scowls at my ridiculous scenario but answers me anyway. "No."

Desperate to figure out how in the hell the universe could be doing this to me, I ask him another question. "Are you a mirage?"

His scowl fades into what I can only assess as resignation. "Nope."

It's a full-on standoff in the middle of the hallway, and he stares back at me with the exact same irritation I imagine I'm throwing his way.

"Are you a ghost?"

"No."

"A zombie version of someone who's already dead but just happens to look like Trent Turner?"

He sighs and slips his hands into the pockets of his dress slacks. "How long are we going to do this?"

"For as long as it takes for me to understand what is happening," I spit. "Why are you here? In my apartment building?"

"I live here."

"No, you don't."

He can't, because son of a wench, I refuse to let this be my reality.

"Pretty sure I do," he responds, and that stupid, smug smile of his grates across my nerves like sandpaper.

"Nope. No way." I shake my head manically. "That doesn't work for me. You're not allowed to live here."

"Doesn't work for you?" An annoyed chuckle escapes his full lips. "That's rich coming from the woman who moved in to an apartment like some kind of gypsy in the middle of the fucking night."

"Oh God. You're my boss, and you live next door. You're the boss next door." I point up at the ceiling at, you know, *Him*, and declare, "And Emory says I'm the one with a sick sense of humor."

"Have you had a psychotic break, or is this something you do regularly?"

# THE *Billionaire* BOSS NEXT DOOR

I move my gaze back to his. "Huh?"

"Should I get used to waiting for you to finish talking to yourself? It could really stretch out the hours of what will already be a grueling workday."

"Blah, blah, blah," I mock with the face of a possessed Martian, shoving past him to make my way to the stairwell. Ever since I read that taking the stairs instead of the elevator is a simple key to maintaining good heart health in *Shape* magazine, I've made sure to implement the practice.

Since working out obviously isn't my specialty and fried foods give me life, it's all up to the stairs to make sure I don't have a heart attack at the age of forty-five.

Trent follows, unfortunately, every inch of his body humming with much the same energy I feel for him.

Annoyance. Loathing. Painful awareness that this is our life now.

How on earth can this be happening? The one person I can't seem to take in stride is not only my new neighbor but my freaking boss too.

*Is the universe trying to kill me?*

And, seriously? Why is he here? I know it's an insanely nice building with apartments that require the kind of rent you need to make well over six figures to afford, but doesn't he have some Richie Rich mansion in the suburbs he can fill with his toxic-ness instead?

Not only will I have to spend hours upon hours with him every day at work, but I will come home every night and have to deal with the fact that this prick is on the other side of my living room wall.

I will have to see him every-fucking-where, all the flipping time.

When I leave for work.

When I get home from work.

When I get my damn mail.

*Jesus Christ, what if I masturbate and he hears me? I won't survive.*

The dramatic thought forces me to a halt in the stairway, and he rams right into the back of me.

I groan as the back of my shoe scrapes a blister on my heel before the day has even started.

"Could you watch where you're going?" I snap snidely as I turn around to meet his infuriating green eyes.

"I was," he spits back. "You're the one who stopped in the middle of the staircase."

"Yeah, well…"

"Yeah, well?" He raises a challenging brow.

"Just go in front of me," I grumble when I can't think of a snappy enough insult.

He smirks like he's won, and I want to slap the expression right off of his handsome face.

*Whoa, whoa, whoa, Greer. Handsome?*

No, not handsome face. Just a face. A completely normal, nothing-to-see-here face.

By the time I make it to the bottom of the stairwell, he's got a head start on me, and I decide to keep it that way.

There's no upside to walking shoulder to shoulder with him all the way to the hotel.

When he rounds the corner out of sight, I increase my pace to one slightly faster than a tortoise. In what must be a personal record, I've given myself plenty of time to make it to the hotel on time, but I really want to stop for a coffee at the shop around the corner first.

*Nobody should go into the day without coffee.*

My brother always told me that my mom used to say *Quick wit is just wit with caffeine.*

I had to reach adulthood to truly understand what she meant, but now, I feel like I have a really clear picture of just how smart she must have been.

The Easy Roast sign with black-and-white lettering hangs over the entrance up ahead, and I can feel my legs start to churn involuntarily.

The smell of coffee beans and fresh pastries floats down the street and into my nose, and I can't get there fast enough.

# THE *Billionaire* BOSS NEXT DOOR

The bright light of the morning makes the transition into the dark shop all the more troublesome, and I have to take a good fifteen seconds for my eyes to adjust before stepping up to the line of customers waiting to order their drinks.

I'm about five people away from the counter when I notice the back of a man.

A very *specific* man who literally won't disappear this morning.

Hunching and leaning, I immediately become an appendage that shoots out of the back of the person in front of me. They didn't ask for this deformity, they weren't expecting it, but at a time like this, they have no choice.

I need camouflage, and I need it *now*. In a coffeehouse in New Orleans, camouflage just so happens to come in the form of a hipster guy with a beanie.

Trent accepts his coffee with a smile and heads for one of the café-style tables outside.

It's January, but this is New Orleans, and it's remarkably pleasant out in the fresh air.

I keep watch on him with a discreet eye as the line moves forward until, finally, I get to put in my order for a large coffee with cream and sugar and a chocolate croissant.

Carbs are my best friend today, and I'll do my damnedest to load up on them right up front.

Until then, I'm going to hunker down in a booth in the back and wait until one of two things happens: Trent Turner leaves, or I have absolutely no time left before I'm late.

Because I won't sacrifice my work reputation to avoid him.

No way. I'll go *Hunger Games* on that bitch.

May only the best of the best survive.

# Chapter Thirteen

## Trent

Seated at a little café table outside Easy Roast, the coffee shop up the street from my New Orleans apartment, I scan the street for signs of the enemy and come up blessedly empty.

Fuck, I'd love to know who is plotting against me. It feels like I'm being sent a death sentence in the form of a snarky, sarcastic woman by the name of Greer Hudson.

First, my dad *hires her*.

Then, she up and moves right next door to me.

Literally. *Right next to me.* Her front door is right beside my front door.

*How is this even possible?*

The odds of that kind of clusterfuck scenario have to be insane. Surely, I'd have a better chance of getting my father to realize he's a controlling bastard when it comes to his son. Or for Cap to stop talking about his dick like it's an actual family member.

Dear God. If that woman is anything but the devil in disguise, the heat of lightning can strike me down right now.

I put my cup to my lips and take a sip of my Americano.

Ouch.

Fuck *me*, that coffee is hot.

I scramble for a napkin to keep the contents from soaking my suit and wipe the escaped scalding liquid from my lips. That she-devil has me so frazzled, I've apparently lost the ability to complete normal human functions like drinking hot liquids without burning my damn tongue off.

Talk about a stellar start to what should be a big, successful first day with the new team.

*Just put her out of your head, you bastard, and focus on the priorities.*

Work. *That* is the priority. Making the New Orleans project the best hotel Turner Properties has ever built. *That* is where my focus needs to be. Not anywhere close to Greer Hudson and her penchant for snark.

With a renewed sense of determination, I grab my phone and pull up the Uber app to call a car. It's only ten or so blocks to the hotel, a distance I could walk if I wanted to, but because I had to stop at Easy Roast and get my shit together, I don't have that much time.

Once I finish putting in a request for a car, my phone starts to vibrate in my hands.

**Quincy Calling.**

What appropriate timing. He's just the man I was hoping to chew out.

"Well, hello," I say obnoxiously.

"Wow," he replies with a laugh. "That's some ominous tone, brother."

"Oh, you bet," I agree. "It goes perfectly with the doom of realizing I now live next door to my actual waking nightmare."

"Huh?"

"Greer Hudson," I say pointedly. "My new neighbor. As of this morning, I've learned that she lives in the same building as me. On the same floor. Right next door. To *me.*"

There's a short pause, and the receiver scratches like he's rubbing it with his fucking palm.

"Tell me you didn't know, Quince."

"I didn't," he responds.

"Your girlfriend's family owns the building, and you're the one who helped me snag this place. How in the fuck didn't you know?" I question.

"I did. But I had no idea Greer was leasing the apartment next door."

"For a man who should have all of the inside info about my building, you really dropped the damn ball here."

He chuckles. "I didn't know I was supposed to be keeping tabs on your building's new occupants."

"Fucking hell." I sigh. "New Orleans is a huge city. How could this have happened?"

"Sorry, dude."

"You don't sound all that sorry."

He doesn't. If anything, he sounds amused. The bastard.

"That's because it's not my fault," he retorts, but his voice never strays from his familiar, calm Quincy tone. "Why would I waste time apologizing for something I'm not responsible for?"

"Take your rationality and shove it. There's no place for it here."

He chuckles. "Why don't you stay at your dad's place? Doesn't he have a penthouse in the city?"

I force a fake laugh from my lungs. "I'm sorry, you must be mistaking me for someone my father likes."

"Oh, come on. Senior likes you. It's just…tough love."

I snort. "Hah. Well. Whatever it is means I'm not staying in his penthouse."

"Then fucking buy a house of your own. It's not like you're a pauper, for shit's sake. Why are you living in an apartment anyway?"

"Because." I shrug. "I don't know if I'm staying in New Orleans after the hotel is done. New York is my home base, you know that."

Cash to spare or not, I'm not a fan of wasting money on uncertainties. And because of everything going on with my mom, my future living situation is one big fat unknown.

"New York is also where your father is." He kindly reminds me of shit I don't feel like thinking about right now. "Maybe it'd do you some good to get some distance."

"Distance from my father means distance from more than just him, Quince, and you know it."

# THE *Billionaire* BOSS NEXT DOOR

I grew up in New York. It's what I know, what I love, what I'm used to. New Orleans is an entirely different animal, and beyond that, it's not where my mom is.

I know it sounds ridiculous for a thirty-three-year-old man, but being close to her is important. Especially since her diagnosis. Who knows how many good years she has left?

"Sounds like you're stuck, then. If I were you, I'd just make the best of it."

"Make the best of it?" I repeat on a sigh. "Why does everyone keep saying shit like that?"

"Maybe because it's good advice."

I snort. "Okay, Dr. Phil."

"Yeah, yeah. My hair is thinning, and I have a mustache. Real original."

"I don't give a shit about your bald spot, Quince. I'm talking about your holy-Kumbaya style words of wisdom."

"That's right, Turn. Wisdom. Even your insults know I'm right."

"Come on, Q." I refuse to believe this is my reality. "Surely, they have another apartment available in the building? Or even another building with an apartment that doesn't put me right next door to a crazy, obnoxious woman?"

"Are you saying you would actually *move* to another apartment, that you don't even know if you're going to stay in for longer than nine months, just to get fifty feet farther away from her?"

I don't even have to think about my answer.

"*Yes.*"

"Wow."

"So, another apartment?"

"Nope," he responds way too quickly. "At least not another apartment rented from Emory's family. This is probably it, dude. When you signed your lease, there were only two apartments available. The one you moved in to and the one next door to yours. This is the kind of building that locals would practically sell a limb to live in. It's rare for spots to become available. Not to mention, the whole reason you wanted it was because of its prime location to the hotel."

Everything he says is right. I rented this apartment for a reason. And I don't have any damn time to go searching for a new place. Not with the NOLA project demanding all of my time and energy. Losing even one day could end in delays I can't afford.

"Great," I grumble, smashing a piece of my chocolate croissant in between two fingers.

I stare out toward the road, my mind racing with all sorts of irrational thoughts. But when I see a Prius with an Uber sticker in the back window pull up to the curb, I throw some money on the table and pick up what's left of my newspaper.

"I've got to go," I say to Quince. "My car's here."

"Okay, dear. Have a good day at work. Kisses."

"Blow me," I say in return.

He's still laughing when I hang up the call and cruise across the sidewalk.

I've got a hand on the door handle of the black car when a different hand, one with red fingernails and owned by the devil, smacks the back of it away.

"Whoops. Sorry, neighbor. This Uber's mine."

And there, as if I channeled her evil spirit, is Greer Hudson, smirking so hard one of her perfectly shaped eyebrows lifts.

"Excuse me?"

She clears her throat and nods to the driver. "Check your information, dear. You'll have to wait for the next eco-friendly hatchback."

She shoves me out of the way, pops the door open, and jumps inside.

And I'm left with the confirmation that she's right as I open the app and compare the license plate as it putters away.

When you're unwilling to share your Uber with your new boss

on your first day of work, you're either asking for trouble or you have a few screws loose.

And, I swear to God, when it comes to Greer Hudson, it's both.

*Fine. If this insane woman wants trouble, I am more than willing to oblige.*

# Chapter FOURTEEN

## Greer

It's been a whirlwind of a morning, and it's only nine a.m.

I left my boss stranded on the sidewalk to wait for his own Uber, even though we were coming to the same place.

*God, why can't I stop doing things like this!*

It's like I'm *trying* to poke the billionaire beast.

And ever since then, he's shown his disdain for me—*his new neighbor* and *employee*—through his annoyed glares, heavy sighs, and overall grumpy demeanor.

But yet he's still managed to run a tight ship. I'm talking spandex-pants-stuck-straight-up-your-ass kind of tight ship.

One hour into our first official work day and we've had our morning meeting, toured the majority of the lobby area and what will be the pool and fitness center, and spoken to at least seven subcontractors working on the property.

After all that, there are two things I know without a doubt. The hotel is going to be gorgeous—God and Trent Turner willing, that is. And my boss is an absolute natural…*at being a prick.*

"Jesus Christ," Trent says, his eyebrows furrowing in irritation. "It's like every time I come here, we have to start over. Is Sergio here? His guys?"

Obviously, the second point proves itself more and more every minute.

"I don't think he's scheduled to be here until tomorrow, Mr. Turner," the lead contractor, George, responds.

"Does anyone other than me realize what kind of a schedule we're on here? We have nine months—*nine*—until opening day, and we're still roughing things in."

"I'll try to get him on the phone—" George responds in an attempt to soothe the raging beast.

"No. I'll call him myself. Give me the number," Trent demands impatiently.

George's hands shake as he scrolls through his phone and rattles off the numbers.

Trent dials as he speaks, and then he glances to the rest of us in the room before hitting send.

"Busy yourselves. I know for a fact each and every one of you has something important to be doing."

Wow. And I thought I made a bad first impression.

Skeptically sour faces litter the room as Trent steps outside to make his phone call, and if I didn't know how aggravating the man was, I actually might feel bad about how deep his hole is getting with these people.

Doesn't he know the phrase *Kill 'em with kindness*?

I decide distraction is the best way to handle the awkward vibe in the room and step up to the plate to take charge. "Hey, Sarah," I call to the assistant of the general contractor. "Did you say lighting was already laid out, or did decisions still need to be made?"

I wish I'd been brought in on this project from day one, but most people don't know how deep a designer's details really go. Lighting placement affects the whole aesthetic of the hotel, and it'll make a huge difference to know whether I'm working off someone else's foundation or if I get to establish my own.

"Uh," she mutters, pulling herself away from the mass interest in the prickish behavior of our new boss, and rolls out the prints on the makeshift sawhorse table. "I think all of the wiring is run, but they still have to cut in the boxes. If there's something specific you're looking for, I think there's still plenty of room to make changes."

*Fan-flipping-tastic.*

"Great. I think we really need to focus on having both soft and hard lighting options in each guest room. There's nothing I hate more in a hotel than too little or too much light. People want options. Edits on the next great American novel require a slightly different ambiance than a night of bow chicka bow wow, if you know what I'm saying."

Sarah laughs, and the two guys who were surreptitiously observing Trent through the windows turn to me and smile.

Tony is the food and restaurant manager, and Marcus is a hospitality specialist I met in New York. He's apparently had a hand in every hotel Trent Turner Senior has ever opened and probably knows more than the rest of us combined, but he's been remarkably quiet the whole day.

It seems like maybe he's just waiting to watch Junior fall on his face.

I wonder if Trent's even considered what an asset Marcus would be to have on his side.

Trent comes back into the room and, of course, immediately the light mood takes a nose dive to the depths of hell.

I shoot imaginary darts at his bright-green eyes and imagine him hitting the ground in pain.

It's almost ridiculously satisfying, and I can't help the little laugh that bubbles out of my throat because of the mental image.

It doesn't go unnoticed.

"Something funny?" Mr. Serious Pants asks sternly.

I raise an eyebrow and hold my ground.

It's honestly like I'm incapable of doing anything else around him.

"Yes."

"Care to share?"

I consider the riotous laughter the other people in the room would experience if I were to tell the truth and make a cost comparison against the undeniable shit I will earn for saying it.

# THE *Billionaire* BOSS NEXT DOOR

The chips are stacked against me, so I decide to keep this little ditty to myself.

"No. I'm good, thanks."

Trent scowls but doesn't say anything else as he waves us out of the fitness room—ironic that I'm still giving him shit in hotel gyms, I know—and back into the corridor that leads to reception.

Sarah bumps me with her elbow while we walk, like some girl-code form of congratulations on my back-talking to the boss, and I'm instantly back in high school, cackling at the back of the classroom with the other class clowns.

*Dear God, how low I've sunk.*

I need to get control of my impulses. Not only do I need this job, but after seeing the foundation of this place, I *want* it.

I can practically smell the fresh paint of my choosing as it goes up on the walls and feel the finest of textures and linens under my fingertips.

I can picture the touches of Creole and charm and everything special this place could be, and I could be the one who makes it that way.

What an accomplishment that would be. It would make all of the hard work and the tears and the struggles worth it, and I know it would make my brother proud to see me do something so significant.

With a renewed sense of purpose, I'm on my best behavior for the rest of the morning. I don't snark when Trent sneers, and I don't crack jokes at his expense when he isn't around.

I am a walking, talking goddamn professional, and I expect some Fortune 500 company owner will be designing a course based on my approach any day now.

Sarah and the guys give me funny looks given that they don't know how a Stepford wife managed to inhabit my body in such a short time, but I don't let it sway me.

There's a head honcho in town, and it just so happens he's the most annoyingly attractive human on earth.

*So what?*

But I'm alone in my endeavors.

Trent is still officially the most pompous boss I've ever worked for, and with the way his sour attitude commandeered the staff's mood this morning, his grave looks to be about forty feet deep at this point.

And that really brings to mind just one thing…

I wonder if Emory's parents will let me bust through the wall when he dies.

## Chapter FIFTEEN

### Trent

I'm halfway through the fourth day of working with the NOLA project team, and it's been a long fucking morning.

I slept like shit last night and woke up at the ass-crack of dawn, arriving at the hotel a good two hours before everyone else, just so I could avoid one particular person on my team before I'd managed coffee.

A she-devil in heels who believes every idea that's ever crossed her mind is the most brilliant idea that's ever been thought.

Greer Hudson is by far the most insufferable woman I've ever met in my life. And trust me, my best friend is Cap, therefore I've met a lot of fucking women.

At work, she is everywhere I am, a sarcastic, pursed-lipped, thorn in my side, and when I get home, she's *still* there. All around me.

There's something about knowing she's on the other side of my bedroom wall that is stealing my sanity *and* turning me into an insomniac.

For a building as expensive as the one we're both living in, you'd think they'd have better soundproofing.

But they don't.

I can hear her every step. Her every cackle. Her goddamn reality show preferences buzzing from her television.

Even the sounds of her shower running reach my ears through the walls.

*If this isn't the definition of hell, I don't know what is.*

I'm tired. Grouchy. And a headache the size of the Empire State Building is taking up residence in my skull.

Needless to say, I'm in need of a short break from the stress that is the job site, and there's only one place that'll do.

The instant the nostalgic sign for Coastal Crepes fills my vision, relief relaxes my shoulders, and I cross the street and head toward the entrance.

This restaurant holds special memories for me. When I was a kid, my mom used to bring me here whenever we visited New Orleans, and just the smell of it brings the woman I used to know to my mind.

Three years ago, she was diagnosed with Parkinson's disease, and the progression has been fast. And she's not the same as she used to be, mostly because of the depression dealing with the disease has driven her to.

She used to be fun and fun-loving and a positive peace-keeper in the tense relationship between my father and me, and while she's still mostly positive when it comes to me, she's become ruthlessly unforgiving of herself.

I still see the woman who gave me care and attention, no matter how much success I garnered, and I want her to know I do.

For the last year or so, I've spent my weekends taking her on coffee dates and to the movies, shopping for a new outfit to make her feel good, and to the park even if it's just to feel the sun on her face. And her quiet enjoyment of each outing only motivated me to do more before I left to head the project that is the Vanderturn New Orleans hotel.

Before I knew it, I was delaying my NOLA departure date just so I wouldn't have to skip out on time with her.

But my desire to be near my mom in New York has only created an even bigger sore spot between my father and me, and when I finally committed to coming down here, she told me she didn't want me to come back. Not on the weekends to visit, and not when anything else came up.

I was to stay in New Orleans, one of her favorite cities in the world, until I finished the hotel.

I don't know if her demands were a martyr-like self-sacrifice in the name of my relationship with my father or something else, but any time I try to bring it up, she shuts me down.

Instead of getting sucked into the sadness of what I wish were different about my life, I shift my focus to the things I can control.

The hotel, and currently, the specifics of my lunch crepe.

Peanut butter, Nutella, banana, and just about as much bacon as one man can handle—the actual cure, I'm sure, for a ravaged soul.

The bell above the door rings when I pull it open, and it doesn't take long before I order my food and sit down at a two-person table in the middle of the restaurant. The great part about this place for workdays is that you can either sit down and a server will take your order, or if you're in a lunch-hour rush, you can order up at the counter and find a seat on your own.

With this restaurant only five blocks from the hotel construction site, I have a feeling I'll be a frequent customer over the next several months.

I cut into the edge with my fork, bring the bite to my mouth, and look right into the ass of Greer Hudson at the counter.

*Seriously?*

I wish I could say my eyes are deceiving me, but they aren't.

I can tell it's her, even from the back.

I'm ashamed to admit that when we *aren't* fighting, I spend way too much time looking at the round, plush surface of her ass.

It's perfectly shaped and just the right size, and if we hadn't gotten off on the wrong foot in the Vanderturn Manhattan gym that day, I might have accidentally told her so.

I stare until she turns around and then jerk my gaze back to my cooling crepe to avoid eye contact.

I make a point not to watch as she leaves the counter with her meal and finds a table of her own, but for some freakish reason, I can sense her anyway.

Back and to the left, her table is in the tiniest corner of the restaurant imaginable. In all of my visits, I've never even seen anyone sit there. The space is so tight that I'm pretty sure the restaurant only put it there so they could advertise more seating than actually exists.

But for some unknown reason, she *insists* on sitting there, in a booth that doesn't really look like a booth. It's basically just a miniature table pushed up against a wall, with a bench built for no one bigger than a baby.

And for what must be caused by a minor bout of delirium from lack of sleep or stress or *something*, I can't *not* look in her direction. I'm powerless to my curiosity.

Quickly and as discreetly as possible, I glance over my shoulder and into the nook where I know she'll be.

She makes a huge fucking effort to slide into the booth, damn near twisting and turning and contorting her slim figure into a pretzel.

Once. Two. Three. Four failed attempts, and I'm practically choking on a piece of banana from the hilarity of it.

It's like she has a beef with the table itself.

She is so damn determined, so damn stubborn, that I'm silently wondering if she'll remove a limb just to prove a point to a restaurant table.

When the fight becomes too much, when she finally gives in, she stands and leans over the table, picking on her crepe like a vulture.

God. This woman. She is something else.

With a slight shake of my head, I go back to focusing on my own meal, and I don't notice immediately when she's up and on the move again. In fact, I don't *really* notice her until the third time she walks in front of my table.

And that's just the beginning.

Greer uses the strip of floor in front of my table like a goddamn

# THE *Billionaire* BOSS NEXT DOOR

runway, stealing glances at me from behind a veil of hair every time she passes.

The first pass, she's flipped her jacket backward and slipped on sunglasses.

The second round included a new part to her hair and that jacket tied around her waist.

It's like she's trying to trick me into thinking it's not her or something.

I'm not sure if she thinks I'm legitimately blind or if she thinks she's somehow engaged a special superpower to make herself invisible, but I'd be lying if I said I'm not getting some kind of amusement out of it.

*Not to mention, each time she walks by, that plush ass of hers does too.*

It's not until the tenth time that she makes a pass, and one of the patrons asks her if she's homeless and in need of money or food, that she drops the act and stops in front of the chair across from me.

She clears her throat, and I smile in greeting.

"Oh, hi, Greer. I didn't realize you were here."

Right. She did everything but flap her wings and throw a shoe at me. Everyone in the universe knows she's here.

Her face melts into a sneer as it becomes undeniably clear I'm lying.

When she still doesn't pipe up but stays rooted to her spot with a blue-eyed glare directed toward me, I have to prompt her.

"Go on," I say and rest my elbows on the table. "I can tell you want to say something. In fact, it looks like the effort to keep it all in is literally killing you. So, by all means, spill."

Her face softens a bit. "Respectfully?"

"Is that really possible for you?" I ask, and she rolls her eyes.

"You'd catch a lot more flies with honey than all that vinegar you've been pissing all over the place."

"I'm sorry, what?"

"You're kidding, right?" she tosses back without hesitance. "You've spent the entire day doing an impression of Sideshow Bob. Sarah's almost worn her teeth down to the nubs."

"Come on, be real," I refute and narrow my eyes. "I wasn't *that* bad."

She scoffs. "Yes. You were. Barking orders and chewing out George."

"George wasn't doing his job."

He *wasn't* doing his job. And, honestly, it feels like George is never doing his fucking job.

"Look," she says and lifts both hands in the air. "I'm not trying to start shit. I'm just saying you might want to dial it back a notch if you don't want an outbreak of stomach ulcers to take down the whole crew."

*Not trying to start shit?* This, coming from the woman standing in front of *her boss* and telling him how to do his job.

It takes everything inside of me to keep my tone calm and neutral. "While I appreciate your attempt at constructive criticism, I think you need to realize, as the head of this project, it's my job to make sure shit gets done," I say through a tight jaw.

Apparently, Greer Hudson is an expert at heading up projects and managing people. And here I just thought she was the designer on staff. Go fucking figure.

"I'm not going to hold George's hand and give him a back rub to boost his confidence because he's not doing his job. I'm going to tell him he's fucking up so he gets his shit together and *starts* doing his job."

She rolls her eyes. "I'm not saying you should sit us around a campfire and make s'mores. Just back off a bit on how hard you're riding everyone's asses. You don't have to be a tyrant to get people to do their work."

*A tyrant?* She's obviously never worked side by side with my father.

Before I can offer up a retort to her holier-than-thou and completely unwanted *and* unwarranted advice, a boy with a dark mop of hair cruises by with dirty dishes in his hand, and Greer reaches out and flicks him.

"Yo, garçon," she says like a lunatic. "Another pickle for me, and a heart for the Tin Man over here."

The kid shakes his head and buzzes back to the kitchen.

# THE *Billionaire* BOSS NEXT DOOR

I fake a horrid excuse for a smile. "Very funny."

"I thought it was pretty good."

"For someone who acts like she knows everything about how to treat people, you sure don't seem to mind the way you treat the busboy."

"The busboy is my nephew."

Skepticism makes my head shake. "No way. He has to be eighteen at least. And you're what? Twenty-six?"

"That's the nicest thing you've said all day. Seriously." Her responding, albeit sarcastic, smile is too pretty for my liking. "But I'm thirty-three."

I laugh. There's no way she's a day over thirty. "No, you're not."

"*Yes*, I am. Don't tell me I'm going to have to show you my driver's license."

"How?"

"How what?" she asks with a raise of her brow.

"How is he your nephew?"

"Uh, biology? See, when a mommy and daddy really love each other, they do something called sex. Sex is—"

I shove back in my chair. "Funny."

She snorts. "Well, what are you looking for here? He's my brother's son, which makes him my nephew."

"Your brother must be older."

She straightens her spine, surprised at how accurate I am. "Ten years. He pretty much raised me after my parents died."

The unexpected admission makes my chest constrict. One second, we're tossing insults, and the next, she's reminding me there's something human under all that hostility of hers.

"I'm sorry. How did they…"

She looks down at the table, pulls out the chair across from me, and takes a seat. I give her the time to collect herself before she speaks again.

"Their plane went down."

"God, Greer, I'm—"

"One of their employees wanted to take over the company, so he paid a guy to put a bomb on their plane."

My jaw drops. "Holy shit."

"They found it before it went off, though, and threw it out the window. But it clipped the engine, and they went down in the ocean. I was by myself at home—except for the staff, of course—and I had no choice but to take over their company myself. Unfortunately, that made Lawrence even angrier. He wanted the company and the contents of the vault—"

Jesus Christ. *I can't believe I let her sucker me like this.*

"You're just reciting the plot for *Richie Rich*."

"Yes. Yes, I am. I thought you'd relate. Being a billionaire and all."

It's on the tip of my tongue to tell her I'm not exactly a billionaire. Turner Properties might be a multibillion-dollar empire, but that doesn't mean my share in the company equates to ten digits in my bank account. My dad is, but I'm not. And he might not even leave the company to me when he's ready to retire. He's threatened to leave it to someone else several times.

"Are your parents even really dead?" I ask, and the instant the question leaves my lips, my stomach turns with discomfort. I'm not trying to be a dick; I'm just trying to gauge how far Greer's snark goes when it comes to conversation. But shit, I might have pushed the envelope a little too far.

"Yes. They are." I wince as she stands from her seat and kicks it back under the table with a shove of her foot. "But asking how someone's parents died within a week of meeting them isn't exactly the politest thing to do."

And then she walks away from my table, leaving me feeling like…*a real fucking tool.*

*Shit.* Suddenly, the allure of my forgotten crepe doesn't seem so powerful anymore.

## Chapter SIXTEEN

### Greer

Ever since my failed attempt of therapy hour at lunch, Trent's been giving me weird looks.

He'll be scolding one of the electrical workers, and then he'll look over at me and the skin between his eyebrows will wrinkle.

It makes his face look broody and interesting, and all of my focus goes straight to the complex mingle of green in his eyes.

I hate it.

As a means of distraction, I've taken to making a list in the notes on my phone. A critique list, so to speak, that includes all sorts of things for him to work on.

Critical? Yes.

A wee bit petty? Maybe.

But completely satisfying? Most definitely.

So far, my list includes the following:

1. Consider addressing employees by their names, you know, so you don't sound like such a dick.
2. A smile never hurt anyone. And a smile while giving orders will make you seem less like the Terminator, Ah-nold.
3. Giving a compliment won't actually kill you. Seriously. Try it. And even better, pepper it in between all of your fucking insults.
4. Skip the gym a few times a week, bro. Your firm ass and tight muscles are distracting your team's focus. And, as we ALL

know, you're all about the focus. To the point of overbearing insanity.
5. For the love of God, switch colognes. It's fucking annoying how good you smell…to your team. We all hate your delicious aroma.

Okay. So, the list is in its first-draft stage, but it doesn't really matter.

I doubt he'll ever see it, what with me having to actually die in order for him to climb over my dead body, but it's at least keeping my mind and eyes occupied and my sexually repressed vagina in check.

"Where are the samples?" Trent asks, his voice stern and his steady, glare-y gaze directed at George. "There were *supposed* to be samples two days ago."

George, the poor guy, flounders like a fish on dry land. "The… samples. Right. I'll check, sir."

Ole George might as well be a monkey sidekick to the Man with the Yellow Hat because all he has when it comes to these "samples" is curiosity. Floor samples, paint samples, fucking urine samples…the mysterious samples could basically be anything. And if I were George, I'd be incredibly tempted to prove my point in the worst possible way.

Lucky for everyone on this job, including me and my big fat impulsive mouth, I am not George.

But I am me. And because of my boss's inability to be clear in his instructions, I have inspiration for item number six on my new list.

I open up my notes and add a new Trent Turner critique.

6. Be specific so people know what you're talking about. On this team alone, we have two male construction workers who literally go by Dick and Beaver. And that doesn't include lovely Carrie Balls who is assisting the painting team.
Shit gets real confusing real flipping quick if you don't explain yourself.

"Greer," Trent calls, and my eyes jerk up like a deer in the middle of the road.

"Huh?"

His face curls into impatience, and the rest of the crowd looks on wide-eyed. Apparently, he asked me a question I didn't hear.

Mental note to self: pay better fucking attention instead of making notes about beavers and balls.

"I *asked* what you had in mind for the reception desk. We need to order materials by the end of this week at the latest."

I'd make a note that he shouldn't emphasize words with attitude, but I'm pretty sure I deserve it this time around.

Instead, I spout ideas for the reception area on the fly and hope they're good.

"I think the front desk should mirror the look of a historic kitchen island. Black woodwork for the base with a light marble top and brass accents and maybe even some shelving with touches of the French Quarter behind. We can build drawers and cabinetry into the employee side to assure plenty of storage for supplies, but the look will be sleek and area appropriate from the outside."

"What about the computer systems for check in?" Trent challenges. "Seems like that will look clunky on top of the streamlined counter."

"We can do a lower tier on the hotel side if you're worried about the look of everything on top. That would solve the problem, and from the front entrance, the reception area would stay consistent with clean and smooth lines."

"Can you sketch something up for tomorrow?" he asks, and I'm nodding before he even finishes the question—despite the hours I know it will take me.

I'm committed to making a good impression with my work and work ethic, even if I can't seem to take my foot out of my mouth.

"Absolutely."

"Good," he says, his voice devoid of disappointment for maybe the first time today.

I give myself a mental pat on the back and promise a cookie or two as a reward. In fact, maybe I'll have that donut I bought at Easy Roast before I came into work this morning.

My purse is a Mary Poppins-style wormhole of varied goods, but I know it's in there somewhere.

And it's that inflated ego and misplaced food focus that get me in trouble. By the time I stop giving myself mental high fives and digging in my purse, the group has moved on, and I haven't a clue where they went.

Shit.

It's not like they're miles away, but this place is still a maze of dark construction hallways and unexplained rooms. They could have gone any of several directions from here, and I haven't the faintest clue which one.

Donut in hand, I jog from one end of the half-constructed lobby to the other, listening for the sound of Trent riding someone's ass.

The silence is deafening.

*Jesus.* Of all the times for him to talk at a normal decibel, he had to pick this one.

Tucking the donut back into my bag, I take off in the other direction at a jog. Two turns in and down a long hallway, with my hearing dialed up to dog-whistle, I finally think I hear the faintest hint of human voices.

My heels clack as I run across the unfinished floors and skid around the corner and into another unknown room—and right into a sawhorse table holding an *open* can of bright-red paint.

Everything around me turns to slow motion, and it's like I'm watching my very own car crash.

The table jolts.

The can of paint jumps into the air.

And pow! A paint explosion splats onto my khaki pencil skirt. I look down with wide eyes to find the entire crotch region—*son of a sugartit!*—of my garment is covered in red. Stephen King's *The Shining*, Redrum kind of red.

# THE *Billionaire* BOSS NEXT DOOR

Well, fuck. Fucking *fuck* me with a super-flow, extra plug-power tampon.

*And seriously? Where in the hell did this godawful paint come from? Thirsty vampires?*

All it takes is a single moment—a tiny little blip in time—to completely refocus your goals and priorities.

Suddenly, I must *avoid* finding the group at any cost.

I drop my bag to the ground and immediately start rifling through it again. I know I don't have a change of clothes—*stupid, stupid, stupid*—but surely, there's something in here I can use.

After a minute and a half of digging, the best thing I can come up with is my phone.

I take it out and dial the only woman in New Orleans who has the free time to take my frantic call.

My moneybags bestie.

"Hello?" Emory answers on the second ring, and I don't waste any time with pleasantries.

"I need assistance, and I need it now. Alert the media, send out one of those broadcast warnings, and change the road signs."

"Oh, good," she sighs. "I see the first week on the job is going well."

"This isn't the time for your jokes, Emory!" I whisper-yell into the receiver. "I've got a red stain on my crotch the size of a basketball."

"Wow. This escalated quickly."

"It's a long story!" I shout. "I don't have time to tell you it. Just know that I got separated from the group, bumped into some paint, and now I look like a shark just took a bite out of shark week!"

"Just relax," Emory commands. "I'm sure it's not that bad."

"It is. It is that bad, Emory, I promise you. I look like a menstrual volcano!"

"Well, it's not actual blood. Just explain that it's paint, and I'm sure everyone will laugh it off."

"Laugh it off? You're kidding, right? I look like I don't know how to use modern sanitary products on the first official week of work, and you think my *coworkers* are just going to laugh it off? I work with mostly men, Em! If anything, they'll all start passing the fuck out from the mere idea of periods and feminine hygiene products!"

"Technically, you're only a contracted employee. They're not really coworkers in the traditional sense—"

"Can we please stay on topic here?" I cut her off. "For the love of God, get on your computer and find out how to get paint out of a skirt with basically nothing. Tell Google to MacGyver that shit."

"I'm not at my computer—"

"Emory Marie!" I screech. "*Focus.* I look like my vagina is a blood geyser. Any minute now, the dragons from *Game of Thrones* are going to show up and burn this place to the ground."

"Fine. But you'll have to hold on for a second because I have to look it up on my phone."

After a quick grumble and grunt of agreement, I start humming the music from *Jeopardy* to put subtle pressure on her.

She doesn't appreciate it.

"If you don't stop that, I'm going to quit my search, get in my car, drive to the hotel, and murder you so violently, no one will be able to see the paint for all the blood."

"Geez. I think you might be harboring some questionable tendencies, E. Answer me this—have you ever *experimented* with hurting animals?"

As expected, Emory ignores me. But it's not like serial killers usually admit to being serial killers. I'll have to keep a vigilant eye, just in case.

"Google says there's no way to get the paint stain out without supplies. All you can do is keep it wet until you get home and then use rubbing alcohol and a toothbrush."

"Oh, good. Keep it wet. Just what I need to do to make it look even more like I'm riding the crimson wave."

"All right, all right. If you can stop freaking the fuck out and find a place to hide out for fifteen minutes or so, I'll bring you a change of clothes."

"Really?" I squeal.

"Yes," she sighs.

"I've been meaning to tell you, E…you're the only woman for me. When do you want to get married? I'm thinking May at the Botanical Gardens. The hibiscus will be beautiful."

"Shut up and lie low. I'll call you when I get there."

She hangs up after I agree, and now I'm left with nothing but time to kill.

I take a seat on a bucket in the corner of the room, pull out the donut that caused it all and my sketch pad, and set to work.

There's a whole hotel here that needs designing, and the least I can do while avoiding my boss and colleagues is work.

## Chapter SEVENTEEN

### Trent

I notice nearly immediately that Greer hasn't followed the group when we move on from the lobby to the lounge on the sixth floor, but at some point, I expected her to catch up.

When she's still missing twenty-five minutes later, I have no choice but to go look for her.

I hand out assignments to the rest of the group, make sure they know I'll be back soon to check on their progress, and take the stairwell back down to the ground floor.

Backtracking is my only means of search at this point. If she's wandered somewhere else on the property, I might not find her until her body starts to smell.

The stairwell is empty as I jog down six floors and bust through the door at the bottom with the weight of my body. There's a long hallway of conference and banquet rooms, followed by a left-hand turn up at the end.

It's a bit of a maze, but it's meant to be that way. The sole purpose of this intricate design is to prevent other guests from stumbling their way into an important meeting or conference.

I'm nearly two-thirds of the way back to the lobby when a pool of red paint in the doorway to the business center catches my attention.

I pause for the briefest of moments and have to force a deep breath into my lungs.

# THE *Billionaire* BOSS NEXT DOOR

*Goddammit.*

My anger fires at the carelessness of the workers, and I pick my pace back up, prepared to give whoever left it to sit on the floor coverings a stern word.

It won't take long to soak through the cardboard we've laid out and stain the tile, and the time and cost of replacing this caliber of marble in the whole area is an expenditure we don't need. My father has laid out a tight budget he expects me to follow, regardless of the necessary margin of error doing a project of this magnitude guarantees.

Careful of my step, I turn the corner…and run right into the sight of Greer's bare back and ass, the thin string of her barely there thong the only fabric covering skin.

It's a millimeter of surface area at most.

*Jesus.*

Frozen in place, I feel my heart speed up and my dick stir.

My eyes do a better job of roving than the robot thing they use on Mars, despite the fact that I haven't given them permission.

Her hair is long and just barely waved and cascades in a perfect waterfall down the center of her back. It highlights the length of her spine, and son of a bitch, I'm now picturing fucking her from behind.

*Dear God, stop thinking about that!*

The effort it takes to remove myself from the doorway is almost too much to conquer, but I know the longer I stand here and stare, the more of a chance there is that she'll notice me.

I duck just outside the door, against the wall right beside the frame, and take a deep breath.

I picture all the skin I couldn't see. Her breasts, her stomach, her—

*Fucking hell, why in the fuck is she naked?*

I scrub at my eyes, trying to unsee the perfect, endless inches and inches of tanned skin, but it doesn't work.

The curve of her hips and the tantalizing tease of her thighs are a permanent image in my mind. For the love of God, I will probably be thinking about it on my damn deathbed.

A noise sounds from inside the room, and panic overwhelms me.

*Oh, fuck. She's coming!*

*That's usually a good thing*, the brain in my aroused cock teases.

Unsure of what to do, I look around for something to make me look busy, make me look, like, you know, I'm the fucking boss and not some Peeping Tom, but I come up empty-handed. Instantly, I just let instinct take the wheel, and next thing I know, I'm off at a run headed back toward where I came from.

*Good God, I'm literally running away from a beautiful, gorgeous, naked woman. Cap would have a fucking field day with this.*

It doesn't take long before I hear the clack of her heels as she follows closely behind, and I dial my run up to a sprint until I make it to the stairwell.

This is fucked. *I'm* fucked. But what else can I do when all kinds of terrifying situations are floating around inside my head?

*Gross misconduct.*

*Sexual harassment.*

*Greer witnessing an erection the size of Texas tenting my pants.*

All worst-case scenarios, yet possible scenarios all the same.

With quick breaths and a racing heart, I hide inside the stairwell like a lunatic and peek through the window until it seems like a good time to pretend I wasn't just ogling her like a fucking pervert.

*Good Lord, Trent. What in the hell are you doing right now?*

I adjust my traitorous cock inside my pants and try to get my shit together and, you know, act like I'm the one in control of this project.

After rehearsing some simple phrasing a couple of times, I burst through the door and steel my voice against the prepubescent squeaks I know lie just under the surface of my normal timbre.

"There you are," I say in a way I'm hoping is normal. "We're up on six. Come on."

I don't mention the change to her outfit, and neither does she.

# THE *Billionaire* BOSS NEXT DOOR

For six flights, we don't mention *anything*.

For two people who've spent nearly every moment they've been in company with each other sparring, we're suddenly doing a hell of an impression of silent-film stars.

Mere footsteps from the doorway to the lounge, she finally pipes up.

"I, um…" I stop, but I don't turn back. I don't think I'll be able to meet her eyes. "I spilled some paint downstairs, and I know—"

"I'll have someone take care of it," I interrupt.

"Oh," she says, clearly shocked at the simple, nonconfrontational response.

I step forward into the room, and she reaches out to stop me with a hand to my elbow. The heat of it burns all the way through my jacket, and I jerk away in response. She takes it the wrong way—because why wouldn't she—and immediately recoils in apology.

"Look, I'm really sorry. For falling behind and for the paint. I know—"

"Don't worry about it," I say curtly. I need nothing more than to put some distance between us before my dick takes over again. Now that I've seen what I've seen, he suddenly thinks he's in charge. "Shall we get on with this now?"

She nods, scoots past me, and doesn't even think about talking back.

And I'm left to wonder why, all of a sudden, it feels like something has changed. As if seeing her in that vulnerable situation has fired up a new part of my brain.

In what feels like an instant, all of that hate I've been harboring for her doesn't feel so much like hate anymore.

# Chapter EIGHTEEN

## Trent

It's been five days since I accidentally saw Greer naked, and anytime I close my eyes, I can still see the swell of her ass where it meets her thigh.

In fact, I see it so vividly, I've started having dreams about catching her without her clothes on in the business center in a way that's reminiscent of the beginning of a porno.

As a result, I've continued to get up an hour and a half earlier for the past several mornings, just to ensure we won't leave our apartments at the same time, and focused on spending as little time with her at work as humanly possible.

She asks me a question; I redirect it to Marcus and relocate to another room.

She makes a suggestion; I nod and move on like my stake in her design is meaningless.

She laughs with Sarah about some secret joke; I avert my eyes and ignore them completely.

Seriously. How has it come to this? A week ago, I couldn't stand her, and now all I do is think about the way she looks beneath her clothes?

I blame Cap and his bullshit for filling my head with all these ideas of sexual tension and letting some "steam out of the pot."

It's not real attraction; it's just biology…*right?*

"Uh…Mr. Turner?" George's voice fills my ears, and I blink from

# THE *Billionaire* BOSS NEXT DOOR

my stupor to find him standing in front of the makeshift desk I currently reside behind, in what will eventually become the reception area of the hotel.

*Get it together, Trent.*

"Yeah?" I ask, clearing my throat and forcing the scattered thoughts of Greer and her silky-smooth skin out of my head.

"I just wanted to let you know the sample shelving for the conference rooms has been installed and is ready for your approval."

Finally. George is actually following through.

"Great," I respond and stand.

I follow his lead, past reception and down the maze of hallways, until he stops inside the first meeting room. My eyes find and lock on to Greer standing in the center of the room talking to a construction guy named Dick. Her hands rest on her slim hips, and her gaze looks toward the ceiling.

*Fucking hell, I can't escape her.*

She is everywhere, all the time, and the brain in my pants can't resist appreciating the vision that is her perfect ass and long, slim thighs encased in one of those tight-fitting skirts she insists on wearing nearly every day of the week.

For fuck's sake, doesn't she own at least one pair of pants?

Capris? *A fucking parka?*

*Anything* but those damn skirts and silk blouses?

"So, what do you think?" George asks, and I turn to find his uncertain gaze locked on me.

"What do I think...?"

"About the shelving."

*Oh, right. The fucking shelving. The whole reason we came into this room.*

Thankfully, no shelving for me to approve is located in the center of the room.

Slowly, I move around the space and take in the way the professional cabinetry and shelf installations create practicality while maintaining a modern and sophisticated appearance. They transform the room into exactly what I'd hoped.

At least one thing is going right today.

"I approve," I say and turn to meet his eyes again. "Go ahead and get the guys working on the rest of the meeting rooms."

"Will do, sir."

George strides back toward the hall, and I'm left to my own devices.

Alone. With Greer.

*Shit.*

She's still standing in the center, Dick long gone with George, and I watch as she moves to the corner of the room to grab one of the brand-new, plastic-covered office chairs.

Her fingers grip the back cushion as she rolls it across the floor until she stops just below one of the newly installed sample light fixtures.

With a lightbulb in her hand, she uses the armrest to steady herself, and I watch in absolute horror as she goes to step onto the chair.

The chair on fucking wheels, mind you.

"Uh...what are you doing?"

"I just want to see how the lighting would look if it were a bit softer."

"You're going to hurt yourself," I say. "Get down and let one of George's guys do it."

"It's fine," she says, too fucking determined. "I do this all the time."

"Greer—"

"It's fine," she cuts me off.

Her heels dig into the plastic covering the seat cushion, and she focuses her eyes on the ceiling.

She lengthens her slim body, stretching her hands toward the fixture, and the chair does not appreciate the movement. It wobbles and wiggles, and I know she's exactly ten seconds away from disaster.

# THE *Billionaire* BOSS NEXT DOOR

"Oh shit," she mutters, and I'm already moving toward her, quick as my feet can take me.

In a matter of seconds, the chair *and* her feet slip out from under her, and she free-falls from standing and heads straight for the floor.

But I jump toward her just in time.

Arms flexed outward and my hands braced, I catch her in midair—before her fall turns tragic—with my hands *directly* on her ass.

On instinct, she leans forward to catch her balance on the back of the chair, and that abrupt movement only lifts her ass more toward my face and pushes the plush, perfect flesh deeper into my hands.

Her ass is literally in my hands.

*What the fuck is happening?*

"Uh…" she mutters through a shocked breath. "I'm so sorry… I… Shit… Just…"

Her stuttered words tell me she's just as confused as I am.

I'm utterly speechless. Probably, I presume, as a means of defense while I'm trying *not* to focus on just how good her ass feels in my hands.

And it does feel good. Better than I imagined.

*Now would be a good time to stop gripping her ass…*

Shit.

Quickly, I move one hand to her stomach, and with a firm grip around her waist, I lift her body away from her complicated situation with the office chair.

Once her heels hit the ground, I put a good ten feet of distance between us.

"Are you okay?" I heave, forcibly pushing the words past my lips.

"Uh… Yeah… Thanks," she says, and with those big blue eyes of hers, she moves her uncertain gaze from the floor and looks at me. "I'm okay."

"Okay…well…" I pause and run a hand through my hair. "I'm… uh…glad you're all right."

"Yeah. I'm all right."

"You're all right. Good. That's good."

Fuck, this is awkward.

"So, I'm just going to get one of George's guys to help me with that…" She pauses, and I nod like a moron.

"Okay. Yeah. That sounds good."

"Okay, good."

Certain we've met our quote for *okays* and *goods* and *all rights* for the next two years, I do the only thing I can do in this situation. I turn on my heels and walk right out of the conference room.

If someone had told me Greer Hudson's ass would end up in my hands by the end of today, I would have bet my entire share of Turner Properties on the contrary.

Yet, somehow, some-fucking-way, that is exactly what just happened.

And I thought seeing her naked spurred some seriously dirty thoughts.

*Touching her…feeling something I've been imagining vividly…was the last thing I needed.*

## Chapter NINETEEN

### Greer

Coastal Crepes is one of the best breakfast, brunch, and lunch restaurants in the French Quarter, and has a convenient location smack-dab in between my office and the hotel.

And it also just so happens to be owned by my brother.

My grandfather opened it in the sixties, passed it on to my father, and then, when my parents died in the car accident when my mom was pregnant with me, he took over running operations again—along with raising his grandchildren.

We spent so much time here when I was a kid, I often wonder if that's what made my brother the passionate chef he is today. When my grandfather died, it only made sense for him to leave Coastal Crepes to my brother rather than to me.

In fact, I'm pretty sure it would be about out of business if it were up to me. I've almost lost my design firm, and I actually know stuff about design. The only thing I know about the food business is how to eat.

The wrought-iron-and-glass door is heavy as I swing it open onto the stone sidewalk and duck inside. Dark compared to outside but lighter than much of the masculine design in the French Quarter, the restaurant settles my soul with everything familiar.

Years of coming here—years of growing up in the seats of the wooden benches of each booth.

It's Saturday night family dinner and the restaurant is closed, so the only people inside are the ones I'm expecting to find—my brother, Heath, his son, Brooks, and his wife, *Rhonda*.

*Rhonda* is everything I've never wanted in a sister-in-law and then some, but for some reason, my brother loves her. She hardly ever speaks, shows little-to-no emotion other than hatred, and wears turtlenecks even in the summer.

They married a year and a half after he divorced Brooks's mom, back when Brooks was ten, and I've been forced to live in close proximity to a cyborg ever since.

I'm half convinced she's got a pussy made of liquid gold or something—a real church lady in the streets, freak in the sheets kind of thing—but I'm determined not to ever find out.

I'm not qualified in that kind of field research, and I don't want to be. From what I hear, it takes three-to-six months of training and a huge investment in elbow-length gloves.

"Hello, hello," I call as I sidle up to the table—the side with my brother and nephew—and try to shove in next to them.

Heath is amused by my antics—mostly because he doesn't know that they're rooted in blistering, hex-casting hate for his wife—and chuckles. "Plenty of room on the other side, Greer. Maybe you should take a seat over there."

Automatically, Rhonda's laser eyes engage, threatening to shoot me where I stand if I dare try. For as much as I can't stand her, I think she dislikes me more.

I entertain everyone by making my own happy medium—a spare chair pulled up to the end of the table.

Spaghetti Bolognese sits front and center, and a dish with pickles hangs out on the side just for me.

I rub my hands together in glee and reach out to get it.

Heath slaps my hand playfully and gives me a huge smile.

"Why don't we start with giving thanks?" he suggests like the daddiest-dad there ever was.

He is sunshine where I am rain, spirituality where I am... I don't know what I am.

I mean, I'm not agnostic, but if you compared my dedication to faith in a bar graph with my brother's, my column would be pretty much nonexistent.

"Start with getting me more pickles. The little hoodlum in the kitchen shortchanged me again."

"First of all, the hoodlum is your nephew."

I shrug.

"And secondly, he gave you three pickles."

"Which isn't nearly enough, *and* if he really loved his aunt at all, he would *know*," I argue sagely, giving Brooks the side-eye dramatically. The overconfident teen-man doesn't even look up from his fucking phone. Not that he ever does. I don't think I've heard more than twenty words from my nephew since he turned fifteen and got an iPhone.

"We're eating pasta," Heath points out. "Not deli sandwiches."

"And?"

Heath rolls his eyes but jumps up from the table nonetheless. Crippled by his innate desire to be helpful, *especially* when it comes to the little sister he practically raised, he can't resist my request even if I am being a pain in the ass.

I know the pickle thing is weird, but if I'm honest, I have no intent to change. On the sliding scale of drugs, cucumbers soaked in juice are hardly equivalent to meth.

After setting the pickles down on the table in front of me, Heath lifts a leg over the back of his chair and climbs into it—the kind of thing only people over six feet can do—and dives right into his prayer.

Apparently, any delay is just another opportunity for me to mess it up.

I glance up a few times to make sure Rhonda doesn't spontaneously combust from the prayer—kind of like what happens when you splash holy water on a demon—but for the most part, I listen dutifully.

When Heath finally finishes, I take a big heaping scoop of pasta and cover the entirety of my plate.

*Mm, carbs.*

A few twirls of my fork later, I'm about to put the glorious food in my mouth when Heath busts right through the force field I was certain I'd constructed successfully by wearing all black clothing and needlessly emo makeup.

"So, Greer. Tell me how the new job is! Is the hotel business exciting?"

"It's great," I say, filling my mouth with spaghetti to disguise my deceit. "No problems whatsoever."

*Besides spilling paint on myself, getting on my boss's bad side* before *my actual interview, giving him constructive criticism he didn't appreciate that led to me wondering if he even knows I exist anymore, and then, accidentally putting my ass directly into his hands,* that is.

Yeah, everything is pretty fucking great.

So great, in fact, that Trent seemed like less of an asshole at work for all of twenty-four hours, *until* two days ago when my ass landed in his hands and served as a catalyst to revert back to barking orders and rampage.

*My milk shake brings all the boys to tyranny. Go figure.*

"Good. I'm so glad for you." Heath's smile beams. "Isn't that great news, Rhonda?"

Rhonda sneers so hard, I'm pretty sure I see fangs.

I jerk my gaze to Heath and Brooks, convinced they'll have seen the evil spirit within her, but they seem unfazed.

What the actual hell? Where are Alyssa Milano, Shannen Doherty, and that-other-one-whose-name-I-can-never-remember when you need them?

"And how about the new place? I still can't believe you're downsizing from the house to an apartment, but if Emory's parents own the building, it must be nice. You got renters insurance, right?"

Yeahhhh. The thing is…my brother has no idea how much

trouble my business was in before I got this job or how little of a choice I had in moving out of my house.

He worked so hard to make sure I had all the things I dreamed of, and to tell him just how close I've come to losing it all... Well, I can't even stomach the thought of it.

I'd much rather soak in the bitter truth of it all by myself.

Luckily, I don't have to lie about the quality of the apartment. Emory's parents own one hell of a classy place.

"It's great. Spacious and modern," I say, trying to give him at least a morsel of something to cling to. "And yes, *Dad*, I got renters insurance."

He smiles at my jab at his smothering worry and points to his shirt.

I didn't even notice it before, but I'm pretty sure it's the only thing I'll notice now.

**Dad Body is the new Hot Toddy.**

Gah, that's terrible.

It's like a dad joke from hell, and the only thing remotely creative about it is that it rhymes.

I smile and nod anyway, just to humor him, but not before reaching to grab the wine bottle and pouring myself another enormously healthy glass.

If I'm going to make it through the rest of family dinner with the Corny Dad, Mute Teenager, and Tina Turtleneck—*aka my lovely witch-in-law*—without saying something I shouldn't, I'm going to need a little *lubrication*, if you know what I'm saying.

Liquid courage.

Hooch.

The sauce.

A little vino for my—

Alcohol. I need alcohol.

By the time I leave The Last Supper, I'm what a college frat boy might refer to as *smashed, bro*. And three large glasses of wine are all it took to get me here.

My tolerance for drinking is on the low end of the spectrum because I don't really drink that much.

Other than a glass of wine here or there, the most I ever drink is at dinner with my brother and his family.

It's not that they're that terrible or anything; I think I'm just… comfortable. Or I need the intoxication to tolerate my sister-in-law's stink eye. Honestly, it's a toss-up.

But I know my brother would never judge me or jump to conclusions, and even though Rhonda doesn't talk to me, she doesn't talk to anyone else either. They see me for who I am and accept it.

Hell, my brother drove me home in his minivan and waved from the curb like a proud father when I finally got the outside door to my building open.

I'm a lucky woman, having such a positive, supportive guy in my life—even if he's got corny dad jokes and doesn't contribute to my bank account at all.

Hah.

Truth is, Heath is such a good guy, he probably would give me money if I asked him to.

But I'd never do that to him. He has his own business to run and family to feed.

My head swims as I force myself to climb the stairs rather than taking the elevator as some form of pseudo-punishment, and I'm only slightly disappointed when I make it to the top without falling down and acquiring a head laceration.

I'm *kidding*. Well, sort of. I mean, I'm currently in a phase of life where a two-to-four-day hospital stay sounds like a trip to the spa.

Basically, a life has many seasons.

# THE *Billionaire* BOSS NEXT DOOR

My door seems nice and very door-like as I sidle up to it and give it a hug. For all my joking, I'm glad to have a home, and that seems like a good reason to give it a hug.

I get a little too cuddly, though, and the door bites back, smacking me right in the forehead.

*Well, that wasn't very nice.*

"Ow!" I yell at my wooden friend. "Our relationship is never going to work if you can't get past your intimacy issues. My other friends might start telling me to leave if you're not careful."

He doesn't laugh, but I do enough for the both of us. I'm just getting ready to take the flirting to the next level with some keyhole penetration when my friend moves away on his own, swinging open... and right into my nemesis's apartment.

Except, holy cotton balls, does he always look this good?

"Well, if it isn't Trent Turner! Juney Junior! Turn the Burn! The Term-i-nator!" I greet him, reaching out with my hand and poking his bare chest with my index finger just to make sure he's not some sort of mirage.

*He's real.*

"Holy shit. You're real," I mutter, and I can't stop my gaze from moving down his body.

He is in nothing but a towel, his hair is wet, beads of water roll down his perfect chest, and dear God...I might pass out.

I'm *pretty* sure I just saw the outline of my boss's penis.

No skin action, no actual visual of the amount of purple power that thing gets when fully locked and loaded, but a penis blueprint, if you will.

And, apparently, the architect who drew up those penis plans didn't hesitate to put in some serious square footage.

Immediately, I start thinking about what Trent's boner would look like, and I giggle.

God, that's such a funny word. *Boner. The bones. Boneville. Boner Time.*

"What about bones?" he asks, and my giggling comes to an abrupt halt.

*Oh my God, WHAT? Did I just say that aloud?*

"Did you just say something about bones?"

*Oh, holy shit, I did.* Someone. Help. Me.

"Don't wah-y, about it Ah-nold." I give him a friendly slap on his bare shoulder, and the smacking sound reverberates around us. "I'm just singing. A song. About bones. It's an old one. You probably don't know it. Almost no one knows it. No one but me. I know the big bone song."

*Nice save, Greer.* Obviously, I do my very best thinking under the influence.

I should probably drink more often.

"What?" he asks again, before adding, "Are you drunk?" His eyebrows pinch together in what seems a whole lot like judgment.

My personality spawns another side—one with absolutely no sense of self-preservation.

"Don't be so judgy, Junior. Everybody enjoys a little bit of wine every now and then. It might not cost one billion dollars a bottle like yours does—"

He rolls his eyes.

"But it's flipping del-i-cious!" I singsong, even adding a bit of jazz hands to pizzazz it up a bit.

"Look, how about I help you get into your apartment, and we'll talk in the morning?"

"Fine," I agree. "We can talk in the morning. But you better put that lightsaber under some heavier fabric before we go to commune with the Lord. It's impossible to focus when that thing is just swinging around like it owns the joint."

Just one side of his mouth hitches up, but I think he might actually be smiling.

*Wow.* He looks goooood with a smile.

"Commune with the Lord? You go to church?"

"On Sunday? As in, tomorrow's Sunday? Of course. It's just that sometimes—most times," I muffle under my breath, "I sleep in a little too late or get stuck in traffic or come down with a cold or—"

"So, you don't actually attend church. You just pretend to plan to so you feel better about yourself."

"I don't know." I shrug one lazy shoulder. "That was a lot of words that just came out of your mouth, but hey, they sounded good."

"Come on," he says with a laugh. I fall into a trance in his eyes like he's the snake in *The Jungle Book*. "Let's get you to bed."

"Yes, sir," I agree. Bed with him sounds mighty fine.

# Chapter TWENTY

## Trent

It's funny how a night can start one way and end in completely another.

At seven p.m., fresh drink in hand, I settled onto the couch and stretched out an arm across the back, the plans for the hotel and a stack of expense sheets stretched across the surface of my coffee table.

I haven't had time to get a TV for my apartment yet, and besides the grandfather clock ticking audibly from the corner of my living room, there wasn't anything but the silence from next door to seep through the walls and into my place.

I hadn't heard her all night, and against every ounce of my judgment, I couldn't help but wonder where she was.

Does she spend all of her Saturday nights out or only the occasional one to let loose?

Is the stress of this job going to be too much for her, and perhaps most importantly, is she going to distract me this much the whole time?

Annoyed with myself, I grabbed my phone and sent a funny meme about a blowfish in the group text with Cap and Quince, but neither responded, and the loneliness became even more painful.

Frustrated, I decided to busy myself with the task of unpacking more of my boxes and trying to make this place have at least a semblance of actual residence.

## THE *Billionaire* BOSS NEXT DOOR

I've been living out of a suitcase like a vagabond since arriving here, and this was exactly the kind of desperation I needed to change that.

I sorted and piled, I tucked and folded, I arranged and rearranged. It took nearly four hours, but finally, I had a closet full of clothes, a medicine cabinet full of toiletries, and a kitchen with at least a few random supplies.

With only one box left, I fully expected to finish the job and be rewarded with at least a pathetic sense of accomplishment.

But expectations are often much different from reality, and the Walter White mask at the very top distracted me.

Stupid thing in hand, I wandered the apartment looking into the chemist's face like he could somehow take me back to that night.

To recklessness and spontaneity and a kiss with a stranger I still think about.

It was the first time in years—hell, maybe *ever*—that I've acted out of instinct and hormones at a work function rather than sticking to a carefully crafted plan.

It was the first time I've been so amused by a woman that I let go of all thought of rationality and responsibility.

It was a dick thing to disappear so quickly, without even the exchange of a name, but the pressure of my dad's judgment was too much. And the fear of losing the NOLA project became too vivid in my mind.

But that doesn't mean I can't fantasize about it.

Which is exactly how I ended up in the shower with my hand to my cock, giving myself something I needed more than I even realized.

I'd only just come when I heard a loud bang on my door.

Quickly, I jumped out of the shower, wrapped a towel around my half-hard dick and hips and went to check it out.

Fast-forward twenty minutes and one extremely drunk employee, and here I am now. In Greer's apartment, doing my best to lift her dead weight into her bed, while trying to keep my towel secure around my hips at the same time.

It's a fucking task.

"Use your legs, woman," I coach, wondering if I need to spend more time at the gym. In all regards, Greer is a petite woman, with just the right amount of curves. I shouldn't be struggling under her weight, but it's like she's lined her pockets with lead or something.

She laughs, of course, because apparently when she's drunk, I am incredibly funny. "Legs. That's a funny word, don't you think? Like, who came up with that? Why aren't they called trunks? Or yims? Or blosts?"

"I'm not sure. But if I run into anyone who was around during the previous millennia, I'll let you know," I mutter and try to avert my eyes when the hem of her skirt moves up her perfect thighs a few inches too far.

What feels like miles upon miles of her silky-smooth skin is right there. In front of me.

*Good God.* My dick hardens immediately.

Before I can even think about doing something stupid, I snag the edge of the wrinkled comforter at the edge of the bed and toss it over her body before that skirt decides to migrate any farther.

Abruptly, she sits back up, squishes my cheeks together and guffaws, speaking in a voice laced with baby talk. "Oh my, my, someone's cheeks are awful cheeky, aren't they?"

When she reaches out with a pesky hand and runs her fingers across the cotton knot at my hips, I shove a gentle hand to her shoulder and settle her back into the bed.

I'm completely unsure what her plans were, but I know they wouldn't have been good.

For her—*she's drunk*. For me—*I wish I were drunk at this point*. For my fucking sanity. Or for my carefully constructed willpower, for that matter.

"Just relax," I instruct. "Go to sleep and forget this ever happened."

"You'd like that, wouldn't you?" she challenges, and I can't help but laugh.

"Trust me, Greer," I say, and like my hand has a mind of its own, it reaches out and slides a lock of hair out of her eyes and behind her ear. "You'd like it too. Probably even more than me."

For a long moment, she looks up at me with those big blue eyes of hers, and my chest tightens.

God, even drunk, even slurring crazy shit I don't understand, *even when she's talking back to me at work*, she's beautiful.

"That's what they want you to think," she says quietly, and her eyelids start to droop with sleep. Each blink lasts longer and longer, and I'm damn near mesmerized by the way her long lashes fan down over her cheeks.

"Yep. That's exactly what they want you to think," she repeats, and I blink from my trance.

"They?" Who the fuck is she talking about?

"The Wimwoms," she says seriously. "They want you to think that I'm a frog and you're a prince or something like that, and that our kiss could cure the world. But it can't. I know because I've pictured it, and all that happens is explosions."

"Explosions?"

"Bombs."

"Bombs?"

"Big ones."

*Sweet Jesus, what did she drink tonight?*

"Greer, did you go to a club tonight? Did someone drug you?"

"A club!" she shrieks with her eyes now closed and devolves into a fit of hysterical laughter. "No way! Just dinner with a witch, a cornball, an iPhone, and a whole bunch of delicious pickles."

I pinch my eyebrows together in concern, and she reaches up to smooth them with just one finger.

"Green eyes," she says. "Goddamn those goddamn green eyes."

And then she's out. Dead to the world and snoring just enough to confirm she's breathing.

I shake my head and take a deep breath before looking down to my now fully hard cock.

*Fuck, this is becoming a problem.*

I turn her so she's safe on her side, shove away from the bed, grab the trash can from her bathroom, and set it beside her bed before leaving.

I don't look back, given my dick's obvious inability to behave, and head straight for my apartment to pass out in my own bed.

It's after midnight, and if I don't end the day now, there's no telling what else will happen.

I step out into the hallway quietly, being sure to lock her door behind me, and walk the five steps to my own. I grab the knob and turn…nothing.

Oh *fuck*.

I jiggle again; no give.

*Nooooo. Are you kidding me?*

I look frantically around the hall for a key that doesn't exist. For all the unpacking and settling I did earlier this evening, not one moment of it included hiding a spare key in case I locked myself out.

And I'm still in a towel. *Only* a towel.

What am I going to do?

Thoughts scatter and dart through my head like rats as I try to grab ahold of one long enough to come up with a plan. By the time I do it, I've settled against the door of my apartment, leaned my head back, and covered my eyes with my hand to block out the light.

My dick, however, the traitor, is still hard.

Luckily, the name that comes to mind does a good job of changing that.

*Quincy.* Quincy is dating Emory, and Emory's parents own the building. Surely, he can get a key to let me in with as little humiliation as possible.

Right?

---

# THE *Billionaire* BOSS NEXT DOOR

Wrong.

Quincy's laugh is downright obnoxious as he comes through the front door of our apartment building and meets me in the lobby.

I would have stayed upstairs in the hallway, but the only public phone is downstairs at the front desk. Plus, the bastard told me one a.m. delivery service goes no farther than the bottom floor.

"Wow, Turn," he greets with a smile ten times bigger than my face is even built to accommodate. "This just keeps getting better and better."

When I called him, I thought keeping the part about being in a towel out of the story would somehow benefit me. Evidently, I forgot that he'd have to find out anyway and that the element of surprise always makes it worse.

"Is there a new fashion trend I should be aware of?"

"Do you have a key or not?" I ask, completely ignoring his question.

"Oh, I've got the key," he says cheerfully. "One I had to procure by waking my girlfriend, dragging her out of bed, taking her to her apartment to get the keys to her parents' place, and then going there to get it."

I wince.

"Thankfully for you, they're on a yacht in the middle of the Mediterranean."

"Listen, I'm sorry for the inconvenience, but do we really have to do this now? I'll take you to lunch one day, and you can give me the third degree."

"Oh no. No, no, no," Quince replies, shaking his head. "I'm not giving you any time to weasel out of this. No details, no key."

"Jesus, Quince. When did you become this ruthless?"

"Around eleventh grade. Now, go. Details." He snaps his fingers, and it's only the reality that I will have to spend the rest of the night outside of my apartment with no clothes that keeps me from reaching out and slapping his slightly chubby face.

"I opened my door, stepped out in the hall, and the door shut behind me. I didn't realize it was locked," I paraphrase, holding out a hand for the key.

He shakes his head, unconvinced. "Nope. Not buying it. No way you're going to go outside of your apartment in just a towel without a good reason."

I growl. "I heard a noise, okay? I was checking it out."

"And you found something, didn't you?"

"Quince."

"What did you find, Turn? Tell your good pal, Quincy," he mocks sweetly, and I sigh.

"Greer."

"Oh, my, my. This is getting interesting now."

"She was drunk and thought my door was hers. I helped her into her apartment, and when I went back, the door was locked."

"Mm-hmm. And what else happened?"

"*Nothing*," I stress. This whole teasing tour is all in good fun, but jokes about something happening when Greer clearly couldn't consent are not.

Quincy steps forward and holds out the key, and I take it swiftly before he has a chance to play any other games.

"Goodnight?" he prompts as I head for the stairs. "Thank you?"

"Fucking goodnight," I say over my shoulder.

"Did you know it's customary to be nice to the person who's done you a favor?" he calls. "Just a little information to tuck away for later."

"Fucking *thank you* and goodnight," I toss back just as the doors to the elevator open.

He smiles and pinches his fingers together. "Close. You'll get it eventually. Keep practicing."

The elevator doors close, and I breathe a sigh of relief.

The only thing I'm going to be practicing is common sense—first thing tomorrow, I'm hiding a spare key.

I need to make sure the only person I have to call for help in the future is myself.

## Chapter
# TWENTY-ONE

### Trent

Waking up at five a.m. to avoid going to work at the same time as Greer is brutal. My eyes are always about as easy to peel open as an apple without something sharp, and I almost *always* smash my toe on the corner of my bed on the way to my bathroom.

Hell, waking up that early is the worst part of every day, which is probably why this particular Monday morning, I don't.

My sleep schedule is all screwed up, alternating between insomnia and sleeping so deeply I don't hear the world.

So, when my alarm goes off, I'm apparently in the comatose phase of my REM cycle.

I sleep and sleep until almost seven, and now, not only am I not extremely early, I'm running *behind* schedule.

My tie is in some form of a knot, but I'm almost positive it's more Clove Hitch than Half Windsor, and my shirt is only ironed on the front.

With a half-baked plan to keep my jacket on the entire day to hide that fact, I scoop my keys and phone off the kitchen island and head for the door.

I have the knob half turned when I hear activity in the hall and freeze.

Greer and I haven't seen each other since I put her in her bed Saturday night.

I know it's a better idea to get that interaction over with rather than having to live out any awkwardness in front of everyone on the job site, but at least there, we have roles to hide behind.

I'm the boss and she's the designer, and there are plenty of things to talk about that don't include the way she looked at me and my only-a-towel-covered cock, or the fact that I saw way too much of her creamy thighs, or that I'd just finished masturbating before her drunken, adorable ass started assaulting my front door.

*Adorable? Really, Trent?*

Hell. I don't have time to think about this kind of shit.

I shake off those insane thoughts in an attempt to gain some sanity, but apparently, I'm all out today. Instead of simply manning the fuck up and walking out of my apartment, I press my curious ear to the wood of my door to listen for sounds of her retreat.

There's a scuffle and a soft whoosh and then a few clacks, but when they stop, I take away my ear and replace it with my eye at the peephole.

And, instantly, I'm faced with a giant eyeball staring back at me.

*Shit.* I jump back a little. *What the...?*

Without even thinking, I engage the peephole again, and this time, instead of an eyeball, Greer's entire face and one raised hand consumes my microscopic view.

She pauses, squinting a little, but she just kind of stands there, hand frozen in the air and her gaze locked on my door like she's trying to attempt X-ray vision or something.

I have to step away, you know, before I do something rational like open my door and ask her what she's doing.

Because, yeah, that'd be too easy, right?

When no knock comes after ten seconds, I tiptoe my way to the door to peek again.

She's gone.

Ironically, I find myself disappointed.

Boy oh boy, do I love the New Orleans version of myself.

# THE *Billionaire* BOSS NEXT DOOR

Crazy. Indecisive. Needlessly pithy and combative. Hiding behind doors and peering through peepholes. The list goes on and on.

I need to get this hotel finished and get back to New York before I'm a complete fucking disaster.

Finally done hiding for the morning—since, you know, she should be gone by now—I turn the knob fully and step outside into an empty hallway.

The door locks easily, and the spare key I put in the potted plant by the stairwell yesterday is still there.

I know because I check.

*Obsessive-compulsive.* Add that to the list of my Louisiana-enhanced qualities too.

Making my way down the stairwell and across the lobby, I push open the front door to a bright and sunny January day. It's warm for winter, but still chilly to say the least.

Silver lining—I shouldn't have any trouble keeping my suit jacket on over my half-wrinkled shirt.

A little homesick and a lot more confused than I've ever felt, I take out my phone and call the one person who will make everything feel better.

My mom.

She answers on the second ring and does a remarkably good job of acting like I haven't woken her up.

"Trent," she greets. "It's so good to hear from you." Her speech is slightly slower than it used to be, and every once in a while, it sounds a little like her words are slurred. But compared to the deterioration of her motor skills, the change is almost imperceptible.

"I know, Mom. I'm sorry I haven't called more—"

"Don't be ridiculous," she interrupts. "You're busy down there. The last thing you need to be worrying about is calling boring ole me. Everything's the same."

I laugh and shake my head. If only I could say something similar.

"Well, nothing is the same here," I admit.

"But it's good, right?" she asks. "I know it must be. Everything is good in New Orleans."

*Yeah. Not so much.*

I'm considering whether or not to delve into any of the details when I spot Greer up ahead, kneeling down next to a homeless woman and unwinding the scarf from around her neck.

She speaks softly to the woman before taking her hand and nodding. She winds the scarf around the woman's neck and then stands, pointing to the coffee shop we evidently both love to frequent.

"Trent?" my mom calls for my attention.

I watch as Greer heads inside Easy Roast, but I force myself to put most of my focus back on my mom.

"Sorry, Mom. I got distracted."

"Ah, a pretty girl, perhaps?" she coos, and I laugh.

"First of all, you'd better hope it's a pretty *woman* if you don't want to read about your son in the paper."

"And second of all?" she prompts, way too much wisdom in her sixty-five years.

"Yes, it was a pretty woman. At least, kind of."

Her laugh is a little shaky, but it makes me smile. If all I get out of all this crap is making my mom's day a little brighter, it'll be worth it. "Well, that sounds interesting and cryptic. I can't wait to find out the rest."

"Someday," I deflect.

She harrumphs.

"Just think of it like *General Hospital*," I tease. "The story will conclude sometime in the next decade."

She laughs. "If then. I think the actors who play Sonny and Carly are going to die before their whole sordid tale is done."

"I'm not going to lie to you, Mom. I have no idea who you're talking about."

"Don't worry about it."

I smile.

## THE *Billionaire* BOSS NEXT DOOR

"It's Jason who really matters anyway," she adds.

I bite my lip to stop myself from laughing. "Listen, Mom, I've gotta go. I'm running late this morning, and—"

"And a pretty woman needs your attention. Say no more."

"Mom, that's not it. I need coffee."

"And a pretty woman," she teases. "Yes, son. Reading you loud and clear."

"No. You're not reading me at all. There's nothing going on with the woman."

"*Yet*," she says knowingly. "Of course, I get it. Love you, honey."

God, I don't want to get her hopes up over something that's not even real.

"No, Mom, there's nothing... Mom? Mom?"

I'm yelling into my phone for my mommy—who's already hung up on me, by the way—when Greer comes out of Easy Roast holding two coffees and a bag and sees me.

It's an intense moment—one that feels like we'd both rather duck and run—but we make brief eye contact before attempting to give each other a smile.

Weird, pseudo-transaction complete, I head for the coffee shop, tucking my head to give her the space to do as she intended without an audience.

Once I'm inside and she's convinced she's off my radar, I go back to watching her as she crosses the street and kneels down to talk to the woman once again.

She hands her a coffee and the bag before heading down the street toward the hotel.

And just like that, everything I thought I knew about Greer Hudson sinks a little further.

Down low, to the bottom of a barrel filled with all sorts of other things I never expected.

# Chapter
# TWENTY-TWO

## Greer

Saturday night, I had a dream that I saw Trent Turner's penis and it was glorious.

The penis, not the dream. The dream was unnerving because he's my boss and my neighbor, and I don't care how good of dream penis he gives—he is the one guy I should not be thinking about in any sort of sexual nature.

But yet, here I am, with visuals of Trent's dream penis still dancing about inside my head.

Unfortunately, I only have me, myself, and my drunken shenanigans to thank for it.

Freaking out is an under-description for the little exhibition I put on Sunday morning when I woke up after Trent and his minuscule towel had to help me into my apartment and put me to bed.

He *literally* had to put my sloppy, tipsy ass to bed.

It truly would be great if I could go just *one* day without putting myself in the worst possible situations with him.

Luckily, a day later, I think I've finally got myself under control.

I mean, I almost went over to his apartment this morning to talk to him about my party-girl display outside his front door—*and quite possibly, apologize for it*—but I couldn't bring myself to actually let my knuckles hit his door and knock.

And while I normally don't applaud cowardice, I'm thankful

# THE *Billionaire* BOSS NEXT DOOR

for it today. Aside from our weird little interaction on the sidewalk this morning, he's been the all too familiar asshole boss Trent.

Abrasive. Noncommunicative.

Hell, I kind of thought he was going to give George a wet-willy in our morning meeting when he said the shower tiling crew was delayed by two weeks. But common decency prevailed, and no wet fingers went into other people's ears.

All in all, he's made no mention or behavior that suggests Saturday night actually happened.

The only explanation is that I did, in fact, have an alcohol-induced dream about my boss and neighbor, and I'm never drinking again.

Okay, that last part is a lie, but I dreamed about my boss's penis, for fuck's sake. That's the sort of thing that would put anyone in a state of denial.

"Sarah," he calls now, making the skittish woman at my side jump. "Do you have the plans for the suite bathrooms?"

"Uh, yes, sir." Rolls and rolls of papers fill the space between her arm and her body, and the way she's searching through them without putting them down means she's either going to dislocate a hip or go pro in contortionism soon.

"Let me help you," I finally offer, pulling the rolls from under her arm and carrying them over to the table in the corner.

Everyone is in such a hurry to jump to Trent's commands that they all forget to work smarter, not harder.

The ends of all the tubes are labeled, so I find the one with the "Suite" sticker on it and unroll it.

Sarah looks at me like I should expect flowers in the mail.

Trent comes to stand next to me, just an innocent move to get a look at the plans.

But harmless or not, the instant the warmth of his body starts to invade my personal space, unbidden thoughts of his penis fill my head, and I nearly trip over my own two feet as I try to put some distance between us.

Quickly, he places his fingers on my elbow to prevent me from teetering to the floor, and the warmth of his hand spreads through the sleeve of my silk blouse, urging unwanted goose bumps to roll up my arm.

"You okay, Greer?"

I choke on spit as I'm trying to answer, and I have to clear my throat three times to stop myself from choking.

Clumsy. Choking. Undoubtedly, I've established myself as extremely ladylike in his eyes.

"Yep, yep. Just fine," I finally manage to push past my lips. "I'm good. To. Go."

And hell's bells, my skin *still* tingles from where his hand barely touched me.

*Is he made of some kind of sexy electricity or something?*

I cringe at my own thoughts. It's like these Trent Turner penis dreams are stealing my brain cells or something.

Before he turns back to the blueprints, I see what I think is a hint of a smirk, and I have the momentary—*and thankfully fleeting*—urge to grab his face and turn it back to mine so I can investigate my correctness.

"I know the plumbing is already roughed in, but I can't stop thinking that the sink should be on this side of the shower," Trent says, and the whole room tenses. And *then* he adds, "What do you think, Greer?"

Just like that. Easy. Direct. Like…like he actually cares. I don't know about everyone else, but suddenly I'm feeling all Taylor Swifty—Greer can't come to the phone right now…because she's dead.

Unfortunately, the delay my excitement causes kind of makes it seem like I might be suffering from a brain injury.

"Greer?"

When I wake from my trance, everyone in the room is staring at me.

*Good God, get it together, woman.*

"Uh, yes. Yeah. Normally, I would agree with you because I understand your perspective. Most hotels, if not all, are going to set this up the way you describe. But I think doing it this way instead is going to give so much more space and functionality, and isn't that what people staying in suites are really looking for?"

You could hear a pin drop as Marcus, Tony, George, and Sarah wait to hear what Trent says. There is some serious bated breath going on here, and Trent's pause is so long, it's doing a mighty good impression of me and my penchant for fucking around and losing track of time.

"You're right," he finally says, and I faint.

Okay, I don't really faint, but I could have if I ever waited long enough to eat to let my blood sugar get low.

As it is, I just perform a super slow blink.

"Great."

And the day moves on from there.

Trent isn't barking orders. He remains direct and to the point, but *calm*.

George doesn't look like he's one second away from getting in his truck and driving away and never coming back.

Even Sarah smiles. Actually *smiles* with teeth and all.

It's like we're all just one big happy, working family. Sunshine and rainbows and fucking leprechauns with pots of gold show up to the hotel construction site and shit.

And there's actually a glimmer of hope blooming inside my chest.

Maybe there's been a change in Trent's normally abrasive tune?

*Fingers and toes and pretty much everything crossed that he sticks with the new music.*

Basically, it's all gravy, baby.

For all of three hours.

*Until* the familiar asshole-voice reaches my ears.

"George!" he shouts, and I look up from the linen samples I'm currently rummaging through and find our poor contractor in the cross hairs…*again.*

"Sir?"

"Why didn't I know about the delayed deliveries for the indoor pool and spa?" Mr. Boss questions, and I swear to God, a vein makes itself known on his forehead and waves to everyone. All five fingers and an open palm. Hell, even his little veiny fingernails are painted blue.

George is terrified. "I didn't know they were delayed, sir."

Oh no.

"You're the contractor on this job, and you didn't know about delayed shipments?"

"I-I'm sorry, sir," he stutters out in response. "I've been assisting Dick and Beaver with the elevator installations since six this morning."

Trent shakes his head, runs a hand through his hair, and continues to channel his rediscovered rage toward George and the construction team.

The sunshine disappears. The rainbows fade away. Even the leprechauns pack up their shit and hightail it the fuck out of here.

*So much for hope.*

And I have to bite my tongue to keep from saying something snarky and sarcastic and getting-fired-kind-of-risky so hard I probably draw blood.

God, it's more apparent now than ever that something with Mr. Asshole Boss has to change.

And I think I have just the idea what to do about it.

———— ❦ ————

The AT&T store is busy but manageable as I step inside during my lunch hour.

As a loyal Verizon customer, I've stepped outside of bounds by coming here, but clandestine acts sometimes call for desperate

# THE *Billionaire* BOSS NEXT DOOR

measures. Trent surely knows how to buy off the people at Verizon into giving him the name and information of the woman on camera in their store when they match my ID to my existing account.

Or something like that. I don't know the exact details, but deciding to go to another carrier seemed imperative at the time.

"Can I help you?" the young man behind the counter—Henry, if his name tag is anything to go by—greets me, approaching me with his iPad to check me in.

I'm immediately defensive, declaring, "No names."

He doesn't understand, but I wouldn't expect him to. We're in the middle of the mall, not a top-level-clearance CIA operation.

Still, my mission is already in motion, and my behavior can't be stopped. I'm going to get some advice to Trent Turner on how to be a better boss and keep my job safe at the same time, one way or another.

"I need a burner phone. Untraceable. I have cash."

Henry's eyebrows shoot up, and I nod.

"This is serious business, Henry. Can you help me, or do I need to take my business next door to Sprint?"

Henry, the chap, comes over to the dark side with surprisingly little persuasion.

"No way, ma'am," he affirms. "You've come to the right place."

"Fantastic," I say with a secret smile and give my new AT&T pal a pat to his polo-covered shoulder. "I have a feeling you and I are going to be great friends."

## Chapter TWENTY-THREE

**Trent**

For the past week and a half or so, I've been getting texts from an unknown number with ridiculous, almost uninterpretable advice.

*Never walk by a pigeon coop with an owl in your pocket.*

*Don't shit on your own doorstep.*

*If you swim with a friend, your chances of getting eaten by a shark go down by 50%.*

*There is no angry way to say bubbles.*

*Real bear hugs are usually fatal.*

*Don't sweat the petty things, and don't pet the sweaty things.*

*In case of fire, use the stairs.*

And my personal favorite came straight from *The Godfather.* **Leave the gun. Take the cannoli.**

At first, I reacted badly. I honestly thought Cap had subscribed

# THE *Billionaire* BOSS NEXT DOOR

me to some fucking text service as a stupid joke. But when the messages kept coming—mostly, at inopportune times while I was busy trying to get an entire hotel off the ground—I kind of lost it. At one point, I even channeled Liam Neeson.

*Me: UNSUBSCRIBE.*

*Me: I'm going to shit on YOUR doorstep.*

*Me: YOU'RE ABOUT TO SLEEP WITH THE FISHES, MOTHERFUCKER.*

*Me: I don't know who you are, but I will look for you, I will find you, and I will kill you.*

Needless to say, I'm now in recovery.

I've found zen and peace and all that shit.

All that's left is to be proactive about finding the culprit.

My first, most immediate assumption was Greer. She's already tried her hand at giving me advice in person, and I wouldn't put it past her to go to these lengths.

Although, I'm using the word "advice" loosely here. I don't know what shit like shark attacks and bear hugs have to do with anything.

But the longer it's gone on, the more that theory seems uncertain.

I've tried to catch her several times at work, even jumping out and nearly yelling *Hah!* one time, and she's appeared busy doing something else on every occasion.

Sketching.

Conferring with Sarah.

Placing linen and décor samples all over the place and taking pictures.

All in all, she's been an efficient and mostly pleasant worker.

Because of that, I've focused my search back to the only other possibilities I can think of: Caplin and Quincy.

Cap is all the way in New York, and supposedly busy with all sorts of important corporate lawyer things—and women—but he's yet to outright deny his participation in the text attack.

And if there's one thing I know about him, it's not to count him out without proof—ever. In court and in life, he is the kind of adversary who will take you down without your even noticing.

Quincy is still a possibility too, especially with the way he's been taunting me about Greer ever since he dropped off the key.

But he also has a tendency to take credit for all of his ideas. It's almost like he can't physically keep any secrets inside his big, goofy body. If he were at the helm of this ship, he'd be skywriting "Sincerely, Quince" over the hotel.

Basically, I'm back at square one.

And more suspicious than ever. Every person in the hotel, every passerby on the street—they're all possibilities.

This morning, I even caught myself giving George rogue thoughtful looks as he went through the weekly rundown of progress.

And I don't even think George really knows how to text.

I'm about to check in on the terrace flooring delivery when my phone goes off with yet *another* damn text.

**Make like a hooker and open your legs to the advice of others.**

Once again, it's quite the gem.

I scan the room, expecting something to jump out and get me any minute, but as always, everyone is ensconced in their work and paying little to no attention to me.

Greer and Sarah are taping out furniture arrangement possibilities, and Marcus and George are in a heated conversation of some kind in the entryway to the men's restroom in the lobby.

# THE *Billionaire* BOSS NEXT DOOR

No one, it seems, is clutching a phone like Dr. Evil and rubbing their hands together.

My foot ticks, agitation bleeding into the muscle, but thankfully, the ring of my phone distracts me from doing something about it.

**Caplin Calling.**

Against my better judgment—and on the off chance that this actually has something to do with legal trouble—I answer.

"Hello?"

"Well, hello, good sir. It's so lovely to speak with you, Turn. I was just telling Janine how much I missed you."

"And who's Janine?" I ask, my voice bland with resignation. Two seconds into it and I can already tell—this isn't going to be a work call.

Caplin's work voice is completely different from his normal one. Commandeering and sharp, it's like the holy "professional" spirit invades his body and turns him into the business version of a television minister.

And he's not using it today. This is the jesting, often enthusiastic tone of my depraved good friend.

"I met her at the ice rink in Bryant Park."

"And?"

"And my apartment has been our sex hovel for the last week."

My body jerks, and an unexpected visual makes me gag. "Okay, too much information."

"Don't ask for what you can't handle, bud."

"Ah, sage advice." The kind of *advice* I've been getting in fucking droves these days. My hackles rise. "So, is it you?"

"Is what me?" Cap asks innocently. Or at least, faux-innocently. For a guy with a third-degree black belt in one-night stands, he's got the chops of a successful actor.

Then again, I guess being a believable liar is something his job requires of him. In my experience, lawyers are all about talking in loops until someone's ears bleed enough that they give in.

"Who's been texting me advice—and I use that term loosely—from an unknown number? If I get one more text about finding my chi, I might kill you."

His laugh is uproarious, and the blood in my ears pounds. "Dude, that sounds exactly like something I would do. But no. I've been more invested in the sex hovel."

I groan. "Stop saying that."

"What? Sex hovel? Is sex hovel the phrasing you have a problem with?"

"You are the biggest pain in my ass."

"The biggest?" he clucks. "Wow, Turn. You say the sweetest things."

I sigh. "Hey, Cap?"

"Yeah, buddy?"

"I implore you...*stop* talking about your cock's extracurricular activities."

"Okay. But only because I'm imagining you just said cock in the middle of the workplace and people are likely staring at you."

I look up, cautiously, and of course, he's right. Several sets of eyes in the room look up from their work, surveying me with new interest. Greer's are wide and way too *something*. Something interesting and *interested,* and fucking hell, I can't go there right now.

*Son of a bitch.*

His laughter carries through the phone, and I come damn close to hanging up on him.

"Wait, wait, wait," he says, somehow sensing my retreat. "I had a reason for calling. I swear."

"Yes," I agree. "Tormenting me."

I cut a stern look through everyone in the room, locking eyes briefly with Greer again, and then step out into the hall.

"Before I tell you the reason, I need to ask you something first."

"And what's that?"

"Have you banged out all your pent-up sexual frustration with

## THE *Billionaire* BOSS NEXT DOOR

the hot designer yet?" he asks, and I can actually *hear* a shit-eating grin in his voice. "I'm just trying to make sure the countdown on my desktop is correct."

Obviously, it was too much for me to hope that he forgot about the whole Greer Hudson situation.

"I told you that's not happening, you depraved bastard." I ignore the fact that my chest constricts at my words and focus on ending this call before Cap has time to say anything else. "And now, I'm really hanging up."

"Wait. Don't do that, Turn." He chuckles. "My reason for calling is Susie Gimble."

"Who?"

"Susie Gimble," he repeats. "Come on. You remember, we went to high school with her brother—"

"Gavin," I supply, finally remembering who the hell he's talking about.

I lean into the wall next to the door and pinch the bridge of my nose. Why the hell is he talking about people from high school right now?

"Well, she's divorced and living in New Orleans now, and I told her you want to take her out on a date."

My eyes pop open, and I jump, shoving away from the wall I've just settled into. "Jesus Christ, why would you do that?"

"Oh, I don't know," he says sarcastically. "Maybe to get you laid?"

"Cap—"

"You're like a month away from becoming a monk, Turn. Just go on the date, fuck the woman, and then you can move on with your life."

An image of Greer's big blue eyes looking over at me after I said the word cock flashes in my mind, and I crumble.

Because maybe Caplin is right, and maybe he's not. It's truly a fucking toss-up, but before I know it, I'm actually agreeing to it. "Fine. When?"

"It's not for a couple of weeks. She's in Greece right now. You'll have plenty of time to shave your balls."

"Yep. It's official. I'm hanging up now." I shake my head and look to the ceiling. The energy his mind must dedicate to coming up with this ridiculous shit to say is mind-boggling.

He laughs. "Good chatting with you, Turn. Good luck finding your midnight mystery texter."

"It's not… They don't text at midnight…" I struggle to explain, hating that he even knows this much now.

"Sure. Listen, I have to go because Thatcher Kelly just walked in, and there's no telling what kind of legal trouble he's in." I hear our friend Thatch's booming laugh in the background and cringe. The two of them in an office together must break some kind of law. I've never met two people with less of a filter than them. "But don't worry, you won't be a virgin anymore in two weeks!"

I tell him to fuck off, but he's already hung up by the time I get the words out.

Everyone is looking at me again when I step back inside the room after getting off the phone, so I say the only three words that come to mind. Words that will get them out of my hair long enough to erase at least a tiny portion of their memories. "Go get lunch."

# Chapter TWENTY-FOUR

## Greer

There is only one thing I do on Tuesday nights—watch *Ellen's Game of Games*.

Which is exactly what I'm doing now, all curled up on my couch in a pair of sleep shorts and a tank top, popping popcorn into my mouth like a heathen with my eyes riveted on my favorite TV shenanigans.

*Emory: I love how all the people always bounce in those sumo suits and flippers. Like, do their legs become rubberier or something?*

And, occasionally—*only during commercial breaks*—I answer my best friend's text messages.

*Me: I think it's Ellen's glee. It fills their legs with springs. Or hell, maybe it's a part of the show. Like, in order to participate, you need to fill out this contract that allows them to do minor surgery on your legs.*

*Emory: You should do it. What's a little surgery for 100K?*

*Me: Hey! Why don't you do it?*

*Emory: Because I already have money. And perfect legs. Surgery to insert springs would ruin them. You, however, could use a little pep in your step.*

**Me: Oh, right. Also, totally unrelated, but I hate you.**

The show comes back from commercial, and I drop my phone and my conversation with Emory like it's a hot potato.

And trust me, a potato has to be pretty fucking hot for me to drop it.

I won't be interrupted from my favorite program—even if it's by my best friend, talking about my favorite program.

I'm a complicated woman.

Ellen brings out the huge contraption she calls Mount St. Ellen, and three fun-loving people dressed up as little Bavarian boys and girls come running out from behind the stage.

This is one of my favorite games to watch because it takes so much fitness and savagery. Opponent below you on the mountain? Bowl over them like the boulders in *Indiana Jones*.

I'm really getting into it as two out of the three contestants come rolling back down the slime-covered mountain after grabbing fake pull ropes, and popcorn litters the floor from my unsuccessful attempts to get it into my cackling mouth.

My wheeze starts up after a snort, and by the time one of the women slides down and boots the guy contestant right in the balls, I'm damn near having a seizure, I'm laughing so hard.

All of a sudden, my laughter and the TV become background noise to a much greater adversary—the pounding on my door.

I jump up and hurry over, completely unsure who it could be or how I feel about their obvious aggression. When I get close and the pounding starts up again, I grab an umbrella out of my stand and wield it like a weapon.

I'm cocked and ready to swing as I reach out cautiously for the knob.

Slowly—painfully slowly, if I'm honest—I peel the door back to reveal the perpetrator.

When Trent Turner's eyes meet mine, I *accidentally* swing the umbrella like a reflex.

# THE *Billionaire* BOSS NEXT DOOR

He ducks—thankfully—but it's safe to say I haven't improved the boss/employee relations at all.

And I haven't been what one might consider neighborly either.

I'm coming up with goose eggs everywhere, people.

"What the hell are you doing?" he yells, putting up a hand to fight off my offensive as—*whoops*—I'm still swinging the umbrella like a lunatic.

I put it down and drop it back into the holder, but that doesn't make my voice any less shrill as I accuse, "I thought you were an intruder!"

He scoffs, and one dark eyebrow climbs toward his hairline. "An intruder who knocks?"

I don't notice anything else about him at all. Nope. Not the way his casual wear—jeans and a T-shirt—seems to suit his body just as well as professional attire, and not the way his hard jaw complements his sparkling green eyes.

His forearms definitely aren't veiny and pulsing either.

"Well, it was a really hard knock, and I don't know that many people who come to see me where I live," I defend somewhat weakly.

He smirks, and my instinct is to jump on it.

"And just what are you doing here anyway? We don't usually hang out and gab late at night."

He glances at his watch. "It's eight thirty. Hardly what I'd describe as 'late at night.'"

"*What* are you doing here?" I snap at the know-it-all.

"Checking on you," he says before laughing. "God knows why. But it sounded like you were being attacked by a herd of feral pigs in here."

I pause, looking back to the wall that I *know* has to be shared by his apartment, and panic. Obviously, I was aware we shared a wall and were in close proximity… I just…didn't remember that would mean he could hear me.

I clear my throat to compose myself, and the result is astounding. Yep, a real demure debutante here.

"I was watching a TV show."

"A show?" he asks skeptically, peeking inside the apartment without permission and looking around. "Watching a show causes you to make *that* much noise?"

"Yes. It's *Ellen's Game of Games*, and it's hilarious."

He frowns. "I've never seen it."

The music changes in the background, and Ellen's voice proclaims the beginning of Know or Go, and I drop the billionaire boss like I don't know the meaning of either one of those words.

"Uh, what are you—" he starts, and I shush him and head back to my couch, front door still wide open.

"Shh, it's back on."

"Greer, we're in the middle of a conversation—"

"Stay or go!" I yell like a psychopath. "But shut up and let me watch this."

I'm perched on the couch like a gargoyle when I feel him take a seat next to me. I didn't expect this at all—I figured he'd cut and run while he could—but I'm too involved in the show to bother thinking about it now.

Ellen opens up the game with a simple question, and I rub my hands together with delight at how hard it is for the lady to answer.

"She'll drop soon," I mutter to myself like some kind of *Game of Games* overlord.

"You're scaring me," Trent says softly through a half smirk. Evidently, he thinks speaking at regular volume will anger the beast.

"Don't be scared," I say. "You'll come over to the possessed side of things if you'll just watch."

"Why is it *so* funny?"

"Are you kidding?" I nearly shout. "Ellen is like a torture tyrant. She has absolutely no shame about making these people suffer for a chance at money. She loves it!" I glance at him as he considers it, and a lightbulb goes off. "You should relate to that mentality perfectly."

He should, actually. That dictatorial mentality of his is exactly

# THE *Billionaire* BOSS NEXT DOOR

what landed me a burner phone and two and a half weeks filled with sending cryptic advice messages.

Which has been incredibly enjoyable, to be honest.

He's threatened his mystery texter's life no less than three times and now walks around the job site like he's an undercover CIA agent.

I'm probably enjoying it a bit too much.

"I should relate to Ellen DeGeneres's game show?"

"Come on!" I shout, actually taking my attention away from the TV to look at his face. "You torture your employees for their paychecks daily. It's like you and Ellen are kindred spirits."

"I do not," he scoffs.

"Trent, come on. George cried into his yogurt so much yesterday, he ruined it."

He barks out an incredulous laugh. "No, he didn't."

"Yes, he did," I insist. It's not actually true, but if it gets Trent to change his behavior, I hardly think George will mind my painting him as an emotional man. Because for all the covert texting I've been doing on my burner phone, I've seen very little results out of this guy. Maybe, just maybe, he needs a more direct approach.

"I don't believe you."

I throw up my hands like it's all the same to me. "Hey, believe whatever you want. I'm just here to deliver the truth. Like how Sarah went to the dentist on Saturday and found out she has to wear a retainer to prevent more wear and tear now."

"You really have a penchant for exaggeration, you know that?"

"No exaggeration here, my friend. Even Marcus had to join a meditation group to bring down his cortisol levels, and Tony's been running through a string of hookers just so he can have a sense of control but without having to commit emotionally. He's basically dead inside now."

Trent shakes his head with a smirk curling the corner of his mouth and stares at the TV. I watch him intently, Ellen's torture chamber all but forgotten.

"And what about you?" he says, eyes never leaving the TV.

I shrug and settle back into the couch, so I don't have to see his reaction if he has one. But he probably won't. The Terminator usually doesn't. "I swung an umbrella at your head."

"So, you did realize it was me!"

"Shh," I say, unable to stop the little smile that settles into my cheeks. I had no idea sparring with him *away from work* could be this fun. "She's about to drop the winner, and she always enjoys that the most."

"The best is always last," he comments easily, and just like that, my head starts to race.

Was that some kind of subtle nudge because I was the last employee on my list? Or is he just spouting sayings like Yoda?

But his eyes, well, they are now one-hundred-percent serious and intently looking into mine.

*Why is he looking at me like that? And, more than that, why am I still staring into those gorgeous green eyes of his?*

I can't stop, though. His eyes are like crack for my eyes.

*Eye crack...*

*Wait...don't I mean eye candy?*

Nope. I don't. Candy is something you can quit. Crack, on the other hand, is something that is incredibly addictive and trouble from the very fucking start.

Trent Turner and those mesmerizing eyes of his are definitely *eye crack*.

I don't miss when his gaze flickers to my lips. Or when he reaches out to brush a lock of hair behind my ear. I don't miss the way my heart picks up in speed or the way my breath gets tangled up in my lungs. Or the goose bumps rolling up my arms.

I don't miss any of it.

But when the quiet but intense moment ends and we go back to watching the show, I do miss something—his eyes. On me. And when he leaves shortly after the show ends, I find myself kind of missing something else—*him*.

What on earth is happening to me?

# Chapter TWENTY-FIVE

## Trent

It's been two days since I watched TV in Greer's apartment.

Forty-eight hours since I nearly kissed her.

It had all been so fucking innocent, just sitting on her couch and watching some outrageous game show, but at one point, it took a turn.

Before I knew it, I wasn't just fixated on the cerulean blue of her eyes; I was mesmerized by her soft, pink lips. I thought about the way they moved when she opened her mouth to spout sarcasm and sass. I thought about the way they curled up at the corners when she smiled or laughed. And I thought about the way they looked, right then, when her teeth pressed into her bottom lip as she searched my steady gaze.

Fuck. Those lips of hers have become a serious problem for me.

One I don't have any time to contemplate right now because shit has really hit the fan in the hotel build. More supplies have been delayed, two workers quit, and the city pulled two of the permits we need to make any progress.

I am a raging bull, and everything in my path is a china shop.

I know flipping out doesn't necessarily help the greater good, but if I don't hold myself rigid as steel, the stress will snap me in two. At least, that's what it feels like.

For the first time in this build, the delayed supplies are the least of my worries. Quincy's got a few connections with different suppliers and some work-arounds, so we're not totally dead in the water there.

But it doesn't matter. We can have all the shit we need and all the workers we need, but without permits, we're fucked in a way that we don't ever grow our hymen back.

"Sarah, where's George on the permits? Has he spoken with the city? Do we know why they pulled them?" I fire off rapidly.

Sarah pulls out her phone and dials immediately, her hand shaking ever so slightly. I pull my eyebrows together, and I find myself dipping down a little to try to see if she's got a retainer in her mouth.

"I'm not sure yet, sir. I know George went down to the municipal building to find out. I'll get him on the phone."

My phone buzzes, and before I know it, one of those damn advice texts is staring me back in the face.

**Unknown: Smile. And say thank you. People mind an asshole a lot less if he says thank you.**

Instead of getting angry this time, I implement it without even thinking.

"Thank you, Sarah," I say softly, letting the corner of my mouth curl up. "Just let me know when you hear from him."

Sarah looks dumbstruck, and when I spot Greer from across the room, she looks impressed—eyes wide and cheeks plump with an approving smile.

My chest feels warm, like melted chocolate is being infused through a port.

Well, *fuck*.

New Orleans me, it seems, has thrown another wrench in the system—caring what Greer Hudson thinks.

It's almost sickening how easily my body slides into the new plan as it gets a little hit of a high from Greer's admiration.

"Also," I say, looking at a shell-shocked Sarah with new eyes. "You don't have to call me sir. Trent is fine."

Records scratch, and activity drops off to nothing. Several

# THE *Billionaire* BOSS NEXT DOOR

sets of eyes on are on me with an intensity that makes me wholly uncomfortable.

"All of you," I amend. "All of you should just call me Trent."

Greer, thank God, finally breaks the ominous silence. "Will do, Captain Trent."

I laugh, and the rest of the team stare at me like I've suddenly grow an additional head.

Time stands still. A fly drops dead midflight. Mouths gape like open wounds.

*Have I really never fucking laughed at work before?*

"Captain, huh?" I look at Greer. "Okay, I kind of like that."

Instantly, she shakes her head with a cheeky smile. "Sorry. One-time thing."

"Ah, well." I shrug and smirk. "I guess it was fun while it lasted."

After that, five more minutes with the pod people formerly known as my staff is all I can take.

Apparently, I am going to need to pace myself when it comes to softening my fist from iron. If not, I might not have anyone left in a week.

For today, though, I've decided to remove myself from the situation completely. It's not like I don't have other important shit to do, and as much as it seems I'd like to, I can't stand around staring at Greer's approving smile all day.

*Wait a fucking minute. Hold. The. Phone.* My mind starts to replay how the entire interaction went down.

Talking to Sarah.

Text advice from that fucking unknown number.

Magically, I use said advice and say thank you.

And Greer smiles—admiringly.

*Well, I'll be damned... That's quite the coincidence right there...*

I glance at Greer one more time, finding her already back to work and holding up linen samples near a freshly painted wall, and I make a mental note to look into this revelation.

Later, though.

Because right now, my focus needs to stay on the job. There are crucial permits we need to obtain because, without them, none of us will have jobs to come back to.

---

Thankfully, the municipal building is only a six-block walk from the hotel, and fifteen minutes later, I'm heading toward the entrance doors.

George nearly jumps out of his skin when he sees me approaching. His eyes are big and round, and his body language is throwing off all sorts of signals telling me to stay away.

But I know what's at stake here, and despite my history, I have no intention of barreling in here with my guns blazing.

When he sees that I'm not stopping my advance, he excuses himself from the counter and meets me halfway.

"They're working on finding out why they pulled the permits now, sir."

I'm almost surprised he didn't get a text message memo about canning the use of sir, but evidently, everyone has actually stayed busy since I left. I'm impressed.

"We don't even know why they pulled them yet?"

George shakes his head. "No. From what I've been able to figure out, one of the city council members was coming by the job site and didn't think something was in compliance."

"An inspector has to make that decision, don't they?"

"Yes, sir. But out of deference to his standing with the city, I guess they're honoring his request until an inspector either confirms or denies it."

"So, it's the reason he felt like we were in noncompliance we don't know."

"Yes, sir."

# THE *Billionaire* BOSS NEXT DOOR

"All right." I sigh heavily and run a hand roughly through my hair. "Well, I guess I'll leave you to it."

He blinks. Rapidly. Like, an abnormal amount, and Greer is obviously right. I am a tyrant.

*Shit.*

"Sir?"

"It seems like you've got everything under control here."

"Yes, sir." George nods and stands up a little straighter. Without the weight of my temper, he's six inches taller.

"I'm going back to the job site to tighten everything up. Until we know what's stuck in this guy's craw, we're going to have to make sure every aspect of the job is clean and correct."

"I agree. I'll have a talk with the guys when I get back for the day."

I appreciate his work ethic, but after a glance at my watch, I wave him off. "It's almost three. Just stay here until you get it figured out, and we'll pick up where we left off tomorrow."

"You sure, sir?"

I nod. "The city isn't going to make any decisions or do any inspections after hours."

"Okay. I'll talk to the guys first thing tomorrow, then."

"Perfect. Thanks, George."

His mouth opens and closes so many times, I just have to walk away and head back to the hotel site. There's no upside to wasting the amount of time it's likely to take him to understand my new attitude.

After a quick check-in with Sarah and letting George's guys know he'll be tied up at the municipal offices for the rest of the day, I head into the conference room I've been using as a temporary office and grab my laptop and suit jacket.

I have a four o'clock meeting with the NOLA hospitality board across town and just over thirty minutes to get there. I'm already pulling my phone out of my pocket, about to call an Uber, but when I spot Greer in reception, I get an idea.

Swift and light on my feet, I step into one of the small restroom corridors and out of her view. And instead of clicking on Uber, I pull up my text inbox, find the anonymous advice-giver, and send a message.

**Me:** *You there, anonymous? I have something to tell you.*

No response. So, I send another.

**Me:** *It's incredibly important.*

And another one.

**Me:** *So important that you're not going to want to miss it...*

And that's when I see it. Greer, reaching into the pocket of her blazer and pulling out a phone. She glances around the room a few times, before turning her back to the workers milling about near reception and looking down at the phone in her hands.
*It's her. It has to be her.*
Instantly, I type out another text as I quietly walk toward her.

**Me:** *Trust me, you don't want to miss this really important something...*

The instant I hit send, I'm standing close enough to see the phone in her hands buzz, and the screen lights up. I watch as her fingers tap across the keys and then, the instant they release, my phone vibrates.

**Unknown:** *Any day now...*

It *is* her! Holy shit. That little fucking minx. *She's* the mystery texter.

## THE *Billionaire* **BOSS NEXT DOOR**

A part of me is shocked, but another part of me knew it all along. Only Greer would use insane, sometimes incomprehensible text messages to try to get advice to me.

And for some unknown reason, I'm smiling like a loon as I type out another message and hit send.

**Me: Okay, fine. I'll tell you right now.**

Stepping up to Greer, I place a gentle hand on her shoulder and whisper, *"Gotcha."*

The instant the little text bandit—with the evidence still in her hands, mind you—locks eyes with me, I smile, lean even closer, and whisper into her ear, "Thank you."

Her mouth drops open so wide, I'm not sure it'll ever close, but the light shining in her blue eyes as they search mine is worth all of those ridiculous texts and then some.

She might be a pain in my ass sometimes, but I can't deny that today, her usual cryptic advice rang clear, and it taught me an important lesson in humility.

And I'd have to be a real weak fuck of a man not to thank her for it.

Yeah. *Thank God for Greer Hudson.*

# Chapter TWENTY-SIX

## Trent

At the gym that evening, while I'm on the treadmill, my head spins.

*Have I really been that terrible of a boss? Have I been that way all along?*

When I'm stressed, which is a lot, I tend to demand first and think later.

I mean, sometimes, as the boss, you have to be a hard-ass. You have to be the one in control. But not to the point of making your employees uncomfortable. And the past two months on this job, I've been more bark and bite than anything else.

The revelation is eye-opening.

And it's all thanks to her. *Greer.*

She's beautiful and can banter with the best of them—and I'm surprised it's taken me this long to notice.

*Why on earth did I hate it so much in the beginning?*

It doesn't take long before I snag my phone from the cupholder and pull up Greer's actual number in my contacts. I type out a message as I run.

**Me:** *It's crazy, you know, because I've yet to receive a single advice text from this unknown number since this afternoon. And let me tell you, they have quite the track record for sending A LOT of text messages...*

Her response is instant.

*Greer: No hablo inglés.*

I grin. I can't help it. This woman is fucking hilarious.

*Me: HAHA. Very funny.*

*Greer: I know I'm hilarious, but what is your current state?*

*Me: My current state?*

*Greer: Are you mad?*

*Me: Why would I be mad?*

*Greer: Oh, I don't know. Because you're the boss. I'm the employee. And I was texting you advice on how to do your job from a burner phone.*

*Me: You got a burner phone? Just to text me?*

*Greer: Uh…I don't remember the details exactly…*

Of course, she doesn't remember…

*Me: LOL. Sure, you don't.*

*Me: But, no, I'm not mad. When I said thank you, I meant it.*

*Greer: Is the apocalypse happening right now? Are we mere seconds away from a meteor crashing to Earth and blowing us all to smithereens?*

I laugh. Outright. Loud enough that a woman on an elliptical glances back to see what's so funny. *Greer Hudson, lady. That's what's so funny.*

**Me: Always the smartass, huh?**

**Greer: Pretty much.**

Her texts come in rapid fire after that.

**Greer: Thanks for not firing me.**

**Greer: Or murdering me.**

**Greer: Or hiring someone to kidnap me and take me to a deserted island where I would live off of coconuts and leaves and have to befriend a lost volleyball named Wilson.**

*Fucking* Cast Away. A soft chuckle leaves my lips as I type out my last message before heading to the locker room to take a shower.

**Me: You're welcome, Tom Hanks. P.S. Your mind is a scary place.**

**Greer: Tell me about it.**

———◦❀◦———

At around nine, I'm back in my TV-less, far-too-silent apartment and wondering if Greer is home. I've been back from the gym for an hour, and I haven't heard her yet.
I attune myself to the wall between us, listening for signs of life. *Has she all of a sudden started being mindful of her noise level?*
I'm ashamed to do it, but for just a couple of seconds, I press my ear up against the damn wall to see if I can hear better.

# THE *Billionaire* BOSS NEXT DOOR

*Nothing. She's not home.*

Disappointment sets in, and to pass the time, I start browsing TV specs on the internet. Clearly, if I've stooped to pressing my face against the wall, hoping to hear my neighbor for entertainment, it's time to purchase one.

There are a ton of options out there, stretching across all variety of price points, and I quickly get lost in the minutia of it.

I wouldn't know which one to pick to save my life. I've never been the kind of guy to focus on the latest and greatest technology and update every time something new comes out. If it weren't for the company, I'd still have the last generation of iPhone.

But Caplin, he's a different story. LED, LCD, HD, plasma, bone marrow…whatever the fuck. He knows it, he's into it, he's got the best of the fucking best.

I grab my phone from the kitchen counter, settle back into the couch, and put my laptop on the coffee table.

It rings four times before he answers, and when he does, he seems out of breath.

"Hello?"

Immediately, I groan.

"Please God, tell me you are not having sex right now."

His laugh is loud and obnoxious, and I have to pull the phone away to spare my eardrums. "Nope. I'm running. But I love that fucking some chick was the first thing you assumed I'd be doing."

"When all you talk about is sex hovels and shit, it's easy to assume. Which, by the way, I hope Janine was able to leave your apartment without a raging UTI."

"Janine?" he asks, and I squint.

"Isn't that what you said her name was?"

"Yeah, but that was forever ago, Turn. This week, it's Lucy."

Forever ago? More like one week ago.

"Of course." I laugh. "How silly of me."

"Yeah, dude, it's ridiculous. Come on."

I roll my eyes and grab my laptop to open the page comparing TVs.

"Anyway, I *am* in the middle of a run. Is there a reason you called?"

"Yeah…" I'm just about to dive into asking Cap's advice on the latest and greatest in all things technology when music comes on next door at a near-deafening volume.

My attention is instantly rerouted.

"Hellllooo," Cap calls. "Earth to Trent Turner. Come in, Trent Turner."

I drag out the sound of my I as I make a command decision. "I-I-I'm gonna have to call you back."

"What the hell? You called me."

I don't explain before hanging up. In fact, it's the perfect moment to give him a little taste of his own medicine.

But not even fifteen seconds later, my phone pings with a text. *Shocker.*

**Cap: *You fuck.***

**Cap: *P.S. You have a date with Susie Gimble. Maybe you should, you know, call me back so I can tell you the details.***

**Cap: *P.P.S. If you choose not to call me back, I will be forced to send her to your apartment at the time and date of my choosing.***

*Jesus.* And here I hoped he'd be too busy with his sick sex hovels to remember the whole Susie Gimble thing entirely.

Whatever. I'll deal with him later.

Right now, my mind is focused on something else.

*Someone* else, actually. A certain someone who is slowly becoming the most intriguing human being I've ever met.

I drop my phone onto my kitchen counter and head for the door, in the direction of the apparent nightclub that's just opened next door.

# Chapter TWENTY-SEVEN

## Greer

I'm halfway into my chorus, shaking my butt and pulling the string of my thong up and out of my pajama pants—you know, to go with the theme of the song—when my door shakes again, kind of like it did two nights ago.

I shake my hips as Sisqó sings about how scandalous I am and head for the door.

With one quick swipe, I put the umbrella up on my shoulder and turn the knob.

He's smiling until he sees the makeshift weapon and ducks, hands up in defense.

I dissolve into a fit of laughter.

"Oh my God, you should have seen your face. Thinking I would actually swing this at you." I drop it back into the holder, leave the door open, and walk back into my apartment as he shouts to be heard over the music.

"You just swung it at me the other night!"

"But is past behavior really a precedent for future?" I challenge.

"Yes!" he yells with a disbelieving smile. "There's even a quote about it. Past behavior is the best predictor of future behavior!"

"Oh well!" I shrug nonchalantly, and then quick as a whip, I'm hit with the realization that this is the first face-to-face interaction we've had since he found out I was playing Dear Abby with a burner phone. "Did you change your mind?"

"Change my mind?" he shouts over the music. "About what!"

"Fire...murder...kidnap... You know, *change your mind!*"

He laughs and shakes his head. "No!"

*Thank everything for that.*

"Okay, good!" A sigh of relief leaves my lips just as Sisqó really starts to get into it and the bass coming from my speakers jumps up a few notches.

Trent winces a little and puts a hand to his ear. "Can we turn the music down?"

"Are you kidding?" I shout. "This is the 'Thong Song.' The only way to play it is at full volume!"

Resigned to his fate, but plainly too stuffy to join in, he watches as I dance around the room from his spot behind the couch, hands tucked casually into the pockets of his jeans.

I sway my hips just like I was before and even drop into a slightly more conservative twerk.

Through all of it, he watches—*intently.*

So much so, the weight of his stare makes my stomach sink and turn over all at the same time.

If I didn't know any better, I'd swear he's...*attracted* to me.

But that can't be right, so I shake my head to clear my vision.

When the song finally comes to a close, he's still looking at me like he can see through my clothes, and I'm still confused.

I chatter to distract myself. "You disrespected the song, you know? Just standing there like that. You don't stand still while the 'Thong Song' is on."

"I was watching you," he says simply, and I shut my big mouth. Because, yeah, I know. "What's with partying like it's 1999?"

"Ah, so you do respect the song. You wouldn't know what year it was from if you didn't."

He smirks. "I guess you caught me."

I fire finger guns at him because I'm awkward and socially inept. Why they even let me out of the womb, I'm not sure.

# THE *Billionaire* BOSS NEXT DOOR

"So, what's with the music?"

"I love to listen to stuff from my youth. Jam out to Sisqó, test my memory on 'Freak-A-Leek' by Petey Pablo, rage out to Linkin Park. What? You don't?"

He shakes his head and rounds the sofa to take a seat. I watch with barely concealed angst as he makes himself at home on my couch and stretches an arm across the back.

*Am I in a parallel universe? Are we friends now?*

*Like, what is happening here?*

I honestly thought he would straight up kill me if he ever found out that I was the burner-phone messenger. But he knows. And I'm still kicking. It's almost too much to comprehend.

I turn down the volume a little, just to make it easier to hear him.

"I haven't listened to any of this music since I was a kid," Trent says. "Junior high, I think. Does that sound right?"

"I don't know. How old are you now?"

His eyebrows pull together. "I'm your age. Thirty-three. You didn't know that?"

"No," I say with a laugh. "How would I?"

He shrugs. "Google. Wikipedia."

My laughter is so manic, it's almost scary. "Oh, that's right. I almost forgot. You're a billionaire."

He rolls his eyes and picks at imaginary lint on his knee. "I'm not. My parents are, but *I* am not."

I plop onto the couch on the other end and tuck a knee to my chest. "Yeah, but it'll be yours one day. Same thing."

He laughs, but let me tell you, I don't think it's because he thinks something is funny. It's scornful and pessimistic in a way that only I, a cynic myself, understand.

"Wow. What's that reaction all about?"

He shakes his head and pauses, but then speaks anyway. When he does, he makes eye contact, and I instantly feel like my skin is too tight for my body. "My dad isn't exactly my biggest fan. I was supposed to take over Turner Properties when he retires, but lately, it doesn't seem like he's too keen to hand it over to me."

"Whaaaat?" I screech. "Is he looking for an adoptive daughter to leave it to instead?"

He chuckles and points at me with a wagging finger. "Very funny."

"You may think it's funny, but I'm serious. Mama could use a little money cushion. I'm even open to servicing him sexually."

"Greer."

"What?" I tease. "Nothing too kinky, probably, but I don't know… I'm undoubtedly willing to let my morals slip pretty far for a billion dollars."

"He and my mom are still together."

"Maybe she likes to watch, Trent. You don't know. Don't be so selfish."

"You're terrible," he says, but he says it with a smile.

I shrug as something occurs to me. "Wait a minute. Why don't I ever hear you?"

"What?"

"In your apartment," I explain. "You seem to hear me all the time, but I don't think I've ever heard you."

My phone buzzes on the table, and he nods at it.

I scoff. "No way. Don't try to distract me with my phone."

"It could be important."

"Trust me, the last time something important happened to me was in the 1980s, and it was the moment I was born. Answer me. Why don't I ever hear you?"

He lifts his shoulders and sighs before chuckling a little. "I don't know. I'm quiet? I don't have a TV? I don't cackle like a hyena? It could be any number of things."

"I do not cackle!" I protest with a smack to his leg. He looks down at the place I smacked him, and I wallow in my embarrassment.

## THE *Billionaire* BOSS NEXT DOOR

*Oh God, what is wrong with me? Hitting the boss is never a good idea, Greer. Even if there is some kind of weird pseudo-friendly neighbor thing going on.*

When he looks up, his grin is a relief.

"You cackle. Trust me. But it suits you."

"It *suits* me? Are you saying I look like a person who cackles? Do I have a deformity I don't know about?"

He shakes his head and reaches out to squeeze my hand.

My fingers feel warm even after he pulls away.

"It just means you have a fun, free spirit. I *like* that you cackle."

My breath catches in my lungs, and my brain reels through a number of possibilities for escape. Finally, it remembers that my phone buzzed on the coffee table not long ago.

I reach forward and grab it, clicking on the message from Emory to see what she has to say.

Incognizant of my company, I read it aloud.

**Emory: You have a date next week, Tuesday at 7 at La Previe. A guy I know. Wear something revealing.**

"Jesus," I say when I'm done, typing across the keyboard as fast as I can.

Trent leans in and whispers, "What are you saying?"

Normally, I'd keep it to myself, but seeing as he's already involved, I run it down for him quickly.

"I said, 'Thanks for the offer, but the chances of me going on a date you set up for me with absolutely no details are about as good as me finding some spare fucks to give. No.'"

"I take it you didn't know she was trying to set you up." Trent chortles and sits back in his seat.

"Other than the fact that she's always trying to set me up? No."

"I can relate to this dilemma."

I quirk a surprised brow. "How?"

"My friend Cap. He's all but strong-arming me into going on a date with a woman named Susie."

All of a sudden, I'm not a fan of the name Susie. Like, it kind of sounds like the worst name in the world, honestly.

"Are you going to go?"

He raises a brow. "Are you going to go?"

*Am I going to go?*

But he doesn't give me a chance to answer.

"You know what," he says, standing from the couch so suddenly, I don't even read Emory's text when it pings. Instead, I follow him with my eyes as he moves toward the door. I'm not sure, but it kind of feels like my face is turned down into a frown.

"You should go on it, Greer." He opens my door and steps through it, facing me again so I can see his face when he speaks again. "And who knows? Maybe it's destiny."

The door shuts behind him, and I'm left reeling.

*Destiny?*

Something doesn't feel right about this. Not agreeing to this date. And definitely not Trent telling me to go on this date.

*Is he going on a date too?*

He said his friend Cap was trying to set him up. *Does that mean he has already set Trent up or still trying?*

My mind spins with a million different questions and no fucking answers.

And, of course, Emory's message is waiting for me when I look down at my phone.

**Emory: *You are a spinster with a sincere dislike for cats. You are going on this date if I have to drag you there by your nipples.***

Nothing feels right about this.

But when faced with the possibility of Trent going on a date and me just sitting at home like a spinster while trying to hear him fuck some tramp through our shared wall, I agree.

And it feels like the exact opposite of destiny.

Honestly, it feels like destiny just up and walked right out my front door.

*Are you sure you're still talking about destiny?*

# Chapter
# TWENTY-EIGHT

**Trent**

La Previe is bustling with ambiance and busy staff and tables filled with people chattering and flirting and doing whatever it is people do inside a restaurant on a Tuesday night.

I sit at the table I requested, off the beaten path but still facing the center of the dining room, and I wait. For what exactly, I'm not sure, but my eyes are fixated near the door as I sip on the fresh drink I grabbed at the bar before being seated by the hostess.

Okay, full disclosure. I know explicitly threatening not to show up for my date if Cap didn't make sure it was at the time and location of my choosing—ahem, the same as Greer's, specifically—was wrong.

But I couldn't help myself.

I haven't felt the kind of jealousy I felt when Emory texted her about her date since high school.

I asked Catherine Gibbs to prom, but she turned me down to go with Harrison Phelps. He was a pompous ass, and I'm pretty sure Catherine turned out to be a stripper, but the point is, at the time, I was blind with envy.

And when Greer read that text aloud, I flashed back to the same exact feeling.

Obviously, I could have agreed with her, told her to stick to her guns about declining, but…something about that didn't feel right either.

So, even though every cell inside my body was opposed, I told her to go.

If I want her to like me—which, for whatever reason, it seems that's the way my mind and body are leaning—I need her to do it on her own terms and with all the information.

If she wants to go on a date with someone else, she should. If her best friend thinks she found a guy who is good for Greer, then Greer should go on a date with him and see what he has to offer.

But just in case, in the name of chivalry, I'll be here to keep an eye on her.

It's a real fucked-up mind-set, but I'm not the most rational guy in NOLA.

Plus, it's not my place to tell Greer what to do or not to do when it comes to dating. I might have a track record for being a controlling bastard on the job site, but when it comes to women, I don't control; I respect. Their opinions. Their feelings. Their desires.

Any man who does otherwise is a real insecure fucking prick and doesn't deserve shit.

Glasses clink and chatter rolls on at a dull roar as I take a sip of my water and glue my eyes to the door.

My date hasn't shown, and Greer hasn't either, but it looks as though her date has.

For the last fifteen minutes, I've been watching a guy at a table by himself check the time on his phone and slam back glasses of whiskey like it's about to be outlawed.

For Greer's sake, if this is her date, I'm hoping he can handle his liquor.

And then I see her walk in. Blue dress, blue eyes, and the most perfect nervous smile.

She looks like she's on the very edge of losing her shit, and I can't help but grin.

It doesn't matter the day, the time, or the occasion—Greer is always herself. Genuine and quirky, and I don't think I've ever met any woman like her.

I'm staring at her as she walks to the table with the mystery man in the middle of the room, and my heart jumps into my throat as she leans down to give him a kiss on the cheek.

Her dress is low-cut, her breasts are magnificent, and I have to hold myself in my seat to keep from running over to offer my jacket.

I can't hear what they're saying, but everything seems stiff and formal enough. I don't want her to have a bad time, but if I said I don't enjoy watching whoever this fucker is struggle to win her over a little, I'd be lying.

I'm settling in for the show when a slender set of hips in a tight red dress block my vision. I follow them up to a face and a mess of blond hair, and her features are unmistakable.

She is the female version of Gavin Gimble, and undoubtedly his sister—my date, Susie.

*Shit. My date.*

Too absorbed in all things Greer, I completely fucking forgot about my date.

She smiles down at me and holds out a hand, asking, "Trent Turner?"

Time warps into a vacuum, and before I know it, I'm answering.

Only the answer isn't at all what I, or she, is expecting. "No."

Her groomed and shaped brows pull together, and my heart dials up to a gallop.

*Holy shit, I can't believe I'm doing this.*

"You're not Trent Turner?" she asks again, just to clarify.

I shake my head like a lunatic and stand up to apologize. "No, I'm sorry. I'm William…" I glance down for some help in my lie, and I'm ashamed of what I come up with. "Table. William Table."

In my defense, I don't have a lot of practice being dishonest.

"Your name is William Table?" she says, her attitude shifting from friendly to inconvenienced in half a second. I take it as a sign that I'm dodging a bullet and hold strong.

"Yep."

She drops a hip along with any ounce of coy flirtiness and snaps. "Great. Just fucking great."

# THE *Billionaire* BOSS NEXT DOOR

"Sorry," I apologize again. Though, it's safe to say at this point, I don't even really mean it.

I don't know what the fuck Cap was thinking would make us a good match, but I'm guessing it had nothing to do with her personality.

She storms back to the front of the restaurant, and I sit back down in my chair. When the waiter comes over to ask if I'm still waiting for someone, I tell him the exciting news.

"No. I'll be dining alone now."

"Very well. Are you ready to put in an order?"

"In a few minutes," I reply.

For the time being, I've got something else to occupy my time.

Greer and her date are fully involved in a conversation by the time my waiter clears the place setting on the other side of the table, but her smile is brittle at best.

I lean forward into my elbows, trying to hear what they're saying, but it's no use. I'd need a degree in lipreading to decode their conversation, and unfortunately, they didn't offer that course where I went to school.

Thinking on the fly, I take out my phone and type out a text. I know the date can't be going that well, because she picks her phone up off the table to read it.

*Me: How's the date going?*

She frowns at little before making some sort of excuse to her date and typing out a response.

*Greer: Fine. Why are you texting me?*

*Me: What does "fine" mean? In my experience, no woman ever uses that word unless she's annoyed.*

*Greer: You must hear it a lot, then.*

I grin. And keep texting her. *Keep stealing her attention away from her date.*

*Me: What's your date doing right now, while you're texting me?*

*Greer: Staring at my breasts, I presume.*

*Me: Sounds like a winner.*

*Greer: Well, I do have great breasts. But yeah, he's a real gem. He just finished telling me about kicking his mom out of her house when she couldn't afford to pay him the rent.*

Good God. And this is the guy her best friend set her up with?

*Me: Wow. That tells me everything I need to know.*

*Greer: Everything you need to know for what?*

*Me: And for the record, you look stunning tonight. And your breasts are better than great. I've been staring at them ever since you got here.*

What's destined to be is motherfucking destined to be.

I started moving before I sent the message, so by the time she looks up, I'm standing right beside her table.

I can't help but feel good when her blue eyes flare thankfully.

Her date doesn't seem quite as relieved.

"Hi," I say softly, and a tiny grin plumps the apple of her cheek.

"Hi."

Her date doesn't delay before jumping in, all misplaced righteous indignation and hero complex. "You know this guy?"

Greer nods, slowly turning her gaze away from me to look back at him. "This is my boss."

He starts to smile at the news when she adds, "And my neighbor. You know what, he's kind of a lot of things."

His patience is obviously thinning as he asks, "And what is this man of many things doing here?"

"Ending your date," I say for her.

Her mouth gapes, and her date jumps up from the table, affronted.

"Excuse me? Who the hell do you think you are?"

I shake my head and offer a hand to Greer. It takes her a moment to decide, but eventually, she takes it. Immediately, none of the rest of how this encounter goes even matters.

I push her behind me a little, just enough to protect her if this guy loses his shit, and answer him. "You've been pounding whiskey for an hour. I'm sure you'll find something to do without her."

My words infuriate him, and before I know it, his fist is cocked and he's propelling his body straight toward me.

But I'm not five whiskeys deep, nor am I intimidated by this prick.

He's inconsequential in this scenario.

The only thing that matters is that I'm leaving this restaurant with Greer.

*My Greer.*

And I don't care who the fuck I have to fight to do it.

# Chapter
# TWENTY-NINE

## Greer

My chest pounds as Trent pulls me from the restaurant by a tight grip on my hand. My feet can barely keep up, but seeing as he just hit my would-have-been date in the face and the cops are probably on the way, I don't complain.

"Holy shit!" I yell, shaking as we round the corner into an alley and fade into the darkness. "You just clocked that guy right in the face!"

He shakes his hand, obviously hurting, and laughs.

Fucking *laughs*. After committing assault.

Clearly, this motherfucker has lost his mind.

*God, he's so hot right now.*

"Yeah, well." He pauses. "He swung at me first."

"And missed!" I yell, completely beyond controlling my volume. "But you didn't. Bam-o! Right in the kisser!"

He shakes his head and pulls me back down the alley toward the street, checking both ways before stepping outside and putting his hand to the small of my back.

We move at a swift pace, and with all of the excitement, it takes me a minute to realize how bad this could be.

"Jesus. Are you going to get arrested?" I question, coming to a complete stop as I do.

He shakes his head and pushes me forward again. "I don't think so. I know the owner, so I doubt he'll give my name to the police."

"My God. This is exhilarating. I've never been a part of something like this in my life!"

He laughs, admitting, "Me neither."

I can't stop myself from blathering on. "Where are we headed now? To see your bookie? A speakeasy? Do you know someone with connections in the clink?"

"We're going to eat dinner."

"Oh, well. That's anticlimactic," I say, and then quickly realize that his presence at La Previe wasn't exactly an expected occurrence. "Wait a minute. How did you even end up there tonight?"

He shrugs. "I just happened to be in the neighborhood."

I quirk a brow. "And then you what, just so happened to show up on my date?"

He grins. "I guess it was destiny."

*Destiny. There's that word again.*

Consider my mind officially blown.

I start to pace the sidewalk, but he stops me and turns me to face him, and the eye contact is strong. I fade into the power of his sharp green eyes with surprising ease.

"Did you eat anything?"

"No."

"Well, me neither. And I'm hungry."

He stays there, silent and stalwart, waiting for me to agree, and it doesn't take me long to fold.

I barely get the word of agreement, a simple *okay*, out of my mouth before he jerks me inside the restaurant we're directly in front of and directs me to a table.

I sit while he goes up to the counter—obviously, we've taken the ritziness down a couple of notches from the place we fled—to put in our order.

I take the opportunity to ogle him freely.

With his suit jacket left behind at the booth with me for safekeeping, his ass is delightfully available for viewing. It's tight and round, and I don't think they had any other ass in mind when they designed those black wool pants.

He rolls the sleeves of his button-down shirt up to his elbows, and I salivate over his forearms like one of Pavlov's dogs.

So much so, I grab a napkin from the holder to wipe any excess drool off my chin as he spins on his heel to return.

I'm shoving the evidence into the bowels of my purse when he sets down a red basket lined with red-and-white-checked paper in front of me, and one identical to it in front of himself.

"Chicken fingers?" I ask, completely flabbergasted that a kid who grew up as rich as he did eats chicken fingers as a grown man.

"Yeah."

I roll my eyes.

"What?"

"It's just…what are you? Twelve?"

He shrugs. "They're good. Especially with fries."

"Oh my God, that's adorable. You're a child."

"I may never be a judge on *Top Chef*, but I assure you, I'm no little boy."

I blush, picturing the absolute naughtiest meaning of his statement, and he shrugs.

"When I'm out, I eat this way. At home, I try to eat healthy."

I smirk. "How often do you eat at home?"

"Lately?" He laughs. "Not often."

"Eh, well. I'm not one to talk. I eat ramen three nights a week."

"Ramen? Really? And you're judging me for *chicken fingers*? When's the sick frat party, Toby? Are you gonna invite the hotties we saw down at the quad?"

"Shut up."

"Well, come on. Don't throw stones at me if you don't want me to shatter your glass house."

"I don't think that's how that saying goes."

# THE *Billionaire* **BOSS NEXT DOOR**

He laughs and lifts his shoulders toward the ceiling. "It's close enough."

"So, um…" I mumble when the conversation gives way to silence. We're both heavily involved in consuming our chicken fingers—which he's right about being delicious—but I don't feel comfortable enough with him yet to sit in silence. "You seem to know New Orleans pretty well. Have you ever lived here?"

He finishes chewing his bite and wipes his mouth before answering. His manners far exceed my own.

"No. But my mom loves it here. We used to visit when I was a kid, often."

Wow. He has a mother. That he talks about.

I don't know why that's so surprising given he's a human and that's biology, but I'd kind of been picturing him as some kind of immaculate spawn of Trent Turner Senior and Mother Earth.

"That's cool. Do you think your parents will relocate down here when the hotel is done?"

"I doubt it." He shakes his head and leans forward into his forearms, dropping what's left of his chicken finger into the basket and sighing. "My mom…" He clears his throat. "She's got pretty progressive Parkinson's. All of her doctors are in New York, and…well, my dad is pretty set on keeping her there."

Wow. I wasn't expecting that at all. I'm not sure why I always assume rich people can't get sick—because obviously, they can—but it still comes as a shock when I hear this kind of news.

"I'm sorry," I say simply, and it's enough.

Trent nods. "Me too. And thank you. That's the reason I didn't come down here when I should have." He shakes his head. "The reason the schedule is so tight. I just wasn't ready to leave her."

My chest constricts and warms, and boy oh boy, am I in trouble.

Not only is Trent incredibly attractive and intelligent…he's also human and vulnerable and…dare I say it, *likable*.

The only thing I can think to say that isn't *Make babies with me* is about work.

"The schedule is tight, but we'll make it. I'm confident. It's a good team, and you're a good leader."

"Really?" He raises a skeptical eyebrow, and I laugh.

"Okay. Look. You have a tendency to be despotic…"

He groans pathetically and covers his eyes. I reach out and pull away his hand to uncover them as I keep talking.

"But I can see now that you mean no harm. And you've been trying. I can tell, and so can everyone else. Keep it up, and I'm telling you, everything is going to click."

"I hope so."

"Hope is a good thing," I say. "Maybe the best of things, and no good thing ever dies."

He shakes his head, but both corners of his lips curve up enough to form a real smile. Not a little grin or a halfhearted smirk. But a real, honest-to-God, motherfucking beautiful smile.

"Okay, Andy," he agrees, showing me that he knows I'm quoting *The Shawshank Redemption* without saying anything else.

"Just getting you used to the idea of prison, Red."

He laughs and reaches out to grab my basket. "Are you done?"

I'm a little disappointed, not knowing if there's anything else to look forward to tonight after we leave here, but I can't even pretend to still be working on it. All that's left in my basket is a teaspoon of honey mustard and my dirty napkin.

I nod.

He grabs both of our baskets and walks them over to the trash before coming back to the table.

I follow him with my eyes the whole way, wondering how things could have changed this much in this amount of time.

After donning his jacket again, he takes my hand, helps me from the booth, and doesn't let go as we walk to the door.

I'm so lost in my butterflies, I don't even bother asking where we're going.

# THE *Billionaire* BOSS NEXT DOOR

---

Jackson Square is nearly deserted as we stroll through the park and stop by an artist right in front of Saint Louis Cathedral. In the coming weeks, Carnival and Mardi Gras will take over, but for now, it's relatively peaceful.

We're still holding hands.

I haven't uttered a word since we left the restaurant, nervous that my normal smartass chatter will ruin the mood.

Trent hasn't spoken either, but he doesn't seem nearly as anxious as me.

He holds up a finger to ask if I can hang out for a minute, and when I nod, he lets go of my hand.

I'm immediately disappointed in myself for not being argumentative.

Nevertheless, I wait silently as he goes up to the artist and asks him a question I can't hear. There's an exchange, the artist nods, and Trent comes back to me.

"Come on," he says. "Come over here."

I do as he says, but not without some questions. The fact that he arranged whatever this is without me is a red flag.

The artist is rearranging his display and getting out a new canvas, and before I know it, Trent is pushing me down onto a little red stool.

I shake my head and try to stand up, but he nods and holds me down.

"Greer, this is Ben. And he's going to paint you."

"Me? Why? Why not you?"

"Because."

"No, no, I think I'm good. I really have one of those faces that's better in real life than in a still shot."

Ben the artist laughs, and Trent smiles, ushering me back into the seat I've just vacated.

"Just enjoy it," he coaches. "Ben is a professional."

Ben nods, and other than telling them both to fuck off, I'm pretty sure I've run out of options.

Nervous and twitchy, I keep my seat and try to remember to breathe as Ben gets to work.

Trent doesn't stop smiling the entire time. But while Ben is watching me, and Trent is watching Ben, I'm watching Trent. His eyes are heated and appreciative, and my stomach turns over on itself.

Thirty minutes pass, and aside from Ben's painting, the only thing that's changed is how much sexual tension is in the air.

I am a live wire and Trent is water, and I'm afraid when we touch again, we just might explode.

Trent pays Ben and takes the painting before grabbing my hand with his free one and leading us back to our apartment building.

I don't think I've ever been this quiet in my entire life.

Trent leads us both to his door and stops in front of it, still holding on to my hand.

My heart gallops like a Thoroughbred on the racetrack.

Time seems to stand still as he sets down the painting, turns my back to his door, and presses me up against it. My breasts heave so hard in my dress, they come into my line of sight with every inhale.

His body is still in motion—which is good since I'm a statue—and he doesn't stop until we're pressed together from chest to hips. I'm an absolute wreck, but I'm also ecstatic, so I don't protest as his lips touch mine.

The contact is gentle at first, just a whisper of a kiss that I feel all the way from my vagina to my toes.

He hovers there, holding the light contact until I can't take it anymore.

My throat feels dry, my chest feels like it's going to explode, and my stomach has a low, burning ache I don't think will ever go away.

Faced with a deteriorating body, I work on fixing the only thing I can, and I lick my lips to moisten my mouth.

Of course, that means I don't just lick *my* lips. His are there too, pressed to mine, and the feel of running my tongue along the pair of them sends us into a frenzy.

I feel a tug on my hair as he digs a hand into it and pulls me closer, melding our bodies in such a way that I *know* I turn him on. His dick is hard and heavy, and dear God, being up against it like this is so much better than dreaming about it.

His tongue pushes into my mouth, curling around the tip of mine and exploring like Lewis and fucking Clark.

It's apt, seeing as we're in Louisiana, and my eyes start to roll back in my head.

A week ago, we were enemies. And now, we're this. We're speeding past friendship in a rocket designed to break the sound barrier, and it's all I can do to keep my footing.

*My God, he tastes good.*

Like mint and chocolate, his mouth is the most perfect flavor of ice cream.

It's only when I start to moan—loudly—that he pulls away and asks the only question that could bring me back to reality.

"Do you want to come in for a little while?"

His eyes are full of longing and persuasion, and I have to look away to get my bearings. The ceiling is just about my only option, and he leans forward to press his lips to the skin of my neck that's now exposed.

I quiver, but my survival instinct kicks in and helps me form a rational thought.

"Did you get a TV?" I ask.

His no is nothing more than a shake against my neck.

It takes everything in me—literally every fiber of my being—but I somehow give him a gentle push away.

He goes without protest, but he pulls his eyebrows together. "Greer?"

"I don't think I should. Come in, that is."

"Why?" he questions bluntly, not pulling any punches.

I do him the same courtesy. He deserves to know exactly what's on my mind and why it is.

Not some frilly excuse that confuses us both.

"Because you're my boss, Trent."

"You think I'm that kind of guy?" he asks, but his tone isn't defensive. Just curious and trying to understand. "That I'd hold our relationship against you?"

"I don't think you're any kind of guy, Trent. I don't even think it's a *kind of guy* who does things like that. I think it's someone who's hurting and lashing out." His eyes soften. "But up until about a week ago, I was still convinced I hated you, and I don't think all that well while experiencing whiplash."

He chuckles, the smile it creates sticking to his face long after the laughter leaves.

"This job means a lot to me. More than a lot. And I'd like to think I'm smart enough not to jeopardize everything I've worked for on an outcome I can't predict."

"You can't see the outcome of this?" he asks. "Really? I've got a crystal ball in the closet. We can fire it up—"

"Trent."

"I get it." My chest releases the tightness, and I'm relieved not to be having a heart attack, but when he takes another step back from me, separating our bodies completely, the emptiness I feel is almost crippling. "I don't *like* it…but I get it."

"I don't like it either," I admit. "But I think it's for the best."

His lips are warm and soft as he presses them to my cheek.

"Goodnight, Greer."

"Goodnight, Trent."

I move just enough that he can squeeze inside his door, and I stand there in the hallway long after he's gone.

I feel justified in my decision, and my mind says it's the right one.

My body disagrees.

If only it were simple.

# Chapter THIRTY

### Trent

My phone buzzes in my pocket and I pull it out to see a text from Cap.

*Cap: What the fuck happened with Susie Gimble the other night? She called me on a tirade, saying you stood her up.*

*Me: Something important came up.*

*Cap: So, you just didn't go?*

*Me: No, I went. I was there. But, like I said, something important came up.*

*Cap: If you tell me it was because of your fucking job, I will personally come down to New Orleans and murder you.*

*Me: I had to go see about a girl.*

*Cap: You fuck. You know* **Good Will Hunting** *makes me emotional.*

Normally, I'd use this opportunity to rile his apparent sensitive ass a bit, but I'm in the middle of something that deserves all of my time and attention. And more than that, something that I *want* to give all of my time and attention to.

I don't make a habit out of taking women on dates to lighting and fixture stores. The atmosphere isn't exactly romantic, and they don't let you drink wine while you shop.

But now that Greer has made it clear that dating is out of the picture, I've had to find ways to date her in secret.

And by "in secret," I mean without her knowing.

I know; it's complicated.

Still, it means I get to spend time with her—quality time I don't get when we're at work with everyone else—and she gets to be comfortable enough to feel secure in both her job and herself.

Really, it's a win for everyone. Especially for me.

"Trent," she calls now, from up on top of a ladder, head inside of a chandelier. "Are you even listening to me?"

The answer is no. No, I was not. Actually, I was enjoying the view that is Greer's mile-long legs and perfectly round ass.

But she doesn't need to know that.

"Yes."

"Well then, what do you think of this one?" she asks, her voice echoing inside of the chandelier. "It would be in the elevator lobby area of every floor. I think it goes with the marble inlay we decided to do."

On a real date, I'd probably just tell her I like whatever she likes. But since this is technically a work outing, I have to think like the boss. And not, like, a naughty porn type of boss either. A regular, this is an employee type of boss.

"What's the price?"

She pulls her head out of the light, cranes her neck to look directly at me, and makes big puppy-dog eyes.

I brace for the blow.

"Two thousand."

"Two thousand times twelve floors is twenty-four thousand. On elevator lobby lights."

I'm skeptical, and she can tell. She doesn't hesitate to start rationalizing. Something, I've learned, she's really good at when she wants to get her way.

"Yeah, but they set the tone. The rest of the floors have boring old recessed lights and sconces. This is your main expense on lighting. You know, except for the main reception chandelier, but let's not even focus on that now."

"How far outside of budget does it put us?"

"It doesn't," she shouts with glee, climbing down from the ladder slowly. I pay particularly close attention to her thighs as her skirt rides up a little. "It's outside of the lighting budget, specifically, but we came in under budget on the bathroom tiling. So, really, it's like it's all even Steven."

"How much under budget were we on the tiling?" I muse.

She frowns, caught. "Okay, so it was only twelve dollars under budget, but I bet we can come under on the furniture budget too. I have some really great contacts who will give us excellent discount pricing."

"What are the chances of you leaving this store without these lights?" I ask, cutting to the chase.

"None. You should give in now."

I sigh and look back to the light she's picked out. It's timeless and classy and *needs* to be in the Vanderturn New Orleans.

"Fine," I say, wagging a finger to put on a big show about giving in. "But don't say I never gave you anything."

She jumps up and down twice, and then, finally, when the excitement is too much, bounds forward to wrap her arms around me in a hug. I inhale directly from her hair.

It smells like lavender and citrus.

When she ends the hug and steps back, putting her professional face back on and moving on to the next line item, I use a little knowledge to balm the sting of the loss.

Knowledge, you see, that I told her the budget was half of what it was, meaning we really did come in below budget *and* I got a hug from the woman I now fantasize about endlessly.

It might make me a spineless prick, but these are desperate times. When I'm trying to play this many roles all at once, I have to be creative.

"So, what else do we need to look at?" I ask as she wanders the store, her eyes little sparkling saucers of wonder.

It's more than apparent that she's chosen the right career. It takes a special kind of person to find this much joy in fucking lighting.

"Bathroom faucets, bar faucet, showerheads, and bathroom lighting. I found everything else already, but these few things have been eluding me like a parolee with crack in his pocket."

I shake my head and grin. She is one of the funniest women—no, one of the funniest *people*, man or woman—I've ever met in my life.

She always has some kind of joke in her back pocket, and it's always effortless.

I swear, I could sell tickets for following her around for the day to people.

Once word of mouth spread, she'd be sold out well beyond her lifespan.

"Interesting analogy," I say, but what I really want to do is kiss her.

If I've replayed that kiss—our amazing fucking kiss outside my apartment door—in my head ten times, I've replayed it a thousand.

Fuck, two months ago, I never would've believed *not* kissing Greer would feel like a near impossible task, but here I am. Constantly wanting to kiss her.

"I don't go to sleep with a dictionary and thesaurus under my pillow for nothing, Junior," she teases, and it takes me a minute to even remember what in the fuck we were talking about. "You gotta be quick-witted and prolific if you want to make it in this world."

"Oh yeah?" I question with a smirk. "How am I doing?"

"Eh," she squints. "Your projected length of survival tapers off around a decade."

"Wow," I bark through a laugh. "That short, huh?"

"Short?" She shakes her head. "A decade is pretty good. Most people I know aren't likely to make it through the week."

"Well, then. I guess I'll take it as a compliment."

I follow her around the store for another three hours, watching and waiting as she picks through fixture after fixture and rejects ninety percent of them.

It's mindless and monotonous and loaded with stupid minutia and detail.

But it's also one of the best afternoons of my life.

I don't know what I'll come up with next, but I start plotting immediately. Secret dates with Greer are definitely going to become a regular thing.

# Chapter THIRTY-ONE

## Greer

"I feel weird coming with you and Quince. Don't you guys want to go alone instead of having a rickety—*though, otherwise fabulous*—third wheel?"

"No way!" Emory says, elbowing me out of the way to use the mirror in my bathroom to apply her fifth coat of mascara. "It's a party. You won't be third wheel-like at all. If anything, you might actually get to pick up a wheel of your own."

"Which perfectly summarizes the other part of this plan I hate. Thank you."

"Come on." She rolls her eyes. "You hardly go out. You eat, sleep, and breathe that fucking hotel. Lately, even your weekdays *and* weekends are suddenly filled with fixture and furniture shopping with your boss. Don't you want to let loose a little? Have fun?"

She's right. Recently, I've been doing a lot of hotel-focused shopping with Trent.

And the funny thing is, it doesn't feel like work at all. If anything, it's become the highlight of my week.

Last weekend, we hit up a flea market just outside of New Orleans so I could scavenge out some interesting vintage items to be used for décor. It rained the entire fucking time, but God, it was a blast.

I mean, I might've been fantasizing about kissing him nearly the entire drive there…and while we were there, and when we drove home, and then when we said goodnight outside our apartments, but that's my cross to bear.

Honestly, when it comes to spending time with Trent, not thinking about kissing him is the only true hardship.

Everything else is simply fun. Enjoyable. Time-of-my-life kind of moments.

But I'd never in a million years tell Emory that.

Because…*it's Emory*. The big ole sappy romantic who still cries whenever she watches *Dirty Dancing*.

"No," I eventually respond, snarkily. "I hate fun and happiness of any kind. I like to suffer and dwell, and when I'm really energetic, I leave myself little insults on my mirror in the morning."

"This is why you don't have a man, you know?"

"Really? I thought all-consuming negativity was attractive."

She elbows me right in the boob, and I wheeze.

*Son of a bitch.*

"Not the faux negativity, sasshole," she growls in my face. "The bitterness that lives in your every word." One manicured finger touches the tip of my nose to punctuate each syllable. It's *really* annoying.

I grab her finger and pull it away, slapping it with my other hand before I release it.

"Isn't the whole point to find someone who loves you for you?" I question with a raise of my brow. "I can't go around hiding my sarcasm. That's what makes me interesting."

"It's what makes you *intimidating*," she corrects.

"You know what, E? Maybe the world needs a few more *intimidating* women. Why the hell do I have to be meek to be attractive?"

She considers me for a second before squeezing my cheek like a patronizing grandma. "I guess you're right." Then she laughs. "It just means there are a lot fewer fish in the barrel to choose from."

"Good," I say. "I'd much rather my barrel have one goddamn superfish than a bunch of stupid ones."

Emory's smile is a little wonky, almost like she's proud of me in some profound way.

I've never felt the love of a mother's touch, but as Emory smooths a gentle hand across my cheek, I imagine that's what it must be like.

"All right, you superfish hussy. Finish getting ready. I promised Quincy we wouldn't be late."

She smacks my ass as she leaves the bathroom, and I wink. It's so cute that she thinks I give a shit about being on time for Quincy. The only people I answer to in a timely manner are my boss and the IRS.

I swipe on some eyeshadow and mascara and run a clear lip gloss over my lips with the tip of my finger.

After one last glance in the mirror, I flick off the light and walk back out through the bedroom, down the hall, and into the living room where Emory is waiting on the sofa, tapping her high-heeled foot pointedly.

"Jesus Christ, it's about time!" she says, jumping up from the couch and grabbing her purse.

I purse my lips and roll my eyes. "All I did was put on eyeshadow and mascara, you freak."

"Greer, you were in there for thirty minutes!" she shrieks.

*Really?*

I glance at the clock over my refrigerator, and it confirms she is, indeed, correct.

*Jesus. What is wrong with me? How do I waste so much time?*

I'm still considering the complexities of my time management when she grabs me by the hand and drags me to the door like a rag doll with only my keys and cell phone in tow.

"Wait!" I snap. "I don't even have my purse."

"Leave it," she says. "If it means getting out of this apartment right this minute, I'll buy all your drinks for the night!"

*Wow. I should play it this way more often.*

"What if they ID me?" I argue as she's closing my door and locking it with what I guess is her parents' key.

"Hate to break it to you, but no one will question that you're over twenty-one."

I flip her off for the insult, and a memory hits me right in the chest and makes me glance to Trent's door.

"Some people think I look younger than I am, you know. They've told me so."

She hoots. "Was it a guy?"

I frown. "Maybe."

"He probably just wanted to sleep with you."

I pull my eyebrows together, and my grateful, wistful expression at Trent's door turns into a glare.

It's not even fifteen seconds before I'm heading in that direction and pounding on it.

Emory's not pleased. "Greer! Fucking hell! We don't have time to visit your damn neighbors!"

Trent answers in under a minute, right when I'm winding up to kick the door with my foot.

His eyebrows jump to his hairline at my raised ankle-boot-covered foot, and immediately, he covers his nuts.

*Man, our relationship is weird.*

I put my foot down to lower the threat level but deepen my glare.

"Um, hello?" he says. "Have I done something wrong?"

"Do you want to sleep with me?" I ask without preamble or context.

His eyes nearly bug out of his head, and Emory smacks me in the arm with her purse.

"Uh…well…wait…what?" Trent stumbles as Emory yells, "What the hell is wrong with you?"

I gesture wildly, pointing to each of us like none of us knows who the other is. "He," I yell, "is the one who says I look younger than I am." I swing my finger over to Emory. "*You* are the one who says that means he wants to sleep with me."

I swing my finger back over to Trent and then wave it between his body and my own like a lunatic. "So, I'm asking. Do *you* want to sleep with *me?*"

Emory jumps between us like a referee and gets directly in Trent's face. "I'm begging you…do *not* answer that."

"Why the hell not?" I shout.

"Because if he says yes, you're going to flip out. And if he says no, you're going to slip into a depression for the rest of the night, thinking you're not attractive or something. And I'd really like to go to the party with the absolute sanest version of you possible, though that's really not saying much."

I flip her off again, and she shrugs.

I look back at Trent, and he lifts his shoulders too. Clearly, he's been convinced not to answer.

Emory thanks him and grabs my hand again, dragging me down the hall as he watches us go.

He even steps out of the doorway and crosses his arms over his chest, like he plans to keep watching until we're out of sight. It's not until we're almost to the stairwell that the urge overwhelms me.

"Why don't you come with us?"

It's out of my mouth in an instant, and surprisingly, I don't want to take it back.

Trent and I always have a good time together, and he's friends with Emory's boyfriend anyway. It works out perfectly. Plus, he seems to enjoy my penchant for snark. Not once does he ever ask me to tone it down.

*Unlike some people I know…cough, cough…Emory…cough…*

"Goddammit, can you do nothing in a timely fashion, woman?" my best friend questions with a high-pitched, incredibly annoyed squeal to her voice.

Trent uncrosses his arms to reveal his sculpted, white-button-down-covered chest as I break free from Emory and approach him again.

"You want me to come?" he asks, looking down at me from his

# THE *Billionaire* BOSS NEXT DOOR

place way up higher in the air. I don't know that I've ever paid attention to exactly how tall he is before now, but he's got to be six two. "Are you sure?"

"Why not?"

"Well, I was going to head back to work. And I am your boss. I might cramp your style."

"Pshh," I say with a wave of my hand. "Take the rest of the night off, you workaholic. And you're not just the boss. You're the billionaire boss next door, and…" I laugh as it hits me that what I'm about to say is true. "My friend." Who knows when it happened, but Trent is one of my friends.

*A friend you keep thinking about kissing…*

I shake off that annoying thought and focus on the facts. Trent laughs at my jokes, keeps up with my tangents, and doesn't flip out when I act like myself. All in all, I'd say he's one of the friendiest-friends I've ever had.

"All right," he agrees then. "Should I change?"

I'm just about to tell him he looks perfect when Emory butts in. "No. For the love of God, you should not change."

In the end, it's probably better that she answered first.

I smile, and Trent does the same.

"I'll just grab my wallet," he says, and I grab his arm with an evil smile before turning back to Emory.

"Don't bother. Emory says drinks are on her tonight."

Trent laughs. Em glares. I grin.

It's safe to say this is turning out to be a fantastic night.

# Chapter
# THIRTY-TWO

### Trent

Quincy's eyebrows are so high as the three of us walk into the party at Bourbon Bar, one of the busiest places on Bourbon Street, they make it look like he's got an actual hairline. And trust me, he hasn't had one of those in years.

Lights flash, music pounds, and a belly dancer prances by, followed by a college-aged girl with no bra and a neck full of beads. The crowd is a mix of working professionals and partying twentysomethings, and a few tourists snap pictures of everything neon like a cop at a crime scene.

Carnival is one of the busiest times of the year in this city, and from what I've seen, the most colorful. I've never been here during it as an adult, but thanks to the strange and unusual shit I've witnessed in New York, the learning curve when it comes to ignoring things is quick. Especially with Greer's ass swaying from side to side in front of me.

"Trent," Quince says after giving Emory a kiss and tucking her under his arm. "Funny how you said you were working when I invited you to this originally, and now, here you are. What in the world could have changed?"

Greer's gone straight to the bar with Emory's credit card without saying hello to Quince or anything to the rest of us, and I take the opportunity to be at least partially candid. I'm not going to go into any details, but I'm not in the mood to bullshit either.

# THE *Billionaire* BOSS NEXT DOOR

"I got a better invitation."

Quince's eyes lock on to Greer at the bar, and he laughs. She's wearing skintight jeans, a tight, low-cut blush-colored top, and little heeled boots. Her hair is down, her eyes are light, and I want to fuck her so badly, my cock hasn't softened since she asked me if I wanted to sleep with her at my door.

"I'll bet," he says, clearly seeing exactly what I see—one of the most beautiful, smartass women either one of us has ever met.

"I never thought we'd make it here," Emory interjects. "I could feel myself aging. I think I have new wrinkles."

Quincy is amused but wisely opposed. "Nope. No new wrinkles, baby. You're perfect."

"What a romantic," a voice I recognize says from behind me. I spin quickly, and I'm right, my ears are not deceiving me. "And by romantic," he adds, "I mean schmuck."

"Cap?" I question, "What the hell are you doing here?"

"Turn!" he yells, clearly already enjoying himself immensely. He claps my hand and pulls me in for a bro-hug before backing away again.

"I didn't get to mention," Quince interjects. "While I was waiting for you guys, I found another surprise guest."

"Oh my God," Emory says, her voice an unconcealed bucket of deep disappointment. "Why is this night turning into torture?"

Quincy laughs, obviously thinking her disgust for Cap is in jest. I'm pretty sure he's wrong, but I'm not going to be the one to let him in on it.

"What are you doing here?" I ask Caplin again, watching in my periphery as Greer weaves her way back toward us through the crowd.

"I had an emergency client meeting. Figured I'd stick around to have a little Carnival fun." He waggles his eyebrows, and the possibilities of what he might mean by that activates my gag reflex.

"Please," I say. "Spare me the details."

"Don't worry, my prudish friend," he says with an obnoxious

laugh. "The details have yet to commence." His attention pulls away from me and to the side, and his voice turns into the one that makes him sound like a creepy, horny bastard. "Though, it might be changing verrry soon."

I follow his gaze, and unfortunately, land right on Greer.

She looks up at me and smiles, and Cap steps right in between us. "Hello," he says, reaching out to help her with carrying her drinks. She's got three in her hand, presumably one for herself, one for me, and one for Emory, as Quincy was already working on a beer when we got here.

She laughs as he swipes two of them into each of his hands and still manages to touch her arm flirtatiously. "That looked like a heavy load for a pretty girl like you," he comments, and I roll my eyes.

I step around him to intervene, but Greer doesn't need me to. No, she's got him handled all on her own.

"Oh yeah?" she says.

"Yeah," he agrees.

Her eyes narrow. "Is this where you transition into offering to grace me with an altogether *different* heavy load? One you'll proudly dispense on my tits or right across my face?"

Quincy chokes on his beer and sprays it all over his girlfriend—who shrieks—while I step up to take the two drinks from Cap's hands. He's still standing there staring at Greer, his mouth gulping like a fish on land as he, most likely, falls in love.

"Woman, what is your name, and where have you been all my life?" he asks with a hand to his chest. I elbow him out of the way and discreetly shuffle Greer to my side as she answers.

"Greer Hudson, and I've lived in New Orleans since the day I was born."

Seemingly waking up from his spell, he does a double take, looking from her to me and back again as he confirms, "Greer Hudson?"

"That's me." She smiles. "My grandfather named me after Greer Garson, his absolute favorite actress."

## THE *Billionaire* BOSS NEXT DOOR

"You're even better than expected," Cap says while I'm busy pondering the little nugget of information about herself she's just given so freely.

"I'm sorry," Greer responds. "It seems you know me, but I have no idea who you are."

Caplin offers a hand and a beaming smile. "Caplin Hawkins. Lawyer and friend to both of these bozos."

He jerks a thumb back and forth between Quincy and me, and Emory jumps in with a comment of her own. "And the most annoying human being on earth."

Greer laughs. "I thought that was me?"

Emory shakes her head and grabs the drink clearly meant for her out of my hand. "I know. So did I. Apparently, the world is full of all kinds of surprises."

I'm left with a beer, and though it's not my preferred drink, it's a hell of a lot better than most of the other options she could have chosen at random. Including the mystery wine Greer is taking sips of and the fruity-looking cocktail Emory just procured.

The conversation only devolves from there.

On the one hand, it's extremely disappointing not to have the alone time with Greer I was expecting. But on the other, it's really great to have a night out with her and my friends.

I haven't done anything like this since before my mom was diagnosed, and it feels good to kick back and have a good time with people who know me.

As an added bonus, Greer and Caplin's banter is among the best I've ever witnessed.

I was jealous at first. Almost wildly so, but the more the night's gone on, the more and more obvious it is what a disaster they'd be if they ever tried to get together.

"No!" Greer yells now, bouncing on the seat next to me and climbing up onto her knees to make herself seem bigger. I'm not sure if she thinks it'll make her argument more convincing or what, but it's fucking adorable. "*Married at First Sight* is the one where they get married without knowing the other person. *90 Day Fiancé* is where they mail-order brides and grooms."

Clearly, they're arguing over groundbreakingly important things.

"What's the difference?" Caplin snorts. "Neither one of them knows anything about the person they're marrying. And for what? Just so they can say they have some shitty piece of paper?"

"*Ha!*" Greer shrieks. "It's obvious you don't watch them. You're just another man who's cynical about marriage. How motherfucking original."

I wince at her volume, putting a hand over my ear closest to her to protect my hearing, but I laugh at her impassioned debate about reality TV.

Caplin sits back, officially frustrated. "I give up."

"Thank God," Emory mutters, dropping her head into her hands while Greer does a victory dance beside me. "Please, baby Jesus, can we have some fun now?"

Greer nods and Caplin shrugs. Quincy throws both of his hands up in the air to shout "Hallelujah!"

I hold out a hand to help Greer up, and she takes it without hesitation. Caplin takes notice, raising an eyebrow at me in question, but I ignore him completely.

There's no fucking way I'm getting into the convoluted details of all this shit with him now. I've already wasted enough of my time with Greer tonight listening to him talk.

As we leave the party and walk down Bourbon Street, the excitement of Carnival dances on all around us. It's still a little while until actual Mardi Gras, but it's safe to say the partying that comes along with it is in full swing.

People hang out on balconies and toss beads down to passersby, and the music booms loudly from every restaurant and bar we pass.

Confetti from the parade earlier today litters the streets, and you can't go five feet without bumping into another body.

The crowds and chaos are everything I hate about being in New Orleans, and yet, I'm having the time of my life.

And I have a feeling it's mostly because Greer is walking next to me, holding my hand.

I take the opportunity as we stroll along to get in some private conversation with her. Her eyes are everywhere, taking in everything like a kid in a candy store for the first time.

"Have you ever celebrated Mardi Gras on Bourbon Street before?"

She shakes her head and laughs. "Nope. Thirty-three years in this city, and I've never done it."

"Why not?"

She shrugs. "I don't know. I guess it was just never the right time. It wasn't my grandfather's thing, and it's certainly not my brother's. We usually do low-key dinners together, and that's about it. His idea of excitement is changing up his usual brand of socks."

My chuckle echoes off the building next to us and lingers. "People could probably say the same about me."

She laughs. "You like a certain kind of sock, huh?"

"Doesn't everyone?"

She shakes her head and laughs. "I put on whatever socks come out of the drawer first. I usually don't even take the time to match them when I pull them out of the laundry."

"Blasphemy," I breathe dramatically.

We're both silent for a minute before she speaks again. This time, her voice is soft, and I have to listen harder to hear all the words. "You know, if you wanted to ask me about my parents now… I'd tell you."

I smile and squeeze her hand. "And I figured when you were ready to tell me, I wouldn't have to ask."

We walk almost another block in silence, our friends running, bouncing, and clowning loudly in front of us before she speaks again. "They died in a car accident. One last date night before they had another kid to take care of. My brother was home with a babysitter, and my mom was eight months pregnant with me. Apparently, they saved me, but they couldn't do anything for them."

"Greer," I whisper.

She shakes her head and shrugs. "I never met them. I wish I had, but in a way, it helps. I don't really know what I'm missing, you know?"

I nod because it's all I can do. I can't speak, and I can't change it, no matter how much I wish I could.

"My grandfather and my brother raised me."

"Is your grandfather still alive?"

She shakes her head. "He passed away ten years ago."

"I'm sorry."

"So am I. But it doesn't matter how much we want them to, no one lives forever. I'm just lucky to have had him be such a big part of my life while he was here."

"Thanks for sharing with me," I say. "I feel privileged."

She smiles then, and my heart swells two sizes. "You listened to what I said, and you put in the effort. You more than earned it."

In this moment, I'm certain that the effort I'm willing to put in when it comes to Greer is both effortless and infinite in its supply. And God do I want to be the kind of man who not only earns her trust and her time and her laughs and her smiles and all of the good, amazing things that are Greer, but I want to be the kind of man who is deserving of her, too.

# Chapter THIRTY-THREE

## Greer

My hand shakes as I apply the lipstick Emory lent me. My hair is professionally blown out, my dress may as well be shrink-wrapped, and my toes are crammed into a pair of wholly uncomfortable but fabulous shoes.

And my stomach feels like its contents might make a reappearance and ruin it all at any moment.

When Trent first invited me to the Mardi Gras ball for the city, I assumed I was an easy plus one for a mandatory function. Ever since the fiasco with the permits, he's done his best to stay on the good side of the city—especially the mayor.

Even though the inspector found everything in order when he came out to the site and the decision was reversed, the whole ordeal put the entire project on the city's radar. The city council even started to make rumblings that the Vanderturn New Orleans is a cookie-cutter establishment being developed by money-hungry billionaires with no real interest in the city or its history.

But Trent has gone out of his way to prove their assumptions false, including accepting an invitation to the Mardi Gras ball with enthusiasm and grace.

Secretly, I'm impressed by the way he's handled it all.

And after nearly two full months of hating me, then getting to know me, *and then*, forming a friendship, Trent and I have reached a level of comfort we both enjoy. On Tuesdays, he comes over to watch

*Game of Games* with me, and at least three nights a week, we have dinner together.

We've fallen into a routine of sorts, and while it's not exactly noteworthy stuff, I thought we'd both come to enjoy it.

But as I found out a week ago when he was asking me to attend the ball with him, that's not entirely the case.

Trent, it seems, had been biding his time, waiting for something.

Something, if I'm honest, I've thought a lot about too but have been way too scared to even consider.

*"The thing is, I want this to be a real date,"* he said after I agreed to go.

*"Trent—"*

*"I want a chance, Greer. One chance to show you what it could be like if you let it happen. If you're still convinced it's not a good idea afterward, I'll leave it alone. You have my word."*

Obviously, right or wrong, I agreed.

And now I'm so scared, I think I might pass out. Though, part of that might be the python-like fit of my dress. Black velvet with a V neck, a scoop back, and a built-in corset, it's everything I'd imagine a Mardi Gras dress should be.

But there's a lot more to this than good formal wear, an expensive dinner, and a good time with the most attractive man I've ever known.

He's my *boss*.

The hotel is my livelihood.

And like some kind of miracle, we've found an amazing rhythm that suits us. We collaborate, we compromise, and maybe most importantly, we treat one another with respect.

In fact, Trent treats the entire team that way now, and everyone is happy and healthy.

Sarah's been able to stop taking Xanax, and George got his scoliosis diagnosis reversed.

I'm kidding, obviously, but, all in all, it's been a month of milestones, and I'm *terrified* that if Trent and I take this to the next level

# THE *Billionaire* BOSS NEXT DOOR

and don't work out, the backslide will be more than any of us can handle.

Fed up with my overanalyzing, I shut off the light to my bathroom without looking into the mirror again and head straight for my living room.

I look to the wall we share one last time, ready to get this show on the road by just meeting him at his door, when music starts to play from his apartment—for the first time *ever*.

I swear, even after all this time, and the acquisition of a TV, Trent Turner makes about the same noise as a church mouse.

But *this*…this is loud.

I walk closer, slowly, listening as the song builds and builds and then bleeds into the chorus.

"In Your Eyes" by Peter Gabriel.

Without thought, my feet start to move, through my living room, out the door, and over to the place where his door should be.

Only, instead, his door is open, and there, in the center of the living room, is Trent, fully dressed and pressed in his tux and finery, holding an 80s style boombox over his head and doing a very impressive John Cusack.

Oh my God.

"*Say Anything* is one of my favorite movies," I whisper.

It doesn't matter that the music is blaring; somehow, he still hears me.

"I knew it would be."

I have to strain my voice to say something back over the music. "That's either really sweet or really creepy."

He lowers the boombox from above his head, turns down the volume, and smirks. "Which one are you gonna go with?"

I scan the room dramatically, bending at the waist and stooping down to look on the shelves of his furniture. When I'm done, I look him in the eye again and put my hands to my hips. "Well, I see no shrines to my womanhood, containers of teeth, bags of hair, or little glass jars filled with questionable preserves, so I'll give you the benefit of the doubt and say sweet."

"I keep all of that stuff in my bedroom."

His snark makes me laugh. It's obviously very delicate and in no way contains a snort.

I check the time on my fancy watch—one that belonged to my mother—that I only wear on special occasions and gasp. "Oh my God, I'm sorry I'm so late. Didn't you say the ball starts at seven thirty?"

He chuckles, puts the boombox on the kitchen island, and grabs his keys, wallet, and cell phone from the surface.

By the time he makes it to me and places one, perfectly tender kiss on my cheek, I've drawn my eyebrows together.

"Trent?" I ask as he spins me toward the door and puts gentle pressure on the small of my back.

We're out in the hall, locking up behind ourselves when he finally answers. "I told you it was seven thirty, but it's really eight thirty. We'll be on time."

Someone else might be offended at his assumption, but I am relieved. My voice is shrill as I congratulate him on his success. "Yes! *Thank you*! I've been telling Emory for years to con me if she wants me to be on time! Well done, you!"

His chuckle makes his smile seem especially radiant, and I get lost in it pretty damn easily.

If it weren't for the gentle guidance he gives my body with the palm of his hand, I'd stand there and stare at him all night.

Instead of taking the stairs as usual, he leads me around the corner and pushes the call button for the elevator. My feet are thankful.

"So, is there anything I should know?"

"What do you mean?" he asks.

"You know, about tonight. Any particular way I should behave? Any topics I should avoid?"

"You think I invited you so you would have to pretend to be

something you're not?" He shakes his head. "Be yourself. I have faith that you'll know what would be taking it too far and what wouldn't be."

I snort. While I appreciate his faith in me tremendously, I'm not sure it's well placed. "Uh…I'm not known for great decision-making in social situations. I understand the sentiment, but I'm not sure you're making the smartest business decision."

The elevator arrives with a ding, opening its doors and beckoning us to step inside. I'm all ready to comply when Trent pulls me back, turns me toward him, and takes hold of both of my hands.

The elevator closes and leaves, and a hive of very busy bees breaks out in my stomach.

"Uh, shouldn't we have—"

"Greer," Trent says, giving my hands a gentle tug to get me to look at him instead of the elevator. When I do, his face is serious and so handsome, it actually hurts to look at him.

Strong jaw, chiseled cheeks, and majestic green eyes are seemingly my weakness.

"Attending the ball *is* about business. You're right. A business you just so happen to be passionate and knowledgeable about and heavily involved in. But *tonight*, the whole experience is about you and me on a date. It's the part I care about more, and the part I'm choosing to focus on. The ball is just the backdrop."

"Is it just me, or have you, like, taken a crash course in swooniness in the last twenty-four hours?"

He pushes the button for the elevator again, leaning away from me momentarily, only to come back and wrap an arm around my waist.

I'm shivering in all my feels, but he seems perfectly composed.

"Nope, no advanced schooling. You're just not used to me as a date."

"Well, shit. If I'd known dating made you this nice, I would have done it from the beginning."

His lips brush the shell of my ear, and he whispers, "It wouldn't have worked."

"Why?" I ask, the anticipation and excitement of this newfound feeling he's giving me making my skin feel electric.

"Because I thought I hated you then."

I laugh. "You're right."

He nods, and then I bring the hammer down because I'm ruthless and inappropriate and, despite what he seems to think, I have trouble not ruining a moment.

"Except, I didn't just *think* I hated you. I did. I've got the voodoo doll to prove it."

"So that's why, way back in January, I had to ingest an unnecessary amount of TUMS and Pepto Bismol." He quirks an adorable brow, and I giggle.

"Okay, so maybe I don't have a voodoo doll, but I can't deny I was tempted."

Trent just grins. "Just so we're clear, I know I had moments of being a real dick, but—"

"*A lot* of moments," I correct.

"Yeah," he agrees. "Okay. But you're weren't a peach either, honey."

I act affronted, and he just laughs and wraps his arm around me tighter as he leads me into the elevator cart. "It's okay, though," he adds and hits the button for the lobby. "Because all that sass and sarcasm are two of my favorite things about you."

Two of his favorite things about me?

As in, he has several favorite things about me.

*Goddamn.* Date Trent is just dropping swoon bombs all over the fucking place.

*Fingers and toes crossed I don't spontaneously combust before I get to enjoy more of this irresistible guy.*

# THE *Billionaire* BOSS NEXT DOOR

Velvet drapes and flower waterfalls cover the walls of Gallier Hall, this year's location for the mayor's Mardi Gras ball, and candlelit tables dot the space of the room like stars.

My eyes flick left and right and up and down, completely unable to latch on to any one thing, there's so much going on.

Performers dance in synchronization in the corner below aerial silks, and I wonder if they've just finished their routine or are about to get started.

Trent's hand is warm in mine, and as a bonus, he hasn't made the barest mention of how sweaty mine has gotten.

I don't know if it's my nerves or the fact that I'm just not used to holding hands with someone for extended periods of time, but my glands seem to be in overdrive.

"Is it hot in here?" I ask a little manically.

Trent smiles at my panic, which just seems to make me panic more.

"No? Just me? Are you seriously not sweating at all?" I ask, wiping at my brow with my free hand.

Trent watches me closely for only a moment before pulling me close and whispering in my ear. "Just relax," he soothes. "Have fun. I promise you don't need to be this worked up. In fact, why don't I get you settled at our table and then go get you a drink?"

I'm shaking my head before he can finish speaking. If he leaves me alone, sedentary at our table, I will die a quick but painfully awkward death. I can feel it.

No, I need to be moving.

"Why don't you go schmooze a little, and I'll go get us drinks," I suggest instead. "It'll give me something to do and a little time to calm down before I have to talk to anyone."

He agrees easily enough—and by easily enough, I mean he gives in when I threaten to throw a shitfit in the middle of the room like a Pixy-Stix-fueled toddler—and leaves me to go say hello to some of the other hotel owners he knows.

When I get in line for the bar, I make sure to pay special attention to the bartender's name—and gender—and paste a huge smile on my face.

This night will require steady drinks, and in the name of making that possible, I'm going to be this bartender's favorite goddamn person if it kills me.

"Hi," I say with a little flirtation, using the fact that this one is really a man to my advantage. He smiles back and glances down at my heaving bosom, and I know I'm in business. "I'll take a Chardonnay—big glass," I emphasize, "And a...a..."

Well, *fuck*. Why in the hell didn't I ask Trent what he wants to drink? Am I the most terrible date in the universe?

The longer I pause, and the rowdier the alcohol-thirsty crowd behind me gets, the more my carefully placed flirtation and big breasts start to wear off.

Frankly, if I don't get something out soon, I'm pretty sure they're going to end up calling an ambulance for me because of signs of a stroke, so I spit out the first thing that comes to mind and move on with my life.

"An old-fashioned."

It's fancy and niche and seems appropriate for the venue, if nothing else.

If Trent hates it, he'll only have himself to blame for not giving me something specific to order.

When I find Trent with a group of people I don't know, but only can assume are important, I'm too focused on the trauma from the bar to worry about anything else.

He takes his drink with gratitude as I hand it to him, and then after taking a quick sip, smiles down at me.

"How did you know I like old-fashioneds?" he asks.

I guffaw. "I didn't. I picked the first thing that came to mind when everyone behind me started to take out their pitchforks and yell. There's a real problem with mob mentality in this country. It was like a—"

Cutting me off with a squeeze of my hip, Trent turns me toward the group we're standing with and introduces me. "This is my date, Greer Hudson." They all nod hello, but their eyes are wide. Probably from the hot mess they've just overheard.

"Greer, this is the mayor, her husband, and a few members of the royal court."

"The royal court?"

"Appointing royalty is a Mardi Gras ball tradition," he explains. "Our mayor is the queen, her husband the king, and Jules, Bonee, and Ty are all local business owners and members of the royal court."

The mayor's face is kind as she asks, "Are you new to New Orleans, dear?"

I consider lying because that'd probably sound better than the truth, given my lack of knowledge of Mardi Gras, but I'd never be able to support it with any details. This is the only place I've ever lived—the only place I've ever really known.

I laugh a little—self-deprecation ripe in the tone. "No, ma'am. I've lived in New Orleans all my life. My brother, Heath, owns Coastal Crepes."

Her eyes light up.

"On St. Phillip Street?"

"Yes, ma'am. It used to be my grandfather's."

"I love that place! Best crepes I've ever tasted, sweet and savory."

"Thank you," I say, and I feel my cheeks blush a little.

Trent's eyes are wide as he turns to face me. "Your family owns Coastal Crepes?"

I nod.

I don't know what he's thinking because he doesn't say anything else, but I don't have time to worry about it because the *mayor* is talking to me again.

"Next year, we need to make sure your brother gets an invitation to the ball too. That's one of my favorite local businesses, and he does a fabulous job of running it."

"Thank you. That's the kind of news that could make him call off the hit man."

"I'm sorry?" she asks, and the Secret Service-looking guys at her back step a little closer. Trent's hand convulses in mine.

*Oh shit.*

"No, no, ma'am," I mumble in a panic. "Not you. He'd never take out a hit on you. I meant on me. Kid sister and all. Lots of trouble." I point to the specific location of my problem. "I have a big mouth."

Trent steps in before I can sink our ship completely, but I've got to tell you, we're definitely taking on water.

"She's a jokester. Her brother is really proud of everything she's achieved. We all are. You know, she's a business owner too. Her design firm, Hudson Designs, is doing all the work for the Vanderturn New Orleans."

"That's fantastic," the mayor says, but she's shuffling her feet discreetly in the other direction. "Well, if you'll excuse me, I've got a lot of people to mingle with."

"Of course," I agree as she turns to go.

She doesn't ask me to leave, but I'm pretty sure my invitation to next year's ball is going to get lost in the mail.

"Oh my God," I say when the whole group has disappeared. "Didn't I tell you I would mess this up?"

Trent laughs and pulls me in for a hug. The smell of his cologne is better than anything I've ever experienced in my entire life, hands down.

I have never smelled a better-smelling human.

"It's fine. She thought you were funny."

"She thinks I'm a threat to national security."

"Maybe," he teases, and I pull back from his hold enough to glare. "But you're the most beautiful terrorist I've ever seen."

"That's not funny at all, Junior."

"It is. You can't see it now, but you will later, trust me."

"Can we just drink and overeat on carbs now, please?" I beg. "I need something I'm good at. And I'm a world champion at stuffing my face."

He places a soft kiss to my lips—just enough to wake my shit up. *Hello, we're on a date, and your vagina, despite low usage, is still very much aware of how this works.*

"We can eat and drink as much as you want. But first, I'd really like to dance."

"Dance?" I question. "You dance?"

"With you?" he clarifies. "Definitely. With you, I dance all night."

---

With teasing and taunting and flirty little kisses, Trent and I spent the rest of the Mardi Gras ball in our own little world. He laughed at my jokes and played with my hair, and by the end of the night, even I thought I was the most beautiful woman in the room.

As a boss, Trent Turner is a formidable man. As a neighbor, he's almost frighteningly quiet and easy to get along with, and as a friend, he's a funny match for my banter and open to a good time.

But as a date…he is on a whole other level. He charms. He swoons. He fucking sweeps you off your feet and catches you perfectly with a tight grip on your hand and a winning smile.

He kisses you when he should and gives you space when you need it, and not once did he try to get me to change something about myself.

It was the best fucking date I've ever had in my life.

We danced. We drank. We talked. We laughed ourselves silly. And now, we're in an Uber, heading back to our building.

Trent's hand is on my thigh, and his long fingers gently massage my skin through my dress.

It's such a simple gesture. A light touch. A little massage. But fuck, it's slowly driving me insane. All I can think about is his fingers sliding under my dress and touching me between my thighs.

I am achy and throbbing, and it feels like sexual tension has been building between us for an eternity.

Even when we were hating each other, it was there, an undeniable pull, an irresistible attraction. And now, tonight, after experiencing what it's like to go on a date with Trent, I feel my mind spinning with all sorts of possibilities of how I want this night to go.

Fuck, I haven't felt this kind of pull since that New Year's Eve party.

And, honestly, even that experience with the man wearing the Walt mask doesn't come close to what I'm feeling right now.

I need him.

I want him.

And hell's bells, I don't want it to end with a simple kiss goodnight outside our doors.

When the Uber pulls up to our building, Trent helps me out of the car, and hand in hand, we head through the entrance, past the lobby, and onto the elevator.

The cart is silent as we step on, and when the doors begin to shut, I have the insane urge to mold my body to his and kiss that perfect mouth of his so hard it might bruise.

I stare down at my heels and try to calm my near-panting breaths.

But the feel of Trent's fingers underneath my chin urge my eyes to his. He is mere inches from me now, his chest just barely brushing against mine, and he stares down at me with an intensity that has my heart kicking up in a fast and unsteady rhythm.

"Greer," he whispers my name like a fucking prayer, and a shiver rolls up my spine.

And before I can respond, before I can tell him I want to spend the night with him, he presses his mouth to mine in a hard and deep kiss.

I moan, and he slips his tongue inside my mouth.

*Fuck. He tastes good. He always tastes good.*

We kiss until we're breathless.

# THE *Billionaire* BOSS NEXT DOOR

We kiss until I'm completely lost in him.

We kiss until the elevator rides up and down the floors of our building more times than I can comprehend.

"Fuck, Greer, I need you," he whispers against my mouth. "Come home with me."

"Yes." I whimper my agreement, and it spurs a sexy as fuck groan from his lungs that I swear I can feel all the way to my fucking toes.

He doesn't waste any time after that, lifting me up by my ass and wrapping my legs around his waist, and walking us off the elevator.

Fuck if I really even know what's happening. I'm too focused on kissing him.

I never want to not be kissing him.

I press my hips to his, and he somehow manages to unlock his apartment door.

I moan against his mouth, and before I know it, we're inside.

And then we lose ourselves to each other. We're all hands and lips and teeth and tongues. We're touching and kissing and panting, and it's like we both want to be doing all of the things, all at the same time.

He tosses me down onto his bed with a sexy ease that makes my stomach spasm.

He steps forward and puts a purposeful hand to the back of my dress.

My breath catches in my throat, and out of desperation, I start to pant. My mind feels foggy but euphoric, and the zipper of my dress isn't even halfway down yet.

"Trent," I gasp, grabbing at his hair as he kisses his way across my breasts, drags the velvet fabric down with his teeth, and closes his mouth tightly over my nipple.

I arch my back and bicycle my feet on the floor, trying to find some kind of metaphorical stability for my spinning head.

I'd say I don't know how we got here, panting and moaning and half naked on the bed, but I do.

I know *so hard*.

You can't have this much attraction, this much sexual tension, between two people without a fucking explosion.

And that's what this is right now. The fucking explosion.

I may be a strong, independent, goal-oriented woman who doesn't need a man, but I need this one.

I need him bad.

My feet give up the fight to find the floor and defer to my legs as they clamp around his hips and pull him closer.

His weight feels delicious and decadent on top of me, and his lips are exploring me so thoroughly, it feels like they're all over, all at once.

"Trent," I moan, wrapping my arms around his shoulders and pulling him closer.

He fights it, though, pulling the straps of my dress off my shoulders and sliding it down my body first.

When he comes back, bare chest against my chest, I nearly pass out from the warmth of it.

"Trent," I call, but he ignores me, kissing my neck with suction just light enough that it won't leave a mark.

I pant his name again, wanting his lips, wanting his eyes, *wanting him inside me* so bad it hurts. But he continues to ignore me, and you could say that was the moment that broke the vagina's patience.

I grab his hair and pull, and he groans, but when I'm done, his eyes are on mine and his attention is avid.

"Stop fucking around and slide your dick inside of me."

His laugh is raucous as he shakes his head, so I bump him to get his attention again, adding a little slap to his ass for good measure.

"I'm serious."

"And I'm serious about taking my time," he challenges.

"Bone me right now," I order. "Take out your hammer and start nailing some wood."

"Greer—"

"Do it! Put your P in my V and—"

## THE *Billionaire* BOSS NEXT DOOR

"Lie back," he cuts me off to order. And suddenly, Date Trent and Boss Trent have formed some sort of super Dom sex mix, and I'm powerless. I am at his command, a willing and able submissive. "I'm going to eat your pussy first, and I'm going to enjoy it. Don't even bother trying to talk me out of it."

"Yes, sir," I say, and he smirks.

"Is this what it takes to get you to follow orders?"

"Ordering me to accept your sexual pleasure?" I say with a laugh. "Yes. Yes, it is."

"I'll have to remember that at the office."

"We don't have an office," I scoff.

"We should get one."

"Less talk, more action, *sir*."

He winks, pulls my panties down my legs, and gets right to work. And holy hell, is he a dedicated worker.

Tongue swirls, sucking kisses, touches, and tickles—he uses it all to work me into a frenzy so hard I'm screaming. I come with his mouth and I come with his cock, and when we're done, I know without a doubt, it's the most noise his apartment has ever created.

# Chapter THIRTY-FOUR

**Trent**

I wake up at exactly six a.m. But not for the reason of work or responsibilities.

I wake up because of Greer.

She is here, in my apartment, in my bed, gloriously naked and sleeping peacefully beside me.

Her eyes are closed, her long lashes fan out across her cheeks, and her lips showcase the hint of a smile. And soft, even breaths encourage her breasts to move up and down gently.

Fuck, she's a glorious sight.

The best thing I've seen in…forever. And the thought of popping this heavenly bubble and heading into a day filled with work sounds horrible.

Quietly, I slide out of bed, toss on a pair of boxer briefs, and head into the kitchen to make some coffee.

Normally, this is the part of the day where I go through emails on my phone and sift through what needs to get accomplished for the day. I obsess over what's been done at the hotel and what still needs to be done and how much time is left to accomplish it all.

But while the coffee brews, I'm lost in thoughts about the sleeping angel in my bed.

I think about her loud, addictive laugh. Her witty sarcasm. The way her beautiful blue eyes look when she's consumed with pleasure. I even think about the fact that she talked about a fucking hit man with the mayor.

# THE *Billionaire* BOSS NEXT DOOR

*Goddamn, she's something.*

Once a fresh cup of coffee is in my hands, I come to a conclusion—I'm not popping this bubble today.

It might be a weekday and both Greer and I are due into work.

But I'm the fucking boss, and I've decided we're going to act like it's a goddamn Saturday.

We're going to stay in my apartment. In my bed. All fucking day. And I'm going to spend hours upon hours savoring the way she feels and tastes and moans.

Yeah. That's exactly what we're going to do today.

Without hesitation, I grab my phone off the kitchen counter and update the team via text.

**Me: Greer Hudson and I will be working off-site today. Call me if any issues arrive.**

The instant I hit send, I feel…*relief.*

And then, I remember that Greer is in my bed. Beautiful and bare.

It doesn't take long before I'm setting my coffee on the counter and heading back into my bedroom. I move onto the bed, pull the blankets off Greer's body, and settle myself between her now-spread legs, and I just look at her.

*Fuck, this is the most perfect pussy I've ever seen.*

Willpower gone, I slide my tongue against her and place one long lick against that perfect pussy of hers.

She stirs a little but doesn't wake, and I continue on with my important business.

My initial exploration of her with my mouth is lazy and slow and…savory.

But the mere taste of her on my tongue becomes too much to bear.

My cock hardens, and I lose myself. Tasting her. Eating and

sucking at her. It's like I'm a man starved and she is the only item on the menu that will satisfy me.

*Goddamn, she tastes good.*

She moans and her thighs start to shake, and it's then that she wakes up.

"Holy shit," she whimpers. "Oh my God."

"Ignore me," I whisper against her with a smile I can't hide. "Just go back to sleep."

"I...*Oh God*...I-I think sleep is pretty much impossible right now."

She arches her back and her supple breasts push forward, and I enjoy the fucking view of her losing herself to pleasure.

And she does lose herself. Legs shaking, breaths panting, incomprehensible moans escaping her lungs. The climax rolls through her body, and her blue eyes do that amazing thing where they glaze over and shine brighter at the same time.

*Fuck. I could spend the rest of my life making this woman feel good.*

Once her breaths slow and her muscles relax, I slide up her body and press a soft kiss to her cheeks, her lips, her nose, her neck. Pretty much everywhere my lips can reach.

"Good morning, Greer."

"Yeah." She snorts. "Talk about some morning."

I grin down at her. "We're not going to work today."

"Huh?"

"We're working off-site. I've already updated the team."

"Oh," she responds, and her lips form a perfect little O. "Where do we have to go?"

"Nowhere."

"Huh?" she asks and scrunches up her adorable nose.

"This is where we're working today. Right here." I waggle my brows. "In my bed."

"I'm sorry...what?"

"We have a lot to accomplish here," I whisper into her ear and reach down to slide my finger inside of her.

"We do?" she asks, and a little moan leaves her lips.

"We do."

I slip my finger out of her, and she whimpers her annoyance. But that annoyance turns to hip-gyrating arousal when I rub the tip of my cock against her clit.

"Fuck," she moans and wraps her thighs around my hips. "I hope you sliding inside me is one of the things on today's list."

"Oh, don't worry, honey," I say with a little smirk and just barely push the tip of my shaft inside her. "That's at the very top of our list."

The feel of her pussy as it touches my bare cock is almost more than I can handle.

*Thank Jesus and all of his disciples for Greer's perfect pussy and the fact that she's on birth control.*

"Well, thank fuck for that!" she cheers, and I use that moment to slide all the way home.

And Greer's delicious moans follow me the entire way.

*Yeah. Today is going to be a fan-fucking-tastic day.*

# Chapter THIRTY-FIVE

## Greer

My head pounds. Not, I should note, from an actual hangover involving too much alcohol, but simply from being in my thirties and staying awake past midnight.

I swear, the body switches off all cooperative function when you enter your third decade, and three years in, my suffering is only magnified.

I cover my eyes to block out all the sunlight and reach to the side of my bed to switch off my alarm.

Only, for some reason, I don't feel my nightstand at all, but the hard yet supple flesh of a warm, naked body.

*What am I doing on the wrong side of the bed?*

*And why does the empty spot on my bed feel like a human?*

I peek one eye open, squinting through the crack of my fingers to find a navy-blue wall and gray drapes. It's masculine and decorated and looks nothing like the plain white box I'm still living in.

Ironic, I suppose, since I'm an interior designer, but I've been really fucking busy.

Finally, after a minute of start-up time, my brain starts to run at full function, and I immediately remember where I am.

In fact, now that I do, I can't even believe there was a scant moment I didn't.

Trent Turner—the billionaire boss next door—and I...had sex last night.

And all day yesterday.

*And* even the night before that.

Basically, for the past twenty-four hours, we've been exploring each other until we can't keep our fucking eyes open.

Wild, loud, *sometimes dirty* sex that I can still feel between my legs.

The craziest part of it, though, is that it didn't feel crazy.

It felt right and easy, and simply…*amazing*.

His bedroom has been our home, and the painting Ben made of me in Jackson Square leans against the wall on top of his nightstand.

When I finally noticed it during a break from our sex yesterday, I took the opportunity to tease Trent about the fact that he *does* have a shrine to me.

I turn to face him, studying the lines of his face. He's still asleep, and all the hard edges have rounded off into softness.

He looks tender and peaceful, and without the hypnotizing spell of his open green eyes, I can almost convince myself I stand some sort of chance against him.

But only almost.

I reach out slowly, carefully, and run the knuckles of my right hand over the tiny stubble that's formed on his cheek overnight.

His hair is a mess, but I don't think he's ever looked more perfect.

Between one blink and the next, he opens his eyes and smiles.

"Good morning," he says softly. Evidently, it doesn't take his brain any time at all to boot up.

"Good morning," I say with a smile. "I guess we're going to have to actually go in to work today, huh?"

"You trying to get your boss to let you play hooky again?" He smirks like the devil, and I snort.

"God, I wish, but I have too many things to get done today."

"You want to hear the silver lining?"

I nod.

"You have another meeting with your boss tonight."

"I do?"

"Uh-huh," he leans forward and presses a soft, too-short kiss to my lips. "Tonight. Eight p.m. Right here." He reaches forward and places his big hands on my breasts. "And you are not allowed to cover these up."

"So, just business casual, then?" My responding giggles turn to a moan when he leans forward to suck one nipple into his mouth and flick his tongue against it.

"Clothes aren't optional, Greer," he retorts in his bossy voice and moves his greedy mouth to my other breast, kissing and sucking and swirling his tongue and me into a frenzy.

I'm two seconds away from climbing on top of his body and riding him until we're late for work, but a pounding coming from the front door stops me before I can even get started.

It's loud and demanding and, in a way, confusing.

Because I swear, I've heard it before. From him.

"How are you in two places at once? Did you clone yourself?"

"Huh?" he asks, too busy jumping up from the bed and putting on pants to follow my logic.

"The door. That's exactly what you sound like when you pound on mine."

He shakes his head with a smile and tosses one of his shirts at me from the closet. I catch it, but I don't make a move to do anything else.

"Are you coming?" he asks, and I laugh.

Oh boy, he's funny.

"Uh, no. I think I'll hide out here until I find out who it is."

"Chicken," he taunts, and I shrug.

"You bet your ass. Now, get out there and answer the door. If I've disappeared when you come back, check the roof."

He charges forward and gives me a quick kiss and a tight hug as the pounding gets even louder.

Whoever's on the other side of his door doesn't like fucking around with waiting.

"No roof. Stay put. I'll be right back."

## THE *Billionaire* BOSS NEXT DOOR

"Okay, no roof," I agree as he jogs out the door. "But I'm not making any promises about the closet!"

I fall back on the bed and pull his shirt to my nose to take a whiff. It smells like fresh laundry and him, and a stupid, sappy smile curls the corners of my mouth.

I *like* him.

All-consuming, thought-hijacking, stalker-making kind of like, and as much as it scares me, it excites me even more.

I'd all but shut down the possibility of finding someone this compatible, someone to love me.

But it seems like, maybe, I'm not out of the game yet.

My ears perk up as Trent's voice carries into the bedroom from the front door. It's loud and surprised and devoid of the lazy ease of just a few seconds ago.

In fact, it sounds like the Trent I met months ago.

I lean forward, wrapping the shirt around my body just in case and listen even harder.

"Dad, what are you doing here?"

Dad? *Dad?* Motherfucking Dad?!

As in, the boss to end all bosses who makes my billionaire boss look like a little baby boss?

Oh *shit*.

I jump like I've been electrocuted and make it from the bed to the closet in one bounding leap. I close myself in quickly and take big, gulping breaths. Unfortunately, that makes me feel like I'm going to hyperventilate.

*Small, normal breaths, dummy,* my brain coaches.

Of course, from my new hiding spot, I can no longer hear what they're saying, but I don't care. I'd much rather huddle in the dark, silent safety of the closet than hang around—*almost naked*—in his bedroom just waiting for his dad to walk in and find me.

Trent finds me fifteen minutes later, apology and disquiet both stark in his eyes.

"I'm sorry," he says. "I had no idea he was coming, but I told him I'd meet him at the hotel in twenty minutes. If I'm not there…"

"I know," I say with a wave of my hand, eager to make him feel at least a little better. The last thing I want is to be another worry on his giant list. "Don't worry about me. I'll get ready and then swing by the office to pick up the new samples and sketches I got in before I meet you there."

He smashes his lips to mine gratefully and pulls away way too soon. "Thank you."

"You got it," I say teasingly. "You've got to be flexible when you're banging the boss."

His eyes light up, and he winks. "Tonight. We'll see just how flexible you really are."

The tectonic plates between my legs shift until I'm squeezing them together to fight against a full-on earthquake.

Trent smirks and grabs a suit from behind me before heading straight for the shower.

I head for home.

I've got a lot to do.

One Trent to support; one to impress.

There's more at stake than a job now.

Now…it's a job and my heart.

---

When we break for lunch, I'm on top of the world. Both Trents have been smiling at me all morning as I go over all of the proposed designs and elements unique to this space.

Tony, Marcus, Sarah, George, and I, we're a well-oiled machine thanks to Junior's new and improved leadership skills, and I can't imagine the presentation we threw together for Senior going any better.

It is dazzling and innovative, and it makes me excited to spend the next six months making it all come to life before the opening.

# THE *Billionaire* BOSS NEXT DOOR

I'm packing up my briefcase to head to lunch at Coastal Crepes—the secret location Trent texted me to meet him fifteen minutes ago—when I remember that I left one of my sketches down in the lobby where we stopped last with Senior.

It's in the direction of the exit and I don't want to forget it, so I decide to stop and get it on my way out of the building.

Down six flights from the lounge area and through the winding halls that confused me so much on the first day, I'm a few steps from the lobby when I hear Trent Senior's voice.

When I hear my Trent say something in return, I freeze on the spot so that I don't interrupt their conversation.

"You're doing a good job here, Trent," Senior says, and I can't help but smile. I know how rocky their relationship has been and what doing a good job means to Trent. Hearing praise from his dad has to make him feel so good. "The staff respects you. I can tell you've won them over and they're working hard. You're keeping the timeline tight, and the jobsite looks good and clean. All in all, I'm impressed with what you've done down here."

I bite my lip to stop myself from squealing for my guy. He *has* worked hard, and he deserves to hear it from his father.

"Thanks, Dad. It's really been a team effort."

"I'm sure it has," Senior confirms. "Hotels always are."

Trent hums his agreement, and I go from ecstatic to impatient. *Okay, boys, enough back-patting. Let's move this thing along.*

I'm about to come out of hiding to give them a reason to wrap it up when Senior speaks again.

"As for the design…"

*Ooh, that's me.* My ears perk up, and I lean in to listen harder.

"She's missing the mark."

*What?*

"I don't say this often, but I think my initial instinct about her was wrong."

My chest pounds and my ears roar, and oh my God, I think I might throw up.

"What?" Trent asks, and I'm nodding like a fucking lunatic over here, even though no one can see me.

Which, now that I think about it, *thank God* no one can see me.

"Some of her design is okay, but she's too eccentric. Too wordy. She makes everything more complicated than it needs to be."

There's a pause. Just long enough to make me stop breathing.

"You should let her go," Senior orders simply, and a crack forms, right down the middle of me. It's all I can do to hold it together. But Trent's going to defend me; I know it.

Sure, that probably won't change Senior's opinion of me, and it probably won't even save my job, but at least it'll save my soul.

I'm practically clawing at the walls in the moments it takes Trent to answer, but when he does, I hold my breath completely to make sure I don't miss anything.

"I respect you, Dad. Always have, always will. In the past, you've pretty much always been right. In fact, I don't think I can even remember a time when you've been wrong."

Senior hums.

"So, there's no reason to think you wouldn't be now."

*No reason to think you wouldn't be now.*

He's *agreeing* with him?

Tears sting my nose, and my gut feels like I've been punched in it.

The crack that Senior made is gone, and in its place, everything shatters.

I don't wait to hear anything else.

I *can't.*

Instead, I run.

Far and fast, I get the fuck out of there as quickly as my legs will take me, and I don't look back.

I had it all right before—before stupid Trent Turner and his stupid green eyes pounded on my door and broke in to my heart.

## Chapter THIRTY-SIX

### Trent

"No reason, except the only one that matters."

My father's eyebrows go up in challenge, but I hold my ground. There's no way I'm going to let him come in here, and after one day of being with everyone, presume he knows what's best for the team. He doesn't know the dynamic, he doesn't know the details, he doesn't know *Greer*.

"You're smart and successful, and you built this business on your back," I continue. "Your legacy is a strong one, so you have to know I wouldn't disagree with you on this if I didn't believe so strongly that I should."

He nods. "I'm listening."

"Greer is the heart of this place. She's had brilliant ideas, unbelievable work ethic, and is the reason this team is running so smoothly."

I swallow, knowing I'm going to have to take another bite of humility and give it to him straight if I have any chance of convincing him. "It was a rocky start. I was headstrong and authoritative and going about it all wrong. Without her steady advice and mediation with the team, we wouldn't be anywhere near on schedule."

I run a hand through my hair, stand up from my chair, and look directly at my father. "Let go of her, and we might as well let go of the progress we've made on the hotel."

He considers me for a moment, his face stoic and his stance

impassive. His hands rest casually in his pockets, and he purses his lips in consideration. Finally, he comes to a decision.

"Fine. If you feel that passionately about her presence, I'm not going to overrule you. But you're the point man. If you do this, you're taking responsibility for any and all mistakes she may make."

I nod. Greer isn't making any mistakes, and I know she won't going forward. But that's not the point. The point is that, for the first time ever, Senior believes in me enough to let me win.

"Understood."

He nods his head, just once, and then sticks out a hand for me to shake. "All right, then. I've seen all I need to. I'm impressed with the change in you, Trent. You're finally learning that your team is there for a reason. Lean into them, and don't lose this humility. I'll see you at the opening at the end of September."

And just as quick as he came, he's gone.

I glance at my watch after he steps outside, and I curse.

Greer is waiting on me at Coastal Crepes to have lunch, and I'm late.

I gather my shit in a hurry and jog outside to catch a cab. Luckily, it's the busy tourist season, and the options are plentiful.

I make it to the restaurant in record time, but when I walk inside and look around, it looks like I might be too late.

I take a second scan, but I still don't find Greer anywhere.

Instead of wasting any more time, I go up to the counter to ask.

After all, her brother owns the place. Someone's bound to know if she was here and left.

I wait in line so that I don't anger the other patrons, and when I get to the front, the kid I now know is her nephew greets me. "Can I help you?"

"Uh, yeah, actually."

He raises his eyebrows as if to say *Get on with it, then*.

I laugh at how stupid I must look, and he grows even more skeptical.

# THE *Billionaire* BOSS NEXT DOOR

I speak quickly to get ahead of myself before they call the cops. "I'm looking for Greer. Your...aunt. We..." I pause, unsure of what she wants her family to know at this point, and then finish with the safest option. "...work together."

"Right," he says. "She came in before and said she wasn't feeling well. Said to tell Trent she said that. You Trent?"

I nod. "Yep. I am."

"Cool. She also said to give you the Kevorkian special. Any idea what she means by that?"

The fact that this kid has no idea who Kevorkian is scares me; the fact that Greer used that name and mine in the same sentence scares me more.

---

I knock on the door for close to a minute before Greer finally answers.

She's in her pajamas and a robe, and her face is an absolute mess.

I know I shouldn't say that. I know I should say she looks beautiful no matter what, but I can't.

There's snot and mascara mixed together to make a brownish goo on both sides of her nose, and her hair looks like it's been pulled out at the roots. Her eyes are bloodshot, and her skin looks so puffy, it seems like she's had an allergic reaction.

Clearly, when she told her nephew she wasn't feeling well, she meant it.

"Oh my God, are you okay?" I ask, shoving her back with a gentle hand to her stomach and stepping into the apartment.

"Yes, of course," she says sarcastically. "Do I look like something's wrong?"

I laugh at her obvious joke, and she glares at me.

"I'm so sorry you don't feel well."

"Yeah," she scoffs. "Me too."

"Why don't you take the rest of the day off—"

"You'd like that, wouldn't you?" she mutters under her breath, dragging her slippered feet into the kitchen and grabbing a package of Oreos.

"No, I wouldn't," I say with a laugh. "But you're clearly under the weather—"

"*Clearly.*"

"So, you should take the time to get better before you come back to work."

"I still have a job?" she asks, and I tilt my head to the side in confusion.

"Of course you still have a job." I nearly want to laugh at the ridiculousness of her question. "Being sick isn't a fireable offense, Greer. Which is why you should take the day off and come back to work when you're feeling better."

"Maybe your dad will be gone by then."

I draw my eyebrows together at the subject change, but I wouldn't be surprised if she's got a fever and is delusional. I decide just to go with it. "He's already gone, actually. Just left."

"He is?" she asks, spinning around so fast, a piece of cookie comes flying out of her mouth.

"Yeah."

She shuffles to the fridge and takes out a glass of milk. I cringe.

"Milk? Do you really think that's the best choice if you're feeling sick?"

She skewers me with a glare so sharp, I put up my hands and chuckle. "Okay. Cookies and milk, it is."

She moves around the kitchen manically, not meeting my eyes, and I take a shot in the dark to try to make it better. "Kevorkian special, huh?"

She grunts.

"I'm sorry I was late," I say with a smile. "I'll make it up to you, I promise."

She stares into a cabinet, her hand on the knob, before closing it and turning to face me. Her face might be the most serious I've ever seen it.

"It's fine. I just...don't feel well. It's gonna take me a couple of days to feel better probably, and then I might work at my office to avoid contaminating the crew."

I pull my eyebrows together.

"Maybe it's a quick bug. You might feel better tomorrow."

She shakes her head. "Doesn't feel like it."

"Well, okay... I'll come back after work with some soup, and we can—"

"No."

I jerk my head back. I step toward her, and she holds up a hand. Something I don't like but can't explain takes hold in my chest.

"Greer—"

"Trent, you're in contact with everyone on the job. If I infect you, I infect them all. No. You'll stay away too. I'll see you next week."

"Can I go on record and say I don't like this?"

"Sure," she allows. "But it won't change it."

"Okay. But I'm unwilling to compromise on one thing."

I start forward and she backs up, panicked eyes all the way until her ass runs into the counter behind her.

I keep going and box her in, looking into her snotty, goopy eyes and telling it to her like it is.

"You're a mess," I say, and she frowns. "But there's still no one I'd rather be looking at."

I press a kiss to her lips and then another to her forehead before doing as she asks.

I close her door behind me with a quiet click and tell myself she's just sick. It's been a weird, long day already, and she's exhausted.

Greer's been on her own for most of her life, and that's how she functions best. If I give her the space to sort it all out, she will.

Yeah, that's it. It has to be. Everything will be better when she is.

# Chapter
# THIRTY-SEVEN

## Greer

Apparently, I do still have a job with Turner Properties and, even though Trent Senior appeared convinced I wasn't the right woman for the NOLA job, no one's canned me yet.

It's taken a lot of irrational inner monologue and talking myself off the proverbial ledge not to do something stupid like quit because of my pride.

At first, I really fucking wanted to, but this hotel means something to me. I've put my heart and soul into it, and dammit, I want to see it become the beautiful, blossoming, thriving hotel I know it will be.

Not to mention, I need the financial stability a job of this magnitude provides more than I need to protect my sometimes thick-as-steel pride.

So, after two weeks of faking the flu and avoiding the hotel—and Trent—by working out of my office and my apartment, I decide it's time to end the charade.

I mean, it was a nice reprieve and all, not worrying about how I looked and put myself together and getting all sorts of get well wishes from everyone I know, but you can only pretend to be sick for so long before people start threatening things like "taking you to the doctor" and "giving you tips for better management of your immune system."

Plus, I've spent way too much of my time trapped in an endless loop of tortured thinking about Trent Turner.

# THE *Billionaire* BOSS NEXT DOOR

The good, the bad, and especially, the complicated.

I thought if I could just spend enough time working out the shrill, nonsensical way I wanted to react to his talk with his dad—and his take on my work—in my head, I'd eventually be able to put it behind me.

And it worked. At least, for the most part.

But even when I work my way past this one thing, I'll never be naïve enough to believe there won't be another. Something—some, stupid thing—will always be there, in the day-to-day of our work, that makes me unable to separate the lines of our professional and personal relationships.

It'll bleed into the work, and before I know it, I'll be back here, pretending to be sick and throwing away parts and pieces of an opportunity I may never get again, just to save face and heartache.

No, working with Trent and being with him at the same time is never going to work out.

I'm struggling with accepting the news, trust me, but perhaps the hardest part of this realization is figuring out how to tell *him*.

Because for the past two weeks, Trent hasn't exactly gone away.

He's texted, he's called, he's stopped by on numerous occasions. And in return, I've been a one-woman show full of excuses.

*My office has better lighting.*

*The internet says I might have bird flu.*

*I'm secreting unknown fluids.*

You name it, and I've said it to my sharp-suited, green-eyed neighbor.

In the end, the only solution I've been able to come up with is to KISS. Keep it simple, stupid.

Literally. I have to get in there, avoid all eye contact if possible, lay out the facts without going into the gory details, and cut and run.

Maybe then we'll be able to finish the job together and move on with our lives.

With so many months left to go, I don't think getting into the nitty-gritty of what changed my mind will be good for either of us.

I know cornering him at work is entirely unprofessional, but I'm completely out of options.

With us living next door to each other, it's better that I break the news to him here, on neutral ground. Where beds don't yet exist, and neither of us can make a scene because of the many ears around us.

At least, that's the best theory I've been able to come up with.

It's somewhat ridiculous and probably irrational, but I'm *hurt*.

I don't know what happened between him and Senior after I left that meant I got to keep my job, but I know what I heard. Hours after waking up in bed together—weeks of doing everything I could to help him succeed—Trent didn't defend me at all.

I know I should be able to separate professional and personal feelings and actions like Trent apparently can, but work *has* been my personal life for the past five years.

I've given my firm everything I can, and an attack on my work feels like an attack on me.

We'll be here again, I'm sure of it, and I don't know that I can keep squashing down the way it makes me feel, which, ironically, is small.

I'm a block from the hotel when my phone rings with an incoming call. I dig it out of my sixty-five-pound purse by the very end of Paula Abdul's "Straight Up"—my ringtone—and don't even get a chance to check the ID before answering.

"Well, helloooo, avoiding whore formerly known as my friend."

"Emory—"

"Wow, I'm surprised you even remember my name."

"I've been busy!"

"Busy avoiding me," she sneers.

"To be fair, I've been avoiding everyone."

"I know. Your brother told me you haven't had dinner with them since January."

"You talked to my brother about me?"

"I've talked to five Catholic priests, two strangers, and a shop clerk at Bergdorf's about you. Of course, I've talked to your brother."

## THE *Billionaire* BOSS NEXT DOOR

"Look, now isn't a good time. I'm about to walk into the hotel—"

"Oh, good. At least you're done avoiding that."

Emory's attitude rubs, and I get fed up. "You know what? You don't even know what's going on. Maybe I'm avoiding everything for a reason, ever think of that?"

"Duh," she snaps. "Maybe your *best friend* can tell something is going on with you, and I don't know, thought you would *come to her* with your problems instead of trying to deal with them yourself like a douchecanoe." She laughs derisively. "Maybe. Just a thought."

"Emory…"

"Yeah?"

I close my eyes tight and say words I'm not very good at saying. I don't like to apologize for how I am—for *who* I am—and a lot of the time, that means I avoid the practice altogether. But sometimes, you wrong someone, maybe someone you love, and you've got to make it right. "I'm sorry."

She huffs. "You should be. But also, it's okay. I love you, and I'm well aware you have issues."

"Gee, thanks."

We're both silent for several moments, and then she heaves a heavy sigh. "I guess your silence means you're still not ready to share with me?"

"I will. I promise. I just…can't get into it now. I just have to focus on moving forward."

"Oh, great. Just sweep whatever it is under the rug," she grumbles. "Sounds like a great idea."

"Shut up," I say with a laugh. "I'm not sweeping it under the rug."

"Yes, you are, but okay. Tell yourself whatever you want. I'll be here when you figure out what a terrible idea it was."

I shake my head and roll my eyes to the sky. It doesn't matter that she can't see me. "Thanks. I'll keep my finger on speed dial."

"Greer," she calls out before I can hang up.

"What?"

"Call me when you need me."

"Thanks, E." My voice is soft and sincere, just like hers. "I love you."

"I love you too." She laughs. "Now get in there and fuck some shit up. I want this story to be really interesting when I finally hear it."

"Oh, it will be," I say. "One for the grandkids. Which will be yours, of course, as I'll be living alone with nothing but my TV and pizza bagels to keep me company."

"I'll get you a fish."

"No," I stress. "No pets. Only carbs and the Kardashians."

"Is carbs spelled with a C or a K?" she asks.

"With a K," I tease. "Cs won't exist anymore by then as the Kardashians will probably have taken over the world. They'll rule us from their cryogenic chambers."

"I'm hanging up now. This has gone to a place I don't like."

After a quick goodbye, I drop my phone into my purse and finally make it the rest of the way to the hotel.

It juts up into the pink and purple sunset-filled sky and dares me to come inside. Even though I want to run, I take a deep breath and put one foot in front of the other.

I find George working in the lobby when I walk in.

After checking to see that I'm not one of the walking dead, he gives me a welcome-back hug and points me in the direction of Trent up on the ninth floor.

I groan.

It's days like today when I realize how desperately we need them to hurry up and complete the elevator install, *Shape* magazine and its heart health tips be damned.

By the time I make it up all nine flights, I've got my heels in my hand and my hair up in a ponytail to control the neck sweat.

There's nothing I can do for the cracks of my cleavage and ass, but if everything goes to plan, no one should be able to notice that.

# THE *Billionaire* BOSS NEXT DOOR

I shove open the stairwell door and stumble into the hall…and right into Trent.

He catches me on reflex, but when he stands me upright and sees that it's me, his warmth drops about twelve notches.

"Greer."

I can't even really blame him. I know he's played a huge part in this, but it was really selfish of me to avoid him for so long, too. The man deserves at least some kind of explanation.

"Trent."

"Good to see you're feeling better."

I force myself to smile even though it hurts. "Me too. Listen, do you think we can talk for a minute? Privately."

He glances behind him at the workers he was obviously in the middle of something with and then back to me and nods. "Guys, I'll meet you down there."

They nod and take off at a near run, thankful to be dismissed from our awkward encounter.

Trent turns and heads down the hall, and I follow. I presume he knows somewhere we can go without being heard—at least, without being heard *clearly*.

He uses his master key to open the door to one of the suites in progress, ushers me in, and closes the door behind us.

When he finishes, he turns his back to the door, leans against it, and crosses his arms over his chest.

I literally hate that our relationship has come down to this. That those sparkling green eyes I love so much look at me so differently now.

But I know it's for the best.

I clear my throat a couple of times to moisten it, and then I dive right into the speech I've been practicing.

"I'm sorry I've been avoiding you. I've had a lot on my mind, and I know…I know I didn't handle it well."

He sighs. "I've been worried about you."

"I know. Again, I'm sorry. I really am, and I don't know if it helps make it sound more sincere at all, but I don't normally say that—apologize."

He nods, and when it's clear that's all I'm going to get, I go on.

"I owe you an explanation."

He nods, and I clench my fists.

*Is he going to do anything other than nod? For Pete's sake, the guy's always got something to say, and now he's all clammed up.*

Deciding to categorize it as a good thing, I charge on.

"I've been thinking…and I don't think a relationship between us is a good idea. Working together and dating…it's just not going to work. I thought maybe it could, but…it can't."

For the briefest of moments, his green eyes glaze over with something that strongly resembles hurt, but it's gone between one blink and the next. So quickly, in fact, I'm not really sure I ever saw it at all.

And then, he shoves off of the door with a foot and walks toward me.

I hold my breath so hard, a balloon forms in my chest.

"I agree."

*You do?*

He turns, walks to the door, and opens it to go. He looks back over his shoulder one last time to leave me with a few clipped words. "We're finalizing the bathrooms on Wednesday. Make sure you're ready."

I nod, but I don't let go of the breath I'm holding until he's gone.

Just as you'd an expect of a popped balloon, I deflate completely.

A simple parting of ways is exactly what I wanted.

So why does it feel so wrong?

# Chapter THIRTY-EIGHT

## Trent

"Sometimes I can't believe this shit," I say, taking a swig of my whiskey and looking out at the bar with distaste.

I fucking hate going out, but thanks to my sassy-tongued, blue-eyed, perfectly terrible neighbor whom I really fucking wish I didn't like anymore, I hate staying in even more these days. Four fucking weeks since she up and declared us over, and I'm still a hot fucking mess.

I didn't want things to end, but Greer was *determined*.

I could see it in her eyes and the defiant way she held her petite shoulders, and I could hear it in the way her voice lacked her usual sassy softness. She was all fucking business. One-hundred-percent ready to break things off.

Call it pride or self-preservation or whatever the fuck you want, even though I hated what she was saying, I just went with it. Told her I agreed. Just laid the fuck down and let her end things between us.

"God, I can't fucking believe the way it all turned out," I clarify. "I can't believe we were ever together, and I can't believe we're apart. The whole thing is a big ole fucking mystery, and I'm the victim. I can feel the blood all over. Brutal. Maybe I should just stick to random hookups. Kiss women on New Year's Eve and forget them. It worked for me once."

It's the first time Cap's been down to visit since Carnival, and the meeting of my best friends' minds and my heartache is long overdue.

Quince snorts, and I turn back to look at him and Cap as they hide their faces behind their beers. "What? What is this about?" I ask, swirling a finger at their faces.

"Should we tell him?" Quince asks, and Cap nods.

"Definitely. I can't wait to see his face."

"What? Tell me what?"

"Dude," Cap says. "Sticking to your New Year's Eve hookup is sticking with Greer. Goofy Gus and his snooty girlfriend set up the whole thing."

Quince glares at the unbecoming nicknames. "You were a part of it too."

"A part of what?" I ask.

"Getting the two of you together," Cap says casually, as if he's doing something other than dropping a nuclear sized bomb. "Once we found out she was the one you kissed on New Year's Eve, it was all hands on deck. The apartment. The dates. Everything."

"What do you mean, she's the one I kissed on New Year's Eve?" I croak, gripping my beer bottle so hard, it feels like I'm just shy of the pressure it would take to shatter it.

"Beyoncé? Midnight? Remember telling me about that shit?" Cap taunts, and I have to fight the urge to drive my fist into his cocky face.

"Well, I told Quince and Emory, and they told me who she was."

"Greer," Quince adds, just in case I couldn't figure it out.

"Yeah?" I ask, my voice heavily laden with weeks' worth of heartbreak and aggravation. "You're telling me the two of you knew all of this, set all of this up, and are just telling me now?"

Cap has the good sense to raise his eyebrows and brace, but Quince is too good-natured to understand how wound up I am.

"Yep. Emory made sure she moved in to the apartment next to you, and Cap set you up on a date he knew you wouldn't keep—"

"You what?" I yell, turning my anger to Cap.

He holds up his hands defensively, and Quince whistles. "Not the right time to bring that up, I guess. I see that now."

# THE *Billionaire* BOSS NEXT DOOR

Definitely not. I shake my head.

"I can't believe you guys. Going behind my back like that. Keeping this from me until now. Letting me wonder about all of it for this long."

"To be fair, we didn't have a hand in the heartbreak part of it," Cap pipes in. "That was all you guys."

*Jesus Christ, give me patience right now.*

"Oh good. That makes it all better."

"Look," Quincy says. "The point is, we were all rooting for you. There's a reason we all thought you'd be good together and pushed to make it happen. And clearly, we were right."

"You were right?" I shout. "You were *right*?" My laugh is derisive. "Then why the hell do I feel this way?"

"Because that's love, motherfucker," Cap, the fucking sage, informs me. "It slaps you in the dick almost as often as it tickles your balls. You gotta balance the two and figure out how to enjoy the pain. Get turned on by it. Harness it. Use it."

"You're ridiculous. What the fuck are you even talking about?"

Quince takes a sip of his beer and chuckles as Cap slaps him on the shoulder and shakes. "Look at this guy," Cap says. "You think that feisty fucking redhead of his doesn't cause him heartache and blue balls seventy percent of the time? She does. I guarantee it. But he's found a way to go with the craziness and embrace it."

"Well, that's all fucking well and good, but Greer doesn't want to date me. It's not like kidnapping her, holding her hostage, and forcing her is an option. What do you suggest I do?"

"I'm a little scared at how quickly your mind went to kidnapping, Turn, but for your sake and the sake of my status with the bar association, I'm going to ignore it."

"I think what Cap's trying to say," Quince says, ever the peacekeeper, "is that you should wait it out. You're not supposed to work together forever, right? When's the hotel done?"

I scowl. "September."

"Then I suggest you get really good at touching yourself between now and then, study up on some videos to learn how to touch her—"

I flip Cap off.

"—and then show her what she's been missing when there's nothing else in the way."

"And I suppose you guys have a plan to help me do that?"

"Dude," Cap says with a laugh before nodding at Quincy. Quincy nods at me.

"Of course, we do."

# Chapter THIRTY-NINE

### Trent

It's been five months since Greer ended things between us.

One hundred and twenty-five days, twelve hours, twenty-seven minutes, and fifteen seconds since she told me she couldn't continue our relationship. That it was too hard to be together and work together.

Okay, so maybe I don't know the exact time down to the seconds, but fuck, time is moving at a snail's pace. The amount of brain power it takes to focus on finishing the hotel and not think about Greer is Herculean.

In summary, it's been fucking *horrible*.

She pointedly avoids me, and when we're in close proximity to each other, it only drives the knife deeper.

I have to see her at work and in the hallway at home, and I have to hear her through the walls of my apartment. She is all around, everywhere, but she's not mine.

It's hell. Which, ironically, was exactly what I thought when I first found out she was hired for the Vanderturn NOLA design.

*My oh my, how things have fucking changed.*

My only saving grace is what the torture of seeing her everyday provides.

I know her work habits. I know her schedule. I know her friends. I know that she hasn't gone out on a single date since we broke up and that she spends most of her weekends at home, in the apartment right next door to mine.

And all of that means I know that Greer hasn't moved on.

Call me a lovesick fool all you want, but that information is like a defibrillator to my battered heart. It means there's hope on top of the despair and light at the end of the tunnel.

But broken hearts and silver linings aside, today is a big day.

And my focus needs to be on the hotel.

We are two weeks away from the opening, and my father is currently doing his walk-through. Every floor, every room, every nook and cranny of the place my team has worked so hard on for the past nine months.

I am proud of this hotel, so fucking proud of what my team has accomplished, but I have no idea what he's thinking as he walks through the reception and lobby area. His face remains neutral and his eyes are investigative, refusing to provide any kind of fucking reaction that would actually give me something to go on, some kind of clue as to what side of the emotional scale I need to prepare myself for.

By the time we reach the outside terrace, where Greer has artfully arranged a cozy and sophisticated outdoor space that demands people enjoy it, my nerves are buzzing like a live wire.

It's only the sense of pride for what she's created that distracts me from my anxiety. I can already picture it at night with the sleek fire pits going and the twinkle lights flickering off the lush landscaping and guests sitting on the cushioned couches with drinks in their hands and smiles on their lips.

But I swallow down the unwanted emotion and focus on the task at hand. Preparing myself for whatever blows my dad is probably preparing to give.

"Well, Trent," he says and turns around to meet my eyes. "Honestly, I'm not surprised."

*Oh, here we go...*

"But also, I am," he adds and walks toward me. "This is beyond anything I imagined or expected for this hotel. You did good, son. You did real fucking good."

# THE *Billionaire* BOSS NEXT DOOR

Wait...what?

"You're happy with it?" I ask, and he nods.

"I one hundred percent approve," he says, and slowly, a smile crests his normally straight and firm lips. "And I'm proud of you."

"You're proud of me?" I question dumbly, but fuck, Trent Turner Senior is never proud of his son.

Disappointed? Irritated? Riding his ass? All the fucking time.

But proud? I can't remember the last time that happened.

"Of course I am." His smile grows. "I know you worked hard. I know you had some serious revelations about what it takes to run a team on a project of this magnitude. But you learned and you grew during the process, and that was all I ever wanted."

Slack-jawed, I don't even know what to say.

But it doesn't matter because my dad apparently has plenty of words for the both of us.

"Running Turner Properties is all I've ever wanted for you, Trent," he says. "It's been my dream since the day you were born. But I know what it takes to run a company like this, and before I could pass the torch to you, before I could finally retire and spend the rest of my days with your mother, I needed to make sure you were ready. I needed to make sure you could handle it on your own." He pauses briefly and looks around the terrace. "This company is important to me. I've sacrificed a lot to get it where it is today."

"I know you have, Dad."

"But now, I'm confident it's in good hands."

"What are you saying?"

"I'm saying it's time," he says. "It's time for me to step down and let a new, talented, and innovative generation take over. And you are more than capable of filling those shoes."

He looks up at the hotel and then back at me.

"And by the looks of what you've created here, you are more capable than I am to create the kind of hotels that go with the times. The kind of hotels that will keep Turner Properties a household name with old *and* new generations."

"Wow. I really don't know what to say."

"Besides signing the contracts my lawyer has already drawn up, you don't need to say anything."

"You're serious?"

He nods and steps forward to wrap me in a manly kind of hug. The one where it's half-hug, half-backslap, and one hundred percent my father. "I admire you, Trent, and everything you've created here. And I'm excited and more than ready to watch you continue on this path. But from the sidelines, preferably on a tropical beach somewhere with your mom."

Once my dad walks back into the hotel, I stay standing outside, reeling.

I've been waiting for this moment for what feels like all my life, and now that it's here, I don't have a fucking clue what to do with it.

Trent Turner Senior is turning over the multibillion-dollar company otherwise known as Turner Properties. To me.

*Holy fuck.* Only, the relief I feel when the realization actually starts to settle in isn't as all-consuming as I imagined it would be.

And it takes me all of one minute to realize it's because something is missing.

*She* is missing.

Greer Hudson might be determined to have space, but I'm determined to be with her.

*Still.*

If anything, the time apart has only deepened my need and want for her further.

When I see my future with Turner Properties, running the company and creating new hotels throughout the world, I can't picture it without Greer.

It's time.

It's time for me to get my girl.

# Chapter FORTY

## Greer

It's been a long road finishing the Vanderturn New Orleans, but I can finally say it's over, and I'm proud of what I've done.

The finished product is immaculate and special, and I've grown as both a designer and as a person.

And I mean that literally. All the carb-loading working so closely with the guy I'm most likely in love with but will never be romantically involved with means I'm six pounds heavier.

I've eaten three decades worth of feelings in five-and-a-half months, and I don't even regret it.

The fluffiness has gone mostly to my breasts, and watching Trent—and every other man in a fifteen-mile radius—try not to stare at them while talking to me is like attending a stand-up comedy special every day.

*Uh, uh,* they stammer. *Blah, uh, blah, uh, blah.*

The only real bummer about the hotel completion is that someone—*I'm betting I know who*—thought the motherfucking masks would be a good idea for the grand opening party.

Like, really?

We're doing this shit *again*?

I didn't even bother getting a different one. I was Beyoncé once, and I am Beyoncé again—if only that meant I also had her wealth and celebrity status.

Emory's obnoxious laugh clues me in to her location despite the fact that she and the Q man have chosen to go with a new schtick completely. They are no longer TSwift and Kanye. Today, they are Lucy and Ricky.

And let me tell you, it's a good thing I love Lucy because Ricky, the fuck, has some splainin' to do.

I come up behind Quincy somewhat aggressively and take out the support of one of his knees. He almost crumples, and many another man would be upset, but not Quince.

He laughs even before he sees it's me.

Of course, when he sees it is me, he laughs even harder and pulls me in for a hug. I've been their little adoptee for the last five months, clinging to the two of them like a leech without the health benefits. Somehow, even after everything I've put him through in that time—and there's been a lot—Daddy Quincy still treats me like the daughter he's too young to have.

"I suppose you're the one to blame for these shit-tastic masks again, Big Q?"

He chuckles. "I might have had something to do with them. Isn't it fun?"

"No, Quince. No," I say with a scowl he can't see. "It's not fucking fun."

"Come on," he cajoles. "Sure, it is! You might be yelling at me, but it's like Beyoncé is yelling at me, and that makes it a lot more enjoyable."

"You're way too positive for me tonight. I don't think we can hang out."

"Good," Emory jumps in, hugging Quincy's waist tightly. "We wanted time alone anyway."

"Gonna bang in the coat closet?" I ask, and she smacks me in the tit. "Ow." I rub at it to make it better, and Quincy's line of sight drops right on cue.

Men. They're all like moths to a flame.

Though, to be fair, this black satin dress is so low-cut, I had to tape my nipples to the inside of it to keep them from showing.

## THE *Billionaire* BOSS NEXT DOOR

Something about it being the last time I'd be forced to see Trent in an official capacity made me want to go all out. Time to quit, here's my tit. Or something like that.

I didn't really think it through. I just put on the dress, and my breasts did the rest.

Okay, I'm done rhyming, I swear.

Time to drink instead.

I make my way to the other end of the King Van Lounge, a beautiful space we've managed to create on the sixth floor with a view overlooking Bourbon Street on one side, and the pool and courtyard on the other. Floor-to-ceiling windows on each side open up the space, and twinkling dots of prismatic light on the accent wall reflect in the glass.

It makes the space feel otherworldly and warm, and if I weren't in such an awkward spot with the owner of the hotel, I could gladly park my butt in one of the spacious chairs here for the rest of my life.

The bar juts up and out of the floor as though it's a part of it, the white-and-gray marble of the top and waterfall matching the tile of the floor. It's elegant and unique, and I'm so proud to say it came from a place in my head.

Preoccupied with the design, I pay no attention to the bartender, and for the first time on record, the whole exchange goes off without a hitch.

I get my Chardonnay, and he goes about his business, no bitchy blacklist in sight.

*Hmm. Maybe I was just putting too much pressure on myself before.*

I pick up the glass from its spot on the countertop and turn, tripping on the overly long train of my dress and dropping that shit straight to the floor.

It shatters and spreads, and every masked head in the room turns to stare at me.

"Hah," I laugh nervously. "Whoops."

A quick glance back at the bartender shows all goodwill has disappeared and confirms that I got ahead of myself.

I'm ostensibly doomed with bartenders until the day I die.

I'm about to leave drinkless when Trent Turner Senior steps up to the bar, maskless, and taps his fingertips on the surface.

"Another Chardonnay for Ms. Hudson, please."

The bartender doesn't even attempt to give him a side-eye. "Yes, sir."

I don't know how he knew it was me, but I feel like it's better that I don't ask.

Lord only knows what the man would say.

I fidget nervously, rubbing the satin between the tips of two fingers on one hand while we wait for the drink in silence.

I'm not sure what to say, given the whole sordid history. He doesn't like me, but he doesn't know that I know he doesn't like me...and yeah, it's a messy, fucked-up thing.

Still, somehow, it seems genuine as he compliments, "The hotel is beautiful, Greer."

I'm thankful for the mask for the first time tonight as my cheeks warm with a small blush. "Thank you, sir."

"I'm impressed with what you've put together here. I have to say, I wasn't convinced initially."

My chest tightens at his honesty. The truth makes the memory of hearing him say it more vivid, and I'm surprised by how acute the pain is.

I have no clue what to say to it, but he doesn't make me figure it out.

"I thought the lines were too modern for this part of the city, and the cultural touches too literal."

I swallow thickly as he laughs.

"But what do I know? I also think these fucking masks are ridiculous, but people seem to be enjoying them."

I snort, and he seems to understand what I mean by it, despite the wide array of possibilities.

"I know," he says good-naturedly. "But Trent insisted they were a good idea, and it looks like, mostly, he was right."

## THE *Billionaire* BOSS NEXT DOOR

My breath catches in my throat, and I have to pound a fist to my chest to force the air out of the way so I can speak. "The masks were Trent's idea?"

"Yep," Senior confirms, handing me my new glass of Chardonnay. I take it as carefully as I can and grip it tightly.

And it's a good thing because the next thing he says flips my world upside down.

"His idea to keep you, too," he adds nonchalantly. "Really fought for you. Said you were the heart of this place."

*He...*

My breathing slows, and my eyes hover between open and closed as I come dangerously close to passing out.

*He fought for me?*

"Turns out he was right."

My heart pounds in my chest, and I suddenly feel like my mask has no air in it.

I grab for it indiscriminately, trying to latch on to any goddamn part of it that will help me get it off.

The speed of my breathing grows and grows as the rubber sticks to me in my panic.

I'm half ready to hulk out and rip that shit off Avengers-style when "In Your Eyes" by Peter Gabriel starts playing over the sound system.

It's completely out of context for the soundtrack they've been playing during this soiree and makes the hair on the back of my neck stand up.

Forcing myself to take three deep breaths, I finally peel the death mask off of my face and look up at Senior.

He's looking behind me with a genuine smile—though, slightly mocking—on his face, and it's all I can do to keep my shit in check as I turn.

There, in the middle of the dance floor, with a boombox over his head, is Walter White.

My mystery kisser.

I shake my head and clap my hands over my mouth and nose.

I know those legs and those abs and those arms.

And, as it turns out, there's more than one reason I know those lips.

All of it, including the kiss with a stranger on New Year's Eve, belongs to the boss next door.

# Chapter FORTY-ONE

## Trent

Saliva pools in my mouth as the weight of an entire lounge full of people's stares bears down on me.

It's intense and off-putting, and the only person I have to blame is myself.

Still, Greer is one of the two hundred people staring, and that at least makes it worth it.

She's taken off her mask, a part of this plan I hadn't even considered was a possibility, and what's left on her face is a complicated mix of hope, shock, and muddled affection.

She's likely wondering how long I've known about our kiss on New Year's Eve, and how much of what I've said to her has been based on a lie. I just have to hope that there's also a little part of her that feels like a missing piece of her heart has been made whole.

The crowd starts to chatter the longer I stand here, boombox overhead, and I'm wondering if she's ever going to put me out of my misery.

The song is almost over, the lyrics coming to a close, when she finally takes her first step.

I watch entranced, her beauty unmatched by anyone in the room or otherwise. She's everything I never knew I needed and more, and I know for a fact that, if by some miracle I can convince her to give me a shot, she'll keep me on my toes for the rest of my life.

When she stops three feet in front of me, I set the boombox on the floor and peel my mask off my face.

She raises a single eyebrow in challenge, but there's not even a hint of a smile.

My throat drops into my stomach.

"Using the same trick twice?" she tsks. "I would have expected more from you."

The humor in her insult gives me just enough confidence to speak my truth, and to do it without caution or censoring.

"What are we talking about here? The mask or the song? Because I thought the mask was a necessary touch."

"Yeah, I get the mask, Walt. I'm just surprised you have such a big crush on John Cusack." She rolls her eyes. "Like, get a room already."

"It was symbolic, just like in the movie. It's the song that was playing the night we—"

She shushes me and puts a hand over my mouth. "I know what night it was."

I smile a little, and for the first time, she seems to notice just how many people are watching us right now. I feel a little bad for doing this so publicly, but it was the only way. If I'd tried to confront her in private, she would have weaseled her way out, one way or another—even if it meant kicking me in the balls.

But that doesn't mean I can't rectify the situation now. "Do you want to go somewhere and talk?"

"Other than here, in the fishbowl of human condition?"

I smirk and nod.

"Yes."

"Then, yes. Make that happen quickly, and I'll give you a bonus point toward your score on whatever argument you're gearing up to make."

I put a gentle hand to her back and lead her out of the crowd and toward one of the storage rooms. My mom winks at me from across the room, and I blush like I'm five years old.

# THE *Billionaire* BOSS NEXT DOOR

Ideally, I'd be taking Greer somewhere more romantic than a closet full of shampoos and table linens, but with this being opening weekend, it's about the only unoccupied ten square feet on the entirety of the property. And at this point, privacy is more important than show quality.

I step aside to let her in first and then follow her in and let the door click shut behind us. The silence is almost startling.

With a mind to that and how she must be feeling, I give her a minute to get her bearings. She looks at everything possible except me. And she doesn't make eye contact with me even once. I'm actually impressed with the talent it must take to pull that off, seeing as I'm the net in the middle of her eyes' game of ping-pong.

"Greer."

"Hmm?" she asks, still taking inventory almost compulsively. I imagine this is the fifth time she's counted the rows of shampoo on the shelf.

"Greer, look at me, please."

When our eyes finally make contact, it's like the spark her questions needed to explode all over the place and out of her mouth. I do my best to keep up—which, I guess, is all I ever really do with her anyway.

"How long have you known we kissed on New Year's Eve?" she asks.

"Since shortly after you told me we were over."

"How did you find out?"

"Cap and Quincy told me."

"They knew?!" she shouts inside the small space, and I nearly laugh at the relief in hearing her so unfiltered, so Greer. It feels like it's been an eternity since I've seen her. All of her. Like this.

"Yes. As did Emory. They set us up to live next door to each other."

That answer stops the questions briefly, but only because I have to pin her to the door to keep her from tearing out of this place and committing triple homicide in the middle of the party.

"I know," I console. "They're assholes. But they're our assholes, and without them, I never would have realized how perfect you are."

She sags in my arms, closes her eyes, and lowers her voice to the barest hint of a whisper.

"You think I'm perfect?"

"I know you're perfect. For me."

"Even when I'm saying 'motherfucker' in public?"

"Even then."

She loosens my hold with a squeeze of her own and lets her head fall back into the door. "Why? Why on earth do you find me attractive?"

"Because you are. You're witty and funny and smart and beautiful. You have one of the best minds I've ever had the pleasure of exploring."

"I'm sarcastic. And mouthy. And highly unprofessional fifty percent of the time."

I shrug. "I guess I find all of that charming, then. Is that a problem?"

She laughs, just one sharp bark before shaking her head with a smile. "Yes. I think there's something seriously wrong with you."

"Only if you leave me here by myself. With you, it just means we go together better than ever."

"Trent—"

"What? You said it would never work while we were working together, and we're not. As of tonight, you are officially off the payroll."

"And jobless," she remarks sardonically.

I shake my head and lean in to press my lips to hers. She's a smartass and she's apathetic, but she can't be either of those things to this.

Her eyes flutter closed as I run my tongue across her lips to open them, and then I touch the tip to hers.

When we pull away, there's only one thing to say.

"There's magic in the two of us. And we both know it."

My voice is soft, but my words are loud. There's no way she can't hear what I'm saying.

"I love you, Greer."

Her crystal-blue eyes widen, and a shaky hand touches her mouth.

"I didn't plan it, but our lives…and our friends…did."

She laughs. I smile.

"We both had a lot at stake when we started this job, but in my opinion, life handed me a lot more than I bargained for."

Finally, she nods. "Me too, Trent. And you know what?"

"What?"

She leans forward and presses her perfect lips to mine. "I love you too."

# EPILOGUE

## Trent

"No way," I argue, tossing a piece of popcorn into my mouth with amazing accuracy. "It's five at most."

"Pshh. Are you kidding? Have you seen her face?" Greer argues. "We're definitely in transition. Seven. I'm calling it."

Emory glares, nostrils flared, while she finishes breathing through a contraction. "If you guys don't stop making bets on the size of my cervix, I'm going to climb out of this bed, baby motherfucking hanging out if I have to, and drag you out of the room myself."

Greer pulls her lips inside her mouth and pretends to shake in fear. I fall a little more in love.

"I thought she'd at least threaten something serious," I whisper. "Mass murder. Mutilation of our genitals. Something."

"Don't tempt me!" Emory yells through her clenched teeth as another contraction hits her.

"Wow," Greer remarks. "You're going to want to remember that childbirth obviously allows superhuman hearing. For future reference."

Goddamn, this woman. She makes my life.

A year and half ago, I dressed up like Walter White—*for a second time*—and convinced Greer to give me another chance, and I'm certain no one has ever loved this woman like I do.

I have memorized all of her smiles. All of her laughs. I know her annoyed sighs and her sassy glares. I know what makes her wet, and I know what makes her come.

# THE *Billionaire* BOSS NEXT DOOR

I know her. *All* of her. And I've never been happier in my entire life.

My smile is unstoppable as I cuddle into her on the hospital couch and bump her with my shoulder. "You want to have kids with me?"

She giggles. "Yeah. Someday."

"Like, how *someday* someday? Should we start trying now? I think I saw an empty room down the hall."

"Easy, Walt," Greer says with a laugh. "You're going to have to give me time to heal from the trauma of watching Emory give birth first."

"You're not watching me give birth!" Emory yells. "Quince, you better get them out of here before I ki—"

"Okay, okay," Cap says, stepping forward from the corner, a surprising peacemaker.

"Quince, you just stay with Emory. I'll handle Mo and Larry."

He grabs me by the shoulder, but I shake him off so I can offer Greer a hand up as she frowns. "What happened to Curly?"

"He died," Cap says stoically before pointing back over his shoulder. "She killed him. So, let's go before you both meet the same fate."

The two of us laugh our way into the hall, poking and prodding and teasing each other all the way to the snack area. St. Luke's Hospital in New York is big and sterile and about as unromantic as possible—and apparently very advanced if Emory's parents insisting that she give birth here is anything to go by—but it's the gesture… the *moment* that I'm after. The one that will suit the woman I've fallen head over heels in love with.

The woman I would have moved to New Orleans for.

Instead, she gave up everything she'd ever known, the city she loved, and living close to the only family she's ever had to move to New York and chase dreams with me.

After taking over Turner Properties, I took it upon myself, as one of my first official acts, to hire an in-house designer for all of our new projects and updates alike.

She's sassy and unfiltered and my favorite human being on the entire planet Earth.

Hopefully, the one I'll get to introduce as mine for the rest of my days.

We stand in front of the vending machine as Greer makes her selection, and I wait nervously to see how well I really know her.

Cap gives the nod from about ten feet away, taking out his phone to be ready.

I'm just fucking hoping he gets pictures of something other than an epic fail.

Greer clucks and hums and hems over her decision for so much time that I can feel a bead of sweat run down my spine.

I'm pretty sure I lose moments off my life, but that's okay. I'll want to go first anyway.

The idea of living without her at this point is…inconceivable.

She finally pushes the button for A7, and everything inside me locks up with anticipation.

*This is really happening.*

Thank God for Greer's mostly predictable love for Cheddar and Sour Cream Ruffles.

When the bag drops into the tray and she bends over to take it, I glance over my shoulder at Cap to see he's giving me a thumbs-up.

A lot of planning—and if I'm honest, a lot of money—went into today, but I couldn't imagine anything more appropriate.

Greer isn't a fancy, hoity-toity kind of gal. She doesn't put on airs, and she sure as shit wouldn't want me to get down on one knee at some stuffy restaurant that serves caviar and outrageously priced champagne.

Basically, it was either this or somehow get us onto Ellen's *Game of Games*. Considering Ellen won't be filming any more episodes for another eight months, this is the option that stuck.

Because *fuck me*, I'm not waiting another eight months.

When you find the person you want to spend the rest of your life with, you don't want to waste any more time. You want to dive headfirst and connect yourself to that person in every way possible.

And that's exactly what I'm prepared to do. Right now. In front of this vending machine while Greer's best friend gets ready to give birth to her daughter down the hall.

Don't worry, the expectant parents approved it with flying colors.

They couldn't think of anything better on the day their daughter was born than giving her "aunt" the beginning of a family of her own.

Greer gives me a weird look when she turns around—I know my face must be a ravaged mess—but I ignore it just long enough to prompt her to open the bag now.

"Can I have one?" I ask nicely, pouting my lip when she seems as if she might hold out.

"All right. Fine," she agrees, plucking the bag open and reaching inside.

Only, as Cap and I know, the only thing she'll find in there is a ring.

Her eyebrows pull together as she fishes it out and pulls it from the bag, but the moment her eyes meet diamond, she freezes completely.

I take the opportunity to get down on one knee.

---

## Greer

Holy mother of mercy.

Holy Jesus Christmas in a choir.

Holy elves dancing around Santa and the North Pole and a whole bunch of other shit I can't possibly focus on right now.

The diamond sparkles in the offensive fluorescent hospital lighting, and my knees threaten to give out as Trent sinks to one of his in front of me.

"Greer, I need to ask you a question."

My nod is the definition of dumb. Up and down with no actual bearing on time or space or life, I watch as Trent takes the ring from my hands and starts to slide it onto my finger.

My heart is racing and my jaw feels numb, and to be honest, I'm pretty sure I'm having a heart attack.

But I wouldn't interrupt this for anything in the whole fucking world.

At least we're in a hospital. They'll be able to get to work on me quickly.

"I love you."

I try to return the sentiment, but I'm pretty sure it comes out sounding like "I mumble schmoo."

Thankfully, he seems to understand anyway.

"I had a tiny idea of how perfect you were for me early in our relationship, but I'm wholly certain about it now. No one makes me laugh like you. No one calls my shit like you. And no one...no one has ever loved me like you do."

It's all I can do not to start sobbing right here.

"You've been there for me and my mom, and you've made me and my family yours without hesitation. I know it won't always be easy...but it will always be right."

I nod and squeeze his hand and give him every indication I can of my answer before he even asks the question.

It's literally all I can do to wait for him to have his moment.

"Be mine forever," he finally says. "Be my best friend in life, my partner in crime...be my wife."

"One hundred times yes," I say. He scoops me up into his arms and tucks my lips to his ear.

It's the perfect proposal. The perfect place. The perfect man.

I laugh as the soft flesh of my lips skims across his ear. "No one else is crazy enough to take me."

"There might be," he corrects, giving Cap a jerk of his head.

# THE *Billionaire* BOSS NEXT DOOR

Cap nods despite not knowing what we're talking about, and it makes me smile even bigger.

"I just got here first."

When the room stops spinning and I finally find my feet, I know who I need to see, and I need to see her right now.

She's been there for me since teatime and sleepovers, and I want her to be the first to know now.

"Can we go tell Emory?" I ask, glancing down at the twinkling cushion cut—*massive*—stone on my hand once more.

Junior doesn't disappoint.

"Of course."

I take off at a run, shoving people out of my way as I go, and likely committing minor assault on several pregnant women.

I don't slow down until I barrel through the door to Emory's room and hold up my hand in victory.

"I'm engaged!" I shriek, to which Quincy responds with a smile.

Emory's happiness is a little less obvious, but evident all the same.

"Congratulations," she groans into a yell. "I'm crowning. Now get the hell out!"

So, I do.

I wait in the lounge with my fiancé and Cap, Emory's family and friends, and even my brother and *Rhonda*.

Everyone's here in New York City for the big event, but I'm the luckiest one of all.

Because at the end of the day, when Hudson Blair Black screams her first hello to the world, I've increased the size of my family by not one, but two.

---

## Cap

The gang is all here, and as of today, we've officially added one more to our crazy group.

Hudson Blair Black. A little beauty who is a mere two hours old. She has a head full of hair that matches her last name to a T, and her eyes are so big and blue and gorgeous that I predict they will one day equate to nothing but trouble for a lot of men.

*Mostly her father.*

Quince stares down at his daughter with nothing but unconditional love shining from his every fucking pore. Just born and she already has her soft-hearted daddy wrapped around her tiny finger.

Emory sits in the hospital bed, gazing up at her husband and daughter, and looking exactly like what I'd think a fucking Kardashian would look like after giving birth. Full face of makeup, some kind of fancy gown thingie that I fucking know didn't come from the hospital, and her hair is damn near runway ready.

Fucking women.

I *love* them—looking at them, smelling them, *tasting* them. I especially love making them come.

But do I understand them when it comes to anything other than pleasure?

Not even a little.

Truth is, I haven't even tried for the last decade or so. I've been more than content to fly by the seat of my dick, enjoy the company of a woman for a short time, and move on with my life.

I'm too busy to get locked down in some kind of soul-sucking, life-ruining monogamous love story like Quince and Trent, and I've never really been the kind of man who pictures marriage and babies and shit in my future—I get bored when things become too predictable.

"Look at how little she is, Trent," Greer says, her voice laced with wonder and awe and a whole bunch of other shit women tend to have when looking at babies and puppies and fucking kittens.

# THE *Billionaire* BOSS NEXT DOOR

Trent, the lovesick bastard, smiles. "She's perfect."

I watch them share a quiet look laced with silent words that we're not privy to, and whatever it is makes my heart clench inside my chest.

*What the fuck is that about?*

I rub at my chest and squint.

Something's got to be coming from the ventilation system.

Carbon monoxide maybe?

Because for as willingly as my two best guy friends are throwing in the towel on their freedom, their fucking bachelor life, and settling down with women who have captured their hearts, I can't even fathom that kind of love.

And I don't want to.

In the span of three hours, I've witnessed—and helped because I'm an awesome friend—one of my best friends get engaged to a woman he once hated with every ounce of his being. And I've watched another become a father.

It's crazy. They're crazy.

I'm, without a doubt, the sanest human being in this room.

Well, me and the handsome fuck who just walked in.

Milo Ives is Emory's cousin and one of my most successful clients. Of course, because of my natural likability, he loves me and considers me one of his good friends.

I've gone along with it. You know, for his sake.

*God, I'm funny. If only I could wink at myself.*

Seriously, though, our friendship means I've seen him in all sorts of situations, including, but not limited to: a drunken brawl, a revolving door of women, and the kind of success that recently put him on Forbes list of richest men in the world.

"Congratulations, guys," he says as he steps toward the hospital bed and takes a peek at a now sleeping Hudson in Quince's arms. "Goddamn, what a beauty."

The brand-new mother and queen of glam smiles proudly. "Obviously, she gets her looks from me."

Greer snorts. "Honestly, it's hard to tell with all that makeup you've got caked on your face."

Emory's responding look is a glare that could penetrate walls. "At least I met my daughter without looking like I just rolled out of bed."

"You and I both know that is exactly how I will meet my future daughter." Greer laughs. "And you know I'm just kidding, Em. You look gorgeous. Kim Kardashian's glam squad fucking wishes they could make her look that good post-birth."

I laugh. I can't help it. No matter how much of a lovesick bastard Greer Hudson has turned my best friend into, she cracks me up.

"Don't even start, Cap," Emory retorts, and I just shrug.

"I didn't say a word."

The conversation switches back to the baby, and it's hard to believe that one little human being holds the kind of power to mesmerize a room full of grown-ass adults.

I'm just about to give my formal congratulations when Greer informs us we need to exit the room. "Okay, it's time for you bastards to get out of here. Emory needs to get her tits out."

"Jesus Christ," Emory mutters. "Stop saying that."

"Fine. Emory has to get her *boobs* out."

Emory rolls her eyes. "I have to breastfeed."

It sounds like the kind of activity I'd love to stick around for, but Quince spears me with a look I can't mistake—a silent threat against my most favorite appendage.

I follow Milo out of the room without spying any nipples.

"Where are you headed now?" I ask as we walk the short hall to the elevators. There's some weird voodoo energy surging through my body still, an aftereffect of all the deadly gas, I'm sure, and I need some way to burn it off.

Manly stuff. Wild stuff. *Bachelor* stuff.

"Back to work."

"That's fucking boring." I groan and tap the down button

between the two elevator carts. The one on the left dings its arrival almost immediately.

Milo laughs before stepping onto the elevator with me, and I scowl.

Why doesn't it seem like he's feeling what I'm feeling?

Agitated, I stir the pot.

I'm pretty sure our friend Evan—and the CFO of Milo's company Fuse—is due to get married soon, and there's no way he's not feeling the same way about it as I am about all of this.

"Is Evan really getting married?" I ask, and Milo tilts his head to meet my gaze as the elevator doors close shut.

"Yeah."

"And how do you feel about that?"

"I mean, he's been engaged for nearly a year. Seems like the natural next step," he says, unflustered.

*Why the fuck isn't he commiserating with me?*

"First, Quince. Now, Evan *and* Trent." I sigh and run a hand through my hair. "Goddamn everyone's dropping like flies."

Milo laughs. "Well, if that isn't the worst way I've ever heard anyone describe marriage…"

"You know it's true, dude. Marriage. Babies. Shit is going down within our friend circle."

"Aw," he teases. "You feeling left out, sweetheart?"

"Shut the fuck up," I retort on a chuckle, and we step out of the elevator and head toward the hospital lobby. "I'm terrified…*for them.*"

"Oh…" He pauses *and* smirks, the collected, self-assured bastard. "So, you're just scared for them. Not scared in general? Or projecting your commitment fears onto them? Of course, that makes total sense."

"You bet your ass, it does," I say without a second thought. "I don't have any fears of commitment. I just prefer not to commit."

"So, this is more of an altruistic kind of concern you're harboring, then."

"Exactly."

"If that isn't a good friend, I don't know what is," he teases, and I roll my eyes.

"You know, I almost forgot how much of a fucking smartass you are."

Just before he opens his mouth to most likely offer some witty retort, his phone pings several times, and he pulls it out to check the screen.

I watch as his brow furrows, and with one tap of his finger, he unlocks his phone to read the messages.

I'm all ready to assume it's some software/techie/business bullshit, but before I can avert my eyes to seek out something more interesting than watching Mr. Brainchild text over boring computer shit, his reaction reels me back in.

"What the hell?" Milo mutters.

"Everything okay?"

"Yeah," he says, but he shakes his head at the same time, scanning the messages on his phone a second and third time. You know what? Fuck scanning. The motherfucker is *staring*. Hard.

I try to sneak a peek, but the bastard snatches it away too quickly.

"What the fuck, dude? What is it?"

"It's nothing."

"That doesn't look like nothing." I grin. I can't help myself. Something fucking juicy is in those texts, and goddamn, I want to see.

I hold out my hand. "Let me see."

"Fuck no." Like a damn teenage girl, he locks the screen of his phone and slips it back into his pocket.

"Someone sending you titty pics?" I ask with a grin, and that simple question has his face scrunching up into something that borders on shock and horror and *intrigue*.

"Don't be a fucking dick."

"What?" I ask and raise both of my hands in the air. "It's a valid question."

## THE *Billionaire* BOSS NEXT DOOR

Because it *is* a valid question.

But more than that, it's that question that riles him the most.

No doubt about it, those text messages are from a woman.

*Looks like another one is about to bite the fucking relationship dust.*

I swear to God, sooner rather than later, I'll be the only sane, single motherfucker left in New York.

THE END

Love Trent and Greer and ready for more from Max Monroe?

Well, we've got news for you!

We have more *standalone* romantic comedies in our Billionaire Collection!

You WILL NOT believe the laughs you have coming for you!

*My Brother's Billionaire Best Friend* is the next book in the collection that you NEED to read!

And the entire collection is currently free in Kindle Unlimited!

———— ✺ ————

Want even MORE from Max Monroe?
Don't worry, girl, we've got you covered!
Here are more Max Monroe books!

### Sweet, sexy, swoony, downright hilarious Rom Com:

*Billionaire Bad Boys Series*
Reading Order:
*Tapping the Billionaire*
*Tapping Her*
*Banking the Billionaire*
*Banking Her*
*Scoring the Billionaire*
*Scoring Her*
*Mother Fluffer*
*Sleighed It*

### Sexy football studs and hilarious, Sports Romance:

*Mavericks Tackle Love Series*
Reading Order:
*Wildcat*
*Pick Six*
*Trick Play*
*4th & Girl*

### Hot doctors finding their hilarious way to love:

*St. Luke's Docuseries*
Reading Order:
*Dr. OB*
*Dr. ER*
*Dr. NEURO*

All of the above series are currently Free in KU, and trust us, you don't want to miss meeting the OG Billionaires, the sexy Mavericks, or the hot docs of St. Luke's hospital if you haven't met them already. Head to Amazon and start with *Tapping the Billionaire* today!

Stay up to date with our characters and us by signing up for our newsletter: www.authormaxmonroe.com/newsletter

You may live to regret much, but we promise it won't be this.

Seriously, we make it fun!

Character conversations about royal babies, parenting woes, embarrassing moments, and shitty horoscopes are just the beginning!

If you're already signed up, consider sending us a message to tell us how much you love us. We really like that. ;)

---

Follow us online:

Facebook: www.facebook.com/authormaxmonroe

Reader Group: www.facebook.com/groups/1561640154166388

Twitter: www.twitter.com/authormaxmonroe

Instagram: www.instagram.com/authormaxmonroe

Goodreads: https://goo.gl/8VUIz2

# Acknowledgments

First of all, THANK YOU for reading. That goes for anyone who's bought a copy, read an ARC, helped us beta, edited, or found time in their busy schedule just to make sure we didn't completely drop the ball by being late. Yeah, that's us—sliding in fifteen minutes behind schedule just like Greer. Thank you for supporting us, for talking about our books, and for just being so unbelievably loving and supportive of our characters. You've made this our MOST favorite adventure thus far.

THANK YOU to each other. Monroe is thanking Max. Max is thanking Monroe. This shouldn't surprise you since we've done this in every book we've published together so far. Or maybe it does surprise you because you don't ever read those acknowledgments. If that's the case, joke's on you. We happen to be hilarious, even in our acknowledgments. But you'll still have a chance to find out next time because we'll probably do this forever.

THANK YOU, Lisa, for being your amazing, hilarious, graciously accommodating, and eagle-eyed self. We SWEAR the next book is coming to you early. We know we've said this before, but we really mean it this time. REALLY. Why are we getting the impression you don't believe us? HAHA

THANK YOU, Stacey, for making the insides of our book look so much prettier than organs. And for acting like you don't hate us when we send you one million updates. ☺

THANK YOU, JoAnna & Sandra, for being superior Counselor Feathers. You ladies amaze us on a daily basis, and you are the reason Camp Love Yourself is the coolest place to be. Seriously, you do a better job of running it than we do.

THANK YOU, Banana, for rocking our covers. And for spending lots of time covering nipples and enhancing crotches when we ask you to. It's a tough job, but somebody's got to do it.

THANK YOU, Social Butterfly PR for doing So. Many. Things. If you were one of our kids, you guys would be our favorite child.

THANK YOU to every blogger who has read, reviewed, posted, shared, and supported us. Your enthusiasm, support, and hard work do not go unnoticed.

THANK YOU to The Bookworm Box for letting us be a part of something so special! Words cannot express how truly honored we are!

THANK YOU to The Bookworm Box subscribers for being so amazing and supporting something as wonderful and awe-inspiring as The Bookworm Box!

THANK YOU to the people who love us—our family. They support us, motivate us, and most importantly, tolerate us. Sometimes we're not the easiest people to live with, especially when there is a deadline looming. We honestly don't know what we'd do without you guys.

P.S. You don't know what you'd do without us either, so suck it.

THANK YOU to our Camp members! You guys make us smile every day! Especially when we pop into camp when we're supposed to be doing something else and we're really easy to please. It's like being really hungry—everything tastes good. HAHA! J/k. J/k. You'd taste good even if we were overfull.

As always, all our love.

XOXO,

Max Monroe